JULIA stood a few feet away. Blocking his path. Her long, wavy hair caught in the breeze, lifting and flirting about her face.

Her face, cast half in shadow, half in pale moonlight, made his gut tighten with longing. It seemed an indulgence, decadent beyond any measure of decency, to stare at her beautiful face.

He'd missed her. Desperately. In every last intervening hour since he'd almost kissed her beside the pasture fence.

She took a hesitant step toward him. Her pale, summer-weight robe covered her from neck to wrist to ankle.

Suddenly aware of his nakedness, he wished he'd pulled on more than a pair of Levi's. Better yet, he wished he'd left the house to walk the fields.

"Nice night." He headed past her to the safety of his own bedroom, planning to lock the French door between them.

"Yes, it's beautiful out." She hugged herself against the cool wind. "Conrad," she added hastily, "I have one question."

Last time she'd asked a question, he'd gotten himself into a heap of trouble.

"Not a good idea." He moved to pass her. Three steps and he'd be safely inside his bedroom.

She detained him by planting a palm in the middle of his bare chest. "Wait. Please."

The warmth of her touch, shockingly intimate, lanced through him. Gooseflesh prickled all over his wind-chilled body. Reflexively, he grabbed her hand.

The wind caught her wrapper and brushed the hem against his bare feet. Her sleeve skimmed his arm.

Her delicate scent provoked memories he didn't want. His hands in her hair. The almost-kiss that nearly destroyed him. The overwhelming need to taste her lips, to accept and to give. His pulse rushed through his veins.

She took a half step closer, slipped an arm about his waist, and brushed her bosom against his chest. The unnerving contact sent heat coursing through him. She felt so warm, alive, intoxicating. He moaned as her sweet-smelling hair caressed his cheek.

"I've missed you," she whispered, a split second before she reached up and pressed her lips to his.

Praise for The Cowboy Steals a Bride

" Wonderful, Clean Western Romance.
The Cowboy Steals a Bride is a great western romance—with the added bonus of being a clean read (a rarity these days). Holt brings the characters to life and sets up a heart-breaking situation with a love triangle: Holmes has written letters so compelling that Julia comes from Baltimore to meet him, intending to marry him. Fortunately—or unfortunately—Holmes' brother Conrad is there and he and Julia are attracted to each other. Weeks pass before Holmes returns—weeks when a delightful friendship builds into love between Conrad and Julia. Another great addition to the Husband-Maker trilogy."

~ *Heather,* Amazon.com, 5 stars

"This was a good read, more on the harlequin level (no sex) but likeable. Two characters feel the immediate attraction when they first meet, however the bride is intended for the other brother --who makes an appearance towards the end of the book. In fighting their attraction they also become friends which is the main concept of this story. All ends well and it is a likeable read."

~ *Winn*, Amazon.com, 4 stars

The Cowboy Steals a Bride

The Husband-Maker Trilogy, Book 2

Intended for his brother, but perfect for him.
What's a cowboy to do?

She's given up *everything* to seize her dream...

Julia Tyndall knows exactly what she wants: freedom and her choice of husbands, far away from Baltimore society.

Holmes's letters won her over, but it's the work-hardened, *beautifully imperfect* reality in denim and chambray that steals her heart. But it's not Holmes she meets on the train platform...it's his brother.

Days stretch into weeks and Holmes is nowhere to be found. How is a bride to remember and honor a marriage agreement when her groom's never around?

He's losing his heart to his *brother's* bride...

Conrad Macquarie doesn't have much patience for women on his dairy, even his brother's bride. She's enamored with the intricate workings of his dairy enterprise, too intelligent, uncommonly beautiful, a far sight too appealing.

Worse yet, she's the only woman who's ever seen past the scarred surface to the man beneath. Every moment spent with her blurs the familial lines, heating friendship into more than he should take. But it's so much less than he wants.

If Holmes doesn't get himself home soon, there's no telling what lines Conrad just might cross.

Dedication

For Diane Darcy and Heather Horrocks, the best critique group ever. Ladies, thank you for the support, kindness, and guidance. You're amazing!

Also for Mark, my very own hero. Our twenty-six years together are the *beginning* of our very own Happily-Ever-After.

"I loved this book! Kristin has a great style of writing incorporating facts and details from the past to give the story clarity and believability. I loved her characters. She writes as if she were standing in the shoes of each person and can really feel their emotions and think their thoughts. Kristin writes the way I have always wanted to write. She has mastered the art of weaving a story through many plots and sub-plots and leaving no loose ends dangling. I started with this book, though it is the second in her series of three. The book stood fine on its own, but I loved how little things made more sense when I then read her first book in the series. I anxiously await the third book.

When I was a young teenager, my grandmother had a shelf of romance paperbacks in the summer kitchen of her home. I read them voraciously always putting myself in the place of the heroine of the story. This book is better than all those I read so long ago. I give it my highest praise! I hope Kristin Holt will continue to write and fill my bookshelf with beautiful literature that I can pass on to my grand-daughters."

~ *Carol Goode*, Amazon.com, 5 stars

"As sweet as it claims.

But also funny and exasperating and although you expect a happy ending, there's still enough suspense as to "when" everything is going to work out. Highly recommended, especially for those who like a wholesome romance."

~ *tbob*, Amazon.com, 5 stars

The Cowboy Steals a Bride

A Sweet Historical Mail Order Bride Romance
(Rated PG)

The Husband-Maker Trilogy, Book 2

By

KRISTIN HOLT

Note: each book in this trilogy stands alone and may be read in any order.

www.kristinholt.com
ISBN-13: 978-1493594252
ISBN-10: 1493594257

This book is a work of fiction. Names, characters, places, and incidents are products of the writer's imagination or have been used fictitiously and are not to be construed as real. Any resemblance to persons, living or dead, actual events, locales or organizations is entirely coincidental.

eBook design by Kristin Holt: www.KristinHolt.com
Cover image www.shutterstock.com
Cover Design © 2014 by Elaina Lee,
www.ForTheMuseDesign.com

The Cowboy Steals a Bride

The Husband-Maker Trilogy, Book 2

Intended for his brother, but perfect for him.
What's a cowboy to do?

She's given up *everything* to seize her dream...

Julia Tyndall knows exactly what she wants: freedom and her choice of husbands, far away from Baltimore society.

Holmes's letters won her over, but it's the work-hardened, *beautifully imperfect* reality in denim and chambray that steals her heart. But it's not Holmes she meets on the train platform...it's his brother.

Days stretch into weeks and Holmes is nowhere to be found. How is a bride to remember and honor a marriage agreement when her groom's never around?

He's losing his heart to his *brother's* bride...

Conrad Macquarie doesn't have much patience for women on his dairy, even his brother's bride. She's enamored with the intricate workings of his dairy enterprise, too intelligent, uncommonly beautiful, a far sight too appealing.

Worse yet, she's the only woman who's ever seen past the scarred surface to the man beneath. Every moment spent with her blurs the familial lines, heating friendship into more than he should take. But it's so much less than he wants.

If Holmes doesn't get himself home soon, there's no telling what lines Conrad just might cross.

Dedication

For Diane Darcy and Heather Horrocks, the best critique group ever. Ladies, thank you for the support, kindness, and guidance. You're amazing!

Also for Mark, my very own hero. Our twenty-six years together are the *beginning* of our very own Happily-Ever-After.

Chapter One

California, Summer 1895

INTENDED DAUGHTERS-IN-LAW looked one hell of a lot different when kissing the wrong man.

Serious kissing. The kind that involved passion and promises and reeked of betrayal.

Phillip Macquarie gaped. Wedding champagne went down the wrong way. His old heart seized in mid-rhythm. The scene was so unbelievable, so gut-wrenching, he couldn't look away.

Before his very eyes, Daphne Browning—the fickle-hearted wench—displayed an appalling lack of moral character. For all to see.

She was supposed to marry his son, Holmes. *Everybody* knew that.

But that didn't stop the crowd from applauding and shouting congratulations. Maybe they were too plowed on wedding champagne to realize Miss Browning had just announced her impending marriage to someone other than her intended.

Phillip plunked down his goblet and shoved back his chair. He had to put a stop to this. Now.

Simultaneously, John and Luke grabbed Phillip's shoulders, pushing him back into his seat.

Phillip shrugged off their hands. "She is Holmes's last chance."

"I'm real new at this daughter-in-law thing." Luke topped off his champagne flute. "But one look at that Browning girl, and it's obvious she's more trouble than she's worth."

"Hey now," John said, always the peacemaker. "She looks happy. Maybe this is for the best."

"She was supposed to be happy with my son." Fury frothed within Phillip.

Luke shrugged. "Looks like she changed her mind."

"Do you suggest I allow her to ruin Holmes's life?" Phillip demanded. "For the likes of that thick-through-the-middle, uneducated baker?"

Luke had the gall to grin. "Good riddance."

Holmes would be brokenhearted. Flummoxed. Destroyed.

To his utter horror, Phillip realized this was worse than he'd first thought. Miss Daphne Browning had been Holmes's predominant reason for returning to Liberty. Without her for his bride, chances were too great Holmes wouldn't return at all.

He split a glance betwixt his lifelong friends. The three of them had discussed this precise topic, once or twice.

Until now, Phillip had felt secure. Confident. Delighted.

He narrowed his eyes at the contemptible, salacious, unfaithful tart. Luke had spoken true. Good riddance.

The shock finally wearing off, Phillip informed the others, "I won't allow that woman to drive my son away from the bosom of his family."

"She isn't the only girl in town," said Luke.

"Who else is there?" Phillip demanded, wildly casting his gaze around the filled-to-capacity Orme Hotel ballroom. Most of the young ladies Holmes once kept company with were now married. The pathetic few who remained were a poor match for Holmes.

Phillip watched as the pudgy baker escorted contemptible Daphne onto the dance floor. They waltzed midst the other wedding guests. How dare she look so happy?

As his best ideas so often did, the solution came in an instant. Such impulses had always paid off. "I'm going to draft an advertisement. There must be decent girls out there who are willing to be mail-order brides."

John's expression turned panicky. He glanced toward Judge Morley, seated two tables away. "You aren't planning another paper marriage, I hope, because—"

"No." He wasn't reckless enough to risk something like that again. At least not yet. He'd give the dust time to settle.

Concern lined John's brow. "You'd best think this through."

Phillip sat a little straighter. "I welcome the challenge. I love Holmes. His happiness is worth any amount of effort."

Luke nodded in agreement.

A moment passed while John considered what had been said. "You can count on me for support."

Pleased, Phillip leaned back, already planning the advertisement he'd circulate in the newspapers.

"I can't resist offering a friendly wager," John added to his pledge. "Twenty dollars says my Andrew marries Lillian before Holmes weds his mail-order bride."

Phillip raised a brow and tried not to laugh outright. Andrew had been courting Lillian for a decade. Andrew and Lillian would still have an "understanding" when Holmes returned from Harvard in nine months' time. "Make it forty. This wager will help finance Holmes's wedding trip."

"Forty?" Mischief twinkled in John's eyes. "That sure of yourself?"

Confident, Phillip offered his hand. "I always win."

They shook to seal the wager.

Luke chuckled with delight. "Last one to prod his son to the altar is a rotten egg."

Chapter Two

May, 1896

AS THE TRAIN PULLED INTO the Liberty station, it was all Julia Tyndall could do to remain seated. She peered through the dirty windows at the people gathered on the platform. Anticipation vibrated through her.

Her grand adventure had truly begun.

As other passengers rose and gathered their belongings, Julia's attention flitted from one man waiting outside to another. She bypassed men with families, skipped over a fellow kissing his girl in greeting—kissing! In public! What a glorious, welcome difference from staid Baltimore society—and searched for *her cowboy*.

She'd painted glorious mental images of a man

clad in denim, chaps, and chambray. A man who lived the intriguing western lifestyle she'd glimpsed in photographs. After hours studying the art gallery, she'd known she had to experience the Wild West for herself.

She grinned widely.

Today, she'd meet her own honest-to-goodness cowboy.

One with work-roughened hands. And a broad, firm body, muscled from a lifetime of labor. His face would be sun-browned and calluses would roughen his never-been-manicured hands.

She *needed* him a little worse for wear.

Given the life he lived, the inevitable injuries cowboys and ranchers experienced, he might be able to look past her physical imperfections hidden so well by proper clothing.

She'd banked everything on it.

Everything.

And traded in Gregory—the narrow-shouldered, soft-handed, pale-faced man her father had hand-picked for a son-in-law—for a chance at happiness with Holmes Macquarie.

Gregory had high political aspirations and even higher expectations of Julia, even though she came with the right family name. Perfection wasn't ever good enough for him.

It had taken her awhile, but Julia had realized Gregory wouldn't ever be good enough for her.

Holmes Macquarie, in comparison, would be an ideal match.

Aunt Portia stood in the aisle and pinned her hat into place. "Do you see your Mr. Macquarie?"

"Not yet." But he was out there. She could feel it.

Portia snapped her hatbox shut. "No time like the present. I'm desperate for a lemonade and an introduction to your groom, not necessarily in that order."

Hastily, Julia took one more look at the sepia-toned image of Holmes Macquarie. She'd memorized every detail of the bust portraiture. The handsome profile accentuated the strong jaw, prominent cheekbones, full head of hair, the masculine form of every feature.

Her heart beat rapidly, making her all the more nervous to finally meet him. She folded Holmes's letter together with the portrait and tucked them inside her handbag.

Portia gathered her belongings. "Starch and steel," she reminded Julia. "Up, up. Let's get the meeting over with." The tiny woman headed for the exit.

Julia turned her attention back to the platform. She knew she'd recognize Holmes on sight. From his letter, she knew he was a perfect blend of city and country, east and west. A Harvard lawyer, true, but one who had grown up on a dairy ranch. He loved his childhood home and wanted her to love it, too.

There wasn't a single thing about Holmes Macquarie that didn't appeal to Julia. She had complete faith that things would work out splendidly between them.

Granted, she was half in love with him already. How could that be avoided? He embodied everything she'd ever wanted. A rancher. A scholar who understood both East and West. A flesh-and-blood man whose letters had touched her heart and given her a fresh chance for marriage and family, with a man of her own choosing.

The platform had cleared somewhat, leaving a handful of scattered people milling about.

Through the grimy train windows, Julia caught a glimpse of a cowboy, standing with his feet braced an impressive shoulder-width apart. His well-worn boots were scuffed and dirty, his denims faded with much wear, and his dusty chambray shirt stretched over a broad torso that had seen years of honest work.

She'd never seen any male with such remarkable musculature. Her heart thumped into her throat and seemed to hover there.

Work-hardened. Masculine, handsome, and so incredibly real.

Oh, she'd been terribly wise to leave the city behind and head west.

Julia clapped a hand over her gaping mouth, grateful he couldn't see her through the dirty windows. It seemed so incredibly improper to ogle him.

In Baltimore, she'd been compelled to behave like a lady, avert her gaze, and control her desire to stare. Julia noted her trusted chaperon sipped the foam off a beer as she strolled the length of the platform. How like Portia to fashion her own set of rules.

Portia's thirst suited Julia fine. Given the lack of supervision, it seemed quite acceptable that Julia soak in every detail.

The cowboy's wide-brimmed hat cast a shadow over his face, but couldn't hide the square jaw and intelligent features.

A very familiar face, indeed.

Julia's heart skipped.

Holmes.

Without warning, he swept his hat from his head and wiped a shirt sleeve over his brow. He strode a few paces down the platform, his profile every bit as arresting. Afternoon sunlight illuminated the red in his auburn hair. The locks curled over his collar. Longer than fashionable at home. Oh, so very appealing.

He'd written of the one detail the sepia-toned portrait hadn't conveyed; the Macquaries were easily distinguished by their varying shades of red hair.

This splendid specimen was *him.*

Absolutely magnificent.

And he wanted to marry *her.*

An unsettling sensation quivered in Julia's middle. She leaned back in the seat, completely unable to rip her gaze from Holmes.

Impatient, he clapped his hat against his thigh. He scanned the train, his jaw set, his gaze lingering on the train windows. Then she noticed a detail his photograph—posed nearly in profile—carefully concealed.

Of course it would. What photographer would intentionally capture so obvious a scar? The reddish line swept from the left corner of his mouth and across his cheek. It wasn't new. She could tell that much. But it must've hurt. Terribly.

And he hadn't mentioned a single word of it in his letters.

He had to have known she'd see the scar immediately upon arrival. So evidently, he didn't think it an issue.

Relief, welcome as blossoming flowers in May, swept through her. He was *perfect*.

Not only was he a little battle-worn, but he had the confidence of a head of state. A body could tell, simply by watching him for a few seconds, that his injury neither defined nor limited him. His very presence commanded attention, respect, seemed far larger than his stature.

His portrait hadn't revealed any of *that*.

A tingle of female appreciation walked up her spine.

As she stared, he replaced his hat, stalking the length of the platform, apparently searching for her.

Oh, yes, she'd definitely made the right choice.

Julia pinned her hat into place and drew a breath for courage. She grabbed her travel satchel, hat box, and handbag, anxious to greet her destiny.

WHERE WAS SHE?

Conrad Macquarie didn't have all day to wait on the platform. Had his brother's bride missed the train or changed her mind altogether?

As if Conrad hadn't a thing to do, Pop had sent him on this errand. Although he'd left the dairy in capable hands, it went completely against Conrad's nature to waste daylight. He had a good ten hours' work to squeeze in before nightfall.

No sign of Holmes—Pop had obviously hoped the Golden Son would arrive today—and no sign of his bride. It seemed this errand had been an utter waste of good daylight.

He'd decided to ask if any passengers remained on board, when one last young woman came down the steps.

Trim, hourglass figure. Gorgeous face. She carried herself confidently.

Whoa, Nellie. Conrad swallowed, acutely aware Miss Julia Tyndall's comely portrait hadn't done her justice.

That was her, all right. Taller than he expected.

Even if he hadn't seen her picture, he would've known that expensively tailored navy blue travel suit had started in a fancy eastern city.

Relieved he'd finally found her, he crossed the platform. She looked up, her features alight. Up close, his brother's intended bride was absolutely arresting.

Her brunette hair shone under her hat, a perfect complement to her large, dark blue eyes. The navy wool of her dress accentuated her coloring. Her smooth, creamy skin was flawless. Not a single freckle, blemish, or crease. Looked a bit too much like one of Katherine's porcelain dolls.

Though the outside packaging was very attractive, this prim city lady wasn't Conrad's type—nor could anyone of her ilk be remotely interested in a common laborer like him—but that didn't mean he couldn't admire his brother's good fortune.

"Mr. Macquarie? I'm Julia Tyndall."

Conrad nodded in greeting and offered his hand.

She slipped her gloved hand into his. Her firm grip surprised him. Just like everybody else, especially females, her gaze lingered on the ghastly scar distorting the left side of his face. And like all dignified folk, she pretended not to notice.

Her gaze returned to his eyes, right quick. “I’m so very happy to meet you.”

“Likewise.” He expected her attention to drift back to his cheek. It didn’t.

“I’m looking forward to meeting your whole family.” Her smile seemed a bit too warm, her attention a tad too familiar. She squeezed his hand. Again. Her fingers slipped from his.

Uncomfortable, he took her travel bag and hat box from her grasp, automatically turning his good side to her. “The family’s looking forward to meeting you, too.” He’d never seen his parents so happy about anything. Ever.

“I’ve looked forward to this for ever so long.” Her appealing smile brightened. “Thank you for meeting our train. I’m glad for the chance to meet *you* first.”

He glanced at her, as leery as a heifer in the bull pen. Why would his brother’s bride want to meet *him* first? He knew he wasn’t much to look at, and that only made him wonder what she was after. Whatever it was, he didn’t want to know.

“You must be tired,” he said, ready to end their brief conversation. “Let’s find your trunks and get them loaded.”

Miss Tyndall pointed out her five matching Saratogas, all trimmed the same with brass reinforcements at the joints. He hefted the substantial trunks one at a time into the wagon bed.

As he shoved the heavy baggage toward the front, he sensed Miss Tyndall’s gaze lingering on him. He caught her watching his every movement. She flashed a smile that slammed into his gut.

This wasn’t concern over her belongings. Nor was it boredom. Whatever the woman’s game, it made him damn nervous. No one—not even Sally—had looked at him like this. He’d heard talk of women making calf eyes at men, but he’d never seen it aimed directly at himself.

Until now.

Maybe if he had a lick of experience, he'd know what to do. Given this particular female was about to marry Holmes only made it worse.

If this woman turned out to be cut from the same bolt of cloth as Sally Tibbs, then Conrad felt sorry for Holmes. He may have thought Miss Julia pretty, in an untouchable sort of way, but her personality wasn't looking all that attractive.

"What did you bring with you?" he asked, all nothing's-bothering-me. "Everything you own?" The drive back home would take twice as long, fully loaded like this, but it couldn't be helped.

Her laughter, sincere and warm, didn't exactly answer the question. "These, too, please." She indicated another stash of three smaller, mismatched, travel weary trunks.

It took some doing, but Conrad managed to cram all eight trunks into the wagon bed.

By the time he'd finished loading, an unfamiliar gray-haired woman approached the rig. Her ridiculously large hat, boasting a birds nest—complete with *eggs?*—wobbled atop her head. The woman was so short, her wide brim didn't come close to meeting his shoulder.

She finished off the last of a beer, and said to Conrad. "Excellent brew. Very fine indeed." Her dark eyes twinkled with perhaps one drink too many. "I've studied Californian wines extensively, but hadn't heard tell your beer was every bit as palatable."

Miss Tyndall took the glass from the older woman's hands. "Mr. Macquarie, may I introduce my aunt, Miss Portia Tyndall."

He wasn't surprised to see Holmes's bride had brought a companion; any proper lady would. Pop hadn't specified, but then Pop had sprung the surprise of Holmes's guest on them suddenly, as if he hadn't known about it himself.

"*Doctor* Tyndall," the matron corrected

immediately. "Twice over. But *you,* young man, must call me Aunt. Family is family."

"My youngest brother's studying medicine. Probably plague you with questions." With the way things stood with Gabriel, Conrad wouldn't be the one to pass on this interesting bit of information.

"Oh, I'm not the kind of doctor that does a body any good. My primary doctorate is in geology, the second in botany."

"Geology. That's..." Rocks? Earth formations? He hadn't any idea what a geologist did, or why they'd want to do it.

"Have you sensed tremors today?" The doctor clapped one tiny hand onto Conrad's forearm. The frippery atop her hat wobbled.

"No, ma'am."

"Vibrations?"

"Most Californians take notice only when pictures swing on the walls." He latched the back of the wagon, made sure it was secure, then herded the women to the front. The quicker he got the ladies back to the ranch, the sooner he could get back to work. Time was a wasting.

Aunt Portia's disappointment was obvious. "Not even the slightest rumble?"

The train engine vibrated the earth beneath their feet. He doubted he'd sense a minor quake if one happened at that very moment.

But the batty old woman wouldn't give up. "Tell me, did you experience the quake of April twenty-eighth?"

Must this conversation happen *here?* Now? He took the doctor's empty beer glass and set it on a piece of unclaimed baggage.

She prattled on, "what I wouldn't have given to be here then. You *were* here, weren't you? I assume, by your mode of dress, that you are Holmes's brother Conrad."

"Yes, ma'am."

"Aunt Portia," she corrected. "I thought so. Holmes's letters detailed the whole family. Four brothers: Holmes, the attorney; Silas, the accountant; Conrad, the dairyman; and Gabriel, the medical doctor-in-training."

"Right." The matron had neatly labeled all of them. "One sister, Katherine."

At her aunt's assessment, the young Miss Tyndall blanched pale as skimmed milk. Panic flickered in her eyes. She seemed to teeter on her high heeled shoes.

Conrad clenched his teeth. He knew that look; Ma fainted too often for comfort.

"Conrad?" she mouthed, hardly making any noise at all.

For a moment, he expected her to topple onto her backside. The only decent thing to do was catch her. Even if that was precisely what she wanted.

He cringed inwardly. He never should have agreed to run this errand for Pop. Next time, he'd say no, and a great deal more.

"*Conrad* Macquarie." Miss Julia wasn't asking a question.

He split a glance between the two ladies, and witnessed their silent exchange. He'd never claimed to understand women or their reasons for doing anything. But in that moment, his heartbeat slowed, and he understood the problem.

Miss Julia had mistaken him for Holmes. *Him*.

It was absurd. But amazing. Despite the obvious similarities, Conrad's spoiled face had kept anyone from confusing them. Ever.

But that had to be the problem. One look at Miss Julia's porcelain skin, flooded with color, and he *knew* he was right.

But surely she knew Holmes well, been courted by him for months, at least. Had it been so long since they'd last seen one another?

Unlikely.

Could it be Holmes had sent for a bride he'd never

laid eyes on? Why would he do such a thing? Daphne Browning had married the baker, and that might have made Holmes do something this risky and impetuous. It sounded like something Gabriel would do--not orderly, methodical Holmes.

No wonder Miss Julia had said those things, looked at him that way. In this light, everything looked a great deal different than it had just moments ago. Flattering, all that attention.

The attention she'd believed she'd given Holmes.

It may have looked indecent a minute ago, but not anymore. She cleared her throat. Stood a little taller. Tucked her discomfort away far better than Conrad had ever seen his little sister or mother do. He found he respected her for it.

"Yes," Aunt Portia said, "You are he, are you not?"

Hadn't Holmes told these ladies anything? Apparently he hadn't spelled things out. *Conrad is the one with the nasty scar ripped from one corner of his mouth—an obvious, unsightly mark that'll make it easy to pick him out of a crowd.*

"Of course you are," Portia rushed on. "One glimpse of those hands, and I knew you hadn't spent the past several years in a classroom. But you do resemble your brother."

Sensing discomfort from sister-in-law-to-be, he spoke to her directly. "A simple misunderstanding. I should've introduced myself properly, ma'am. I'm Conrad Macquarie."

Miss Julia nodded. Tried to smile. Straightened her spine. "My mistake. Your hair color, the strong similarities in your features... I believed Holmes would meet us."

Her uneasiness seemed to fade. "Thank you." Her smile took on a genuine quality. "For meeting our train."

"My pleasure," he told her.

"For all the talking you've done, Dolly," Aunt Portia said as she climbed aboard the wagon, evidently without expecting his assistance, "about identifying a man's chosen work by with a cursory inspection of his hands, I would've thought you'd take notice."

"I was otherwise occupied," Miss Julia said to her aunt, even as she cast Conrad a glance. Her gaze dropped to his hands—rough, callused, scarred—and her quick smile returned.

So she liked his hands. Fine by him. Made him want to smile back. If he'd been a man prone to such, he would've. For in that moment, he caught a glimpse of the woman beneath the flawless, too-citified-to-be-human facade, and decided she wasn't as bad as he'd feared.

Could be Holmes was a very lucky man.

JULIA IMMEDIATELY recognized the ranch house as the beloved home Holmes had described.

Two-and-a-half stories, painted white, verandas circling both the first and second floors. Clusters of chairs formed comfortable groupings as if the family spent warm evenings outside enjoying the view. Lilac bushes burst with vibrant lavender and purple blossoms, celebrating the arrival of spring.

The Macquarie family home was welcoming. Spacious. Appealing. Well-tended. But one thing was missing from the grand picture of this first arrival.

Holmes.

Julia tried to hide her disappointment.

Two women—easily recognized as Holmes's mother and his only sister, Katherine—waited on the front porch with a pair of welcoming smiles. They waved.

Portia waved back and called, "Hello!"

Julia waved, too. Still no sign of Holmes himself. Surely, if he were at home, he'd join the others momentarily.

Having grown up in company of politicians, she understood the demands upon Holmes's time. If he wasn't occupied in the law office in Liberty, he would undoubtedly be sequestered in the library at home, working until the moment she arrived.

It was a romantic and foolish notion to expect him to wait on the veranda for her.

But that didn't mean she hadn't wanted him to.

So, where was he? No one watched from behind the freshly washed windows. The door stood half open. No sign of Holmes.

Why hadn't his mother called to him, the moment she'd seen the buckboard clear the rise? The answer was obvious. He wasn't home.

Julia sighed, called a greeting to Mrs. Macquarie and her daughter, and reminded herself Holmes would surely be home in time for supper. He must be equally as anxious to meet her, as she was him. She ought to be pleased by these turn of events. Now she'd have the time to wash her face, brush road dust from her dress, and prepare to make a better impression.

Conrad eased the pair of horses to a stop and set the brake. He leapt to the ground, circled behind the wagon, and offered her a hand down. "Ma, Katherine. Meet Miss Julia Tyndall, and her aunt, Doctor Portia Tyndall."

A flurry of warm welcome enveloped Julia. The sweet, light fragrance of lilacs scented the breeze. She glanced at the empty house, one more time.

The women exchanged pleasantries and asked about the comfort of their journey. After a few moments, Portia asked, "When can we expect to meet Holmes?"

The moment the words had left her aunt's lips, Julia knew there was a problem. A sinking feeling tugged on her nervous stomach. The disappointment was familiar. How many times had she watched her father put his political responsibilities ahead of family?

She glanced from Holmes's mother and sister and

their dour expressions, to Conrad. A moment's silence told her she wouldn't find their answer pleasant. Mrs. Macquarie seemed to plead with Conrad to handle the situation.

"Last I heard," he finally said, "Holmes won't get home until sometime next week."

Chapter Three

PHILLIP LEANED BACK in his chair at the head of the family's dining room table. This long-awaited evening had turned out almost as planned...except for Holmes's glaring absence.

Punctuality had never been his firstborn son's strong suit. The boy had been two weeks late for his own birth. Yet one might assume Harvard capable of instilling discipline if naught else.

Other than that one significant detail, Phillip was immensely pleased. Miss Julia Tyndall had proved to be exactly what he'd ordered. Every bit as pretty as her picture. As fine a lady as her letters had indicated.

It was unfortunate those same letters hadn't warned about Aunt Portia's penchant to dominate supper conversation.

Weary of listening to Portia relate stories of her first safari, Phillip masked a grimace behind his coffee cup. Who cared one iota for Africa? He'd banked everything on Julia's adoration for California, specifically the five mile radius surrounding this ranch house, and he grew impatient waiting to talk about that specific topic.

At the first hint Portia's tale might be winding down, Phillip asked, "Miss Julia, tell me, what do you think of our ranch, now that you've seen some of it?"

Interest flickered in Julia's blue eyes. "Our ride in from town, and what I've glimpsed from the veranda, has made me anxious to explore it all."

Exactly what Phillip wanted to hear. But he wanted details.

Portia didn't give Julia a chance to elaborate. "My thoughts, precisely." She turned to Julia for confirmation. "No matter how much one sees, there's always something more. Africa *called* to me. I was helpless to resist."

Now seemed like a good time for Africa to extend another invitation.

Seated at Phillip's left, Violet took his hand. She gave a little squeeze, tipped her head slightly toward Julia's Aunt Portia, her green eyes twinkling. *Do you believe these two Miss Tyndalls are related?*

Without a single word passing Violet's lips, Phillip understood her message completely. A nice bonus after almost four blessed decades of marriage. At sixty, Violet's red hair had only begun to gray, her plump cheeks still soft, and she still possessed the temperament of an angel. Given the present company, he saw that as a plus.

At first glance, he'd have to agree with his wife's assessment. Miss Julia and her aunt didn't bear much resemblance. Tiny Portia chattered like a caged monkey, her tight, gray curls bobbing with every turn of her head. Miss Julia, in stark comparison, had manners fit for supper in the White House.

Holmes should be here.

The mere thought irritated Phillip all over again.

He glared at Holmes's empty chair at the foot of the table.

At a minuscule break in Portia's tale, Katherine rose and gathered empty dessert dishes. "Excuse me. Do continue, Dr. Tyndall."

"Call me Portia. Family is family." A quick smile, a nod that bid Katherine to go on with whatever, then launched back into her story. "It was on my second tour of Egypt that my guide's boat capsized on the Nile. Some said he had it coming, for running a shoddy operation."

She speared a nibble of spiced apple cheesecake. Her rapid speech was effused with energy. "But I knew differently. The newspaper reports were quite glamorized, regardless of the specific details I provided."

Violet's grip tightened. *Truth?* she asked, without murmuring a word.

Phillip shrugged. *Possibly.* Listening to Portia wore him out. If the loony woman intended to remain in this household after the wedding, Phillip imagined he'd eat a lot of suppers in his bedroom.

"Shoddy operation," Portia murmured between sips of dessert wine. "Ha! That guide saved my life. As the boat overturned, a crate toppled over the edge, snagged my skirts, and dragged me under. If it hadn't been for his quick thinking and a blade to rival any Bedouin's—"

Violet blanched. Her grip tightened. From the end of the table, Phillip heard a suspicious snicker from one of his sons. The guilty party—Gabriel, apparently—sucked down water to hide his laughter.

Katherine returned from the kitchen, just in time to hear mention of the blade and slashed skirts and heroic rescue efforts. Phillip watched his only daughter's pale skin turn completely white.

"The pyramids, Aunt Portia," Julia inserted smoothly. "Do tell our hosts about your experiences there."

Aha. Clever girl. Excellent use of diversionary tactics. Holmes would appreciate Julia's quick mind and even temperament. Phillip shot his wife a look. *Didn't I tell you? Perfect match.*

"An absolute wonder!" Portia plunked her wine goblet upon Grandma's tatted tablecloth—an heirloom used for the rarest of special occasions—and drew a deep breath. "The mathematical symmetry is astounding."

Phillip only half-listened to Portia's rapid speech, detailing everything from the colors of the sand to the genera and species of vegetation she'd encountered in Cairo. He glanced down the table at his two sons, Conrad and Gabriel, both as fidgety as penned bulls.

Conrad seized his opportunity for escape, following Katherine into the kitchen with an armload of Grandma's good china. Desperate, Gabriel gathered up a handful of napkins and trotted after his siblings.

Completely clueless she was losing her audience, Portia turned her rounded eyes on Phillip and Violet. "I know you're wondering how I managed to survive my ordeal."

Supper had already dragged on twice as long as any Thanksgiving feast Phillip could recall. He saw little reason to torture the family one moment longer. "Indeed I am."

Violet nudged him. *She's our guest.*

Phillip immediately amended his tone, for Violet's sake. "We all are. And we wait with much curiosity for tomorrow night, when I hope you'll share the conclusion." A wee bit of emphasis on the conclusion part.

"Yes, yes." Portia glanced at Holmes's vacant seat at the foot of the table. "I suppose I ought to save *some* of my adventures, until Holmes is in residence."

"Grand idea." Maybe Julia would have more to say, if her aunt ever stopped talking.

"When will that be, exactly?" Portia looked from Phillip to Violet, and back again.

Phillip considered giving specifics, then thought better of it. Holmes would be otherwise occupied, and unable to properly greet either Miss Tyndall, because the minute his errant son got home, Phillip intended to tan the boy's hide. The kid's telegram stated he'd been delayed in Boston. *Delayed?* What on earth for?

On a whim, Holmes had mucked up everything.

Now The Plan—which had been meticulously organized—required serious adjustments. The Three had already decided to take turns keeping an eye on the depot. They couldn't allow Holmes to show up unannounced at the ranch, having no inkling who Julia was.

If Holmes had returned on schedule, he would've had ample time to get used to the whole idea of a bride. This had been necessary because Phillip had no doubt that Holmes, forever contrary, would balk. At first. But he'd come around, and see Julia was everything he'd ever wanted.

When that was all said and done, *then* Portia could regale Holmes with fantastic tales of Africa and Egypt and Timbuktu.

"Next week?" Portia prompted, gesturing vaguely. "Does that mean Monday, Friday, somewhere betwixt?"

"Early in the week, surely." Phillip pasted on a smile, even as his stomach turned queasy. Confidence. Certainty. Those were some of his best assets. Even if Holmes hadn't been precise or generous with the details.

"Well." Portia brightened and turned to her niece. "We've trunks to unpack. Let's get started, shall we?"

"Miss Julia." Phillip rose. His old knees complained. Sitting at the dining room table for three hours had wreaked havoc. "Join me in the library, will you? The women have monopolized your time this afternoon." Once Holmes saw her, Julia likely wouldn't give an old man the time of day. She'd be understandably too enamored with her intended. "I want a turn."

Violet, bless her heart, herded Aunt Portia into the kitchen. She'd offer more coffee and listen with patience as their house guest continued her stories.

Within minutes, Phillip finally had Miss Julia's complete attention. He offered her a seat in one of the matching upholstered chairs before the library's hearth. A few pleasantries, a compliment or two, and Phillip was ready to discuss business.

"If it hadn't been for the trial running a full day longer than anticipated, I would've met your train myself."

She smiled demurely. A hallmark of fine breeding. "Yes, sir. Thank you."

"I'm so pleased Holmes found you. Mrs. Macquarie and I are certain you two will be very happy."

Guilt pricked Phillip, but he wasn't about to spoil an ideal arranged marriage with too much truth. "Holmes was terribly disappointed to miss your arrival. He's waited eagerly for you. Counted down the days. I hope you understand this case in San Francisco was of utmost importance."

"I understand completely."

Of course she did. As the daughter of a United States Senator, she knew all about a man's obligations. "Very important case, indeed. That's one thing I admire about my son, his dedication to his work. He'll be a tremendous asset to my law practice."

"His letters mentioned his desire to join you."

"Why, yes. I'm pleased he told you." Another twinge of guilt. He ignored it, aware he dug himself in a little deeper. It couldn't be helped. "I wondered how much he'd said about himself."

"He shared a great deal."

"Good, good. I hope he extended an invitation to your parents. They will, of course, want to be in attendance for your wedding. I realize they have a great distance to travel, and we'll want to consider their time limitations."

"My parents will not be coming."

Surprised, Phillip took a moment to answer. His smile melted. "No?"

He'd planned to introduce Senator and Mrs. Tyndall to his friends. To hear they wouldn't come disappointed him to no end. Why not? What could possibly be more important than their own daughter's wedding?

He tried to respond with refinement. He chose his words with care. It would never do to reveal he knew too much. "Your father must be busy. All business-men—"

Her sad smile stopped him in mid-sentence.

When she didn't speak, he knew a moment's panic. Did she know he'd researched her family? "If he's not too busy, then what's the problem?"

"My parents did not," she averted her gaze, paused, "support my choice to come to California."

"Why *not?*" Phillip didn't even try to keep his voice down. He knew every last word written in those letters. He'd given them no reason whatsoever to doubt Holmes's ability to provide a comfortable living. He couldn't imagine why the illustrious senator wouldn't wholeheartedly approve of a Harvard-educated attorney for his daughter.

"They believed I was making a mistake."

Mistake? This match was no mistake. This bride and groom wouldn't be any happier if they'd fallen in love the old fashioned way and chosen each other themselves.

How could she sit there, so serene, so calm? Phillip wanted to bellow, "*Objection!*"

"With due respect, you needn't worry about my parents."

"I'm not worried, not in the slightest. They couldn't help but approve, on some level." He grappled for any justification he could find. "They sent your aunt along as your traveling companion." It occurred to him that the senator may have merely wanted a bit of quiet in his household.

A moment passed. Julia's expression filled with remorse. But she said nothing.

With a groan he couldn't quite stifle, Phillip pushed to his feet and paced toward the window. So Julia's father hadn't agreed. At all.

Indignant, he took several seconds to gather his composure. How dare the senator think a Macquarie wasn't fit for his daughter? Phillip took exception to Tyndall's judgment of Holmes. A mistake, indeed. Tyndall undoubtedly expected the marriage to fail.

Ha. Tyndall had no idea who he was up against. Phillip Macquarie didn't know the meaning of the word failure. He'd never grown accustomed to losing—because he always came out on top, in first place. Always.

It was most unfortunate the honorable senator hadn't accompanied his daughter west, rather than allowed his spinster sister to chaperon. Phillip had plenty to say to any man who dismissed his sons.

"Once you meet Holmes," Phillip told Julia, his tone as soothing as he could make it, "you'll see you've done the right thing."

He searched her expression for any sign of distress. She seemed calm enough, but he'd misread jurors faces before.

Uneasy, he considered that the last thing he needed was Julia heading home, back to her disapproving parents, before her much-anticipated meeting with Holmes could take place.

This was one wager he had no intention of losing; his firstborn's life-long happiness was at stake. He would see it through to a favorable conclusion.

"I already know I've done the right thing." Miss Julia, serene and certain, held his gaze. "Holmes's letters have convinced me this is where I want to be."

He heard the quiet conviction in her voice. He liked this pretty lady more and more. "I'm very glad to hear that."

She stood, met his gaze and held it. Her soft smile

eased some of Phillip's anxiety.

Julia had come west to marry Holmes, despite her father's judgment. Phillip never would've guessed, from her well-mannered letters, that she'd prove defiant. But he liked defiant. Meant she had pluck. An admirable quality.

And she wanted to marry his son.

Yes, indeed. He'd chosen splendidly. A woman who knew her own mind and had the sense to choose Holmes, despite the lack of her father's approval. Her family would come around. Before or after the wedding, it didn't really matter. Whether or not the esteemed politician bothered to come west to witness the blessed event, it would take place.

"I'm happy to find you're everything Holmes says you are." He chuckled softly and took her small hands in his own. "You two will be very happy together."

From the beginning, he'd planned to do whatever it took to make her so content and happy here, she'd never want to leave. Given Holmes's absence, he'd have to work a little harder to make sure she didn't grow weary.

Julia's letters had convinced him of her love of the west, of her craving to experience everything a ranch had to offer. She'd expressed an enthusiastic desire to see the Pacific, to live among the giant redwoods, and to experience rural life.

She'd written an endearing list of things she wanted to do: gather eggs, learn to ride, milk a cow, plant and tend a vegetable garden, stroll the open fields. Her wishes were simple, and lengthy in number. Both of which pleased Phillip to no end.

The girl couldn't have loved the area more, had she been born a native. Which was precisely why Phillip had recognized Holmes's bride the moment he'd read her letter. For the more attached she became to this spot on earth, the less likely Holmes would ever want to leave again.

"It's most unfortunate Holmes missed your

arrival, but I have just the thing to make the next few days pass quickly. Holmes told me you wanted to see the workings of a dairy."

"I *do*."

Phillip liked the way her melancholy over Holmes's absence quickly turned to enthusiasm. At the library door, he bellowed, "Conrad!"

No one knew more about operating the dairy than Conrad. He lived and breathed this place, and loved no topic of conversation more. It would take Julia *days* to see it all, and begin to understand all the ins and outs. No boredom. No errant thoughts of returning east. No time to worry overmuch about her parents' disapproval or Holmes's absence.

Phillip welcomed Conrad with a hearty clap on the shoulder.

This addendum to The Plan would work out fine, indeed.

CONRAD CONSIDERED SHOOTING himself in the foot, just as an excuse to avoid driving Miss Julia around the ranch.

Instead, he settled for showing up at the house right after morning chores. He expected to find the citified china doll still abed and far from ready to go out.

To his surprise, Miss Julia wasn't only awake and fully dressed; excitement glittered in her eyes as she met him on the porch. Her upswept hair shone in the morning sunlight. The green skirt, shirtwaist, and bow tied about her neck were freshly ironed.

He stopped the buggy, not sure he liked her enthusiasm. Ladies like her could not possibly enjoy driving past fields and pastures, circling outbuildings, and hearing about the dairy. She had something—probably some*where*—else in mind.

Conrad wanted no part of it.

"Would you mind if we walked?" she asked.

"What?"

She opened her green and white striped parasol to shade her skin. "Walking gives a better perspective. I've been watching for you, but didn't see you before you hitched the buggy."

Walk? In high heels? He saw the toes of fancy boots peeking from beneath her piping-fringed hem. Ten minutes, and her shoes would be ruined. Blisters would sprout on her tender feet.

"I could help you unhitch the team," she offered.

She meant it. Shaking his head, he conceded this tour was going to take three or four times longer than it should have.

"No need." He led the pair of Saddlebreds toward the barn, and handed them off to one of the crew.

Seeing to it Miss Julia walked on his good side, Conrad led her down the lane that led between fields of alfalfa and toward the red brick creamery. He told her everything he knew about raising feed crops.

"Some dairymen," he told her, keeping his tone as flat as possible, "feed their stock all sorts of ill-suited fodder. Beets and turnips, for example. People food. Completely unsuitable for a milk cow."

"As are grains and cabbage."

He slid her a glance. How did *she* know that?

"True," he agreed, still attempting to bore her. "Results in an inferior milk quality. Flat. Watery in texture."

Another fifteen minutes of this—in addition to her fresh blisters—and she'd be sure to yawn, feign tiredness, and want to return to the house. If he quickened their pace, he could cut all this nonsense down to five minutes.

"I see you irrigate." She kept up with his long stride, heedless to the dust clinging to her hem. "Progressive."

"It's necessary."

"Aunt Portia and I discussed the method, at great

length. She's an intelligent woman, quite capable in her own fields of study, but had some misconceptions about the nutritional quality of alfalfa, specifically for cattle."

Conrad cast a glance at Julia. Was the woman serious?

"Portia would enjoy seeing this for herself." She drew breath deeply, an expression of contentment on her features. "Smells so clean, so fresh."

"Hmm. Portia's still sleeping?"

"She went for a walk, before dawn. Exploring. I won't look for her until supper time."

"I see."

"Will it shock you to learn I've never actually seen a cow?"

"Not surprising." When they approached the pastures, he expected she'd hold a lavender water-sprinkled hankie to her nose.

"How many head do you have?"

"About two hundred, including calves."

She seemed impressed. "A large operation."

"Compared to some."

"Some?" Her soft laughter sounded sweet. "In several recent issues of the *Transactions of the California State Agricultural Society*—"

"You read that?"

"Yes. I pride myself on thorough research."

Now she sounded like Aunt Portia. "Why?"

"It seemed prudent, given Holmes's wish for us to live on this ranch." To his surprise, she kept up the brisk pace, without sounding winded. "I may have never seen a cow, Mr. Macquarie, but I can thoroughly diagram her digestive and reproductive systems."

Conrad fairly choked. *Reproductive* system? Holmes's bride was one odd female. Looked like a lady. Dressed and spoke like a lady—usually. But had the oddest sense of what constituted light reading. And appropriate topics of conversation.

"They teach you this in college?" he asked.

She laughed softly, poked him in the shoulder

with her silly parasol, and gave no answer.

Within minutes, they reached the red brick creamery. He held the door for Miss Julia to enter before him. Morning sun streamed through tall windows lining the east wall, flooding the high-ceilinged space with light. "This half of the building houses the cheese-making equipment."

He watched her survey the machinery and implements, her gaze soaking up every detail. She wandered through the room, spinning her closed parasol. She paused to examine a press from a different angle.

Last night, he'd figured the tour was Pop's idea, but he realized Miss Julia had genuinely wanted to see the dairy for herself. That shouldn't amaze him. Like she'd said, she'd come to Holmes's ranch, to be his wife. The woman had spent time reading agricultural reports. No one Conrad knew—especially not women—read those for fun.

Glancing over her shoulder, Julia smiled. "I smell a hint of Monterey Jack."

"Our specialty."

She skirted a work table and peered into the adjoining storage room. "Macquarie's cheese has been on my family's dining room table for years."

"I see." Over the past five years, he'd sold hundreds of shipments to various east-coast cities. Macquarie Dairies enjoyed a fine reputation and lucrative business, both locally and nationwide.

She hesitated on the threshold to the storage room, holding his gaze for a moment. "May I step in here?"

He nodded, then followed her inside. Within these thick walls of stone and brick, the near-constant temperature allowed the cheese to cure to perfection.

He lit a lamp, and watched her stroll the aisles. Her skirts swirled about those silly high heels and closed parasol.

"My mouth's watering," she said softly. "My

favorite breakfast is a slice of Monterey Jack, melted and bubbling over soft-yolk eggs and toast."

"Delicious," he agreed. "It's also tasty melted on a slab of apple pie."

"New Englanders prefer cheddar on their pie."

"Ignorant heathens."

She chuckled, a rich, throaty sound that quickened Conrad's gut. "Luckily for me," she murmured, "I'm a New Englander by education only."

"Ah. Smith College." Pop had mentioned this, just last night at supper. Quite an accomplishment. "You *are* a New Englander."

"Not truly. They'll never convince me cheddar is superior to Monterey Jack."

An unspoken agreement passed between them, and Conrad was stunned to discover he enjoyed Miss Julia's company.

Somewhere, in the past half-hour, he'd forgotten this tour was his duty. It no longer seemed like a chore. He found he didn't care two days' work awaited him.

"What's your favorite way to eat this cheese?" she asked.

"Fresh."

"Ah. You have me at a disadvantage there."

He bypassed the newest of the cheese, heading for the full-flavored wheels that were due to be shipped out the following morning. He sliced a wedge and offered it to Miss Julia.

He found himself watching with anticipation as she took a nibble, held the morsel on her tongue, and closed her eyes. Faint lamplight glowed on her smooth skin. She chewed delicately.

He'd proudly displayed his wares at wine and cheese tastings throughout the county and beyond. His Monterey Jack was touted as the finest in the state. Just last year, the governor had presented Macquarie Dairies an award of excellence.

But no praise had ever come close to Miss Julia's expression of utter bliss.

Seconds passed. She took another nibble. Sighed.

How long had it been since he'd eaten cheese, for pure enjoyment? He taste-tested. Ate to slake his hunger. Appreciated, true. But never like this.

Julia's eyelids fluttered open. She focused on his face.

Not his spoiled cheek...but *him*.

Conrad's mouth dried.

He found himself staring back. The moment stretched.

She said nothing. There was no need. He'd heard her praise. It resonated within him, humming, filling him in a way nothing ever had before.

He took a half-step closer. Surely as if she'd thrown a lasso around his neck, he felt an unmistakable tug in her direction. The kick of attraction startled him.

She pivoted away and the spell was broken.

He blinked. Turned his bad side away from her. Where had *that* come from? He shrugged off the uncomfortable thoughts and pushed them far away. He had no desire to even consider what had just happened.

"Delicious, isn't it?" He put the knife back in its box and headed for the door.

"Yes."

Her sigh sent a ripple of awareness through him.

"You must take great care with the milk," she commented, "every step of the way."

He cleared his throat. "Always."

"I'd like to see what you do. All the stages."

He held the door leading outside, and followed her into the bright sunshine.

She opened the parasol. "If I promise to stay out from underfoot, may I observe the milking tomorrow morning?"

How smart was that, he wondered, to let her come along, especially after what had just happened? She savored his cheese, and he lost all sense of reason. It would be better if he didn't risk something like that again.

"I'm an early riser," she added. "I won't be any trouble at all. It's something I want very much to see."

What could he say? Pop had told him to show her the operation. That couldn't be done in a single day.

He glanced at Miss Julia's face, in the shade beneath her parasol. "We milk at four."

Her quick smile slammed into his gut.

Holmes's bride, he lectured himself. *Off limits. Untouchable.*

"I'll be ready."

Chapter Four

BEFORE SUNRISE the following morning, Julia eagerly followed Conrad and his crew to the milking shed.

"I'm one man short this morning," Conrad informed her, when she stood out of the way to observe the men as they went about their duties. He escorted her down a row of low-walled stalls. "I'll put you to work."

"You want *my* help?" Giddy excitement vibrated through Julia as she took in every detail illuminated by glowing lamps. The building was freshly scrubbed and smelled of strong soap.

All down the line, men worked in teams of two per stall, preparing milking machines with rapid efficiency. This operation hardly resembled picture book images of a farmer's daughter, milking a single cow from her perch on a three-legged stool.

How gloriously menial. Jordon Tyndall's daughter, milking in a cowshed? Laughable. And freeing, unlike anything had ever been. Until now.

Midst these dairymen, she was nameless, of little importance. No one expected perfection from her first try at milking. Exactly the way she wanted it.

"It's a working ranch. Everybody—including company—earns their keep." Conrad did not smile. No change in the deep melody of his voice. But she felt the warmth of his gaze on her, as if seeing her as an entirely different person this morning.

And his teasing felt oddly wonderful.

His easy manner made her instantly at home—in the barn, as well as amongst his family. Almost as if she belonged here. "I'm not company."

"That's right." His gaze took in her serviceable navy muslin—quite possibly the most drab, plain thing she owned—as if he found the dress more appealing than the stylish green ensemble she'd worn yesterday. "So get to work."

Conrad's father had asked him to show her the dairy. Keep her busy. Humor her wishes to see everything. He could've done that by sitting her on a stool in the corner and telling her to stay out of the way.

She could see the crew had work to do. And so did he. But he'd shown her courtesy, in allowing her this experience.

How very sweet. His kindness sent a wash of appreciation through her.

At the end of the aisle, he plunked down a bucket of sudsy water and hung an over-sized lantern on a peg. He spent a minute checking the milker, uncoiling and attaching hoses.

She watched his every movement. In this narrow stall, he seemed larger. Broader. Completely in his element.

"What, exactly, do you want me to do?" she asked.

Before Conrad could answer, his younger brother, Gabriel, slid open the shed door. Cold early morning air swirled into the building, carrying with it the pungent odors of animals. Cows pushed inside.

Julia drew a breath as panic flickered in her middle. "They just *walk* in here?"

"Twice a day, like clockwork."

"So easily? No leashes? No shepherd?" She retreated deeper into the milking stall.

Conrad closed a steadying hand around her upper arm, and spoke close to her ear as the stampede headed in their direction. "Leash? These are cows, Miss Julia, not dogs or sheep. They want to get milked."

"Want to?" In all her study, in all her reading—

The thought evaporated as a cow barreled into the stall where she and Conrad stood. Up close, the great beast was enormous. Warm breath puffed her face. Big, brown, bovine eyes stared back, far too near her own. Julia grabbed up her muslin skirts and bolted to safety behind the milker.

"She won't hurt you." Conrad patted the cow's rump.

"Oh, I doubt that. I *sincerely* doubt that."

Conrad put himself squarely between her and the cow. The gesture made her feel a little better, even as a second creature barreled into the stall.

Conrad spoke over his shoulder, stroking one beast on the forehead. "Gentle as a summer rain, these two."

"In this close proximity, fifteen hundred pounds seems more than a little threatening." She eyed the deadly hooves and great bulk of muscle beneath black-and-white splotched hide. Her heart beat rapidly in her throat.

Curiosity warred with the instinct to put plenty of room between herself and certain danger. But the only way out was directly past the hind-ends of a dozen head of cattle. Did they kick?

Conrad sat back on his heels, bathed the teats and swollen udder with sudsy water. His motions, quick and sure, drew attention to his broad shoulders and bulky arms. He pivoted, to wash the cow on the other side of the narrow aisle. He dunked the cloth and wrung it out.

He glanced up, catching her staring at his every move. If it bothered him, he gave no sign. "This one's a lightweight. Not more than twelve hundred pounds."

"Oh, so it outweighs me by a mere eleven hundred pounds. I'm sure I'll be able to protect myself."

Conrad actually grinned. Very briefly, even as he turned his face away from her view. He dried his hands, muscles bunching in his shoulders. "They are cowards at heart. Won't do you a bit of harm. You're safe with me."

Yes, she was safe with him. He knew this business, lived it every day. From what she knew of him so far, he would've left her at the house, rather than put her in harm's way. "Promise?"

His slow grin made her lightheaded. Straight, white teeth caught the reflection of the lanterns. What a honey of a smile. This must've been the first real one she'd seen—surely she would've recalled if he'd smiled at her before now.

"I promise," he said.

Heat rushed through her. It may have been the press of too many cows in close quarters, but she knew better. "You should smile more often."

Their gazes held for a moment, then he turned away and set the bucket of wash water out of the way. Was that disbelief she'd glimpsed in his eyes? Or was it disappointment?

"Your whole face lights up," she told him. What was so wrong with paying a compliment to her brother-in-law-to-be? There was nothing inappropriate about it, neither here nor in Baltimore's ballrooms.

"Right. And see children run in terror?" He nudged one cow aside and deftly maneuvered Julia out from behind the machine. "Sit." He indicated the milker's bench.

She dropped onto the seat. "Run? That's nonsense. Why would—"

"Women, too. Screaming."

Was he serious? She watched him lift rubber cups from a shiny tin pail. He gave the hoses that led to the milker a cursory once-over.

"I find that very hard to believe," she said after a moment.

He cast her a pointed glance.

"Running?" she asked. "Screaming? That's preposterous." If he thought one little scar—decently healed and clearly dating back to the seventies or earlier—held that kind of threat, then he was sorely mistaken. She opened her mouth to tell him so.

Apparently, he didn't want to hear it. "No time to waste. Put 'em on there." He indicated the implements in her hands.

A set of four flexible cups. She peered at the udder. Four teats. Within a matter of seconds, he had the other cow's appliance in place. The soft whirring of five other milkers blended with the animals' lowing and the voices of men. At this rate, the rest of the crew would have the balance of the herd moved through the shed before she got these two milked.

She fumbled with the cups, doing her best to position them all. "Like so?"

"Yes. Now work the pedal. Back and forth, nice and even."

"Just like a treadle sewing machine," she noted. The milker whirred softly, generating a vacuum. To her amazement, the first trickles of milk flowed through the glass tubing leading to the holding tank. "This doesn't look much like the models I examined in *The Dairy Farmer Journal.*"

"You read that one, too?"

"If it has to do with a dairy, I've read it."

"This dairy already has a foreman." He cast her a pointed, but teasing, glare. "We're not hiring, especially for that position. It's *mine.*"

The worst of her anxiety under control, she actually chuckled. How wonderful, this freedom to laugh. Out loud, if she wanted. Here, no one would censure her choice to wear a humble day dress amid male company. Nor her wishes to milk a cow. With her own two hands...sort of.

"I know milking machines," she told him, "because I've studied numerous patent drawings. This one is different."

"Thank you. If you're as well-read as you claim, that's a fine compliment. These machines are my own design."

"They are?" Why that surprised her so, she couldn't say. Hadn't she fully expected to find him—*Holmes,* rather—to be a man who knew how to work with his own hands? An appealing blend of cowboy and scholar?

"OK, that didn't sound like a compliment."

She laughed softly.

Very little about Conrad's milker design paralleled the sketches she'd studied. Where did he figure this out? How did he know about developing working machinery? "It was meant to be complimentary. I'm in awe. I had no idea. Tell me you've applied for a patent."

"First thing. Couldn't allow someone to beat me to it."

"Surely your own men wouldn't steal..."

He shook his head. "Dairymen all over the world face the same problems I do, every day. Someone in Pennsylvania is probably mulling over the same design issues I am."

She lost the rhythm of the pedal, and noticed the flow of milk ebbed. Every so often, air bubbles washed through the lines. "I'm doing this wrong."

"The machine is functioning just as it should. The suction's supposed to be intermittent. Works best that way."

Who'd ever heard of such a thing? "The articles I read glorified constant suction."

"And glossed over the resulting damage from that method, no doubt."

"They mentioned it. Briefly. Pooling of blood in the mammary tissue, permanent damage to structures, forcing milk deeper into the udder..."

Conrad nodded, leaning a bit closer. Was that appreciation glittering in his eyes? "Constant suction equals injury, and I like my cows too much to hinder their production."

With him so near, she completely forgot what other mentions of injuries she'd read. She moistened her lips and tried to sound coherent. "And therefore, your profits."

"A milker that does the work of four men in half the time, without decreasing output, equals money."

Mesmerized, she found she couldn't look away. Didn't want to. "But not if the herd suffers irreparable damage in the process."

"Precisely." A ghost of a smile tugged at the corners of his expressive mouth.

She examined the milker much more closely, knowing Conrad had designed the mechanisms to meet his expectations. This wasn't something he'd bought from someone else. He'd invented it. Her estimation of him rose. Significantly.

"I've done my reading, too," he said. "Nothing out there looked quite right to me. We tried rollers and other mechanical devices, but they're not much better than continuous suction. Over the past several years, I gradually developed a working prototype, then constructed six like this one." He indicated the milker with a jut of his chin.

"And it works."

Lamplight ignited streaks of fire through his hair. In the glow of a dozen lanterns, his scar might have shown up in stark relief on his freshly-shaved cheek—but all she could see was the amusement in his remarkable green eyes. Her heart kicked, and the heat shimmering in her chest seemed to worsen.

"Yes, it works," he agreed, as if creating a new machine was a simple process. "The milkers tripled the pounds of milk extracted, with one quarter the employees needed to do the work. Even with the time needed to steam the equipment, it still frees me to concentrate on the other aspects of the dairy, like breeding stock capable of keeping pace with my milking machines."

Never, in all her studies of dairies, had she anticipated the experience to be anything like this. Impressive.

Dairy, when viewed by Conrad Macquarie, wasn't merely farming; it was a science. By the tone of his voice, she had no doubt he loved his work.

"Sorry," he muttered, and bent to check the holding tank. "I'm boring you."

"Not at all. I'm intrigued."

"Careful. Talk like that, and you'll find yourself on that milking bench, morning and night."

Comfortable with his easy way of teasing, she shook her head. "Twice a day? That's impossible." She smiled at him and caught the corners of his mouth hinting at a grin. "I've far too many other things to do, to milk for you full time, you understand."

"Such as?"

In all likelihood, he'd find her Must-Experience-On-A-Ranch list a bit overwhelming. She might never check every item off, given her whole lifetime.

It seemed a good thing she intended to remain in California. Forever.

He kept his hands busy, adjusting a suction cup on one teat, checking the tubing on the machine, then studied her face.

Voices mingled with the soft thud of shifting hooves. Some of the other crewmen had finished milking, and let the cows out of the shed near Julia's back.

"Tell me what you need to do," he prompted.

"I want to gather eggs."

He shrugged.

"And see how you make cheese. I'm fascinated by

the methods modern dairies employ."

"Shouldn't get in the way of your milking."

"You're a harsh taskmaster." Clearly, he wasn't put off by that confession, so she offered another. "And make butter—rather, watch your crew make butter. Help, if you'll let me."

She caught a glimpse of Gabriel Macquarie as he shut the sliding door behind the last cow. He passed by, headed back to his own workstation.

She noted the brief glance Gabriel tossed at Conrad. The flicker of unrest in his eyes, the tension lining his forehead, his angst intense.

Conrad turned away from his brother and adjusted something in the workings of the milker, but not before Julia witnessed the grim set of his jaw.

He ignored the interchange as though it hadn't happened, almost as if Gabriel didn't exist.

Curious, and worrisome, all at the same time. But what bothered her the most was witnessing all traces of light disappear from Conrad's eyes.

In that moment, Julia realized something was terribly wrong within the Macquarie family.

Julia's feet slowed on the milking pump's pedal.

What could these two brothers possibly have to fight about? Holmes hadn't eluded to any trouble in his letters.

Last night at supper, the conversation had seemed relaxed enough. She couldn't recall a single disagreeable moment between Conrad and Gabriel.

She had the uncomfortable feeling their issues hadn't anything to do with the morning's work. She suspected it was more serious than that.

What kind of family problems would she marry into?

She sensed Conrad's gaze on her profile.

She met his gaze directly. It would be impolite to ask any of the dozen questions running through her head. She decided it would be best to pretend she hadn't seen their interchange. "So, how do we know when this cow's empty? Does the flow slack off?"

She knew the answer, of course, from her hours of reading. By the look on Conrad's face, it was evident he knew that too.

He didn't answer. Instead, he tightened a clamp. "Gabriel's problem's with me. Don't worry about it."

She nodded. Julia wanted to ask, now that he'd brought it up, but she made herself keep silent.

After a few more minutes, Conrad mentioned, "The crew's making butter today. We could use your pair of hands."

Excitement chased away her preoccupation over the trouble with Gabriel. "Butter?"

"Be warned, it's work. I expect you to earn your keep." That light teasing peppered his tone again.

"Work doesn't scare me." She glanced up the row of stalls, finding Gabriel at a safe distance, busy with his own tasks. "But that Gabriel. He's an ornery cuss. If he's going to be there, well, I declare—"

Conrad's chuckle was so unexpected, as he dropped onto his haunches beside the milking bench, that she forgot whatever else she'd planned to say. He propped his forearms on thick, muscled thighs, hands hanging down between his knees.

"Gabriel's problem is with me," he said again, slowly, and with certainty. "And I agree. He's ornery." He leaned closer, to confide a secret. "He'll be out with Doc, as soon as breakfast is over. And you said yourself you want to see my creamery. Macquarie butter boasts a fine reputation."

"Yes, I know."

"Did you know my creamery services the surrounding dairies? The others cart their milk here to be run through the separator."

The thought of actually watching machines separate the fat from the milk, and churn cream into butter filled her with anticipation. Everything she'd read tumbled through her mind, gaining momentum.

She enjoyed the light teasing between them. She

found it amusing. And fun. “You say Gabriel will be away?”

A slow, easy grin lit up his handsome face. “Yeah. Gone. All day.”

“Then put me to work.”

He must’ve noted the excitement in her voice.

“After breakfast, I’ve got a brief meeting with Pop. Once a month, whether he’s interested or not, I tell him how well his dairy is doing. Then, we make butter.” He paused, holding her gaze for a moment. “You’ll like my new pasteurizing machine.”

“That’s an offer I can’t resist.”

“I don’t expect you to resist. I anticipate you’ll drool over this shiny new piece of equipment. I’ve had it all of four months.”

She giggled in a most undignified manner. His answering smile turned intoxicating. This cowboy had proved to be much more than brawn or sinew, more intelligent and fun than she’d imagined.

And he most definitely should smile more often.

For one dangerous, long moment, her traitorous heart forgot he wasn’t Holmes.

Chapter Five

A PAIR OF HOURS later, fragrant aromas of coffee, bacon, and biscuits greeted Julia and the Macquarie brothers at the ranch house. A mixture of happy laughter and conversation invited them inside.

Portia met them at the back door, tying her hat strings. "I've an opportunity too scrumptious to resist. With your intended nowhere in sight, you don't need my supervision. So I'm off."

Julia half expected Portia to be long gone by this hour. Curious, she asked, "Where are you going?"

Gabriel muttered "Excuse me," and slipped between Julia and her aunt, headed for the kitchen and breakfast.

"With Mr. DeLaigle." Portia's eyes sparkled with barely contained glee. "He's promised to show me ground fissures from the quake in ninety-two."

"Who?"

"Mr. *DeLaigle.*" Portia waved her little gloved hand with dismissal. "A neighbor. Macquarie knows him well. Anyway, I've got my lunch packed and a full day ahead—" Portia planted both hands against the door frame. She gasped. "Did you *feel* that?"

Conrad glanced at Julia, concern lining his features. "Feel what, exactly?"

"A temblor," Aunt Portia whispered with reverence.

"A temblor?" Conrad echoed.

"A seism," Portia clarified.

"Ah." He covered his skepticism well, showing nothing but courtesy for Julia's peculiar aunt. She found she appreciated his consideration.

"How long would you say it lasted?" Portia whispered, ever hopeful she'd sense another subtle shifting of the earth. "One second? Less?"

"I didn't feel anything," Julia said.

Portia ignored her. "You?" she asked Conrad.

"Sorry."

"That's a shame. I suppose I'm simply more sensitive to such things than either of you." She tugged down the hem of her coat. "Mr. DeLaigle awaits. Wish me luck."

As Portia headed into the front hall, Julia turned to Conrad. "Who's DeLaigle? I ought to invite myself along."

"DeLaigle's harmless. Been our neighbor since before I can remember, and widowed almost two years. Your aunt will enjoy herself." He paused, a hint of a smile on his lips. "Butter," he reminded her. "And don't forget my pasteurizing equipment."

His teasing made her grin. "Of course."

"You won't want to miss watching dairymen work magic with cream."

Oh, he was good. Smooth. Charming. Attentive.

All his father had asked him to do was show her around the property. Her heart pumped a bit too hard. At his nearness, she did feel tremors and upheavals, but knew the sensations had nothing to do with movement along the fault.

Light, she reminded herself. "And to think I believed you little more than a cowboy."

He raised a rusty brow. "Cowboy? Miss J, I prefer the term dairyman."

Miss J? That sounded almost like a term of endearment. It reminded her of the sweet, affectionate things her many brothers-in-law called their wives.

Conrad's playful attention seemed almost like courting behavior. Kind words, polite invitations, gracious compliments. She ought to know, because she'd seen plenty of that. For no other reason than she was a Tyndall, had witnessed her seven older sisters' courtships, and happened to be cursed with a pretty face herself.

But Conrad, who hadn't cared one whit for Jordon Tyndall's notoriety, seemed to genuinely like Julia for herself. He looked past her father's political connections, ignored the Tyndall fortune, and taught her to operate a milker. And he teased. Not something a man generally did when blinded by a lady's face and social standing.

For the first time in her life, a man ignored the superficial, and seemed to like *her*. He didn't want a boost to his political career, wasn't in the market for a wealthy bride, and looked at her the same way whether properly dressed or laboring in a cowshed.

He merely wanted to be her friend.

A very effective ploy—*if* he wanted her affections.

Which of course, he didn't. Of course he wouldn't. In a matter of time, she'd be married to his brother.

She found herself wishing Holmes would turn out to be a great deal like Conrad. But she knew better. Numerous letters had passed between herself and Holmes. She knew he loved this ranch, but not the way Conrad did. Holmes was pleasant, gentlemanly. But she doubted he knew how to tease. Even a little.

She hadn't known she'd desire something

inconsequential like that.

It was a sobering thought.

"Dairyman sounds fitting," she managed at last.

"I wear the name with honor."

"I see you do."

"Breakfast!" Katherine announced from the kitchen.

"Want to taste what fresh Macquarie butter can do with fried potatoes?" he asked.

Julia nodded. She followed him into the washroom to scrub up to the elbows with strong soap, then into to the kitchen.

This loud bunch of Macquaries had a way of enveloping her in their family without a hint of hesitation. Eating around the kitchen table, as compared to the formal dining room, she felt a sense of familiarity, as if they had become her kin.

But she paid closer attention to the way Gabriel and Conrad interacted—and realized they didn't. The two brothers had the art of ignoring one another down pat.

"I've a grand idea," Holmes's father announced. He spread cream cheese liberally over golden toast, then topped it with strawberry preserves. "Since we've a bit of extra time on our hands, let's plan a welcome home celebration for Holmes."

Julia noted he'd addressed the comment to her, rather than to the family at large. Her pervasive good mood evaporated.

"And as an introduction," Holmes's father continued, "of his lovely bride. We can't wait to show you off to all our friends."

Oh, heavens. She hadn't anticipated anything like this. Just the thought of a gathering such as Mr. Macquarie suggested washed all her happy plans away. Occasions such as those required far more planning than any male could possibly fathom.

To buy herself a moment to collect her thoughts, Julia took a bite of Macquarie Monterey Jack cheese.

Tangy, rich, and flavorful.

"A simple reception," Mr. Macquarie went on, "to formally welcome Holmes into our business partnership. Everyone will be delighted to meet you, Miss Julia. It will be absolutely perfect."

"Yes, indeed," Holmes's mother, Violet, exclaimed. "We must." Dressed in a spring-green everyday dress, her coloring seemed improved over yesterday.

Katherine set a skillet of spiced apple crisp on a trivet in the table's center. "A party's a wonderful idea!"

Gabriel forked a sausage link and took a bite. "I don't see why we need to make a big stink about Holmes getting back. He left. He's coming back. I don't think it needs more than a howdy-do."

"I'm certain," Mr. Macquarie said with authority, "Miss Tyndall doesn't see it that way at all. She understands the importance of a proper welcome."

He turned to Julia, obviously expecting her to agree.

If it wouldn't sound rude, she'd tell him she'd hoped to never see another gala in her lifetime. All she wanted was fresh air, sunshine, alfalfa fields and milk cows.

And the creamery. Today, the crew was making butter. She couldn't believe how disappointed she was to think of missing it.

Mr. Macquarie may have no idea how she felt, but Julia saw that Conrad did. Their eyes met across the bustling breakfast table, and in that moment, she glimpsed his understanding.

His father rushed on, "Violet and Katherine will help you with the guest list. I want a sit-down supper. Music. Reception line." He gestured broadly, barely containing his enthusiasm. "All that. The Friday night, right after his return will be ideal. Can't let Holmes get too busy with wedding plans and work at the office."

This wasn't good at all. She had a mere week to pull off the performance of a lifetime. And some of those days didn't count, because once Holmes was home, and she'd want to spend her time with him.

Macquarie went on, "We'll celebrate while his return is still fresh news."

All her glorious plans to visit every inch of the dairy, to watch each process, to experience and to learn, burned to cinders. There wouldn't be a moment to do any of the things she wanted so badly to try.

Mr. Macquarie sipped coffee. "You'll make quite an impression on Holmes and all others in attendance."

Oh, she'd make an impression, all right.

This would undoubtedly be the most difficult reception she'd ever arranged, without her favored list of chefs and decorators to call upon.

Conrad added cream to his coffee. "Sounds a bit fancy for the likes of us. Wouldn't a simple family dinner do? We'll invite Silas and Nadine—"

His father chuckled. "Holmes will expect nothing less than a full celebration. He's written home about one too many fancy receptions. Wouldn't want him to make unfavorable comparisons, now would we?"

It was one thing to attempt to please her future in-laws, and another to find her rushed efforts judged by her would-be husband.

Julia's stomach turned an odd little somersault and she feared she'd be sick. Of all the things Holmes had indicated he expected in her, an accomplished hostess wasn't one of them.

That was the way she wanted it. Her future had seemed so bright—without a single social engagement in sight. But now, failure seemed inevitable.

Why hadn't she insisted upon tagging along with Aunt Portia? She could be bored to tears examining rocks and vegetation, and blissfully unaware of this reception she wanted no part of.

To refuse would be unconscionably rude.

Ultimately, her first priority was to gratify Holmes's family. She wanted to exceed their expectation, especially where her commitment to

Holmes and their future was concerned.

Holmes's father held her gaze. Last night, he'd seemed accepting during their interview in the library. Yet this felt like test, as if he'd thought it over during the night and now doubted her intentions.

"I'll get started immediately," Julia assured him. "I'm honored to do this for Holmes, for all of you."

"Good." Holmes's dad returned to his breakfast. "I'm certain you'll do splendidly."

CONRAD RETURNED to the house at noon, preoccupied with thoughts of Julia. All through supervising the creamery operations, he'd felt badly for leaving her to face his parents' party plans alone. Ma might think she was good help, but Conrad had his doubts.

He wished he'd done more to dissuade Pop. Postpone. Point out that planning a party of this size, on such short notice, simply wasn't fair to Julia.

He must've reminded himself, a half dozen times, that Julia obviously had her reasons for agreeing to do it. What right did he have to prevent her from planning this party? From where he stood, the party showed excessive favoritism, but no one cared what he thought.

As he lathered his hands in the washroom, he heard Julia and his mother in the kitchen, making a guest list for Pop's party.

The whole welcome-home nonsense sounded just like the prodigal son story: killing the fatted calf, inviting the whole village to the feast, pretending the honored son hadn't ever left home.

All the while, ignoring the ever-faithful son.

Sounded exactly like Conrad's life.

Holmes left for law school at Harvard years ago. Meanwhile, Conrad had invested every waking hour to keep the dairy productive and turning a profit.

Had Pop ever said thank you? Not once.

Had the old man complimented Conrad's management, the way he raved over Holmes's accomplishments? Never.

If Conrad were the one to be married, what were the chances Pop would throw this kind of celebration? Slim to none.

Conrad wouldn't care so much about all that, if only Pop would show him the courtesy of taking his purchase offer seriously. He'd dismissed it, loudly. Again.

Holmes, the golden firstborn, would inherit the law practice. Conrad—*if* he stayed on—would live the rest of his devoted life as little more than a hired hand.

It was good he found his work satisfying, because that was all the thanks, other than a regular paycheck, that he'd ever get.

Shrugging off his irritation, he dried his hands and headed for the kitchen and his dinner. Hunger burned a hole through his belly. He needed to eat. Now.

Immediately, Conrad noticed Julia, sitting at the table in the same navy work dress she'd worn to the milking shed. He noted her straight posture, the tidiness of her papers, and calmness masking her pained expression.

The woman was upset. Couldn't his mother and sister see that?

"A newspaper announcement simply won't do, not for something this important." Ma tapped her pencil against the tabletop. "We must have printed invitations. And placards for seating. If they cost twice as much, given the rush, then they do."

Katherine kneaded bread dough on the counter. "Julia and I can go to town right away and deliver the order to the print shop."

Conrad inhaled deeply, but there didn't seem to be any aromas of cooking food. The bread dough wouldn't be a crusty loaf for another couple hours.

The coffeepot was dry, the cookie jar held nothing

but crumbs. Someone had eaten the last piece of spiced apple cheesecake from last night's supper. He checked the breadbox, found it empty, and slammed it shut.

What was wrong with these women, that life came to an abrupt halt the moment someone mentioned throwing a party for Holmes? Weren't they going to eat in the meanwhile?

If Sally had proved loyal, he might've had someone to take care of him, make sure his basic needs were met.

Hadn't it occurred to Ma and Katherine that Julia might be hungry, too? Undoubtedly, she still felt like a guest in this home and had manners too fine to root through the pantry and scrape together her own dinner.

Daylight streamed through the window at Julia's back, catching the highlights in her dusky curls. An empty coffee cup sat among the numerous pages of notes littering the tabletop.

She looked up from her papers and smiled, weakly, in welcome. That brief second was all the confirmation he needed to know how little she'd enjoyed her morning's work.

Despite his sour attitude, Conrad offered a nod of greeting. This ridiculous party was giving his sister-in-law-to-be an interesting initiation into the family.

Returning his attention to finding something to eat, Conrad checked the stove. Nothing in the kettle, nothing in the oven. He sliced a thick wedge of Monterey Jack and ate it plain. If he wanted a hot dinner, it seemed he'd have to find it at the bunkhouse kitchen with the hired men. Or cook for himself. As if he had the time for that.

He sliced several more pieces of cheese onto a plate and set them within Julia's reach. She glanced up at him, appreciation evident on her lovely face.

Ma pulled a hankie from her sleeve and blotted her brow. "Katherine, do take Michael a few pounds of cheese, along with the request. And make sure he knows his name's on the guest list. That ought to rush our invitations through his press."

"What's Michael's full name?" Julia shuffled through her papers then added a note in the margin of a previous page.

"Michael Hendricks," Katherine supplied.

"But he's a different Hendricks," Ma said, "than is already on the list. That's Effie and Hubert's oldest son, but he doesn't reside with his parents. Oh, that reminds me. Hubert, Junior. We mustn't forget him."

Julia rested her forehead on her palm for a moment. Her lips moved, forming silent words. The poor girl clearly didn't want to throw a party in a new town, inviting people she didn't know from Adam.

As if she'd finally noticed he'd returned, his mother glanced up. "You're back early."

"It's after twelve."

She glanced at the clock on the wall. "So it is." Her color seemed poor, as if the stresses of helping Julia with the initial party plans had put too great a strain on her. Whenever she breathed this shallowly, it usually meant her heart pained her. She needed to lie down.

"You look tired, Ma." Conrad took two glasses from the cabinet and filled them with cold milk from the icebox. He set one in front of Julia. "Go rest awhile. I'll read over the guest list with Katherine and make sure you haven't forgotten anyone."

"I'm fine, dear." Ma turned back to Julia, worry lining the soft flesh about her eyes. "We mustn't forget to order several hundred chocolates from Cadence Chocolatier. I don't want to imagine what Luke will say if we fail...to serve chocolates."

Her breathing was shallow, somewhat uneven, as it tended to be when her heart was beating too fast. "Holmes is partial to the Bavarian crèmes. We'll want to order plenty of those."

Julia hesitated, watching his mother with concern. She set down her milk glass and scrawled another note.

Conrad had seen enough. This party had been Pop's idea, then he'd run off to work and left Ma to fret over the details.

The old man had clearly hoped to give Julia a chance to do what she loved most—couldn't he see how wrong that assumption was, that she hated it?—and to show her off to the neighbors. Bottom line, this was too great a tax on Ma's health.

Conrad had no choice but to intervene. "Where's Alberta?" The housekeeper should've been here by now.

Katherine plopped the kneaded dough into a greased bowl. "The minute she heard about the party, she went to town to hire more help."

She covered the bowl with a clean towel, then picked up her conversation with Ma. "Chocolates will be good. But we still need dessert. Something uniquely Macquarie."

"Holmes is quite fond...of ice cream." Ma blotted her upper lip with the lace-trimmed hankie. "And cheesecake, too. Which...do you think?"

"Let's leave the rest of the details to Julia." He had no intention of allowing either of these women to move forward with plans so grand. He'd talk to Alberta, and make sure she hired more than enough extra help.

Conrad slid an arm about his mother's plump waist and eased her to her feet. "She'll do a fine job. Pop has complete confidence in her."

"Katherine, you'll help Julia find the print shop?"

"I'll take her." Katherine hung her apron on a cupboard door. "Won't take me but a minute to tidy my hair."

Conrad understood exactly why his sister was so eager to go to town. Katherine had always made excuses to spend her days in Liberty. Shopping. Girls' luncheons out. Tea parties. Volunteering her time with church service projects.

Conrad had known, for some time now, that her other interests had long since been abandoned in favor of one very important reason to traipse into Liberty. David Orme.

Ma, bless her failing heart, hadn't caught on to

Katherine's ploys. Just one more indication of how poorly she felt. By the time the party, complete with dozens of guests, had paraded through their home, Ma was likely to be worn to a frazzle.

Conrad didn't like it.

"How nice of you," Ma told Katherine, patting her hand softly. "You girls deliver...the invitation. Order an extra dozen. We'll think...of someone else to invite." She shuffled toward bed, leaning too heavily on Conrad for support. "Then have a bite to eat in town."

One glance at Katherine's delighted expression as she bolted for the staircase, and he knew if he didn't go along, Julia would likely find herself wandering the streets of Liberty alone. He couldn't imagine Katherine was ready to introduce David Orme, thereby giving Julia information that might get back to Pop.

Fine. He'd go. Despite the fact that this time of year, he worked from before sunup until sundown. Every minute counted. There was enough work to make a rest, for any reason, virtually impossible.

He didn't have fifteen minutes to spare, much less an entire afternoon.

Frustrated compounded his hunger, shortening his fuse.

Katherine wouldn't argue. She'd see his presence as endorsement of her time spent with David.

He glanced at Julia. Concern tugged at his conscience. Whatever the demands on himself, Julia was in a fix. A party to throw together and no one else to rely on.

Aware his clothing was filthy, he determined to change after he got Ma settled in her bed, then hitch the team. He'd have to delegate his afternoon's work to Gabriel before leaving. And collect the cheese Ma wanted to give the printer as a bribe.

"Give me five minutes," he told Julia. "I'll bring the buggy 'round front."

Chapter Six

CONRAD ESCORTED Katherine and Julia out of the print shop. "You're welcome," he called to Michael, who'd thanked him for the package of Monterey Jack. "We'll see you at the party."

"Wouldn't miss it," Michael turned back to his printing press.

On the sidewalk, Katherine confirmed Conrad's theory about her reasons for escorting Julia into Liberty. "All right. We'll cross that item off our list. Now, lunch. I know just the place. The Orme Hotel serves the best roast lamb in town."

A hearty bowl of soup at Gino's, or a thick steak at The Goldmine were more to Conrad's liking. Before Katherine had said a word, he'd known she'd want to head for the hotel—and not for the food.

He'd resigned himself to cooperate. For Katherine, he'd do just about anything.

"And their herb potatoes are worth the trip, all by themselves." Katherine giggled and linked her arm through Julia's.

"Sounds delicious."

"You'll like the atmosphere, most of all," Katherine promised. "It's a very stylish place to eat."

Katherine had put on a fancy dress Conrad hadn't ever seen before. The spring-green getup, in the latest fashion, showed off her tiny waist. He had no doubt she'd worn it to please David.

Julia had dressed up for their outing, too. Her eye-catching skirt and jacket, in a deep red, complimented her pale skin and dark hair.

Conrad walked behind the two women as they made their way across the street and one short block to the imposing three-story brick hotel.

Once in the dove-gray marble lobby, Julia's gaze flitted over the ornate mezzanine railing and stained glass ceiling panels that glowed with afternoon light. The purple velvet draperies and furniture, far too presumptuous for anywhere else, seemed right at home in this grand building. Music from a single violin floated through the open doors that led to the dining room.

He watched Miss Julia appreciate the finely appointed hotel. Dark, curly eyelashes, so thick and long caught his attention. How had he not noticed before?

Julia agreed that Orme Hotel was, indeed, very stylish.

Mouth-watering aromas made Conrad's stomach grumble. Last time he'd eaten here, the pot roast had been tender and delicious. Perhaps he'd have that again.

As a well-dressed gentleman led them to a table near the window, Katherine whispered to Julia, "Excuse me, will you? Washroom visit."

Conrad watched his sister scurry toward the side hall he knew led around to the hotel offices. Katherine wasn't here for the herb potatoes or roast lamb, and had little intention of wasting a scant thirty seconds in the ladies' room.

He'd been right to assume Katherine would abandon Julia to her own devices. He couldn't blame his sister. Her opportunities to see David were scarce. Most importantly, she had secrets to protect.

The dining room was comfortably full with other diners. Crystal and silver gleamed upon white linen tablecloths. The signature lavender china, a hallmark of the Orme Hotel since its opening, was rimmed with purple pansies.

Many wealthy older couples dined in small groupings. A few well-dressed matrons visited over coffee and Neapolitan ice cream. Several of them noted Conrad's arrival with Miss Julia. Given their surprise that a beautiful, unfamiliar woman would keep company with the likes of him, Conrad figured they hadn't heard Holmes had sent for a bride.

Seated at a table near the spotless front windows, Conrad perused the menu. His stomach growled loudly. That hunk of cheese felt like hours ago. Quickly, he settled on the pot roast.

Noting Julia still read through the course selections, he did his best to exercise patience.

A young man with thinning pale hair took their wine order and suggested a chilled mint soup.

Julia flicked Conrad a glance. "Shouldn't we wait for Katherine?"

"I suspect she'll eat in the back."

The waiter nodded. "Likely best you don't wait, sir." It seemed the boy had seen Katherine here with David, before today.

By Julia's expression, she evidently couldn't fathom not waiting for Katherine, but she agreed the mint soup would make an excellent appetizer.

"Pardon my curiosity." Julia leaned forward as to not be heard by the other diners. Her impish smile made her pretty face even more appealing. "What's his name?"

He held Julia's gaze. Perceptive, wasn't she?

Before he could decide whether or not to give her

that bit of information, she said, "I have seven sisters, three aunts, four nieces, and one mother. I had the privilege of knowing both my grandmothers. I'm an expert on female behavior."

"And you are one."

Her full smile, ripe with amusement, charmed him. "An expert? Of course I am."

"I don't question your expert status. I meant *you're* a female. Ought to simplify matters some when it comes to figuring out what goes on in a woman's head."

If he'd only understood women, he might've had a fighting chance with Sally.

Julia leaned a bit closer. Sunlight streamed through the spotless windowpanes, illuminating the brick-red plume in her hat. Delicate, dusky curls wisped about her ears and neck. He noticed small, gold hoops through her pierced ears. Her eyes sparkled with something far more appealing than sunshine.

Conrad swallowed, then took a drink to chase the dryness. Holmes had chosen himself a beauty. The good cut of her snug-fitting jacket emphasized her tiny waist and feminine curves. The dark red wool, trimmed with black cording, suited her pale skin.

Made it a real challenge to look anywhere else.

Funny. His only other sister-in-law, Nadine, didn't affect him this way at all.

He liked Nadine, found her company enjoyable, even thought her pretty. Never once had he found himself so interested in every fine detail. Maybe that was because he'd had years to get used to her.

Julia was altogether different. When she smiled, the soft pink blush of her lips held his attention.

He brandished both raised hands in surrender. "I've only got one sister and one sister-in-law. All I can tell you is they like to shop, talk, cook, and bother men."

"Bother men?"

Conrad chugged his water. That one didn't need an answer.

A moment passed, then Julia whispered, "I

deduce Katherine's clandestine meeting isn't something your parents would delight in hearing."

"Bull's-eye."

"And it seems this young man is employed on the premises."

"His family owns it."

Julia's finely shaped brows rose with appreciation. Her gaze flitted over the dining room tables, settled on the violinist for a moment, then returned to Conrad. "I see."

"Pop's a bit fussy about Katherine's beaus."

Conrad noted Luke Wakefield, passing by on the sidewalk outside the hotel. The old goat had been Pop's friend since dinosaurs walked the earth. Along with the minister, the men were thick as thieves. Folks called them The Three.

"Yes, I would imagine your father's a bit picky about whom Katherine sees."

Conrad noticed Luke had paused just outside the windowpanes, to supposedly examine his reflection in the glass. He straightened his worn flannel shirt, but Conrad wasn't fooled. He suspected Luke had noticed Miss Julia sitting with Conrad, and wanted to get a close look at Holmes's intended.

Conrad decided to ignore Luke. "David's too old for Katherine. Or so says Pop," he confided to Julia.

"David Orme, is it?"

"Yes."

"How old is he? Fifty? Fifty-five?"

Conrad hid a grin behind his water goblet. "About twenty-five."

"And Katherine's what? Twenty-two?"

"She will be, come fall."

"Much too old for her, isn't he?" She laughed softly. "A crime. Stealing a mere child's affections."

"Pop claims Katherine doesn't know her own mind."

"Pity," Julia commented.

"And David's life is in town." He indicated the

hotel. "Won't move into the family ranch house. So he doesn't fit Pop's idea of the right man for Katherine."

"Poor girl. What a sad turn, being forced to live in this kind of opulence."

"I never said I agreed with Pop's ideas."

A smile flirted about her pink lips.

"Katherine's of age," he added. "If she wants to keep company with David Orme, it's not my place to protest."

"Do you like him?"

"David's a fine man."

"Good enough for your sister?"

He considered her question, surprised to find it easy to talk to her. He'd never thought female company all that comfortable, but he supposed Julia wasn't just any woman. She'd be family, soon, and that made it easier to be himself.

"Yeah," he said, "he is."

Their spindly waiter approached with two teacup-sized bowls on an ebony tray and a bottle of wine tucked beneath his arm.

They fell silent as the young man set the pale green, frothy soup before them. Little sprigs of green plant matter floated on the surface. He glanced at the narrow-shouldered boy who dared recommend this concoction as soup.

Where was the beef? There wasn't any sign of a potato. How could something be called *soup,* without potatoes? If he ever again found himself in town for a midday meal, it would definitely be at Gino's.

With a dainty sniff, she picked up the soup spoon from among the full place setting. "So fragrant."

Luke ambled past the window, turned and retraced his steps. With undisguised interest, he gawked at Julia. She didn't seem to take notice.

Conrad angled his chair toward the dining room, presenting nosy Luke Wakefield with a better view of his back. If the old man wanted a closer look at Julia, he could very well come inside and introduce himself.

Once their waiter left them in peace, Conrad tasted the chilled soup and decided it was meant for a female's appetite. Julia tipped the bowl of her spoon into the froth and lifted it to her lips.

The soup was lousy. Too hungry to care the mint soup wasn't entirely to his liking, Conrad downed his portion and watched Julia savor her own.

"Well," Julia said as she set her spoon in her nearly empty bowl, "I think it's splendid."

"This?" He'd starve to death before the pot roast ever made it to the table.

"I'm talking about Katherine's romance."

"You call sneaking around romantic? I call it painful. Pop won't allow David in the house, so they don't see each other much. Except when Katherine comes up with excuses to run into town."

"Intriguing," Julia whispered, just loud enough to be heard over the soft strains of violin. "What sort of excuses?"

"It isn't my story to tell."

"You're a man who keeps confidences."

"I'd like to believe I do."

"It's good to know you won't share my secrets."

That sounded a bit personal, coming from a woman who was engaged to his brother. But then, nothing about this new sister-in-law was as he'd expected.

She sipped her wine, watching him closely. Whenever Sally had eyed him like that, she'd always had something on her mind. Usually, the topic was something he hadn't wanted to hear.

"That's commendable, considering it's hard to keep secrets in a household such as yours."

He wasn't sure he liked the sound of that. "Is that so?"

"I couldn't help but overhear your argument with your father this morning."

Any ease he may have felt in Julia's company disappeared. The thought of her, a newcomer to the family, overhearing that particular conversation, made him feel as naked as the day he was born.

He couldn't expect her to understand his viewpoint, much less the desperation behind the argument. A woman like her would pass judgment on his actions, probably lecture him about respecting his elders and behaving the gentlemen, regardless of the circumstances. He doubted she'd ever raised her voice, even once in her life.

He wasn't sure why, but Julia's opinion of him mattered.

He risked a glance, finding her pretty face marred with pity. Pathetic, misguided farm boy, who must beg his father for a bit of ground. A meager aspiration, but what could one expect, given his circumstances?

Julia averted her gaze and neatly folded her linen napkin upon her lap.

Dismissal. Pure and simple.

In that moment, he knew she'd never look at him the same way.

Damn if it didn't hurt like the dickens.

He shook off the suffocating loss. Julia's opinion didn't matter. He didn't care, one way or the other, if she looked at him with disgust. He couldn't expect a citified, college-educated, too-pretty-to-be-believed, society lady to understand. He had no intention of explaining himself, especially to the likes of her.

"It was nothing more than a spirited discussion. It's the Macquarie way. You'll get used to it." He stared out the window, gulped water, and hoped she took the hint that particular topic was off limits.

"Your father's an opinionated man."

Oh, yes. Pop saw everything in black and white. His way was right, and everyone else was wrong. Their battle over the ranch echoed about in his head, compounding the tension knotting his shoulders and neck.

She didn't seem bothered by his lack of a response. "He and my father are quite similar."

Conrad turned the stem of his water goblet between his fingers, but didn't answer. He sensed Julia's close attention on his face. Out of lifelong habit, he turned his good side toward her and glanced toward the exit.

He ought to toss a few coins on the table and leave. Julia's opinion of him couldn't drop any lower, no matter what he did.

She leaned nearer. "Conrad."

He slid her a glance intended to warn her off.

She reached across the tablecloth and touched his forearm. It may have been a normal gesture between easterners, but to him, the touch was so unexpected, he nearly flinched.

Her hand lingered, almost caressed. Air seemed to lodge in his throat. The sight of her narrow, feminine fingers on his shirt sleeve brought a twist of emotion he couldn't identify. He stared at her hand, unable to pull away.

Damn. This simple touch felt so good.

She withdrew. "I do believe our fathers would be fast friends, if they ever meet. Until this morning, I thought my father the most overbearing, insistent man in the United States, perhaps the entire western hemisphere."

Had he misread her, a moment ago? She didn't seem disgusted, nor critical of him, at all. "Are you saying Pop's worse?"

"Oh, yes."

She laughed, a soft, musical sound that echoed in Conrad's lonely heart. Something in her eyes made him wonder if she might understand.

How was that possible? Fancy Miss Julia couldn't be more different from himself if she tried.

"But by a narrow margin. Father and I have had arguments that would mortify even a Macquarie."

"What's that supposed to mean?"

"While you were in the library, sparring with your father, your mother and sister ignored the interchange completely. They went about their work and carried on a conversation as if they've heard the argument so many times, it's merely the noise of traffic rolling past on the street."

"That's my mother." He could only imagine how it must've made Julia feel, to listen to a personal argument, and witness the family's lack of reaction.

"Evidently, she believed you could hold your own."

Through narrowed eyes, Conrad searched for any hint of condescension in her expression, and found none. He found it very hard to believe Julia could overhear most of that argument and side with him. Wasn't she a dutiful daughter, with proper manners polished to a high shine?

"I'm glad to see I'm not the only grown child who argues with her father." Her grin bordered on wicked. "You and I have a great deal in common, Mr. Macquarie."

He doubted that. She, a city-bred, college-educated, gorgeous and pampered daughter of a wealthy man. He'd never gone anywhere, done anything of merit, didn't even own a patch of land to call his own.

To top it all off, he had the misfortune of a disfiguring scar. She didn't know the first thing about prejudices; he had lived with a mask of ugliness from childhood.

What could she possibly assume they had in common?

Nothing.

Except a link through Holmes.

Soft conversation mingled with the chink of silver against china. The violinist finished one piece of music and began another, this one vaguely familiar.

Julia tipped her head a little to the side. "If you'd heard our last conversation, you wouldn't label it spirited. More than likely, you'd call it war."

"War? That's a strong word."

"Oh, yes. Battle. To the death."

Conrad swallowed. That revelation colored everything. He couldn't imagine this well-mannered, city lady yelling at her father, even in the privacy of their home. The idea of her standing up for herself—over what, he didn't know—made him look at her in a new light. Could be she was tougher than she seemed.

"For the record," she said, "Macquarie arguments are mild, in comparison to the harm Tyndalls inflict."

"I thought you said Pop was worse than your father."

She raised one shapely brow, and leaned even closer, to better share confidences. "Given you're a man who keeps secrets, I don't mind admitting the argument between my father and myself, just before I left home, was infinitely worse than anything I heard this morning."

Conrad considered that for a moment. He could think of only one topic father and daughter would've battled over, on the eve of her departure. Her journey to California, and her impending marriage to Holmes.

She must have wanted Holmes, very badly.

Newfound respect welled within Conrad. This china doll had fought with her father, very likely severed ties to home and family, and cast her lot with Holmes.

How would it be, to have a woman like Julia give up *everything* in order to spend her life with him?

Without a doubt, Holmes was the luckiest man that ever walked the streets of Liberty. Make that the whole world.

Conrad held her gaze for a long moment, the yawning void within him expanding. Something dark, hollow, that could only be jealousy, rose within him. Holmes already had everything a man could want. Now he had the unflappable devotion of an amazing woman.

"You and I," she murmured, "are quite a bit alike."

Her smile, radiant and full of sincerity, made his stomach cramp. For half a second, he found himself wishing she meant what she'd said, in a non-familial way. He wanted to believe it was merely hunger, knew it wasn't.

With every conversation, with each minute he spent in Julia's company, he found it harder to remember she wasn't interested in him. This dinner out wasn't about them getting to know each other; this was nothing more than misplaced duty. He was babysitting. He'd be wise to remember that.

Moments passed, and Conrad continued to remind himself Julia's words were meant only as a brother and sister thing. If they had anything in common, it was only their mutual experiences with quick-tempered fathers.

"Have you been to the coast?" The enthusiasm in her voice surprised him as much as the change in topic.

That way women dropped one thread of conversation and dived into another never ceased to baffle him. Just one more thing about females that wouldn't ever make a lick of sense to him.

He grabbed hold of the more comfortable subject. "Twice." He paused, trying to remember his geography lessons. "Isn't Baltimore on the Atlantic shore?"

"Chesapeake Bay, actually." She pulled her lower lip between her teeth, as if hesitating. "I hear the Atlantic and the Pacific aren't a thing alike. My father took us on holiday to the seashore on numerous occasions, but I'd truly love to see the Pacific."

He almost blurted the first thing that came to mind. *I'll take you.* It wasn't his place to take her anywhere. So he settled for, "An ocean's an ocean."

"Is that so?" she asked pleasantly, as if she couldn't have disagreed more. He could see the wheels turning in her head. Calculating the distance, the time, the list of party plans at home on the kitchen table that required her attention. She took a sip of water from her goblet, then neatly lined up her silverware.

He didn't want to disappoint, but she didn't understand the terrain. "As the wind blows, we're about forty miles from the coast."

"And the Coastal Range provides a significant

obstacle, does it not?"

"Passes are few and treacherous. Even by train, you're looking at a several day outing."

She seemed to consider this for a few moments. "From the photographs I've seen and articles I've read," she said in an off-handed manner that did little to hide her eagerness, "the geology would captivate Aunt Portia."

Had she forgotten about the party? Had she forgotten Holmes's impending return?

"I imagine so." But it was Julia's image he saw as she inhaled deeply of salty air, wriggled her toes deep into the sand, and lifted her skirts above the ankles as she waded in the chilly surf.

"Surely my aunt will be enamored with the vegetation. She told me she's determined to sink her toes in the sand before it's time to return."

Conrad raised a brow. He had no trouble imagining Julia, her bare feet caked with sand. He found it hard to keep a straight face.

"Did you just say *toes*, Miss J?" He chuckled. Since when did a proper, city-bred lady mention such body parts, in mixed company?

She ignored his question. "But of greater fascination, to my aunt, of course, is everything we've read about the petrified forest."

"Petrified Charlie?"

Her face lit up. "You know him?"

"Not personally. Everybody around here knows about his operation. Charges fees to show the curious old trees that turned to stone eons ago."

"Portia may have come here with me, under guise of providing adequate supervision." Miss J sipped her wine, a grin teasing about her pink lips. "But I know the truth. She came to see these petrified specimens."

"Ah."

"Have you seen them?"

"Me? No."

"You live how far away? And you've never been?

Pity."

She didn't seem to want an answer about mileage; he suspected she already knew. He also wondered if Miss J was as enamored with the same stuff as her aunt. He couldn't tell. But with all the reading she did about non-traditional topics, he wouldn't be surprised.

After a moment, she said, "Handsomest spot in the Californy mountains."

He'd heard that before. Who'd said it? "Oh, right. Robert Louis Stevenson."

"*The Silverado Squatters*."

"I'm not as back woods as you think."

"Would you like to see it. Someday?" She tipped her head slightly to the side.

He may not be an expert on females, but he wasn't dense, either. Julia wanted him to take her, and Aunt Portia, to Petrified Charlie's forest. For whatever the reason, she'd tried to get him to suggest it, rather than simply state her wishes.

Another female thing. Sally had hinted the same way, a few times. Sally's hints had sometimes fallen on deaf ears. Given his limited experience with the matter, Conrad counted himself lucky he'd caught on quickly.

He gave a noncommittal shrug and hoped it passed for an answer to her question. He took his time spreading butter on crusty bread and avoided meeting her gaze.

Julia's ardor made wild, irresponsible notions flit through his usually sound mind.

She made him want to forget he had a dairy to run, employees to supervise, a dozen head yet to calve, and a crop in the field.

Never before had he felt this itch to abandon all responsibility.

Why was he even considering spending one very long day taking her to see trees that had been dead and buried for literally millions of years?

Even if he wanted to, which he certainly did not, it was impossible. It was too far to go this late in the day.

Besides, she had a party to finish planning before Holmes got back, within the week.

"I hear," she said, her tone most casual, "that a remarkable geyser's not far from there. Portia mentioned it to me...erupts like clockwork, every fourteen minutes. What's it called?"

"Old Faithful." Somehow, he suspected she already knew that.

He chewed the tangy bread, satisfied with the sweetness of the butter. Rich, flavorful butter from Macquarie Dairies. He rubbed his tongue over the roof of his mouth, savoring the last of the creamy richness.

"These natural wonders," she said as she buttered her own bread, "sound absolutely marvelous. So different than anything I've ever seen back home."

Julia, expert in the mysteries of females, waited patiently, nibbling at her bread and sipping wine as if she had all the time in the world. Waiting for him to offer to take her there.

He could see her behaving just like this, while waiting for her father's answer on just about anything. Evidently, this woman not only understood her own gender, but exactly how to persuade males to do her bidding, as well.

Why not? It would be so simple to suggest the trip. It would please her and Portia, both. The outing would keep the ladies occupied and content, just like Pop wanted.

What was so wrong with wanting to show his sister-in-law-to-be a good time?

Everything.

He had paperwork piling up on his desk, an argument between two of the crew to settle, and a backlog of orders to ship. He'd already set himself back another day's work in order to carry her to town today. The errand to the print shop, together with this two-hour lunch would eat the rest of his afternoon. She'd been in town all of forty eight hours, and already, he was three days behind.

Worst of all, he felt inexplicably drawn to her like flies to honey. A moth to her flame.

That was the mountain-sized reason why wanting to show her a good time was so incredibly wrong.

So very wrong, this affection for his brother's soon-to-be-wedded-wife.

Chapter Seven

CONRAD CLOSED his eyes. For the briefest of moments, he justified that there wasn't a thing wrong with liking Holmes's bride. He ought to like her. She would be part of the family.

But this wasn't merely affection for a new sister-in-law, or even appreciation for her beauty. This was the kind of admiration that sneaked up on inappropriate.

What honor was there in falling, even in part, for a woman promised to his brother?

None.

Absolutely none.

Conrad glimpsed movement at the restaurant entrance. Pastor John Proctor and his wife following a waiter to a table. John paused to greet several of the other diners, then noticed Miss Julia seated with Conrad.

In that moment, it seemed evident the pastor

found it commendable Conrad would take the time to dine out, in the middle of a workday, with his brother's bride-to-be.

Everybody in the Orme Hotel Dining Room saw he was only doing his brother a service.

The family expected as much.

Holmes would thank him.

But if anybody—especially Pastor John, who'd known Conrad since he'd been in long dresses—looked closely, he just might see there was a problem.

Because Conrad knew he wasn't looking at Julia the way he did Silas's wife, Nadine.

His interest in Julia wasn't proper, and sure as sunrise wasn't prudent.

Unchecked, it could get him in a great deal of trouble.

That meant there could never be a trip to visit Petrified Charlie's Forest or Old Faithful geyser. Even with her chaperon along, it wasn't his place, nor his right to spend that kind of personal time with Holmes's bride. Holmes would want the opportunity to show her the coast, Clear Lake, the vineyards, the redwoods, anything and everything around here.

It was a good thing Holmes would be home before the end of next week. Conrad didn't like the thought of babysitting the bride any longer.

He didn't know if his sanity could take it.

Shutting down her unspoken request for an outing or two may not be what he wanted, but he sure as shooting had to. "I'm sure you'd rather go with Holmes."

At the mention of Holmes's name, her expression brightened. Anticipation danced in her eyes. "Well, yes. Of course. I only meant to express interest in the area."

He'd made the only honorable choice. She'd said the right and proper thing.

So why did his chest ache with disappointment?

WELL PAST A respectable hour, Aunt Portia finally returned from her outing with Olaf DeLaigle. Julia glanced at the clock on the bedroom mantle. Forty minutes past nine.

These day-long outings with Mr. DeLaigle had to stop. They'd been going on for three days straight. Portia, it seemed, had no inkling of time and no consideration, whatsoever, for their hosts. Although Portia had made it home by dark the past two days, tonight, the sun had long since set. Julia had very nearly made herself sick with worry. She hurried downstairs.

Portia chatted happily, exclaiming about everything she'd seen and experienced, and oh! wasn't Mr. DeLaigle the most charming, knowledgeable guide that ever lived?

Katherine, in her nightdress and robe, took each item Portia handed over. The large handbag, overflowing with loose sheets of scribbled notes. Her over-sized hat. An umbrella.

Julia intercepted her aunt in the front parlor. Portia unwound her scarf, removed her gloves, and prattled on about the geological wonders she'd seen with her own eyes, sketched, and with help from Mr. DeLaigle, *photographed.*

Katherine juggled the armload of accouterments and accepted Portia's coat. "I've kept supper warm for you. Come into the kitchen."

Portia fell silent for the space of a second or two. "Supper?" She laughed aloud. "Why, I am hungry. Haven't paused a moment. Completely forgot about eating."

Impatience warred with relief, and impatience very nearly won. "Aunt Portia, I'm relieved you've finally made it back."

"Oh, there you are, Dolly. I have the most remarkable finds to tell you all about. I've started a new journal, and when I return to Maryland—"

"*Portia.*" Julia drew a breath and waited until she had her aunt's attention. "Everyone in this household is asleep," she whispered, hoping Portia would lower her voice.

"Asleep?" She sounded genuinely surprised. "At this hour?"

"We rise before four." Katherine carried Portia's belongings toward the staircase.

"Why, yes. Of course. I remember now." At least Portia had quieted enough that the others could go back to sleep. "Pardon me." Mumbling something to herself, she drifted to the kitchen and her waiting supper.

Julia found her aunt pulling a soup plate from the warming oven. Making herself at home, she located a fork and sat down to eat. She took several bites, sighing with appreciation. "This is delicious. A bit dry, but tasty, just the same."

Julia's irritation wouldn't fade, simply because Portia returned unharmed. "It's been in the oven several hours, awaiting your return."

Portia paused with a fork, loaded with mashed potatoes, halfway to her mouth. "Aren't you peckish tonight."

"I was worried about you."

"Worried?" Portia abandoned the bite of potato. "Why?"

"I wondered if you'd eloped."

Portia blinked. Then smothered laughter behind her napkin. They both knew marriage was the furthest thing from Portia's mind.

"I hardly forgot about you, Dolly. I thought about you twice. Once when Olaf told me all about the Macquarie family—he told me quite a bit of commendable details about our dear Holmes. And I thought of you again, when Olaf suggested he give me a guided tour of a nearby stand of redwoods tomorrow."

"Again?" How much more was there to possibly see around here? And why did Portia consider herself an adequate chaperon? Julia could do whatever she pleased, and Portia would be none the wiser.

"Of course, tomorrow. I can think of nothing else I'd rather be doing than see these magnificent trees. You hardly need my services as chaperon until the young man is in residence."

"You're leaving me to my own devices?"

Portia chuckled and picked at the beef stew that had congealed on her soup plate. She speared a chunk of carrot and chewed, regarding Julia closely. "Violet and Katherine are home, are they not? I don't see why I must watch you every moment."

Dropping her fork, Portia leaned forward and grasped Julia's hand in her own. She squeezed tightly. "I feel an urgency to seize the opportunity while it presents itself. I have only a handful of days until Holmes will be here, and then what choice will I have?"

Julia understood, all too well, her aunt's wishes to explore, to witness everything, to smell the foliage, to revel in the beauties of this place. Julia wanted to do the same thing. But with the welcome home party rapidly approaching, she had more than enough work to do. Most of it must be set in motion before Holmes returned, or the guests wouldn't know they were invited, much less have anything to eat.

"Don't look so downhearted," Portia urged, squeezing Julia's hand between her own two tiny ones. "What are you going to do tomorrow?"

"Consult with Alberta. Make certain the foods are ordered. Deliver the invitations." Why did it sound so simple? Those two things would take the majority of her day.

"Surely you don't need my companionship for *that*. You could easily accomplish those tasks in your sleep." Her aunt sighed, contentment mingled with anticipation. "Now, once those pesky party things are out of the way, what do you *want* to do with your day?"

Julia couldn't help but grin. It was so like Portia to look forward to her next adventure. How Julia wished she had the freedom to explore the ranch at her leisure, to try some of the much-anticipated things on her list. Weren't eggs supposed to be collected first thing in the morning? Surely that half hour wouldn't sabotage the day's work.

"Before I even begin to see to the party details—"

"Yes, yes. I do like the way you think."

"I will gather eggs."

Portia blinked, her expression blank, as if the thought of Julia wanting to gather eggs hadn't ever crossed her mind. "Splendid!"

"And, given time, I want to watch the crew run the separator. There's still so much left to see."

"That settles it," Portia announced, returning to her stew and mashed potatoes. "You see to your plans, the eggs, the separator. I don't see any need to supervise such routine tasks, do you? I promise to be home from my grand outing in the redwoods with ample time to spare. You and I won't have one iota of difficulty making it to the depot to greet Holmes Macquarie properly."

"Didn't Holmes's father tell you? He wants to pick up his son alone, so they'll have an opportunity to discuss the case in San Francisco. We'll meet Holmes when they arrive at home."

"Just as well." Portia's grin widened. "That gives me another hour or two to explore the trees."

BY LAMPLIGHT, Conrad shaved at the washstand in his bedroom. He drew the blade in smooth strokes down his throat. He swished off the lather in the washbowl.

Finished, he splashed a bit of water over his face and toweled off. He peered into the mirror, turning to the left and right, and ran hand over his cheeks and jaw, checking for any missed spots.

He leaned on the washstand and turned his left

cheek to the mirror. The scar looked exactly like it had for as long as he could remember. Always with him.

Julia's haunting words taunted him. *You should smile more often.* Right. And brown cows gave chocolate milk.

His smile was lopsided, crooked and ruined by his deformity. He ought to know. It belonged to him.

Baring his teeth in a feral grin, he noted his teeth didn't look too bad. White. Clean. Straight as they'd always been.

He squinted. Leaned closer. Took a real close look at the symmetry of the right side compared to the left.

In this light, he didn't look all that disgusting. Almost balanced. Not the way he remembered it at all.

He didn't want to think about it anymore, so he rinsed out his shaving mug and swished the brush. Dried and stored his razor. Threw the towel back over the bar.

And looked in the mirror. Just one more time.

An image of Julia, in the milking shed, feminine shyness dancing in her eyes as she made that ridiculous comment, flitted through his mind.

She liked his smile.

He tried it on for size, just for a second.

He grimaced. Pulled the smile too tight, expecting a butt-ugly, twisted distortion of his lips.

He looked ridiculous.

Look at him. A grown man, pulling faces at himself in the mirror. What was he? A kid again?

His stomach turned an odd little flip. Yeah, he did feel like a boy again. Julia and her infatuations with everyday things like milking machines and cheese presses and smiles had a way of doing that to him.

Remembering the city-girl terror in her eyes as she bolted behind the milking machine, he couldn't help but smile.

He met his own eye in the mirror. And let his gaze slide to his mouth.

His heartbeat doubled on itself.

Not perfect. But a country mile from being as bad as he'd thought.

"NINETEEN EGGS!" Julia shouted from the hen house door. She hefted her basket in a show of triumph. The startled chickens clucked and scattered, tearing across the yard in a maelstrom of brown and white. "Nineteen!"

Conrad fairly choked on a mouthful of cold well water. He plunked the dipper back into the bucket and wiped the back of his hand over his chin.

In all his life, he'd never seen a woman celebrate the somewhat unpleasant task of looting the hen house. As a young girl, Katherine had whined and wheedled her way out of the chore as often as possible. Conrad narrowed his eyes, wondering how his sister had convinced Julia to do her dirty work.

"Do you think there are more?" Julia called to him. Her delicate skin was flushed with happiness.

He'd always thought her pretty. Yet she was more than a lovely face; something about her was different, more appealing, than any other woman. Funny thing was, he couldn't say what.

Somehow, that odd thought made his chest hurt and his stomach ache.

One white feather hung precariously from the curls at her right temple. Although her gown was fashioned of unadorned cream-colored muslin, it was a far cry from the work dresses his mother and sister wore. This city girl didn't belong in the chicken coop.

"Could be a few more." He crossed the yard toward her.

The poor girl only wanted a spot of conversation. With her aunt roaming the mountains with Olaf, and Katherine conspicuously absent from this chore, Julia must be quite lonely for company. Conrad couldn't take her to see any of the sights, and shouldn't invite her along to spend much time with him. But where was the harm in keeping her company, for just a few minutes? As a favor to Holmes.

"Then I'll find them." She set down the basket with care, spun with a whirl of skirts, and ducked back inside the coop.

Conrad laughed, amused by her enthusiasm.

"I've heard some chickens hide their eggs. Is it true?" she asked. Two more hens escaped, protesting loudly.

"Old Goldie's been known to stash hers. Have a look in the northeast corner."

"Where?" He heard the soft rustle of her skirts and the crinkle of hay as she thrust her hands into the recesses. The unpleasant, sour odor made him wonder why she'd go back inside. It seemed Katherine, distracted by David Orme, had failed to give the hen house its usually thorough cleaning.

Curious, he propped an arm above the low door and peered inside.

A faint shaft of weak early morning light filtered through the roof's vent. Dust motes hovered, reminding him of delicate snowfall. Julia tucked her skirts behind her knees to keep the hem off the floor and balanced on her toes.

Conrad tried not to notice her slender calves in silk stockings. Fancy, high-heeled city shoes. Hopelessly out of place in this dirty outbuilding.

In the patch of pale illumination, Julia looked like an angel. Radiant, resplendent, captivating, ...perfect.

Conrad's pulse slowed. The moment stretched as he watched her work, both hands thrust elbow-deep into the straw. How could a city-bred lady, wearing costly shoes, smile with glee while rooting around in search of eggs?

Julia glanced up from her task and held his gaze for the breadth of perhaps three seconds. "Found it!"

She blinked, a soft smile teasing her lips. The joy

of discovery glittered in her eyes, streaking through him with a flash of fire so unexpected it raised gooseflesh on his arms.

His stomach turned an odd little flip, and somewhere in the back of his mind, he knew he was in deep trouble.

With startling clarity, Conrad knew this wasn't a general run-of-the-mill kind of distraction.

This unwanted attraction to Julia was *far* worse than that.

A serious, life-altering inconvenience that would inevitably lead to disharmony in the family.

If he acted upon it.

Which he most certainly would not.

If he caved to the growing temptation.

Which he most definitely would not. He'd learned that wretched lesson the hard way. One foray into that nightmare was enough for the Macquarie family.

This woman would never, could never, be his.

"Two more!" Julia squealed with childlike delight. Her skirts teased his trouser leg as she passed by into the yard.

Conrad closed his eyes and gave himself a stern talking-to. This, this *thing,* whatever it was, would pass just as soon as Holmes got home and tended to Julia himself.

After all, it wasn't meaningful, far-reaching, because he wouldn't allow it to be. A few days from now, it'd be completely forgotten. History. Nothing more than a pleasant memory of a few days spent passing the time, waiting for his brother to return home.

Liar.

Guilt burned in his gut, the flames licking, rising higher in his chest. Who was he fooling?

Julia set her bounty in the basket, taking her sweet time arranging the eggs just so. She didn't seem to have any inkling of the turmoil she caused, innocently walking past him.

He scoured his palm over his face and tried to

turn away. It wasn't even half-past six. The day had barely begun, and already, he'd completely forgotten what he'd intended to accomplish. He'd stopped for a drink of water, and Julia's egg-gathering had derailed him.

"Twenty-two."

With a gleam of triumph, she tucked the basket handle over her forearm. "These aren't the days- or weeks-old eggs delivery services peddle house to house. *These,*" she confided in a low voice, leaning a bit closer, "are as fresh as they come."

Fearing emotion showed clearly on his face, Conrad attempted to wipe his features clean. He tried to concentrate on what she'd said. "Yes, they are. The genuine article."

"For the first time in my life, I *gathered* eggs."

"Yes, you did." Friendly, he reminded himself. For Holmes's sake. Normal, everyday conversation. "Tell me," *sister-in-law,* "how did Katherine get you to paint the fence?"

"Paint the fence?" She paused, then her smile brightened. "*The Adventures of Tom Sawyer*. I see you do read! And you think Katherine compelled me to do her work?"

Her light laughter tugged at something deep inside Conrad.

"I wanted to do this. I've always wondered what it would be like, and now I know."

"Yes, you do."

"Might you guess what else I've always wanted to do?" She whispered the question with an air of secrecy.

He didn't want to share any more secrets. Hesitant, he asked, "What?"

"I want to learn to ride."

"A horse?" he asked stupidly. What else would she want to ride? A cow? A Border Collie?

She nodded, anticipation shining in her eyes. "I've never even ridden a pony. My friend, Sarah, had a pony at her seventh birthday party. All the girls had a turn to ride, but me. Father wouldn't allow it."

"Sorry to hear that." Around here, everyone learned to ride when they were small. That's just the way it was.

"From what Holmes wrote in his letters, I'm not sure he'll have the time nor the inclination to give me a lesson."

That surprised Conrad. Before she'd begun feeling poorly, Ma had ridden often. Katherine was an accomplished rider, too.

"But I didn't let that discourage me," Julia said with certainty. "I had the most wonderful riding habit made before I came, hoping I'd have the chance to wear it."

A riding habit? Ladies around here wore everyday dresses. "Your father must've had something to say about the costume."

"If my father wanted to know every scrap of detail, he shouldn't have given me an open account at Mrs. Bingham's Emporium."

"Bought it in secret, did you?"

"I rarely showed him the gowns Mrs. Bingham delivered." She leaned closer, lowering her voice in confidence. "But I made certain he never saw this fawn-colored, absolutely wonderful outfit. Not that he'd recognize a riding habit if he saw one."

She sounded just like Katherine; it must be a woman thing.

"I had my bridal gown made, too, with my father none the wiser." A sly grin flirted about her pink lips. Obviously pleased by her feat.

Knowing how his sister skulked around, keeping plenty from their parents, he could well imagine Julia unwrapping her parcels from the dressmaker behind locked doors. She likely stashed a huge wardrobe in her five matching Saratoga trunks.

Her expression brightened. "Suffice it to say I'm relieved to be free of my father's dictates. And, since I've yet to learn Holmes's views on the matter of ladies riding horseback, I'm inclined to take this opportunity. This may be my last chance."

Her bright tone didn't do much to conceal her concern. Conrad didn't dare speak for his brother. He saw no sense in reassuring Julia that she'd have plenty of chances to climb into the saddle. Years in Boston may have changed Holmes's view on all sorts of things.

She looked up at him, hope in her eyes. "Will you teach me to ride. Today?"

The today part caught him, square in the gut. He knew what she meant. Over breakfast, Pa had reminded everybody today was the big day. Holmes would arrive on the afternoon train.

Julia's request made Conrad uncomfortable. It wasn't his place to say yes. Or no. Desperation to agree, to grab whatever time he could with her, stampeded over his good sense.

He grasped at any glimmer of sanity he could find. What about the upcoming welcome-home? "Don't you have party plans to work on?"

"The arrangements are all well underway. I consulted with Alberta while we prepared breakfast. The food's arranged, the—"

When she broke off, he met her gaze, wondering why she'd stopped.

His heart turned a slow backwards somersault. He held her gaze, trapped.

"Please?" she asked softly. "This is something I desperately want to do."

He cursed beneath his breath. He found he couldn't deny her this one simple request.

In that moment, he wondered if he could deny her anything at all.

"All right, Miss J."

"Yes!"

Far too pleased by the huge smile he put on her face, he turned her toward the kitchen door. "Take the eggs into the house. I'll saddle your horse while you put on your—"

The word *habit* died on his tongue, for at that moment, Julia kissed his cheek. She ran for the house, protectively clutching the egg basket to her chest.

She couldn't possibly have paused to think about it, because she'd kissed him on the scarred side of his face.

It was just the kind of thank-you his mother or sister might've given him, if they'd been the type to bestow a kiss.

But it sure as sunrise hadn't felt like a sisterly peck. Before he could examine that unwelcome thought too closely, Conrad headed for the barn to saddle the horses.

Chapter Eight

HOURS LATER, Julia sat in the formal parlor, her nerves in complete upheaval. How could she bear sitting still one more minute? Mr. Macquarie should've been back with Holmes a full hour ago. Had his train been delayed?

Violet reclined on the sofa, her stocking feet on a pillow. Katherine read aloud from *The Strange Case of Dr. Jekyll and Mr. Hyde.* Aunt Portia, apparently worn to a frazzle by her outings with Mr. DeLaigle, snored softly in an upholstered chair.

The married brother, Silas, had arrived with Nadine and their son half an hour ago. Nadine was rocking the baby to sleep in an upstairs bedroom, and Silas had gone to collect Conrad and Gabriel.

Julia wished she'd invited herself on the errand, because that would've gotten her out of the parlor.

How she wished she could walk out the stiffness

in her muscles and joints. The horseback riding, albeit at an easy gait, had been glorious and invigorating.

The time had flown past.

But now that it was time for Holmes to arrive, the minutes dragged by at a snail's pace.

There wasn't a thing left to do. She'd dressed carefully in a fashionable dark green bodice and skirt, spent twice as long as usual in styling her hair, and felt confident she looked her best.

She'd spent the better part of two hours going over the party preparations with Violet and Alberta, the housekeeper, so they'd see matters were well in hand. They'd finalized details and delegated the cooking entirely to Alberta's newly-hired help.

Holmes's bedroom had been aired, thoroughly cleaned, and prepared for his arrival with fresh bed linens and cheery sprigs of lilacs stood in a cut-crystal vase. The dining room table was set. Alberta was putting the finishing touches on supper.

The aromas smelled heavenly, but Julia's appetite had fled. Dread had replaced the enjoyment and relaxation she'd experienced while horseback riding with Conrad.

That morning, she may have felt some semblance of hope the celebration would come together in time. But she'd misjudged before.

Her father's criticism, delivered after many of the galas she orchestrated for him, made it clear he expected better. She tried to remind herself this wasn't Baltimore, and her father's opinion didn't matter anymore. All she had to do was pass Holmes's inspection.

What if Holmes found fault in her preparations? Worse, what if he found fault with *her?*

She'd become comfortable in this home, adored Holmes's family. She wanted to keep them all.

Violet had welcomed her with open arms. Katherine had shown her much kindness. And Conrad was the closest thing to a best friend she'd ever had.

Through Holmes's letters, she knew him to be every bit as wonderful as Conrad. He'd easily persuaded her to leave home and family and move to California to be his wife.

So why the hesitation?

She'd told him everything—almost—about herself. And what remained couldn't be addressed in correspondence. The rest would have to wait until they knew each other much better. Probably once they were wed.

At last, she heard the rumble of the buggy's wheels on the drive. Anticipation bubbled through her, just as it had the day she'd arrived at Liberty's train depot. Finally!

Katherine tucked a ribbon into the book and hurried to part the curtains. Julia's saddle-sore muscles twinged as she looked over Katherine's shoulder.

Mr. Macquarie drove the buggy, alone. His shoulders slumped.

Katherine turned to Julia, a question on her face.

What had happened? Where was Holmes?

"Are they here?" Violet sat and smoothed her skirts. "Oh, finally."

"Yes. It's Pop." Katherine put her book in its place on the shelf.

Portia stirred, smacked her lips, and blinked. "Did I doze?" She glanced at the watch pinned to her bodice. "Surely I didn't miss their arrival."

Julia patted Portia's hand. "Mr. Macquarie's just driving up to the house."

Alone. Julia could see that much.

Her spirits wilted further.

Familiar disappointment stole through her, leaving her cold. How many times had her father's trips to Washington been delayed? He'd put his duties to the public first. His wife and children got whatever time was leftover.

Not a pleasant way to live.

Oh, how she'd hoped Holmes would prove

different. Better. More interested in nurturing a relationship than her father had been.

The thought felt disloyal.

She shouldn't make assumptions about Holmes's motives. He was a good man—she knew that. He'd proven himself in his letters. She owed him better.

Maybe he had reason to follow behind. Perhaps he'd come along on horseback after he finished his business in town. Maybe his father had received another telegram saying Holmes would be on tomorrow morning's train.

It had to have something to do with the important legal case in San Francisco.

Otherwise, Holmes would be here. With her.

Wouldn't he? The Holmes she knew would've been waiting, on the porch—no, at the depot—the moment she arrived. Eager to greet her.

Something was wrong. In her gut, she knew it.

Holmes's father trudged slowly up the stairs. A solitary set of footfalls.

Julia's stomach turned over.

Violet rose and hurried across the carpet. She pulled open the front door.

A long pause stretched before Phillip Macquarie finally crossed the threshold.

"Where is he?" Violet peered past her husband, to the buggy.

No answer. Mr. Macquarie, speechless? Julia couldn't believe it.

Dread curdled in her stomach.

Phillip Macquarie looked from one face to the next, apology evident in his every movement. "I'm very sorry, ladies. Holmes wasn't on the train."

AS MOST OF THE family prepared to retire for the night, Conrad found Julia seated on the west side of the house. The last rays of evening sunlight glowed on her smooth skin. She folded her arms against evening's chill. Her posture sagged under the weight of disappointment.

Her sadness tugged at him. She'd waited so long to meet Holmes. No definite word about when he'd be here, either.

Conrad's boots thudded on the wooden porch as he approached.

She glanced up, making a brave effort to hide her sadness behind a smile. To his surprise, she seemed pleased to see him.

The cane chair groaned under his weight. For a moment, he sat beside her, trying to see the view through her eyes. Birds twittered in the trees. Wind tossed the leaves. Out behind the barn, one of the collies barked, then fell silent. Must seem awful lonesome to her, no matter what she'd said about liking the quiet.

He glanced at her. "When I'm feeling low, I find the best medicine is a ride in the hills. I know you're probably still saddle sore, but would you like—"

"Yes." She scooted to the front of her seat and slapped her knees. Enthusiasm brightened her words and expression alike. "Right now? Could we?"

He'd made the suggestion in good faith, but hadn't thought, even once, that she'd agree to go. He'd only intended the offer to cheer her and help shake off the melancholy.

"You want to?" The lady was still as inexperienced as they came.

She stood. "Rule number one, Mr. Macquarie. Only extend invitations you intend to honor."

"Yes, ma'am." Conrad rose, grinning. He worked with a half-dozen men who could take a lesson from Julia. When life doesn't go your way, you may as well smile. Grumpy cusses didn't get what they wanted any faster than pleasant folk.

"Give me five minutes to saddle the horses." He couldn't help but grin all the way to the barn.

Yep. Worked like a charm. She looked more cheerful already.

Suggesting a ride was the right thing to do.

AN HOUR LATER, Conrad stood beside Julia on the crest of a foothill. He waited in silence as the last sliver of sun slipped behind the tree-lined horizon. Insects buzzed softly, interrupted only by an occasional chirp of a bird and Junebug's whinny. The pair of Saddlebreds nipped at tender spring grasses at the edge of the meadow.

Taking a ride into the hills always soothed Conrad, made his tensions and worries ebb. Maybe it was the chance to remember he was only one small part of creation. And the chance to clear his mind and enjoy an hour to himself.

In the valley below, lamps burned in the ranch house windows. Smoke rose in lazy tendrils from the chimneys. From this viewpoint, the house looked rather lonesome, down there all by itself. To Julia, it must look unbearably desolate, with Holmes still away.

Conrad slid a glance at Julia. She sighed and folded her arms against the growing chill. Getting away from the house seemed to ease her homesickness for Holmes, at least temporarily. Good. But it'd be full dark within half an hour, and they ought to head back.

"Ready to saddle up?"

She held his gaze for a long moment, a smile teasing at her mouth. "Five more minutes?" She grasped his forearm, giving a squeeze. "It's so peaceful here. *This* is precisely what I wanted to find in California. Space to breathe. Quiet to hear myself think."

He nodded, mute. How could he speak, for the rush of awareness surging in his veins? Her touch, familial though it was, felt too good. Warmth from her hand seeped through his sleeve.

No woman, other than his mother and sister, had ever touched him this way. Not even Sally.

Until that moment, he'd believed a woman's casual touches mostly unnecessary. Something he could live without.

To his dismay, he realized just how wrong he'd been.

Her hand lingered on his arm, much longer than the glorious moments over the Orme dining room table. Conrad didn't dare move, for fear she'd pull away. An urge to touch her, simply to brush a curl away from her face, or drag a thumb across her cheek, came strong.

Her touch on his arm wasn't permission to respond with familiarity.

Weren't citified ladies too reserved to be all touchy-touchy, even with family members? Especially with men? He wondered if Julia had intentionally left behind all concern for social rules.

Fine by him.

But she did release him, much too soon. She took two steps toward an outcropping of rock, planted one shoe upon it, and scanned the view. Fading, golden rays illuminated her profile, turning her dusky curls into a halo. He watched her scan the buildings below, as if seeing them all for the first time.

"This is the most provincial," she murmured, "picture-book view I have ever seen."

His sentiments, exactly. But his attention was trained on Julia. Again, he was struck with her beauty. Her fancy riding getup seemed so out of place. Like it had been fashioned to wear on a Sunday ride in a big city park. Not here, where normal folk wore denim and chambray and serviceable cottons.

Maybe that's why he couldn't help but think her so appealing. A flawless red rose in a garden of daisies.

"The fields and pastures look like quilt blocks from up here." She turned a little circle, taking in the mountainside and valley below. "This is *all* yours?"

"Macquarie land, sure."

She turned to him, her smile quick and full. "I'm not surprised you want to buy it." Tucking her riding skirt about her, she sat on the smooth face of the rock and patted the space beside her. "Come, sit."

Before he considered resisting, he found himself doing exactly as she asked. His arm brushed her shoulder. Only then did he realize he'd put his bad side toward her.

"Most of the ranch is on flat rangeland, right?" Her gaze seemed to penetrate his profile.

Seconds passed, and he grew increasingly uncomfortable with her staring at his ghastly, disfiguring scar.

It was high time they left, anyway. When morning came, he'd regret staying up late.

He swallowed and risked a glance in her direction. To his surprise, he found Julia looked him squarely in the eyes. How many thousands of times had people stared with undisguised revulsion at the jagged, ruddy scar, only to quickly avert their gaze the moment he looked toward them?

Not Julia.

The way she sat beside him, as if they were old friends, made him feel more acceptance than he'd ever known, from anyone but immediate family. Almost as if she had some uncanny ability to ignore his flaw altogether. But he knew that wasn't possible.

Julia smiled and edged a little closer. "Was it a foolish question? I suppose if your father bought this hilly land, he had a reason. I see you don't grow crops up here." She cast him a teasing smile. "I guess it's the family's favored picnic spot."

He couldn't help but chuckle. "Picnic? When? *Why?*"

"You've lived here all your life. And never once took an afternoon to picnic on your own hillside?" She prodded his arm with her shoulder, with mock disbelief. "What a waste of prime property. What an unconscionable decision to ignore the beauties of nature."

"No, I—"

"Are you so committed to your work, then? No time for play?"

Her teasing tone made him smile. His discomfort faded, even with her attention on the bad side of his face. "That's me. All work, and no play. Makes a man healthy, wealthy, and wise."

She chuckled and seemed to lean, just a little heavier, on his arm. "You've got your adages mixed up. That's early to bed, early to rise."

"Since you got here, Miss J, I seem to have forgotten how to get my sleep."

"Me?" Pretend offense rounded her mouth to an O. "Portia woke you at an indecent hour, not I."

Conrad had awoken to voices, true enough. But Portia hadn't caused him one wink of sleeplessness. Julia, on the other hand, presented a challenge. "Disavowing responsibility, I see."

With one raised brow, she refused to answer. Instead, she looked at him, her expression changing subtly. "This place is in your blood, isn't it?"

He nodded, turning his gaze out over the acres sprawling below. Intimately familiar. He knew every inch of the place, lived for its success, loved it deeply.

She waited, and he had the odd sensation that she genuinely wanted to know more. Her interest surprised him. "It's my home. I took Pop's humble operation and developed it into what it is today."

She smiled at him, softly. It was unsettling to see a woman looking at him like she understood him. No one ever had. He wasn't sure he liked this one thinking she did.

Time to change the topic of conversation. "You must miss your home."

"Not at all."

"That's a bull-sized lie."

Her ready laughter made him smile.

She noticed with glee. "You really *should* smile

more often."

He didn't want to think about it, do it, or talk about doing it. Didn't like the way her gaze ran over his face when he smiled, not unlike a caress.

He looked away. "Why don't you miss home? If I left here, I'd die of acute homesickness."

"So don't go anywhere."

"I won't."

She gazed off into the distance for the space of a few breaths. "What will you do if your father won't sell?"

Conrad shrugged, feigning patience he didn't feel. Restlessness coiled within him. The urgency to make his own way had worsened lately. Why? He didn't know.

"Outlive him, I guess."

She chuckled. "Can you wait that long?"

"Don't know if I'll have a choice." Without land of his own, he'd never amount to anything. He knew that. She knew that. Any woman of quality knew that.

He changed the subject. "My turn to ask you a personal question."

"You can ask," she said with a teasing smile. "But I may not answer."

"What made it so easy to leave home?" He genuinely wanted to know. She'd come west to marry Holmes—that much was evident. Holmes would make a fine husband any woman would be honored to have. But none of that explained why she claimed to have no homesickness.

"Baltimore has nothing to offer me."

"Nothing?" He'd seen her clothing and had a fair idea what her father had spent on her wardrobe alone. What about her fancy university education? Sisters. Those nieces she mentioned.

"No, nothing."

"It's obvious you had parties. A social life. A fine home. I doubt your parents denied you anything."

She shrugged. "None of that made me happy."

Conrad wondered if she'd grow bored out here, without those things. Yeah, the ranch house was solid and sturdy and adequately furnished, but she wasn't the mistress of the estate. If Pop had his way, she and Holmes would always live with the extended family.

"If all that finery didn't make you happy," he said, "I have to wonder what will."

"Little things."

"Like what?"

"My needs are simple."

"I suspect Holmes will be happy to know that, even if it is a poor answer. Come on," he cajoled. He found he desperately wanted her answer. "You can tell me. What would make you happy?"

She chuckled. A warm, rich sound that stirred his blood.

Maybe this wasn't such a good idea. The two of them talking about such personal stuff.

"You know what I want more than anything?" She turned to him, captivating his attention.

He swallowed. Blinked. Found her still staring him straight in the eye.

That gnawing ache in his stomach was back, full force. Something about the way the woman looked at him had a way of twisting his insides.

Finally, he had the presence of mind to shrug.

"I want life away from Baltimore, away from anyone who's ever heard of my father." She paused, as if expecting a response.

"That ornery, huh?"

"No, that well-known. Everyone in Baltimore, in all of Maryland, knows exactly who my father is, and therefore, who I am. But you can't ever tell anyone that."

She was serious. "Sounds rough."

"Don't you ever just want someone to like you for who you are?" Sounding exasperated, she pressed a palm to her breastbone. "In here?"

She didn't pause, didn't really look at him. If she had, she might've seen the naked longing that surely registered on his face. He understood. More than she could possibly know.

"I wish people, especially bachelors in want of a wife, could look past everything that *Tyndall* means and forget all of it. How was I supposed to find a husband in that environment? Someone who wasn't just looking for a profitable match? Someone who didn't have expectations of what a Tyndall bride would most certainly be?"

She did glance at him, then, for a brief moment.

He had an image of life as she described it. When she put it that way, he found it incredibly easy to understand.

She turned away. "I doubt this makes sense to you."

"Makes perfect sense."

Despite the passion fueling her words, she smiled. "Are you one of those money-hunting bachelors?"

"No, Miss J. It never once occurred to me to choose a woman for her money. Truth be told, I'd have to pay her, plenty, just to marry me."

"*Pay* her?" Julia stared at him, her features blank. "What are you talking about? Any girl would be proud to have you. *Honored.*"

Stunned, he couldn't pull his gaze away from the sincerity on her face. What was he supposed to say to that?

"Surely you're keeping company with someone."

At that, he turned away, gazing sightlessly over the Macquarie spread. The old pain returned, worse than ever.

He thought Julia would press. Or at least make some light-hearted comment. She didn't. And that was his undoing. He wanted to tell her things he hadn't told a soul.

"Used to be." It sounded so final.

He sensed her gaze on his face. She seemed to lean a little closer, the warmth of her body surprisingly soothing. Something about her nearness, the way she'd shared her personal thoughts made him want to confide.

But he couldn't. Not yet. Maybe not ever.

Moments passed, neither of them speaking.

"Someday," she told him with conviction, "you'll make some lucky girl a wonderful husband."

An odd, but welcome sensation tingled through his belly, making him a little lightheaded. Something in Julia's eyes—probably only glittering reflection of the sunset—was too easy to mistake for tenderness and endearment.

Of course, she was showing only familial affection. Sisterly interest. Nothing wrong with that.

Except that it made him crave a great deal more.

Someone who laughed easily with him. Who didn't care if she sat on his ruined side or his good one. Somebody who looked at *him,* and loved him for who he was, for what he'd accomplished with the dairy, for everything he was inside.

Someone like Julia.

But women like that only existed in a fairytale.

Despite Julia's optimism, Conrad had always known he'd have a hard time finding a woman capable of wanting him, spoiled face and all. Sally was the only woman who'd entertained the idea of marrying him. Losing her had cost him the possibility of marriage and children.

He knew it wasn't rational to believe Sally had been his only chance, but it sure as sunrise felt like it. With a great deal of perseverance, he might locate a respectable, hardworking farmer's daughter to be his helpmate on the dairy.

He knew he'd be darn lucky if this wife would ever get used to his face, and eventually love him enough she couldn't see the scar anymore.

Through the years, he hadn't dared hope he'd meet such a female so easily.

But he had.

Conrad pulled his attention away from Julia. His heart beat triple-time, making it difficult to catch his breath.

Impossible.

She likes me. Me. *Despite my ruined face.*

Whoa, Nellie. Stop right there.

Despite his delusions, he recognized the danger in entertaining such thoughts.

Even if she had *some* of what he thought he wanted—say, honestly enjoying his companionship—that didn't change the fact she couldn't ever be his.

Not ever.

He was delusional. Crazed. She was promised to Holmes.

Julia might like him, in a brother-sister sort of way, but that didn't mean she'd ever want to marry him.

Beside him, Julia leaned closer, brought her shoulder into solid contact with his arm. She didn't pull away.

The connection felt so very right; it felt so wrong. His heart turned over. He ached to reach for her, to take her hand, to put his arms around her. The mere thought brought a fresh onslaught of guilt.

Ever so slowly, he eased away.

This couldn't go on. Not one more minute. It pained his conscience to realize thoughts of her—his brother's bride—had consumed his every waking moment since meeting her. A very bad omen, indeed, considering Holmes would return any day now, to claim his wife-to-be.

Conrad's heart might be desperate for Julia's affection, but he was no fool.

He couldn't continue to delude himself where Julia was concerned. It was utter stupidity to toy with something he wanted so desperately. Did he think he could spend time with Julia, under the guise of friendship, and not cross the line?

Did he *want* to tempt certain disaster?

Absolutely not.

He prided himself on being a man of character. The time had come to rely upon discipline to change this course.

He pushed to his feet. Courtesy demanded he offer Julia a hand up, but given the weight bearing upon his conscience, he opted to forgo the gesture. "Daylight's about gone. Time to ride."

She followed him to the horses, but said nothing.

As inexperienced as she was, she couldn't mount without help. Conrad gave her a boost into the saddle, avoiding eye contact.

During the interminably long ride back to the house, Julia carried on a light, easy conversation.

Conrad answered most of the time.

By the time they reached the house, he'd made himself a solemn promise. He owed it to himself, to Holmes, and to Julia, to keep his distance.

It was a vow he had no choice but to keep.

Chapter Nine

AFTER BREAKFAST, Conrad's mother caught him and Gabriel before they could make an escape. She shut the back door, apparently for privacy.

"I hate to ask this of you," Ma whispered, "but I need you to carry Julia to town to pick up the invitations and walk them around to each guest."

Conrad stilled. Oh, no. Absolutely not.

With his vow to keep his distance merely hours old, he intended to head straight for the creamery and stay there until he forgot all about Julia Tyndall. Eating breakfast at the same table with her had been torturous. He'd had to remind himself—every five seconds—that she belonged to Holmes.

Immediately, Conrad turned to Gabriel. "You take her. I've got—"

"Don't pawn this off on me," Gabriel interrupted as he stomped off toward the barn. "You leapt at every chance to spend time with Julia before now, and left me with the work."

Conrad's temper spiked. "Don't walk away from me."

Days of abrasive silence. Now this attack, over Miss Julia. She wasn't involved in their dispute, and it was wrong of Gabriel to drag her into it.

"Conrad," Ma whispered. "Don't."

Out of respect for his mother, he swallowed his fury and fought the urge to lash out at his idiot brother. He forced himself to calm.

A moment passed, then Ma said, "Gabriel can handle things here before he heads out with Doc." She sounded tired. "I need you to do this errand for me."

"Pop hasn't left for the office yet."

Distress lined Ma's plump face, and guilt swamped him immediately.

"Katherine?" he asked, hoping for any reprieve at all. It wouldn't do to forget his vow. Despite his solemn promise, he'd spent a sleepless night, haunted by Julia's smile and the way she'd looked at him. How his lonely heart ached whenever he wasn't with her.

No matter what he did, he couldn't get her off his mind. Every little thing brought up thoughts of her. He didn't like it, but hadn't any idea how to keep it from happening. He'd never been this obsessed before, not even with Sally.

"She's promised all day to Mary Leigh's care. I don't know who else we'd get at such short notice."

This could be another of Katherine's ploys to spend the day with David Orme. But Conrad had heard the ladies at church dividing up care for Mary Leigh—confined to bed with a threatened pregnancy—and her seven children. With her husband unable to earn a living and also care for the young brood, the ladies had each given one day's help. He wouldn't be surprised if Katherine did have a legitimate commitment.

Even if she didn't, Conrad wasn't about to bring her sneaking around with David to Ma's attention.

He nearly asked why Ma didn't drive Julia into town herself. But one close look at her pallor, the rapid pace of her breath, and he knew he couldn't ask his mother to spend the day delivering invitations all about town. His conscience wouldn't bear doing anything to tax his mother's fragile health.

That meant he wouldn't, couldn't, say no.

"When?" A weight settled upon his shoulders. How would he possibly manage to keep a rein on his emotions, with Julia so near?

"You've got an hour."

It felt like a death sentence. "I'll give instructions to Gabriel and hitch the buggy."

Ma sighed, her smile payment enough. "You're a fine man, Conrad. So good to help Holmes like this."

He hugged his mother quickly, then headed at a brisk walk toward the creamery.

A fine man? Not by his own measuring stick.

Good to help his brother? Ha!

If Holmes knew how far from honorable Conrad's well-meant intentions had strayed, he'd get himself home and claim his bride.

Agitation churned in Conrad's gut. Just as he reached the barn door, an idea came to him. A dozen men were on the ranch payroll. Any one of them could drive Julia into town.

Once there, the driver could pay somebody else to escort her around Liberty and deliver invitations. The Waters twins or any one of Katherine's friends. A generous wage ought to guarantee cooperation.

Finally, a solution he could live with!

FORTY-FIVE MINUTES later, Conrad realized how wrong he'd been.

Unfortunately for him, he'd found three of the men gathered around the dismantled separator, elbow-deep in repairs. Another had come close to severing two fingers slammed in the barn door; Gabriel was practicing his doctoring.

Given the state of operations, that meant no driver.

Except himself.

A dangerous proposition, considering he found it nearly impossible to forget how Julia's selective blindness made him feel.

Was he thick in the head? Did he honestly believe hiring someone else to help deliver invitations today would solve his problems? It might be a temporary patch, but tomorrow would come, and so would the day after that.

From where he stood, there was only one surefire way out of this fix.

He'd make her detest him.

Damage their so-called friendship beyond repair.

Make her see the very worst in him so she'd keep her distance.

From here on out, she'd avoid his rotten company. That would be best for everyone involved. Everything would turn out just like it was supposed to; she'd wait for Holmes, and Conrad wouldn't be caught in the middle any longer.

And he'd stop wanting Julia for himself.

Time to hitch the team and get on with it. The sooner he proved himself a wretch to be around, the better.

He yanked open the barn door, caught off guard to find Julia perched on a crate. Until this morning, she'd always worn sedate hues like navy blue and brick red and cream. Her yellow gown, trimmed with scads of lace, proved hard to ignore. She looked fresh as springtime, with her hair all done up fancy in a loose bun.

She belongs to Holmes, he sternly reminded himself.

He nodded in greeting and went to work hitching

the team. He made certain he put his bad side toward her and kept his eyes on his work.

He'd spent a lifetime presenting the world with his unblemished side. Flaunting his scar, making sure Julia saw it in all its horrid glory, he felt as exposed as if he paraded around buck naked.

Her gaze lingered on his scrunched, distorted cheek. His stomach turned sour. It was almost more than he could stomach, to ignore her perusal. He fought the impulse to turn his good side to her.

She came closer and hovered at his elbow while he harnessed Saturn. "Your mother kindly put the guest list in geographical order. But first, we need to pick up the invitations. Several days later than the printer promised, but I suppose that couldn't be helped."

He tossed her a dark glance.

This close, he couldn't ignore the subtle floral fragrance of her fancy perfume. His mouth fairly watered at the scent of woman and flowers, all done up in that daffodil-colored gown that accentuated curves he had no business noticing.

He'd planned on behaving like an ornery cuss; he hadn't expected her appealing perfume to provoke him to it.

She held his gaze, steady as they come. "Your mother suggested we go to your father's office and use his counsel room table to address the invitations. We've got a full day's work ahead of us."

His heart lifted, and there it was. That renegade wish to abandon all sense and spend every possible second with her.

Remember Holmes? This is practically his wife. *She's spoken for.* He emphasized the word *wife* to himself, a half-dozen times. *Off limits. Forbidden.*

But Holmes hadn't ever actually seen her, in person. They'd never met. Never touched. Never kissed.

It wasn't as though they were actually married.

Had Gabriel rationalized his betrayal with these very words?

Self-disgust flared, hot on the heels of the lingering anger. Where was his honor, that he'd even *think* such a thing? Especially after Sally.

Hadn't his heart gotten the message? This woman was not for him. He wouldn't feel anything for her, because he mustn't.

He scowled at her and took his time leading Jupiter out of his stall. Minutes passed as he fastened the tack and she watched his every move.

"I'll drive you to town," he told her as he finished with the team, "then hire someone to take you around."

Disappointment dampened the light in her eyes. She merely searched his face for the space of a few seconds. "Is there a problem?"

"I've got work to do here." He slid open the wide barn doors. *Irritable,* he reminded himself, *make her detest me.* "I'm too far behind. Can't spend the day gallivanting around with you."

Daylight flooded the interior, illuminating Julia's yellow dress. It took concerted effort, but Conrad managed to ignore her as he led the team into the yard.

She followed close at his elbow. "I'm aware you're busy. But the pervasive theme in your household, at the moment, is the family pulling together to celebrate your brother's return. I need your help, if I'm to succeed."

"I am helping." His tone echoed with impatience. "Anybody can show you around town. It doesn't need to be me."

"I don't want someone else," she argued. "I want you."

Conrad winced.

She sounded so earnest, so hopeful, that his lonesome heart turned over. He shouldn't want to spend the day with her, but he did. *Why* wouldn't his traitorous heart get the message?

No matter how badly he wanted to, no matter what he'd decided to feel, he simply couldn't look at her the way he did his sister-in-law, Nadine. Just another member of the family; his brother's wife.

"Ready?" He boosted her into the buggy before she could protest. The quicker he left her with the Waters twins, the quicker he could be free.

"No, sir, I am not." Her gaze snagged his.

"That's too bad."

Couldn't she *see* what he was? Simply a man, whose heart was having the darnedest time remembering she was off the shelf, spoken-for, forbidden fruit.

She blinked, her unblemished features clouding with confusion.

He ought to blurt out the truth; he wanted her for himself. *That* would scare her off.

She had absolutely no idea what it was like to be ugly or ignored. She'd never been an outcast, one day in her pampered life. No one stared at her with disgust, called her names, or heckled her with cruel jeers. Anyone who paused to stare did so in awe, not revulsion.

Since she couldn't understand his loneliness, she hadn't a chance of comprehending the desperate craving he felt whenever she touched him, looked at him with compassion and friendship and kindness.

"I don't care if you're ready or not," he told her, his tone sharp. "We're going to town. I'll do you the favor of finding you someone else to spend the day with."

He rounded the buggy and climbed into the seat. The team lurched forward at the first flick of the reins. He urged the Saddlebreds into a canter. Just as quick as they rounded the bend at the end of the drive, he'd give them their heads.

Instead of hanging on with both hands, as he'd expected her to do, Julia snatched the reins and wrested the horses to a stop. Dust clouded about the wheels and rose in the morning sunshine.

On the off chance she'd decided to return to the house, and thereby save him four miles of utter hell, he let her tie off the reins. Her hands shook with what he could only imagine was fury. Good. He was tired of being the only one to suffer.

She hiked up her skirts and leapt to the ground. With her feathers good and ruffled, she headed back to the house.

Conrad shook his head. Good riddance.

To his surprise, Julia stomped around the back of the buggy and up to Conrad's side. "Get down."

He had half a mind to let his Macquarie temper tell her exactly how it was. He wanted her. The way a man wants a woman. He'd kiss her, hard. That would illustrate the truth of it for her; she had no business wanting anything from the likes of him—especially friendship. She had no business causing him an ounce of trouble, yet that's all she'd been from the moment she'd stepped off the train.

"If you're going to town," he said, his tone low, "it'll be now. I've got work to do, and this errand has already taken too long."

"What did I do?" she demanded. "Yesterday, we were friends. We had a nice ride into the hills."

He snorted. If she didn't know what the problem was, he wasn't about to tell her. *I'm on the verge of falling in love. With you.*

Acknowledging the truth horrified him on so many levels. This was more than desire, more than coveting his brothers soon-to-be-wife. His foolish, damned, lonely heart was stampeding toward certain disaster...teetering on the precipice of falling in love with Miss J.

No way, not no how, not in this lifetime would he commit that crime. He'd lived through the pain of that betrayal once, and that had been more than enough of a hard-learned lesson. There would be no confession. No theft of a woman's affections. He'd lie as long as he had to to hide the wretched truth from Julia.

Holmes would *never know*.

Temper sparkled in her eyes. "Next thing I know, you've decided we're not friends. I want to know why."

"Look at me." He clambered to the ground, coming nearly toe to toe with her. Ached to pull her hard against him. Desire to kiss the woman into silence ripped through him. Felt his nostrils flare, his pulse spike.

She blinked up at him, showing no fear whatsoever.

"*Look* at me."

"I am." She stared him directly in the eye.

Nope. If she were really *seeing him*, right now, she'd glimpse the truth—lust and love and desire all rolled into one great big ugly ball of unwanted emotion.

"No, lady, you're not." *Lie*, his conscience screamed. No room for the truth here. He fell back to the only truth he could safely blame it on.

"Do you see this?" Chest heaving, he jabbed a finger at the jagged line that cinched the left side of his mouth toward his ear. "This scar is hideous. So gross a disfigurement, children turn on the street to gawk. Adults pretend to ignore it, but they don't."

He raised his voice, aggravated beyond the limits of his control, his words really giving voice to the truth that no woman could ever *love* him. "They can't. No one can."

Her features softened.

No! He wanted her angry. Irritated. Ready to slap his face for raising his voice at her. Not pity him. Why didn't the damnable female have sense enough to flee in terror?

"You won't help me deliver invitations because you have a little scar?"

"*Little?*"

"Yes, it's little. I don't understand, not at all. Why is this a problem now, and yet it hasn't been before?"

For the first time since she'd clapped eyes on him on the train platform, she examined the scar good and proper. Her expression remained mildly confused. "I've seen your confidence, the way you carry yourself."

She took her time, her gaze roving over every

uneven margin, around his eye, and across his lips. Still, she showed no sign of revulsion. "So? Looks to me like it healed. You speak. You eat. I've seen you smile. This isn't a devastating injury."

"What's wrong with you? You must see it," he bellowed. This wasn't going the way he *needed.* He paced one step away, then remembered he must make her look at his face. He flanked back, nearly trampling her toes.

Bearing down on her, his nose a mere inch from hers, he yelled, "Everyone notices it, every time they look at me. You're no different, Miss Tyndall, despite your highbrow upbringing and fancy education."

He expected her to scamper to the house and tattle to his mother. Or at least slap his face. He'd treated her abominably, and he knew it. He deserved a fist to the jaw and much worse.

Surprisingly, she did neither.

"Do *not* tell me what I am or what I am not," she said, her tone too calm. "You think you know everything, do you?"

"Hell, yes. I'm the expert here, Miss J. Not you."

Her shoes crunched on pebbles as she headed for the edge of the drive. Without saying a word, she sat upon a stump in the dappled shade and calmly worked the long line of buttons along her right shoe free.

This was, by and far, the most bizarre reaction a woman had ever had, when confronted with his hideously scarred face.

His chest heaved with labored breathing. He itched to continue bellowing until she screamed back. She'd said she'd fought with her father, so why wouldn't she fight with him? Infuriating woman.

The fancy high-heeled shoe finally unfastened, she pulled it off and tossed it carelessly into the grass. Showing minimal concern for decency, she reached under her skirts and began unrolling her cream-colored stocking.

"Whoa." Pale silk, almost opaque, conforming to

the shape of her leg. He couldn't pull his gaze away. "What are you doing?"

No answer.

He groaned in pain. Why couldn't she wear thick, serviceable, unattractive wool stockings like his mother?

The confounded woman completely ignored his order.

"Stop, Julia." Whatever she was up to, he didn't want to see any more. He glanced toward the house and outbuildings, finding the yard completely deserted. Where was everyone?

She pulled her right stocking completely off and bared her pale skin. She lifted the hem of her lacy yellow skirts until she'd exposed her feminine ankle and most of her calf.

He couldn't have been more perplexed. He may not know diddly about ladies, but he knew refinement dictated they never show their lower limbs. Ever. It was indecent. Improper.

And incredibly arousing.

No wonder it was improper.

"Miss J—" Tried to force his gaze away, but failed.

"Take a look at this, Mr. King of Blemishes." She raked a vicious line from trim ankle, up the side of her calf, nearly to her knee.

Oh, he was looking, all right. Couldn't wrestle his gaze away from her creamy white flesh. Feminine turn of ankle. Before he could stop himself, he took two paces closer. Ached to touch that expanse of slender calf.

Conrad's heart slammed against his ribs, the rhythm so mucked up, he thought he'd pass out for lack of circulation. He ought to turn away. He should run for the house. He must flee, for his very soul. But his feet seemed to have taken root.

She looked up, her blue gaze piercing. "Do you *see* this?"

Oh, yeah. He'd seen enough to haunt his dreams for the rest of his life.

Silk stockings.

White, smooth expanse of skin.

Long toes accentuated a delicate arch.

No wonder ladies kept their feet and legs hidden because showing them to men provoked the most indecent of reactions.

"*Look,* Conrad," she demanded. She traced a fingertip along her leg once more. "Now you've seen disgusting. So don't tell me some five- or *maybe* six-inch hairline scar is hideous. Now you really know the meaning of that word."

This time, he finally noticed what she'd tried to show him. A jagged, pearly-white scar stretched from the top of her shapely foot, slashed across her shin, and continued toward her knee, under the privacy of her skirts.

He found his throat constricted and speech impossible. Mixed emotions collided in his chest. Whatever she'd suffered, it must've hurt like the dickens.

Finally he found his voice. "Miss J, that's nothing. It's not unsightly." He could get used to seeing her shapely pair of legs. He stumbled closer, his conscience still screaming at him to run, far and fast.

"This is worse, cowboy," she told him, her voice saturated with loathing, "because no one knows it's there."

"How can that possibly be worse? *No one knows.*" He dropped to his knees near her abandoned shoe. "You don't limp. Your shape is..."

"Discernible, even under my stockings," she finished for him. Lifting her skirt to her knees, she displayed both legs, side by side. One deliciously bare, one encased in stocking and buttoned-up high-heel shoe. "My legs are not symmetrical. The injured one did not grow properly."

They might be a little different, but all he knew for sure was a desperate need to run his hands over her foot, up her calf, kiss the tender spot behind her knee...

She lowered the hem to modestly cover her naked toes.

He wrenched his gaze up to meet hers. She looked so distressed, her pain eclipsed his own misery.

He wanted to smooth away the creases in her forehead. He ached for the pain she must've suffered. If only he could take that agony from her, he would've gladly endured it himself.

"What happened?" he managed.

"I slipped from the carriage when I was small. The wheel ripped open my leg."

"You walk fine."

"The bones didn't break, miraculously." She held his gaze for a long moment. "I didn't walk for close to a year. The doctors said I may never run again."

He considered what she'd suffered. "I'm sorry."

"Don't tell me I cannot understand scars, Conrad."

His frustration returned, tenfold. Did she honestly think her silver scar, hidden beneath stocking and petticoats, began to compare with the thick, red line snaking from the corner of his mouth, nearly to his ear? Everyone, who ever passed by, saw his deformity in all its wretched glory. "You have no idea—"

"No?" she interrupted, her tone sharp. "Have *you* no idea how I've dreaded allowing my husband to see this? It's not a topic of conversation a lady should discuss beforehand, now is it?"

Conrad tried to understand her fears. He imagined Holmes, a new husband, exploring—The image sliced white-hot and sharp.

Squeezing his eyes closed, he banished the images.

"See? Even you can't deny this scar is an issue. It's hideously ugly."

"Julia—"

"It's degrading." Her anger gave way, her words snagging on hot emotion. "*Every time* he looks at my legs, this is all he will see. The smaller, *deformed* one."

Conrad clamped his eyes shut and tried to

obliterate the mental image of Julia's shapely legs. He tried to smother a groan, but failed. "Miss J, I doubt that."

"He'll expect perfection. Why wouldn't he? When fully dressed, there's no indication. No hint. Unquestionably," she said, pain echoing in her voice, "it will spoil my wedding night."

There she went again. He didn't want to talk about anything that had to do with Holmes and Julia sequestered behind locked doors. "It will not, I can promise you that. He'll take one look at your beautiful legs and never notice your scar again."

She seemed to sense his interest. Her pupils dilated some as she shook her head with disbelief. "How can you possibly believe such a thing?"

Scare her, his conscience reminded. "Because I'm a man with a heartbeat."

Terrify her into running. "I know all I see is a beautiful leg. *Your* beautiful leg."

Remember the desperation to shoo her away, make her keep her distance. "You've got shapely ankles, Miss J, the kind to make a man obsess."

Her blue eyes widened, with something he couldn't quite label terror. Was that...interest?

No, no. Not what he wanted. He pressed forward, blood surging hot in his veins. "Makes me want to take that limb in my hands. Kiss your instep. Drag my lips from arch to kneecap."

"Sounds delicious. You're sweet." Her powerhouse smile nearly knocked him off his feet.

Sweet? *Sweet?* He scowled.

She grinned. Poked her bare toes out from beneath a froth of lace and wiggled them at him.

He stalked toward the harnesses, determined to lead Jupiter and Saturn back to the barn. He was a monster. An ornery cuss who dared make comments about her bare legs. Somebody she ought to despise.

"You want the honest truth?" She didn't pause, clearly wanting no answer. "When I look at you, I do not see *your* scar."

"*Julia—*" His tone held a bull-sized warning.

"It's one of your features. Nothing more. Like your nose, or your green eyes, or your lustrous head of hair."

He glared at her. "You're blind. This disfigurement—"

"I'd hardly call you disfigured. A little rough around the edges, perhaps, but it fits with your whole rancher-dairyman persona. It looks like you don't hesitate to take risks, like you earned it doing something remarkably heroic."

He snorted. "Heroic?"

"I think you must've been very brave."

He'd have to try harder to wipe that awe from her beautiful face. "It was stupidity. A stupid kid, taking stupid risks."

"Tell me about it."

There she went again, romanticizing everything.

"I leapt off a running horse."

"To save baby Katherine from being trampled?"

He blinked. Gaped. Is that what she thought? He shook his head. "It was a bet. I lassoed a calf, jumped off a horse, and caught my mouth on barbed wire. Ripped my cheek wide open. *Stupid.*"

He expected a wince. Or a gasp. Instead, she gave his face another once-over. "First thing I thought when I saw it was you must get into fights now and then."

The woman had no sense of reality. "Fights?"

"I find the whole tough cowboy image—and your scar—quite appealing."

Heat shot through his abdomen.

She blinked, all innocence. "Is it *supposed* to bother me?"

"*Yes.*" He didn't want to be appealing. He wanted to revolt her tender sensibilities.

The breeze flirted with loose, dusky curls about her face. "Sorry to disappoint, but it doesn't. I think it's cute."

Stunned into silence, he searched for mockery in

Julia's expression. Must she seem so earnest? The urge to bolt, to run far and fast, came on once more with overwhelming urgency. He abandoned the team and headed for the barn with long strides.

"It's too late to see the scar and not the man," she called after him. "All I see is you."

Chapter Ten

AN HOUR LATER, Conrad strode through a field of sun-warmed alfalfa, the odors of earth and grass pungent under the late morning sun. The heated air pressed close, almost suffocating. Conrad's shirt stuck to his sweat-soaked back.

He'd walked a good five miles, and still, he couldn't shake the honesty he'd glimpsed in Julia's eyes.

All I see is you.

How did she expect him to deal with that? Pretend she hadn't said it?

She wasn't supposed to see him as anything more than Holmes's brother. Must she look at him, all doe-eyed, as if she was as attracted to him as he was to her?

His potent reaction to the sight of her bare leg had proved they couldn't be so much as friends.

What did she think he was? A gelding? A steer?

Pathetic, lonely, starved for a woman's affection—

that's what he was. But definitely *all* natural male.

He stormed through the nearly mature crop, headed for the wooden fence on the far side. He ducked between the railings and emerged on the path that circled toward the outlying pastures. He glanced back in the direction of the house, relieved to find himself completely alone.

Breath rasped in and out of his lungs. A fly buzzed about his face. He pressed the heel of his hand over the offensive scar. Heat washed through him, leaving dizziness in its wake.

I think it's cute.

Julia's fanciful words—uttered in an effort to prove her point—had knocked him out of the saddle. He couldn't be positive she'd even meant it.

But he'd glimpsed her sincerity. So either the woman desperately needed spectacles to clear up her vision, or she might actually find him attractive.

Perhaps another man could brush off the simple words as foolish nonsense. But Conrad found it damn near impossible to ignore the surge of hope that flooded him every time he remembered.

All I see is you.

He'd never heard the likes of that from anyone. Chances were, he'd never hear it again.

If he could only pin down what made her so different from every other female, he might have a fighting chance to get her out of his system. He might even find someone else, given enough time.

But Julia was a riddle he couldn't figure out.

From the first hello, she'd been warm and friendly. Genuine smiles and graciousness...and she'd wanted him.

How could he hope to forget the way she'd looked at him that afternoon? With hope and anticipation, admiration and complete acceptance. As if he could do no wrong, as if he were capable of making the earth spin backward upon its axis.

How could he hope to forget she'd thought him

her groom, and seemed pleased by the prospect?

In those brief minutes, she'd shown him more about her character than he'd understood at the time.

Holmes's letters had obviously won her over. Completely. That was evident because she'd had the opportunity to flee. She'd walked right up to him, delighted to make his acquaintance.

In the minutes before she learned he wasn't Holmes, she'd never once indicated she'd changed her mind about marrying.

That made a very attractive package, all dolled up in a daffodil-yellow gown. He found it almost impossible to remember he wasn't supposed to entertain romantic feelings.

But he must, because those romantic feelings were multiplying faster than a hutch of rabbits. He couldn't presume, for even one moment, that he had any hope of a future with her because she hadn't truly accepted *him* that afternoon at the depot, but Holmes.

Holmes had sent for Julia. *His* letters had won her heart, persuaded her to be his wife. In a matter of weeks, they'd be married.

That fact left Conrad no room to entertain delusions of his own happily-ever-after.

It wasn't going to happen.

Not with Julia.

He had no choice but to forget about her and the way she made him feel.

He knew only one way to manage that. Work.

CONRAD STOMPED into the red brick creamery, which housed the pair of De Laval separators in one half of the building, the cheese-making equipment in the other, and the dairy office in an extension.

Physical labor might burn away the frustration, but could not occupy his mind the way paperwork always did. A few hours buried in invoices and reports, he wagered, and he'd forget all about her.

At least for the moment.

Late morning rays streamed through the four east-facing windows, illuminating dust motes in the air. The white plastered walls reflected the daylight. The machinery sat idle, the building gloriously quiet.

Good. All the better to lose himself in the bookkeeping end of the business.

Conrad's boots echoed dully on the freshly scrubbed floor. Just as he reached the office door, Gabriel emerged with a neighboring dairyman, Sims.

Sims, meeting privately with Gabriel?

This was *not* a good sign.

Was this why he'd refused to drive Julia to town? Why he'd claimed he had to doctor Linc's cut fingers? Because he had business to conduct with Sims?

Betrayal slammed into Conrad's gut. He clenched his jaw. Narrowed his gaze at his cheating, lousy brother.

First, Sally. Now, the only thing Conrad still had—managing this dairy.

He never should've trusted Gabriel to handle the day's workload, even for a few hours.

"Glad we could work it out." Sims barely glanced in Conrad's direction as he shook Gabriel's hand. His whiskered jowls wobbled above the collar of his crisp chambray shirt.

Too cocky for his own good, Gabriel shook Sims's hand. "I'll see you Tuesday."

"Tuesday?" Conrad demanded.

Sims tossed Gabriel a glance as he shuffled outside. The door banged shut behind him.

Conrad stared his younger brother down. He'd tucked in his uncharacteristically clean shirt. Conrad glared. "What have you done?"

"Nothing you need to fret about."

Conrad's frustration, barely held in check until that moment, flared to life. "We are not in business to keep Sims's operation afloat. I owe Sims nothing more than a fair price for use of the separator, on *Thursdays*. There are reasons for the scheduling, and I won't have you negotiating changes or giving him preferential treatment without first obtaining my permission."

"Good morning to you, too." Gabriel headed into the small, private office. Conrad's domain. But Gabriel seemed to have forgotten that, too. On the north side of the building, this room didn't get much direct sunlight, but felt too warm.

Conrad peeled off his hat and threw it toward the peg on the wall. The brim caught, momentarily, then toppled to the floor.

Conrad ignored it. "Sims is only one of ten dairies that rely on us. Do you understand?"

"'Course I do."

Irritated, Conrad claimed his seat. He dropped into the leather-covered chair and found it still warm—proof Gabriel had barely vacated it. "I'm gone two hours, and you immediately assume privileges that aren't yours."

Gabriel scratched the crown of his head, making his fiery red hair stand on end. "What, Sims?"

"Yes, Sims. My decision stands. End of discussion." His life may be in complete chaos, with Julia in the house and under his skin, but that didn't mean he must lose control of the business, as well.

He plunked the current ledger onto the scratched desktop, prepared to focus all his attention on *anything* but the turmoil eating him alive.

"That's an interesting assumption," Gabriel said, obviously going for the jugular, "about Sims, I mean."

Conrad surged to his feet, slapping both palms on the desktop. "If I say he stays with Thursday, then he stays with Thursday. That's not going to change, no matter what you promised."

"Our agreement had nothing to do with the dairy."

"You can't expect—"

Gabriel's temper flashed. "Not that it's any of your business, Mr. Foreman, but because you don't know how to let a subject drop, I don't mind saying Sims asked me to drop by to check on his wife on Tuesday. A house call for a medical matter. He doesn't have cash money, so we found another way for him to pay me. But you naturally assume the worst."

Conrad knew a twinge of embarrassment, but he was too proud to admit it.

"Don't bother to ask," Gabriel went on. "Just pass judgment. What's wrong with you lately?"

Provoked, Conrad couldn't hold his tongue. "What am I supposed to think? This dairy is *my* responsibility. I, alone, make the decisions, and I, alone, bear the consequences of those choices."

"Since you started cavorting around with Miss Julia, I'd have to say you've forgotten that."

"I've forgotten *nothing*." He stared Gabriel down. Betrayal surged to the surface again, the wounds Gabriel had inflicted ripped open and bleeding. Some breaches of trust a man couldn't forget, much less forgive.

Sins he would *not* perpetuate.

Awareness flickered in Gabriel's eyes, leaving little doubt they both knew the basis of this argument didn't lie with Hubert Sims, but with Sally Tibbs.

Conrad hadn't wanted to hear Gabriel's excuses six weeks ago, and he didn't want to hear them now.

His brother didn't see things that way. "It's time we talk about what happened."

"Nothing to say."

A few seconds passed. Conrad tried to focus his attention on his work, but failed miserably.

"You shouldn't care that Sally's with me now. You don't love her," Gabriel insisted, "you never did."

"That's not true."

"Be honest," Gabriel demanded. "You're not angry because you lost Sally. You're angry because you *lost*."

Conrad itched to scrabble over the desk and knock

Gabriel's head off. Fire surged through his veins. He locked gazes with his brother, wondering why he hadn't finished this weeks ago.

But he knew why. He'd wanted to blame the demise of his courtship on Sally's fickle affections, on Gabriel's too-handsome face and impulsive character.

But the stark truth was too awful to face; Conrad had no hope of hanging onto a woman like Sally. It was a miracle she'd stayed with the likes of him as long as she had. She'd been the only decent woman who'd ever looked at him twice.

Losing her had hurt. But his heart was in for much worse.

He flipped through pages of the ledger, barely noticing the headings. "Get out. I have work to do."

Gabriel held his ground. "I'm going to live on this ranch, at least for a while. Someday, I'll probably marry Sally. I say we settle this. Now."

"What? You want my forgiveness?"

"Is this my cue to apologize? Why?"

"You *intentionally* stole her affections."

Gabriel's glare could've dropped a bull at fifty paces. "You can't believe that."

"Yeah," Conrad spat, "I do."

"I've got news, brother. She has damn good reason for preferring me to you. I not only bother to show up when she invites me for nice suppers she spends all day preparing—"

"Hey, I forgot."

"*Four* times, you twit. She's supposed to overlook that? Did you expect another invitation?"

Gabriel must be exaggerating. Conrad would swear that supper thing had only happened once. If Sally had cared for him, at all, she would've understood. If Gabriel hadn't been there, ready to tempt away her affections, she would've asked Conrad to supper, plenty more times. "I had work to do."

"So busy with your cows you can't remember Sally? What's she supposed to do? Pine for you, week after week, while you don't bother to call on her?"

"I'm a dairyman. I thought she understood what that meant. And I treated her well," Conrad bellowed, desperate to defend himself from Gabriel's unfounded accusations.

"You were surly. Cantankerous."

"I was not! I took her flowers. Asked her to the Founder's Day picnic. Invited her here for supper, regularly."

"You never had room in your life for her, Conrad. No room at all. She deserves a hell of a lot better than you."

That was the bald truth, and it stung.

Conrad knew he had nothing to offer any good woman. With or without Gabriel's meddling, Conrad never would've held onto Sally.

Gabriel's tone lowered. "I swear I'll be the man who wants her in his life. I learned from your mistakes."

Conrad glared at his brother.

Gabriel didn't have the sense to shut up. "You go right on trying to believe you treated Sally with common courtesy."

Conrad slammed the ledger against the desktop. Fury pumped through his veins. "*Get out.*"

Gabriel stood his ground. His gaze bored into Conrad's.

Conrad ignored his kid brother for a few seconds.

"Your fight is with me," Gabriel said, his voice almost normal. "Not Holmes. You remember that."

What the hell? Conrad knew exactly who'd stolen his would-be bride.

"From the moment Miss Julia arrived here, you foisted all your work off on me. Fine."

"I asked you to take her to town. You refused."

Gabriel ignored the rebuttal. "You'd give her twenty hours a day, if you could manage it. You're all over her—"

"*What?*"

"You're courting Miss Julia. Trying to win her

over. Before Holmes ever gets a chance to meet her."

Bile seared a fiery path up Conrad's throat. He clenched his fists, aching to throw the first punch, to take out his frustrations until Gabriel cried uncle.

"No," he emphasized, "I'm," paused, fired, "n*ot*." Anything but.

Seconds passed. Still, Gabriel refused to admit the truth.

The too-warm room seemed airless. A lone fly buzzed through the open doorway, hovering in the space between Conrad and his brother. The insect's annoying hum resonated in Conrad's ears.

Instead of waning, his frustration escalated. He fought to control himself, to find the right words to put an end to this nonsense, before it went any further.

"You forced bitter medicine down my throat, Gabriel. I know what it's like to have a brother steal the girl I wanted to marry. I'll *never* do the same thing to Holmes."

"No? You're in love with Miss Julia."

The accusation stretched Conrad's patience to the limit.

"I'm *not*."

"Don't lie to me." Gabriel shook his head with derision. "You've got feelings for her."

Several seconds ground past. Conrad fought his rising temper. "Nothing's going on between myself and Miss Tyndall."

Gabriel headed for the door, shaking his head with evident disgust. "You hurt Sally real bad. Don't do the same thing to Julia."

He'd hurt Sally? He didn't like that idea. "I'm not going to hurt Julia. How can I, when there's *nothing* between us?"

Gabriel gave Conrad a look of utter doubt, and shut the office door behind himself. His footfalls faded.

"I know right from wrong," Conrad bellowed at his retreating brother.

The outside door banged closed.

Alone with too much silence, Conrad felt the weight of his brother's accusations nearly crush the breath from his lungs. He *did* know right from wrong.

Damn it all!

The whole sordid mess with Sally, regardless of why she'd left him, had taught Conrad a powerful lesson. It had hurt like hell. He would *not* inflict that upon Holmes.

No matter what Gabriel said, Conrad knew he had the strength to avoid any further entanglement with Julia.

He couldn't allow himself to harbor any affection for her, in any degree. Not anymore.

"NO."

"Yes." Pop paced across the dairy office, then flanked back.

"No." Quickly, Conrad tallied the numbers in the ledger, penciling in the total at the bottom of the page.

"*Yes*. Your mother asked you to drive Miss Julia into town. You agreed. Imagine my dismay when I found forlorn Miss Julia, sitting beside the abandoned rig."

Conrad didn't want to think about her, one shoe on and one shoe off. So he kept his attention on the numbers swimming before his eyes. The total was wrong. It had to be. He added the column again.

Pop leaned heavily on the desk. His gaze bore into Conrad's face. A moment crept past.

Where was Pop's long-winded argument? The old man was king when it came to persuasive speeches. He'd honed the skill through years in the courtroom.

The very place he ought to be, at this hour.

A sinking sensation tugged on Conrad's gut. He fought the urge to make eye contact.

Why was Pop at home?

"You're headed back to town," Conrad said rationally. "You carry Miss Julia to the print shop."

"I'm not going back to work."

Surprised, Conrad met his father's gaze. Pop never took a day off. Not even a few hours.

"Today, I'm sitting at my wife's bedside." Worry tightened Pa's voice. "My place is with her."

Conrad swallowed the hot, heavy lump that immediately formed in his throat.

"And you, son, will do what you promised your mother you'd do."

Chapter Eleven

"YOU'RE EMBARRASSING me!" Julia stopped on the tree-lined street, too mortified to glance back at the house they'd just delivered an invitation to. "You scared that woman, nearly kicked her dog—"

"I did not." Conrad kept walking. Giving her surly attitude.

Whatever demons had possessed him about his scar seemed to linger. She thought they'd been through all that.

He'd been rotten from the moment he'd stomped back to the house and informed her they were going into Liberty. He wasn't behaving like the friend she'd come to know.

The man's crabby disposition need a swift kick in the pants.

"Do your parents always send you to deliver their invitations?" she asked sweetly.

He halted. Turned. Narrowed his eyes and pinned her with a glare. “Look, Miss J, if you don’t like the way I’m doing this, you’re on your own.”

Oh, he’d like that, wouldn’t he? Too bad.

“You can count yourself quite lucky, Mr. Macquarie.”

“I’m the luckiest man on earth. Lucky, lucky.”

Ignoring his sarcasm, she fell into step beside him. She noticed with satisfaction that he’d forgotten to make her walk on his “good” side.

“Yes, you are lucky,” she told him. “You can be most grateful my nanny isn’t here to witness this display of poor manners.”

“Now I’m scared.”

“You should be. Five minutes in her company, and you’d have a profound respect for her methods. She’d reform you. Teach you proper decorum. Give you a lecture you’d never forget.”

He took her elbow as they crossed at an intersection. “There’s nothing wrong with *my* methods. Everybody on that list gets an invitation. I see no reason to make this chore take any longer than it must.”

She blinked, all innocence. “I see that. I also suspect your parents sent you on this errand on purpose.”

“I didn’t ask for it, if that’s what you’re getting at. I’m a rancher. It’s daylight.” As if that explained his sour attitude.

She understood the work that consumed his day, from before sunrise until sunset. “Precisely! And you’re strolling city streets, without a care in the world. A man of leisure. So stop your bellyaching.”

A ghost of a smile tugged at his lips.

She smiled pleasantly. “As I see it, you have one of two purposes. Either you don’t want anyone to know how much you enjoy taking time off work,” she slid him a glance, and found an expression of incredulity on his face. “Or you intend to offend all the would-be guests.”

“You have no idea, Miss J.”

"I think it's both. See, this way, you get a day off work, and your household will be calm and quiet when it would've been overrun by guests."

A smile flickered over his mouth. He forced a scowl.

Good. Her attempts were getting somewhere. "That would be nice, wouldn't it?"

"Yeah." He sounded a tad less grumpy.

Sunlight spilled through the leafy canopy overhead, igniting fiery pools in his hair. For the briefest of moments, he looked far too much like her portrait of Holmes.

So incredibly handsome. So tall, he seemed to tower over her, even with her shoes on. His stature appealed far more than it should.

"Actually, I'm on this fool's errand because Pop insisted on it."

She'd suspected as much. "Why would he send a cranky old man like you?"

"Because he's an idiot."

"Oooh. Nanny would most assuredly wash your mouth out with soap."

"She's no worse than Ma." His lips twitched. "She taught me manners. With soap."

She'd have him smiling, yet. "I see that she did. And a fine example of manners you are."

"That's right." He didn't want to let go of his angst, but she could see it was almost gone. "I'm such a gentleman, I'm going to buy you a sarsaparilla."

"Will a drink sweeten your disposition?"

Conrad chuckled. The rich timbre of that beautiful sound affected her clear down to her toes. His laughter made her join in.

"That would take something a great deal stronger," he said.

They turned a street corner and climbed a slow hill. Business lined the street on either side. Folks crossed the street, moving in and out of shops.

"Here we are." Conrad ushered Julia through an

open door, into the soda fountain.

Two couples sat atop high stools at the bar, sipping frothy drinks out of tall glasses. Display cases showed off pedestal dishes of chocolates in various shapes and hues of brown. The whole shop smelled delicious; a mingling of sugars and vanilla, spice and citrus.

They took their sarsaparillas and small box of chocolates to a circular table for two in a quiet corner. As Julia sipped the frothy, effervescent treat, she enjoyed the respite and Conrad's improved mood.

"Look who just came in." He nodded toward the door.

Julia turned, a bit surprised to find Katherine in the company of a young man. Exceptionally well dressed, dark-haired and handsome. "David Orme?"

"That's the one."

"I thought she was supposed to be tending to Mary Leigh and her family today."

"That's right." Conrad's disappointment at discovering his sister's fib was evident.

Julia slid her chair a bit closer to Conrad's for a better view of Katherine and David. Watching them together, she knew within minutes that David reciprocated Katherine's affection.

Julia stirred her soda with the straw. She watched the young couple with something akin to jealousy lodging in her throat.

But it was more than that. Longing. Loneliness.

She missed Holmes.

Absurd, given they'd never actually met.

"Are you going to tattletale?" Conrad asked, his tone light and teasing. "Ma will ask Katherine, at supper, how Mary Leigh's getting along. You'll have a prime opportunity to spoil Katherine's story."

"I wouldn't jeopardize Katherine's good fortune."

She simply wanted a piece of that pie for herself.

They watched as Katherine and David took their sodas to a table. The young couple, immersed in private conversation, took no notice of anyone else in the establishment.

What would it be like to have someone so focused on her, that it didn't matter where they were? Conrad had given her a glimmer of that special connection, as they'd watched the sunset from the hilltop.

Holmes's letters had promised much more than that. He'd written of his desire to meet her, to know everything about her, to develop a relationship that would last.

He should be here.

He'd promised.

He'd fallen short of that vow, hadn't he?

She'd expected better of him.

Sure looked like he was as all-consumed with his career as her father had always been.

Not a good sign. Not good at all.

Watching David Orme, so absorbed in Katherine, his adoring smile for her alone, Julia's pangs worsened. David leaned close to whisper something in Katherine's ear. Something tender and sweet, given the giddy smile on Katherine's face.

Julia turned away. Why couldn't Holmes be half as interested?

Her conscience twisted. It wasn't wise of her to pass judgment without knowing the details. Holmes's letters had made it clear he had serious, genuine interest in her. She shouldn't think critically of him.

But how could she not? Compared to Conrad, who'd set his work aside, on several occasions in order to give her assistance, Holmes didn't seem to care one way or the other if she'd even arrived.

Mercy, me, she chided. This wasn't appropriate thinking. It wasn't kind nor necessary to doubt him now, after all these months.

She sensed Conrad's gaze on her face. Instead of looking at him, she twirled her straw through her drink.

"You are going to tattle," he said, his tone light and teasing, "I can see it all over your face."

With one last glance toward Katherine and David, Julia sat up a little straighter. "I won't say a word."

"Then what's on your mind?" He sounded truly interested.

She met his gaze and glimpsed genuine friendship. It eased her loneliness and yet made it worse.

"Why did Holmes send for me?" The question fell out of her mouth before she had a chance to consider the implications.

Conrad took his time answering. "He hasn't said a word about it to me."

She needed to talk about this. Even if Conrad hadn't talked it over with Holmes, or written about his plans, he could probably guess his brother's intentions.

"Why would Holmes go to all the effort to send for me, provide ample funds to cover train fare, knowing full well when we were due to arrive, but then hie to San Francisco and stay for so long?"

A moment passed. Something unidentifiable clouded Conrad's eyes. "Holmes told you he was in San Francisco?"

He pushed an almost empty soda glass away.

"No, your father did." Her irritation worsened. "That's what bothers me so much, I suppose. Holmes didn't bother to tell me so, himself."

Conrad fell silent. Leaned back, folded his arms over a broad chest. His expression revealing nothing.

She couldn't hold back. "He assures me this case in San Francisco is of the utmost importance. I understand that. How could I not? I've lived with such my entire life."

Unease flickered over Conrad's calm features. He didn't want to hear any of this. She could see that. But the doubts multiplied, and she needed to talk about it.

"I'm not criticizing," she told Conrad. "But I would've thought he'd send a letter or telegram. I don't understand why he missed his train yesterday, and has made no attempt to let me know when he'll be home."

He took his time selecting a piece of fudge from the sea foam-green box.

Whining like a brat, she realized. If only he understood the depth of her feelings on the matter he wouldn't judge her. "I simply want to feel..." Needed? Desired? Loved? She labeled it, "Wanted."

He bit into the nutty confection and chewed slowly. In that moment, she would've sworn she saw the exact same emotion mirrored in his gaze. She'd swear he did understand, on a visceral level.

He swallowed. Dragged the palms of his hands down denim-clad thighs. "You'd best talk to Pop."

That was it? No reassurance, no explanations, no encouragement? She would've sworn she'd seen complete understanding in him. Perhaps not. She broke eye contact and focused on her hands knotted in her lap.

He pushed the box toward her. "You've never tasted fudge like this. Have some."

Julia stared at the box of candies, but her mind wouldn't stop churning. Conrad knew something. Or at least had his suspicions. She knew him well enough to see that much.

But he was loyal to his brother and father.

Admirable traits.

And bothersome to be excluded. How would it feel to have his fierce loyalty for herself?

Searching his vibrant green eyes, she asked, "Do you think your father knows something?"

"Probably. I bet he knows what's keeping Holmes."

She thought that through for a moment.

"The party's still on, right?" Conrad sipped the last of his soda. "That must mean Pop knows Holmes will be back in time."

Something in Conrad's tone made Julia uneasy. Sadness lurked. His eyes refused to meet hers.

What was he refusing to disclose? A wave of dizziness swept through her.

Conrad wolfed another piece of candy. And studiously avoided looking at her.

He knew something, all right.

Something he didn't want to discuss.

From everything she knew about Conrad, she'd have expected him to look her in the eye. He'd have no qualms about informing her he would not discuss this topic. Despite his loyalty to his brother, his reticence made no sense.

"What aren't you telling me?" she asked, just as Conrad pushed back his chair and rose.

"Want another soda?" Without looking at her, he stood and pulled a coin from his pocket.

Nice dodge.

Let him think he'd safely deflected her question. She'd get her answers. One way or another.

"No, thanks." She didn't want a beverage nor sweets. She wanted the truth, and if Conrad wouldn't give her answers, she'd ask forthright questions of Phillip Macquarie.

Chapter Twelve

SEATED AT THE kitchen table, Julia peeled potatoes and listened to the comfortable, easy talk between Katherine and her mother. This was nice. Just as she'd always imagined mothers and daughters working together must be.

Unfortunately, Phillip Macquarie hadn't joined the family for supper last night or for breakfast this morning. Some important legal trial had taken him out of town. Julia's questions would have to wait.

Or, perhaps not.

"Mrs. Macquarie?"

Violet turned from the cabinet where she put away a stack of mixing bowls. "Yes?"

She'd had ample time to gather her thoughts, phrase her questions. "I've been thinking, and have a couple of questions about Holmes's reasons for sending for me."

Violet closed the cabinet and took a seat beside Julia. Her undivided attention was reassuring. In many ways, Holmes's mother was more approachable than his father. "I don't know much. But I'll answer if I can."

"Why *did* he send for me? He's handsome, accomplished, appealing." She gestured weakly; it had all made far more sense in her head. "I don't understand."

Katherine took six loaves of fragrant bread out of the oven. "Pop told us Holmes announced he was ready to marry, what with his schooling over with. And since he had nobody to come home to—"

Violet interrupted before Katherine got any further. "Katherine, that's enough." Kind, soft-spoken, even in reprimand. Julia liked that about her mother-in-law-to-be.

"Ma! If Julia doesn't know about Daphne, she has a right to hear the details." Then to Julia, "Did he tell his girl married somebody else?"

"Only that the young lady he kept company with had married recently. He didn't blame her, knowing he'd been absent so much of the past many years." Holmes had sounded a tad bitter in explaining his reasons, but she had no interest in condoning him to his mother and sister.

Julia decided to narrow down her question. "From what I've seen of Liberty, there are many marriageable women. Plenty of choices, it seems. I don't understand why Holmes sent for me while still at Harvard. Why not come home, see if someone here catches his fancy?"

Violet's gaze slid to her daughter's. They exchanged a wordless bit of communication Julia couldn't understand.

After a moment, the older woman shrugged. "Holmes didn't share that with us." A sigh. "He's been rather mum on the subject."

Katherine laughed. "He's a grown man. Busy with schooling."

"I know. I suppose the sad truth of it is I don't

know. I could guess—but that wouldn't be anything more than speculation. Could be you'll just have to ask him."

Julia nodded in acceptance.

Katherine tipped the hot loaves out onto a cooling rack. She tossed aside her hot pads, quickly rolling each steaming loaf of bread onto its side. "Speculation, sure. But I have an informed guess as to why."

Surely Katherine's guess would be informative; she knew her brothers as well as anyone.

A pleasant breeze swept through the open kitchen windows. It would be another glorious early summer day.

"First Daphne Browning—that's the girl we all thought he'd marry—announces her choice to marry Charlie. Second, Holmes wrote about two of his pals from Harvard are marrying this summer. Plans are all set. I think Holmes sees marriage as the next step to take."

Violet nodded, a thoughtful expression on her features.

"He hardly knows anyone here at home anymore. All the young ladies are more grown up. And since he spent time in Boston, might've supposed an eastern lady would suit him better." She shrugged. "That might be all it is."

Julia digested Katherine's comments, seeing the probability of truth in them. "Thank you, Katherine."

"Of course. But I might not be right."

No worries. If there was more to Holmes's reasons, his family seemed most unaware of it. The likelihood of Phillip knowing more than the women did seemed poor. In the end, it really didn't matter. No sense worrying about it until Holmes got home. If it still mattered then, she'd ask him for an explanation.

Through the open windows, Julia overheard Conrad and Gabriel arguing. The brothers squared off in the dooryard. Their conversation ceased abruptly.

As did the women's talk in the kitchen.

Apprehensive, Julia watched the men stare one another down. One long, uncomfortable moment crawled past. Gabriel stomped toward the outbuildings.

"I wish those boys wouldn't fight." Violet blotted her brow, her breathing somewhat labored.

"Conrad's never going to let it go," Katherine said, cracking two eggs into her batter.

"I wish they'd *try* to get along."

"Ma, things will never be the same between them. You know that."

"I know. I know."

Julia's curiosity blossomed. What had happened?

Katherine glanced at Julia, then back to her work. "Conrad believes he's entitled to fight with Gabriel. He's right, Gabriel's wrong. Conrad's fighting just to prove his point."

Julia couldn't disagree more, but she didn't say so.

She'd known the kind of men who thrive on a good fight—her father, and much of his political party—for example, and could not label Conrad as like them. Obviously, Conrad wasn't enjoying this. From everything she'd seen, Conrad would choose contentment and harmony over war, any day of the week.

The back door banged shut and Conrad came into the kitchen. His gaze met Julia's briefly. His jaw set in a hard line, his whole frame strung tighter than Grandmother Tyndall's corset.

"Ma, let me do that for you." He reached a skillet from the top cupboard shelf and helped his mother down from her stool. He offered her a supporting arm, despite his agitation.

Surprised, Julia couldn't think of one time Jordon Tyndall had paused to assist his wife or daughters. But then, what little time her father had spent at home, he'd been too consumed with his work to notice much else. The contrast between the two men was sharp.

It made Julia glad she'd left Tyndall ways behind, and had chosen a Macquarie. Surely Holmes would be much more like Conrad than not. A family man, who thought his mother's needs important.

"I'm capable of cooking in my own kitchen."

"I know, Ma. I know."

Julia noted the respect and genuine concern Conrad held for his mother. Very admirable, in her book.

"Promise me, before I die, you boys will get along."

Conrad grunted. Sliced off a heel of warm bread. Refused to make eye contact with any of them.

Julia knew enough to keep quiet.

"I told you not to talk to him," Katherine muttered.

Conrad shot his sister a dark look. He spread butter liberally on the heel of bread, then opened a jar of berry jam.

"What?" Katherine demanded. Loudly.

Their mother sighed.

"Don't blame this on me." Katherine hastily measured flour into the bowl. "I warned Gabriel to leave you alone, too. But do either of you listen to me?"

"Stay out of it." Conrad downed a glass of cold milk in three swallows.

"How am I supposed to do that?" Katherine stirred the batter vigorously. "Ignore you both?"

Conrad's expression, an odd mix of regret and frustration, spoke volumes. Couldn't the others see he didn't want to fight with his siblings? To Julia, it was evident he was mad at himself for being upset with Gabriel.

The tension made Julia's stomach ache. She had to do something. Smooth things over. Change the subject. "We made a batch of fresh chocolate cookies. Would you like—"

He didn't meet her eye. "I gotta go."

With his jam-laden bread in one hand, Conrad banged out the back door.

Not something Julia would've chosen to witness,

but she couldn't just ignore it. These weren't household servants or even close friends. They were her new family and she cared about them. She had to ask. "What was that about?"

Katherine paused. Exchanged a look with her mother.

Julia's stomach tingled with anxiety.

"Don't take his snappishness wrong." Violet said soothingly. "He thinks Gabriel took Sally from him."

Oh my. She'd had no idea. No wonder the brothers were at each other's throats, when they weren't pretending the other didn't exist.

Who was this Sally person? Julia didn't like the idea of Conrad being so in love, his entire world was turned upside down, simply because he'd lost her.

Unbidden jealousy tingled in Julia's stomach. Curiosity got the best of her, and she had to ask, "Sally? Who's she?"

"Sally Tibbs." Katherine finished greasing her cake pans, then plunked the brush back into the crock of lard. "Doc's daughter. Conrad kept company with her over the past year or so, but now she's with Gabriel. I guess he spent too much time over there, apprenticing with Doc and all."

Julia swallowed. No wonder Conrad behaved the way he did, avoiding unnecessary contact with Gabriel, keeping to himself. Her heart ached for Conrad, even as she took an instant dislike to Sally. "What is she like?"

"Darling," Violet said. "She'll give me beautiful grandchildren someday. And she's well mannered, patient." Violet took two onions from the bin and another paring knife from the drawer.

"That's the problem, right there," Katherine added. "Conrad's the king of impatience, but Sally got tired, patiently waiting for him to change."

Julia begged to differ on that one. Conrad had let her work—slowly—alongside him. He'd taught her to ride, with the tolerance of a saint. Impatient? Him? Not in her experience...except for when delivering invitations all over Liberty.

Katherine poured cake batter into two prepared pans. "Even when he was courting Sally, he didn't know what to do with her. Never spent much time in her company."

"I don't understand that." Julia dunked a peeled potato into the bowl of water and reached for another. Considering Conrad's kind treatment of her, Katherine's assessment seemed odd. "He willingly spends a generous amount of time with me."

"But you're family, and here all the time." Violet peeled an onion, dropping scraps into the pail. "Sally isn't for him. Conrad doesn't see that, though. Poor boy thinks he's no great catch and he's lost his only chance," Violet commented sadly, "but I see his value."

That, Julia could agree with. Wholeheartedly.

"He's such a good looking boy." Violet stared through the window, not focusing on anything. "I wish he'd believe me when I tell him so. His scar has caused such bitterness."

Julia rinsed her knife. "He'll find someone else. Someone who'll make him happy." How she wanted that happiness for him.

"You know he never will, the way he snaps at everyone." Katherine sounded exasperated. "He's surly, more often than not. His negativity chases all the girls away."

"Hmm." Julia had seen both sides. Ornery. Pleasant. Quarrelsome. Content. An intriguing mix. But he didn't frighten her. Or scare her off. She liked him, just the way he was.

Now that she understood the gist of what had happened between Conrad and his brother, she wondered why on earth Sally had chosen Gabriel. Not that Gabriel was all that unappealing, of course, but compared to Conrad...well, it wasn't difficult to see who was the better husband material.

Violet said, "If only he were more charming."

Was his mother so blind? "I think he is charming."

"My brother doesn't know the first thing about charming." Katherine tested the oven's temperature, then slid the two cake pans inside.

Violet patted Julia's hand. "You know what Conrad needs? A wonderful girl, just like you."

With that, Violet chopped the peeled onions and slid them off the cutting board and into the skillet. "But that's neither here nor there. Now, let me tell you all about our dear Holmes, as even-tempered as the day is long. He won't ever snap at you the way Conrad does. He'll treat you like a queen."

Julia only heard half of the continued compliments Holmes's mother paid him, for her thoughts and worries were centered on Conrad.

AFTER A FULL DAY in court in Ukiah, Phillip's first priority was to find out if Holmes had returned. Today, Luke had taken his turn meeting both morning and afternoon trains, on the lookout for Holmes.

The last thing they needed was the boy sneaking into town, unannounced. It wouldn't do to let Miss Julia meet Holmes, face to face, only to learn he'd never heard her name.

"Any sign of him?" Phillip asked when Luke looked up from his paper-strewn desk at the mayoral office. Fragrant cigar smoke hung in the still air.

"Come in, come in. I have the most *wonderful* news." Luke's whole countenance shone with happiness.

Phillip's heart leapt. "Where is he?"

"I'm going to be a grandfather!"

A second passed. Phillip must've misunderstood. Weren't they talking about Holmes's arrival? "What?"

"Mitzi's with child. Isn't that the best news you've heard all day long? All month?" Luke rubbed his hands together with glee.

"Fantastic. Now, how about Holmes?"

"I just heard the glorious news myself, this very morning. The babe is due at Christmas. Can you think of a better Christmas gift for an old man? I can see us now, all wrapped up in Yuletide cheer. A baby in the house. It's about time!"

Exasperated, Phillip gave Luke the commendations he wanted. "Congratulations! I'm very happy for you." And he was. A man's posterity was the most valuable asset he had. Family meant everything. "Do give my best to Garth and Mitzi."

"Thank you. I will. Have a cigar, in celebration of my happy news."

Phillip took a fragrant Havana from the box and proffered the end for Luke to snip. Phillip struck a match and puffed once.

Five quick, soft taps sounded on the closed door. Phillip turned, recognizing his friend John's customary knock.

"It's open," Luke called.

John cracked the door and stuck his head inside. One look at him, and Phillip immediately knew something had happened. Something *good.*

Phillip pulled John into the office. "You met the train? Any sign of Holmes?"

John brushed off the question, his face alight with enthusiasm. "Guess what Andrew said at the breakfast table?" Without pausing for a response, the preacher rushed on. "He said to me," paused for emphasis, grinned ear to ear, "'Father, I'm ready for marriage.'"

At trying moments such as this, Phillip wondered how he and John had stayed friends for the better part of forty years. "Do I care about Andrew's *talk* about marriage? No. Because my son is due home, at any moment, to actually get married."

"When I questioned Andrew," John said to Luke, who apparently proved a better audience, "he assured me that he indeed was ready to marry. Isn't that the best news yet?"

Luke chuckled. "I can top that. Mitzi's with child. *I'm* going to be a grandfather."

"Congratulations!"

Phillip stared at his two best friends, avidly shaking hands.

"I'm going to win our wager," John said, a smug smile on his too-handsome face.

"Braggart."

"Mark my words, Phillip. You'd best start saving your pennies, because I'm looking forward to that forty dollars."

Luke took his seat and slumped back onto the upholstery. "Phillip, you okay? You don't look well."

"Do I *care* about this wager?"

"You'd better care," Luke said, peering over his spectacles. "And you'd best hurry and get Holmes back here to marry Julia, if you hope to win the bet."

"Oh, Merciful Heavens, I nearly forgot." John's jubilation faded to ashes in a twinkling. "I have terrible news."

"He wasn't on the train?" Phillip's mood plummeted even further. "What can possibly be *so damn important* in Boston that my son won't come home?"

With every day that passed, Phillip's fears grew. He'd offered the boy everything he could think of to entice him to return, despite the Browning wench's betrayal.

What would he do if the boy never came back?

"I'm not talking about Holmes." John dropped into a seat. "I take it you two haven't heard about Doc Tibbs."

Phillip split a glance between his friends. "Heard what?"

"Damn shame." Luke set his cigar on the ash tray. "Sitting at his own birthday dinner today at noon, the whole family gathered 'round the dining room table, and he suffered a heart attack."

"Dead?" Stunned, Phillip leaned forward in his

chair.

"No," John assured. "But laid up. I wonder what we're going to do now."

Tibbs was the only doctor in Liberty. And Phillip's own Gabriel, apprenticing with Doc, wasn't anywhere near ready for the responsibility. He had years left to go before he could practice medicine on his own.

Panic clawed at Phillip. His family was slipping away.

With Doc laid low, it didn't seem irrational to assume Gabriel would want to enroll in a medical school, all of which were far from home, to continue his education.

"He'll get someone to replace him, won't he?" Phillip's mind raced. "Another doctor. Tibbs will have to bring someone to Liberty. If he can't do it, then the City Council will have to." Gabriel could continue his apprenticeship right here, at home.

"Probably so." Luke leaned back and laced his hands together over his belly. "So, are we through jawing about all the news? I thought you wanted to know about Holmes."

"I do." Amusing, Luke's sense of humor. Phillip concealed his impatience behind his courtroom face.

Luke smiled, raising both white brows.

"Well? Any sign of him?"

"Not a glimmer."

Phillip turned to John. "You hear anything?"

"No. Sorry."

Phillip didn't know whether to be relieved or angry. Since that first telegram informing his parents he intended to stay in Boston a few extra days—*what the hell for?*—Phillip had been forced to change his strategy. First, he'd had to send Conrad to fetch Holmes's bride, then he'd had to come up with an alternate plan to apprise Holmes of his windfall.

After all, he couldn't disappoint Miss Tyndall. She'd corresponded repeatedly with Holmes—via Phillip, naturally—accepted his matrimony-minded invitation to come to California, and assumed a formal offer of marriage to be forthcoming. Phillip intended to fulfill the contractual agreement. Everyone would get precisely what they needed, and in doing so, everyone would be blissfully happy.

"What will you do now?" Luke puffed his cigar.

"Just what we have been doing," though it galled him. He was a man of action! "Wait for another telegram or for him to show up." For the last, interminably long nine months, all he'd done was wait. But he was a patient man. He could wait a few more days.

"No more contact from him?"

"None. Tell me, what is wrong with telephone service? One time, I can get a call through to Boston. The next, no dice. And Holmes ignores my telegrams. Absolutely no response."

"Disrespectful kid," Luke muttered.

"Hey, now," John said. "Holmes is a good boy. I'm sure there's a perfectly good explanation for everything."

Phillip grunted. "I'm stuck in court all day tomorrow. The jury's caught in deliberations, with little hope of reaching a verdict during my natural lifetime. Will you two watch the train tomorrow for me?"

Luke chuckled, tapping ash from his cigar. "I'm beginning to think you're hoping for a stay of execution."

"What's that supposed to mean?" Stay of execution. Bah.

"If you think I'm going to break the news to Holmes," Luke said with a smirk, "you're wrong."

"Break the news?" Phillip narrowed his eyes. "This isn't about *breaking the news*. This is about my son learning he has a beautiful, intelligent woman anxious to be his wife."

"On second thought," Luke said, "maybe I do want to be there."

John chuckled. "Holmes is slower than cold tar.

Andrew will be happily married, with five children, before Holmes gets back here. He may not show up on either of tomorrow's trains."

"Keep dreaming, Preacher." Phillip glared at his friends, but neither man had the courtesy to stop smiling like idiots. "Holmes's last telegram said he'd be home before Saturday. That means tomorrow at the latest."

"Yeah, yeah," taunted John.

"For the record, gentlemen, I'm *anxious* to give Holmes the good news of his bride and impending marriage."

Luke puffed, sending a smoke ring toward the ceiling. "So what am I supposed to do if he shows up while you're tied up in Morley's court?"

John laughed aloud. "Keep him away from Julia. That'll give Andrew even more of a head start."

"Yes, keep him away from Julia." Phillip stood, gathered his satchel and suit coat. "But this has nothing to do with the likes of Andrew."

"No," Luke added, smirking, "I'll bet not."

"You two owe me big for all the times I've helped you," Phillip reminded them. "This is important. Remember, no matter what, I must show him Julia's letters before he meets her."

Luke leaned back in his chair, an amused grin on his face. "We'll do our best, won't we, John?"

BY MIDMORNING on Friday, the entire Macquarie household was in an uproar, preparing for the Prodigal Son's return. The whole Killing of the Fatted Calf routine made Conrad positively ill. Call it concern for Julia, who'd run herself threadbare, or plain old jealousy. He didn't care which.

He swung the ax, severing the balanced log with one stroke. He kicked splintered firewood aside and plunked another log on the stump. He crashed the ax blade through the wood.

Six extra cooks, hired for the overblown welcome home party, had been hard at work in the summer kitchen since before sunrise. They'd burned through a cord of wood already, and demanded more. Alberta's additional four housekeepers set up dining tables and chairs. Each family member scurried from one task to the next.

Conrad would've been fine with all that—if it hadn't been for watching Julia slave away.

Holmes, the ingrate, hadn't bothered to send a wire and offer Julia assurances he'd be home on time. What on earth had possessed Holmes—whom Conrad had always admired—to leave his bride to fend for herself?

If Julia were his, Conrad swore, he wouldn't be able to stay away. He'd put her needs first.

Delicious aromas of cooking food wafted through the summer kitchen's open windows. Conrad's mouth watered. He loved the tangy, rich sauce that accompanied Ma's special recipe for Cattleman's Shredded Beef.

Apparently nothing was too good for Holmes.

Too bad Holmes wasn't good enough to deserve any of this hoopla: the celebration, accolades, and full-time attention of every member of this household. He didn't merit the party to be held in his honor.

Most important of all, Holmes didn't deserve Julia.

Conrad had no trouble seeing that. Why couldn't anyone else?

He carried another armload of wood to the chopping block and dropped it in a clattering heap.

Inside the house, Julia called to Katherine. The sound of her voice twisted in Conrad's gut. She put on a good front, sounding calm and in control. But he heard the underlying tension and anxiety.

He didn't want to care, didn't want to feel a thing.

He cursed Holmes for staying away. If he'd come home on time, none of this would've happened. Julia would be happy, content, and well-cared for by her husband-to-be. Conrad could've met Julia, just as he had his sister-in-law Nadine, and their brother-sister relationship could've been normal.

Instead, he'd gotten too close. He cared too much and felt too damn protective.

The nagging desire to make her happy, to soothe her troubles scared him more than anything.

It was hell, just to be near her.

He thrust another length of wood onto the chopping block. It wobbled and fell into the dust. Conrad dropped the ax, upended the log, and balanced it in place.

The late morning sunlight heated his skin. Wiping his shirt sleeve over his wet brow, he reclaimed the ax.

The log wobbled and tipped. Conrad's temper surged. He lunged, striking the wood with an ineffectual blow. With a growl, he whacked it to pieces where it lay. He kicked the uneven chunks toward the firewood stack.

He couldn't go on like this—hating Holmes, hating Gabriel, taking sides with a woman he'd just met, allowing his feelings for that woman to drive him insane.

For the tenth time that morning, he glanced toward the dining room windows. Instead of merely glimpsing Julia move past the windows, he caught her headed straight for him.

Didn't that put whipped cream on the cow pie.

He caught a hint of her floral fragrance and tried to ignore the play of sunlight on her shiny curls. He split another log clean in two with a single stroke.

She folded her arms against the cool morning air. "Is your father back yet?"

It couldn't be easy, waiting for Pop to return from the depot with Holmes. "Haven't seen him."

"I see."

Must she look at him as though she expected him to fix everything? He had no control over Holmes. Or Pop. And especially not Pop's wild tale about Holmes being in San Francisco, when Conrad damn well knew Holmes hadn't yet returned from Harvard.

Helplessness compounded his anger. It roiled within him, gaining momentum, threatening to explode. Why all the lies?

He turned his back. His shoulders and arms burned with the exertion. His chest heaved with every breath. And still, he felt Julia's gaze on his back. He bent to gather the firewood.

"Why ya breathin' so hard, cowboy?" Laughter echoed in her voice, but couldn't quite mask the quaver, the frustration lurking beneath. "That looks like easy work, compared to what I've been doing today. Give me that."

She gripped the handle in both little fists, testing its weight. "Heavier than I thought."

"Careful, you'll cut yourself."

"Chopping wood is on my list." Half-dragging the ax on the earth, she approached the chopping block.

He caught a glimpse of the worn, functional, low shoes she'd brought out of one of her many trunks. Just like Ma wore, with wool stockings. They were plain, average, and rather homely. Work shoes. Made sense with a whole day on her feet.

Fancy, stylish high-heels flashed in his mind. Silk stockings. Slim, feminine ankles. Dainty toes.

Conrad scrubbed a palm down his face, trying to erase the image. No matter what Julia wore on her feet, all he could see was shapely ankles and white, white skin.

Julia's sissy plunk of the ax caught the upended log off-center. The blade bit into the wood and stopped cold. She turned her attention to him. He could see she had something on her mind, and it wasn't cutting firewood.

Whoa, Nellie.

The time had come to recapture yesterday's light, teasing banter between them—quick, before she started some serious topic of conversation.

She'd successfully teased him out of a foul mood. He'd try to do the same for her.

"You want some help with that, Miss J? If you want wood for the stove, all you need do is ask. I'll carry it right on in the house for you."

She slid him a dark look. "I'll have you know I came to California to split firewood. And ride a horse and gather eggs and grow vegetables and milk a cow."

"I know. So what's next? You planning to ride in a roundup?" The closest anyone got to that, anymore, was sending the dogs to pasture to herd the last few dawdling cows in for milking.

Julia had romanticized ideas about everything. Unfortunately, that was one more thing to like about her.

Her smile seemed shaky. He sensed her hesitancy, and decided he didn't want to know what was on her mind.

"I came to California to stroll through alfalfa. I want to hang out sheets to dry. I want to ride morning and night. I want to *live*." Emotion trembled in her voice. "I want to be happy."

Something twisted deep inside him, compelling him to fix everything, to see to her happiness. He'd do it. If he could. But it wasn't his job. "You and Holmes will be the happiest couple around. You'll see."

She looked him squarely in the eye. "I used to think Holmes and I *would* be happy. But now, I..."

Distraction. That's what she needed. Something else to keep her mind on. What if Holmes showed up with Pop, in less than an hour, and found Julia in this state? "What else is on your list? Want to help brand the calves?" He grabbed the ax handle to wrest it loose. "I'll warn you, it's hard work—"

"I want to finish." She snatched the handle from his grip, the weight of the implement catching her off balance.

Feisty thing, wasn't she?

With a yell that sounded a little like an Indian war cry, Julia whacked the ax into the log. This time, she managed to split it a few inches, but left the blade embedded.

She widened her stance and choked up higher on the wooden handle. "You know what I want to do, Conrad Macquarie?"

Whatever she had to say, he was certain he wouldn't like it. "I see you're fixing to tell me."

"I want to pretend this damnable party never happened."

"It'll all be over—"

She silenced him with one pointed look, her mounting frustration obvious. "Do you think I *want* this headache? I'm having a very hard time caring about a man I've never met, who is several days overdue, and who may *or may not* show up for his own party."

Conrad tried to soothe her, as he would an agitated filly. Soft words. Nonthreatening posture. "No need to get riled up. By this time tomorrow, it'll all be over."

Cold fire flickered in her blue eyes. "If I'd had a choice in the matter, I would've told your father to hire someone else. But did I have a choice? No. If anything, this party ought to be held in celebration of Katherine and David's engagement. Not for Holmes."

"Engaged? That's good news." At last! A chance to turn this conversation onto safer ground. "When did this happen?"

"Yesterday, I think." Julia's expression fell flat, just like whipped cream let sit too long.

"I thought you wanted to celebrate their plans. But you don't look happy." Women. What man had an inkling what went on in their heads?

"I *am* happy. For Katherine and David. But not for me. Nothing is working out the way I'd imagined, and I can't help but regret everything—"

Whoa. Where'd that come from? "No, Miss J—"

"—and I wish Holmes hadn't sent for me."

He shook his head, warding off anything more with two upraised palms. "You're tired, Miss J, that's all. You don't mean it."

"Oh, *yes, I do*." Fire sparked in her blue eyes. "What's more, I wish *you* had."

Chapter Thirteen

JULIA CLAPPED a hand over her mouth.

Had she actually said that?

Mortified, she gaped at Conrad.

He was obviously scandalized and appalled.

She'd just let something utterly stupid fall out of her mouth, and shocked the socks off him.

By the disgusted expression on his face, he didn't even *like* her.

Several horrible seconds passed. Evidently, Conrad wasn't going to answer. He wasn't even going to laugh it off as a silly joke.

The chilly wind cut through her wool dress, but couldn't douse the heat churning within her.

She ought to apologize. Recant. Explain it away as a fit of nerves. Say she meant to say she wished Holmes were more like Conrad—but that would be just as bad.

Of course she didn't wish Conrad had sent for her.

Why had something so scandalous tripped off her tongue? Holmes's inconsideration chafed and irritated, but he was the one she wanted.

Wasn't he?

Conrad was simply her friend. A very good friend. But his expression made her doubt he'd claim her.

"No, ma'am. You don't wish that." He sounded frustrated. And hurt.

Oh, no. She had to fix this. Had to make everything all right. "We're friends—"

"I showed you the ranch, because Holmes wasn't here to do it himself. End of story."

The wind tossed a few loose curls about her face. She tucked one behind her ear, noticing her hand trembled with the effort. "Yes, I know, and—"

He shook his head, pain flashing in his eyes. "We were only passing the time. Tonight, you'll meet Holmes and everything will be fine."

Without saying another word, Conrad stalked toward the outbuildings, his ax clenched in one fist.

She watched him go, his broad shoulders tight. Her stomach twisted into knots, awash with humiliation.

She saw no possible way to correct what had just gone so terribly wrong. She hurried back to the house, determined to immerse herself in Holmes's party.

And pray Conrad and she both could forget this conversation happened.

ON FRIDAY afternoon, Phillip met the train in Liberty. The celebration, set to begin in a mere three hours, was virtually ready. The food, wine, music, speeches, guests—all set to go. All they needed to make the party a success was for Holmes to arrive in time to see it.

Good thing Holmes was a man of his word. His

brief telegram had said he'd be home before Saturday. That guaranteed he would be on this train.

Phillip stood on the platform, hat in his hands, as the last few passengers dispersed. He turned the brim slowly, then tapped it against his leg.

Something was wrong with Holmes. Terribly wrong. He could feel it in his bones.

Coming toward him across the platform, John Proctor waved in greeting. His eager smile faded as he seemed to realize Holmes was nowhere about. "No sign of him?"

"None." Anxiety made Phillip's pulse race. It was past time he *acted.* He had to do something to find his son.

"What a shame." John's shoulders slumped.

"I'm going so send a wire to Kinsley at Harvard. Then Boston Police. Hospitals."

"Surely you don't think he's ill."

"I'm beginning to wonder if he's dead." The thought worried him sick.

"Oh, now don't borrow trouble. I'm sure he's just run into a delay somewhere along the line."

"Only a dead man would abandon his bride and refuse to make an appearance at his own welcome-home celebration."

John cleared his throat. "He doesn't know about either of those two things."

"That's an excuse?" Phillip paced the platform, nearly consumed with apprehension. He had to know, had to *do* something. He couldn't wait idly by, for one more minute.

"You're right." John's brow lined with worry. "Send those wires. Then get on home. Violet's going to need you."

Phillip sighed. He knew his dear wife would be terribly disappointed. And worried.

"Tonight's celebration must go on." As he led the way to the street, John clapped Phillip on the shoulder.

"I'm in no mood to entertain."

"Oh, yes you are. Your daughter's needs are important."

"Katherine?" Phillip stumbled to a halt. "What's this about Katherine?"

John sucked in a breath. "I'll come with you to the telegraph office. Once you've learned something from Boston, you can go on home and—"

"Tell me, this minute, John." Katherine needed this party? What had happened? Dread congealed in his gut. This wasn't about a new gown or a chance to socialize. "This has something to do with that David Orme. I'm right, aren't I?"

"Hey, now. David's a good man. He'll make you a fine son-in-law."

"He proposed, didn't he?"

John nodded.

Phillip winced. So much for the boy asking for her hand, like any decent boy would do. He tried to hide his despair. "You knew before me? Why doesn't anybody ever tell me anything? Why am I always the *last* to know?"

He didn't want an answer, and John knew it. He couldn't spare a moment to think about this turn of events until he'd done what he could for Holmes.

But two hours later, they'd received only one response, from the police department. They had no information, either good or bad.

"You know what I think?" In the privacy of the law office, Phillip put his cheek upon his desk. He fisted his hands in his lap, where John couldn't see. "I think the kid's changed his mind completely about returning home. I think that unfaithful tart Daphne Browning broke his heart."

"Hey, now. All you'll do is make yourself feel worse. Holmes never wrote a word about that light skirt in his letters. I don't think he cares one way or the other."

Phillip noticed John passed by the opportunity to gloat. At this rate, Andrew *would* marry first.

Phillip didn't care. Let John win. What did forty dollars matter? Absolutely nothing, if Holmes was lost to him.

After a minute, he said, "I think he took another job somewhere else. I believe he's trying to exert his own will."

"That's possible."

"I fear he'll never come back. Ever."

A minute ticked past. John finally spoke. "Come on. I'll drive you home."

Glad for his friend's support, Phillip merely nodded.

EXHAUSTED, irritable, and aching from head to toe, Julia found sleep impossible.

The welcome-home party had gone remarkably well, given the guest of honor never showed. The company had been delighted to celebrate Katherine and David's engagement. The Macquaries put on a good show of support for Katherine and had introduced Julia to all present as Holmes's bride-to-be.

Somewhere midst all the hoopla, Julia had noticed Portia had sneaked out. With Olaf DeLaigle.

Rain pattered on the rooftop. The cadence, soothing and beautiful, failed to lull her to sleep. Through the open window, the air smelled fresh and clean. How she loved the covered veranda, making it possible to sleep with the windows open and enjoy Mother Nature's symphony.

Downstairs, the grandfather clock struck two. The chimes echoed through the still house. Had Portia lost all sense of propriety?

Julia couldn't ignore her aunt's absence much longer. Something could be desperately wrong. Olaf's horse could've thrown them both. They could be hurt. And Julia hadn't a glimmer of where to start searching.

She wasn't foolish enough to ignore the probability that Portia was safe and sound, in Olaf's bed.

How embarrassing.

That was something she absolutely could not bring to anyone's attention.

The Macquaries had been too busy with the party and cleanup afterward to notice Portia's continued absence. How would she explain, once the family learned about Portia's suspicious behavior?

That was only the beginning of her worries.

Conrad, who'd hidden from her all evening long, had apparently refused to sleep in the house.

Eventually, he'd tell someone about the unfaithful thing she'd said. Word would get out. Everything would change.

She'd already spoiled her friendship with him, forever.

The last thing she needed was the rest of the family to turn on her.

What could she possibly do?

Light footfalls sounded in the hall outside. Oh, good. It was about time Portia decided to come home. Thank goodness. Maybe no one else would notice she'd been out so indecently late.

Besides, Julia desperately needed to talk to her aunt. Ask her advice. Figure out what to do now that she'd made such a stupid mistake.

Door hinges creaked... but not hers. In the hall, Conrad's door shut with a soft bump of wood against jamb.

She lay very still, her heart pounding double time.

How would she ever face him again?

She lay motionless, her weary legs and back aching, and listened to every small sound coming from his bedroom. Boots thumped to the floor. The water pitcher's thud on the washstand. A soft creek as his bed frame took his weight.

Perhaps a minute passed. A cool breeze drifted in

through her open window. His bed squeaked softly as he turned over.

Still, no sign of Portia.

Oh, what could she do?

She couldn't very well wake the family to ask for their help. Before this afternoon's big mistake, she could have turned to Conrad.

Not anymore.

Julia was shocked to hear Portia tiptoe inside and shut their bedroom door quietly. Faint moonbeams filtered through one open window. It was just light enough to be certain this was indeed Portia, finally come home.

Julia tossed back the covers and sat up. "Do you know what time it is?" she whispered loudly.

Portia brought a hand to her throat. "You scared me."

"*You* scared *me*. "What possessed you to stay out so late? It's indecent."

"I know, I know." Portia sagged onto the chair and bent to unfasten her shoes.

"I've been worried sick about you."

"You're right. It's late. It's scandalous. Ridiculous." Portia giggled. "But Olaf is... he's..."

"I'll tell you what he is. *Trouble*."

"Nonsense." Portia waved away the very idea.

"You're on a first-name basis, I see."

"I don't see why not. We're the same age. Friends, too." Portia unfastened her shoes. "This evening, we took a drive through a woodland. The wildlife were extraordinary. I sketched a dozen pages. We saw a black bear and spotted owls and banana slugs—"

"You missed the welcome-home party." Almost two weeks of preparations, an utter waste.

"There was no one to welcome home. And I assure you I congratulated Katherine and her young man, quite properly."

"I was worried about you. You could've told me you were leaving."

"You knew I'd gone. And with whom." Her voice had taken on that dreamy quality, as if Olaf DeLaigle had stolen her good sense along with her heart.

Julia saw no sense in admitting she had known.

Portia carefully removed each item of clothing and hung it over the chair to dry. "I heard Phillip explain a half dozen times, at least, that Holmes was delayed. What a shame."

Portia didn't seem to want an answer as she hung a few things in the wardrobe. After a minute elapsed, she asked, "Were you terribly disappointed?"

"No, of course not," Julia fibbed, lying down on the feather tick and tucking the sheet back around herself.

"I know how much effort you put into this party, all for his enjoyment."

"It doesn't matter. The guests had a wonderful time. It pleased Holmes's parents."

"You don't fool me," Portia said in a loud whisper. "I can hear how upset you are. And you have every right to be."

Maybe. But her disappointment felt disloyal. Especially after the stupid thing she'd confessed to Conrad.

Apparently Portia wasn't the only one to forfeit her good sense along with her heart.

"I'm sure Holmes would be here, if he could." Portia pulled off her shoes and unrolled her stockings. "Assume he's doing his best, won't you?"

"Of course."

"Starch and steel, Dolly. If there's ever been a time when you needed a bit of faith in Holmes, this is it."

Oh, if her aunt only knew how true that was. "Yes, Aunt Portia."

"This is no time to sit around, feeling sorry for yourself. And I have just the thing to keep you occupied. Tomorrow, *we* are going to the petrified redwoods and the geyser with Olaf." Enthusiasm vibrated in Portia's voice. "I'm so excited, I doubt I'll be able to sleep."

"The geyser?" Julia sat upright. She'd heard that tone in Portia's voice on many occasions—usually in the context of one of her many sisters attempting to sneak time alone with her beau. "Aunt, you mustn't go so far with him, not after—"

"You need the respite more than I do. You see, I have no intention of allowing your courtship to end in tragedy. I've traveled that road, and believe you me, that's a road best unvisited."

All her life, Julia had thought her maiden aunt immune to matters of the heart. She'd been far too enamored with geology and biology to give a fig for males of her own species. Julia didn't know what to say.

"Don't act so dumbfounded, Dolly. I'm a grown woman. I've been in love before."

"Before?" No one had ever said a word to her about Portia having had a romance. But her current devotion to Olaf DeLaigle was apparent for all the world to see.

Portia stepped behind the screen to change into her nightgown. "Why else do you think I invited myself along? I couldn't allow your courtship with Holmes to go awry. And I'm doing my part to make sure that doesn't happen."

"Nothing will go wrong." Julia wouldn't let it.

"You desperately need a break from this house."

"What if Holmes returns and I'm not here?" Julia asked.

"He's made you wait long enough. It won't kill him to wait a few hours for you."

"I can't argue with that." Julia lay back on the bed, completely worn out. The outing did sound inviting. She drew a deep, tired breath. She wanted to get away almost as much as she wanted to avoid Conrad.

"It'll be wonderful, Dolly. You need fresh air and sunshine and a day with nothing to do."

And no chance of crossing paths with Conrad. Perfect.

"It's raining," Julia commented. "There may not

be sunshine tomorrow."

Behind the screen, Portia prattled on about her eagerness to examine petrified redwood trees. Picnics, Olaf's photography, and the beauties of unspoiled nature. To her, rain wasn't a deterrent.

Portia padded toward bed and climbed in. "Mr. DeLaigle will be here at half-past six, so you'd best get your sleep."

On cue, Julia yawned. Already, visions of a much-needed day of rest flitting through her mind.

Outside, the rain shower intensified.

"Oh, there's no need to worry you'll be lonely." Portia settled herself in and pulled up the bed covers. "Conrad's driving us."

CONRAD'S BED was close enough to the open window, despite the rainfall, he could easily overhear every word exchanged between Julia and her loony aunt.

If they didn't want an audience, they ought to shut their window and keep their voices down.

Batty Aunt Portia could make all the highfalutin plans she wanted. He hadn't agreed to drive them all the way out there tomorrow, and he wouldn't, even if Batty Aunt Portia bothered to ask. Nothing could make him go along. Especially in Julia's company.

Miss J had a way of sneaking past his defenses, getting around his determination to see her as nothing more than Holmes's bride. Avoiding her during the party had been hard enough. He'd glimpsed her too often.

He'd felt drawn to her.

Wanted nothing more than to take her in his arms and soothe away her disappointment, her frustrations.

He missed her company.

Even though she'd claimed she'd wished he'd been

the one to send for her.

Her passionate words kept hovering in his mind, never far away. After all this time, her claim had a way of shocking his battered heart. And wearing down his defenses.

If that wasn't a monstrous clue he was in deep trouble, he didn't know what was.

The important thing was he'd managed to avoid her altogether. He wasn't about to let Portia's wild plans undo all the good he'd accomplished in the past twelve hours.

Portia's supposition that he'd join their little outing had barely been stated when Julia whispered, loudly, "No!" She sounded panicked. Almost terrified.

Relieved, Conrad relaxed. See? She was smart enough to understand they couldn't be friends.

"Don't be like that," Portia exclaimed, as if unaware anyone else was in the house. "He's your friend."

A few seconds slid past. Friends? Yes, they had been. He hoped they still could be, but didn't see how that was possible. Not with his unorthodox feelings for her.

Especially not after what she'd said about wishing he'd been the one to send for her.

And showing him her bare leg.

And confiding her private thoughts.

And kissing his cheek.

Far too much had happened between them.

"We're not friends. Not anymore," Julia said softly, and Conrad lay very still, trying to catch the rest of her response. "I don't want him to come along."

Disappointment stole through him, leaving him cold.

This is the way he wanted it. He'd vowed to bury himself in work. Work from before sunup until after sundown. Work, work, work. No time for Julia. So much work, he'd never even think about her.

"Nonsense," Portia said, her tone full of dismissal.

"I'm packing a picnic for four. We're all going."

"If he's going, then I'm not."

That was the most level-headed, rational thing he'd heard Julia say all day.

"We need Conrad to drive the rig." Portia's voice muffled a bit, as she apparently turned over. Bedclothes rustled. The guest bed creaked.

"Olaf's perfectly capable," Julia argued.

Portia said something, but Conrad missed most of it. Something about mud and buggy wheels.

He lay still, listening intently.

"Oh, all right." Julia sounded resigned. "You can ask, but I have no doubt he'll have too much work to consider your request."

His thoughts, exactly.

He rolled over, more determined than ever to be out of the house long before either Julia or her aunt awoke. He'd stick to his plan to use work to avoid Julia completely.

He folded his pillow in half and crammed it beneath his head. *Sleep,* he commanded himself.

No doubt, he'd made the right decision. It should be simple enough to stick to it.

CONRAD COULD count on one hand the number of times Pop had shown up in the field. Every time, he'd wanted something. Something big. Conrad had no doubt this meant trouble.

Trouble that included Julia, a dozen hours trapped in her company, and a run-in with Petrified Charlie.

Conrad squinted into the rising sun at Pop's back and set his jaw.

The old man still rode with ease, but his age showed in the dismount. He grimaced, shook out his stiff left leg, and offered his most persuasive smile.

"No. Can't do it, Pop." Conrad thrust the shovel blade deeper into the moist earth, wrenched the handle back, and tossed the heap of dirt to the side. A cold breeze chilled the sweat on his brow.

"I haven't uttered a word." Pop's smile poured on the charm. "What makes you so sure I've come to ask you to do something?"

Conrad tossed his shovel aside and thrust the fence post deep into the hole. He kicked loose earth around its base. "My answer's no."

"Then I suppose it's fortuitous I haven't got a thing to ask you to do. Nope, no chores, no errands, no work assignments." His pleasant argument could've persuaded any jury to his way of thinking.

Conrad slid his father a sideways glance.

Pop surveyed the line of new fencing Conrad had made good progress on in the past four hours. "Whew! I feared I'd find you up to your elbows in something you couldn't leave until another day. The good thing about fencing is it'll still be here tomorrow or next week."

"I intend to lay another mile of fence, so don't—"

"Consider it done." Pop grinned. "Easily hired out. You deserve a day off, son. A day of rest and relaxation. Lots of good food. A nap in the sunshine."

"No, thanks."

Pop clucked his tongue and patted Saturn's neck. "The whole family's taking a day off. After working so hard for the past few days, we all need a holiday."

Conrad tamped down the wet earth around the post, packing it solid. He picked up his shovel and headed four paces away. He judged the proper position by sighting down the row of standing fence posts.

"Don't want a day off." Final. No room for argument.

Pop followed along behind. He surveyed the lightening sky and thrust his hands into his vest pockets. "It's going to be a glorious day for a picnic. Sun's a shining."

The old man had a reputation for arguing any side

of any argument—and winning. He could spin a yarn that would convince anybody the sky was green and the alfalfa field a hundred shades of blue. When he had his mind set, there wasn't anything a body could say to convince him otherwise.

Conrad shook his head, irritated that Portia had known exactly how to force him to climb in the wagon and head to the petrified forest and geyser with her. He cast Pop an impatient glare and bit the shovel blade into the mud.

Pop grinned, apparently tickled to do Portia's bidding.

"No need to be so industrious, son. Drop your tools. The ladies have their picnic and supplies all packed in the wagon. Time's wasting."

Aha! Proof Portia had convinced Pop to paint the fence. "I've got my own lunch right over there." He indicated the cart he'd brought from the barn, loaded with fence posts, implements, and enough food and drink to last him through tomorrow.

Pop's expression lost all traces of joviality. "Listen to me, son. Julia wants to go sightseeing with Portia and Olaf."

Oh, no she didn't. "Pop—"

"Hear me out." He raised a palm, in a plea for cooperation. "We both know Olaf's not the best of long-distance drivers, and in the interest of our house guests' safety, it's only right you go along to handle the team."

He dismissed Pop's argument. What a load of manure.

Pop clapped a hand on Conrad's shoulder, his expression solemn. "We've done a great job thus far. Miss Julia is content, and I won't spoil it now. The young lady will have whatever her heart desires. Do you understand me? She desires your accompaniment on this outing."

No, Portia wanted him along. Hell if he knew why. "Pop, it's impossible."

The old man, far too accustomed to getting his

own way, refused to admit defeat. "They expect you momentarily. Must get a jump on the day. Portia's determined to stop and smell the dirt and kick the trees along the way." Pop chuckled, as if Portia were the most amusing person he'd ever met.

"Fine." Conrad narrowed his eyes. "Send Gabriel."

"You know he's doing his best to fill Doc Tibbs's shoes. Old Doc is still recuperating."

Conrad snorted.

"What, exactly, is the problem?" Pop asked, his impatience obvious in his stance.

Despite his faults, Pop had a quick mind. Always had. Conrad found it very difficult to believe his father could be so blind, so completely unaware of Conrad's reasons for refusing to go. Perhaps he'd have to spell it out. "I cannot spend time alone with Miss Julia."

Pop waved away the comment. "She's going along to chaperon Portia and Olaf. Craziest thing I ever heard, but those Eastern ladies have their own way of doing things. You'll hardly be alone with her. So no need to fret about her reputation."

As he stared down his father, he knew another refusal would yield nothing. He considered confessing his feelings for Julia to Pop, but couldn't bring himself to do so. The family had to live together, in harmony for years to come. The last thing he needed was a critical audience, watching his every move, reading too much into every word and look that happened to pass between himself and Julia in the months and years to come.

"I," he stated with fierce emphasis, "*can't*."

"This isn't about you, Conrad. This is about our family pulling together to help Holmes." Pop stepped closer, his features softening with concern. "He's not here to help himself. He'd do the same for you."

Conrad shrugged and pulled away. He headed for the cart and another armload of fence posts.

"Times are desperate." Pop dogged Conrad's every step. "Critical. We can't quit now. We've come too far. Julia's too quiet this morning. Sad. Resigned."

Conrad winced inwardly.

"She *needs* this day out," Pop insisted. "It'll be good for her to get some fresh air and think about something besides Holmes. Our family is in this together. All of us."

"I know that." Conrad gathered up a bundle of posts and held it like a shield between himself and Pop.

"I know you've had your difficulties with Gabriel as of late, and for that I'm very sorry. But you and Holmes have always been close. You know he'd do anything within his power to help you, were circumstances reversed."

"Are you listening to me?" Was the old man completely oblivious to the turmoil going on in his own household? "There's no way I can spend the day with Julia—"

"No, Conrad, *you* listen. I know you've got work here. It hasn't been so long since I operated this ranch that I don't have any idea what still goes on here. You're not the only one inconvenienced by Holmes's absence.

"Your mother's exhausted with worry. I've put off four clients this week alone, and I'm already *hours* behind on sleep. Alberta's work load has nearly doubled, trying to keep up with Aunt Portia's mud-caked laundry. Katherine, the poor dear, has been doing everything she can to pick up the slack."

Put that way, how could he possibly refuse? No matter what argument he posed, he'd sound exactly like the self-centered idiot his father believed him to be.

He tossed the bundle of fence posts back into the cart. "Fine, Pop. You win."

Chapter Fourteen

WITH THE SUN high in the afternoon sky, Julia carried a straight-backed chair from the wagon to where Olaf DeLaigle fiddled with his camera equipment.

Portia checked her timepiece, for the fifth time, at least. "Less than seven minutes remain."

"I'll be ready," Olaf assured Portia as he checked the camera's view.

A sinewy widower with thinning gray hair that blew every which way, Olaf stood a good two or three inches shorter than Julia. If Portia noticed he wasn't passing attractive, she gave no indication.

Olaf had already taken a dozen photographs that morning: Portia examining the rings on a cross section of fallen redwood, Portia and Julia sitting together on an enormous tree stump, Portia's delighted smile as she looked up from a banana slug she'd been inspecting. He'd spent a good forty-five minutes staging a portrait of himself with Portia, and gave Julia instructions for operating the camera.

Julia situated her chair as far from Conrad's napping spot as reasonable. She shoved out a sigh and sat. It was going to be a very, very long day.

From the moment Conrad had climbed aboard the wagon, he'd spoken as briefly as possible, and only when asked a direct question. He'd stretched out on a sunny patch of earth, covered his face with his hat, and gone to sleep.

Fine.

Given her own discomfort, she didn't want to talk to him either.

Who needed conversation?

Portia and Olaf provided excellent entertainment, carrying on a dialog about the geological structures necessary for a geyser to exist.

Fascinating, although Portia had been talking about this kind of stuff for as long as Julia could remember.

"Heat source, heat source," Olaf pondered. He straightened his stooped posture. "Magma? That's the right name, isn't it?"

"Precisely!" Portia exclaimed. "Magma heats the subterranean water supply to extreme temperatures, which, due to expansion, is forced to the earth's surface through natural fissures and fractures!"

"Fascinating," Olaf whispered, with evident awe.

Julia had no difficulty discerning he was more enamored with Portia, than with her knowledge of earth sciences.

"Oh, it is. I witnessed—" Portia fanned both hands in glee "—the most utterly amazing things during my two-year tour of southeast Asia. North America's geothermal activity has absolutely nothing on that region of the world."

Olaf took a step closer, his attention riveted on Portia's tale. "Whereabouts in Asia?"

Portia launched into a list of the places she'd

explored, pausing to emphasize why each location had captivated her interest. The accounting was lengthy. Portia had always adored a rapt audience.

"It was while my company was there," Portia told Olaf, her features scrunched with intrigue, "exploring the geothermal lakes and vents, that my right foot broke through the surface. I assure you, I believed I was at a safe distance. With one shoe ankle-deep, the superheated discharge..."

Julia's ears began to buzz. She'd heard tales of these travels so many times, she could almost quote the stories, verbatim. She lost interest, completely.

Closing her eyes, Julia tipped her face up to the warm sunshine filtering past towering treetops, and wished she were somewhere, *anywhere,* else.

Why was she here? To babysit two gray-haired adults who were so enamored with nature and photography and each other that they wouldn't notice if Julia drove the wagon back to the ranch.

The isolation underscored how badly she'd mucked up the best friendship she'd ever had.

He lay sleeping, twenty feet away. The rift between Conrad and herself made the distance seem like an entire continent.

Regret lurked and churned within her, just like the heating waters within the geyser's chasm.

Julia squeezed her eyelids tighter, enjoying the cooling breeze washing over her face—even if it was tainted with characteristic smells of sulfur and other gasses.

"Portia." Olaf's breathing came in irregular gasps. "I never met a woman like you."

Julia opened one eye and peered at Olaf. He stood a respectable eighteen inches from her aunt.

"Of course you haven't, Mr. DeLaigle," Portia answered breezily. "You've never been more than twenty-five miles from home."

Julia sighed. It was going to be a *very* long day.

"I aim to change that." Determination effused

Olaf's claim.

"Where, exactly, do you intend to go?"

"That depends." Olaf took a hesitant step closer to Portia, reaching for her hand. "Where you going, when you leave here?"

This was insufferable.

Julia groaned. She didn't even try to keep quiet about it. But neither chatty Portia, nor the love-struck beau paid Julia any heed.

Portia's response to Olaf's question was limited to a quick smile, for at that moment, steam billowed from the fissure in the earth. The hiss of hot air surged higher, carrying hints of boiling water to come.

Portia whooped for joy.

Julia knew precisely what to expect. She'd seen it three times already this morning.

Superheated water chugged upward. Churning air whispered from beneath the earth. The frothy mass gained momentum.

White, fluffy steam engulfed the pillar of water. The shroud caught on the breeze and slowly drifted.

Olaf photographed the moment, capturing the geyser's eruption and Portia's undisguised delight. The image would be hopelessly blurred. But Portia didn't seem to care.

Boiling water and steam surged nearly one hundred feet into the air, then cascading in a clouded mist to the ground.

Portia shouted over the roar, "...consistent! Equivalent, almost...to the previous!"

Olaf's laughter blended into nature's background music.

Watching the pair, a pang of unexpected emotion slammed into Julia's chest. It caught her so off guard, breath lodged in her throat.

What was this?

Her gaze slid to Conrad. He lay motionless on his back, his hands laced on his chest, his boots crossed at the ankle. And then she knew, precisely, why tears threatened.

She missed him.

He was right there. So close, she might be able to hear the sound of his breathing, if it weren't for the geyser's booming eruption and Portia's excited chatter.

Loneliness swept through Julia. She pushed to her feet and paced into the grove of trees. She needed air. And space.

In the shade, she still felt overly warm. She pressed a palm to one heated cheek and squeezed her eyelids closed.

She had good reason to long for his company. She'd never had real friendships, the kind that flourished for all the right reasons.

Until Conrad.

His companionship had helped her ease into her new life here. The time they'd shared had been filled with invigorating conversations about inventions and machinery and the making of cheese. It didn't matter to her what topic they discussed, because it hadn't had a thing to do with her family name or position.

But most of all, she missed the way he'd made her feel. As though he saw through superficial layers: the Tyndall name, an attractive face, family money, connections. He saw the woman inside.

He'd shown her such connections were not only possible, they were rewarding. And precious.

And she'd spoiled it all.

She cringed. Again. The memory of that imprudent, senseless confession washed over her. Would the embarrassment ever fade?

Missing him so bad her chest ached, Julia turned back and allowed her gaze to travel from his boots, past his Levi's, over the chambray shirt pulled snug over his arms, to his face.

Despite the shadow cast by his hat brim over his cheeks and jaw, she caught him smiling.

She drew up short. Her lips parted.

The turkey was awake! Feigning sleep. Ignoring

her. Leaving her to chaperon the older couple. Alone.

Smiling!

How ridiculous!

She'd upset him with her foolish, impetuous comments. Fine. He'd proven his point. But did something petty like that have to spoil a perfectly good friendship?

After all, they were just words. A few little words, spoken in haste. She hadn't meant to say it. It'd just happened.

The longer she let the matter go, the worse it would become. Matters such as this were far better dealt with immediately. Years in Baltimore Society had taught her that much.

She also knew they could move past this misadventure without actually discussing it. No need to examine the details. Just move forward.

If this were a relationship worth redeeming—which of course it was, given they'd be in-laws before long—she must do something to set it aright.

She'd been the one to cause the problem, so she should be the one to make amends.

No time like the present, considering Portia and Olaf were obsessed with the geyser's waning discharge.

Julia ignored the thump of her heart against her breastbone. Avoiding the rivulets of steaming water trickling away from the geyser's mouth, Julia headed straight for Conrad.

FROM BENEATH the shade of his hat, he saw her coming.

His amusement vanished. He lay perfectly still.

Until this moment, everything had been going just like he wanted. Julia on one side of the picture-taking company, he on the other.

Her fancy high-heeled shoes came to an abrupt

halt not six inches from his shoulder. She tapped one foot beneath dark gray skirts. He caught a glimpse of lace-trimmed petticoat.

He concentrated on breathing evenly, deeply.

"Hey." She nudged his shoulder with one shoe. "I know you're awake."

"Go away. I'm sleeping." Gruff. Unaccommodating. Even a tad bit rude.

"You're a native Californian, right?"

Couldn't the woman take a hint? He didn't want to talk to her. OK, he did, but wouldn't allow himself to.

"What else is there to see around here?"

He grunted. As grouchy as he could make it.

"Interesting vegetation?" She paused, waited. Then continued, "Creepy, crawly insects, other than that disgusting banana slug?" He heard the shudder in her voice.

He fought a smile.

And remained mute.

Her hand settled upon his shoulder. Her skirts pooled against his arm. Awareness trotted up his spine.

Maybe he should've yelled at her. Scared her away. 'Cause, sure as sunrise, she was scaring him.

"Listen, Conrad. Portia's driving me insane. I can't stand this geyser, for even five more minutes. If somebody doesn't tell her what else there is to see nearby, we'll be stuck here, in this very spot, until sundown."

Conrad counted to ten. *Slowly*.

Julia sighed. With emphasis. "Maybe until sun*rise*."

This was kind of fun. He liked getting a response out of her. It meant he was doing a good job of irritating her, just like he'd planned.

So he counted to twenty.

While he recited the numbers to himself, as prolonged as could be, he overheard Portia carrying on loudly about where to set up the camera next.

Julia was right. Left to her own whims, loony Aunt

Portia would stay here until next week. Unfortunately, that trapped him right here, with Julia.

"We should pack up," she suggested, sounding unruffled. "Go for a drive toward Petrified Charlie's."

"Nah." He stretched, careful to avoid bumping her. "I'm tired. Go away and let me sleep."

Before he could fold back into a comfortable position, she knocked his hat clean off his face.

He squinted into the bright sunlight, zeroing in on Julia's face hovering directly above his.

Propping one hand on either side of his chest, she looked him directly in the eye.

Captivated—trapped!—he held her gaze. She leaned an inch or two closer, but for his traitorous body's swift response, she may as well have touched her lips to his.

Her hip pressed against his side, and he realized she'd cornered him. He couldn't lower his arms. Mustn't sit up, or he'd bump squarely into her.

Cry uncle? Not today. Not ever.

So he scowled. "Woman, I said no."

Her slow, easy smile kicked his heart into a gallop. This wasn't supposed to happen. No looking her in the eye. No personal conversation. And absolutely no physical contact.

He rolled away from her.

The arm she'd planted at his side tightened. "Not so fast, cowboy."

He hesitated. Her touch, so impersonal, and yet so incredibly intimate felt wonderful. He closed his eyes, selfishly absorbing the amazing sensation of her almost-embrace.

He could get used to this.

Dangerous. Utterly stupid. Still, it felt so incredibly good.

"You and I," she whispered, "are in this together."

"No—"

"Yes, we are. Truce."

"Nope." Over his shoulder, he glared at her.

"Oh, yes. Truce," she insisted, "or I won't let you up."

This little city woman didn't stand a chance. He could shoulder a calf without breaking a sweat. Pulling free of her would be easy.

But, did he want to?

Seconds passed.

He ran his tongue over dry lips. "Name your terms."

"Friends."

He let that sink in. What was wrong with that? Something was. But snuggled like he was, between a round hip and her forearm, he didn't want to remember.

"We're friends," she repeated, leaning closer to his ear, "and we act like it, from this second on, or I don't let you go."

"Hmmm."

"That means you have to persuade Olaf and Portia that the petrified forest is infinitely more attractive, before that geyser even thinks about spewing again."

PHILLIP LOOKED UP from a very important case file, to find Portia darkening his doorway. Two days had passed since the outing to see the geyser and petrified trees, and he hadn't so much as heard Portia's voice in that length of time.

With all of fifteen minutes remaining until he had to be back in city court, he didn't have a second to spare, even to ask after Julia. Unfortunately, Portia's two specialties were earth sciences and idle chatter—neither of which Phillip had patience for at the moment.

"Good afternoon, Mr. Macquarie." Portia entered his private office without waiting for an invitation. Her peacock-blue hat matched her wool suit impeccably. Even the overlarge peacock handbag, dripping with beads and tassels, had been dyed to match. The woman usually wore drab, plain colors and fabrics—all the better to forage through the woods. Obviously, this was an important visit.

"Afternoon." He expected Portia to get right to business, yet she merely wandered through his office, past the volumes of case law, running a gloved finger over the leather spines. She muttered exclamations.

If Phillip weren't so pressed for time, Portia's dawdling might've made him nervous. He returned his attention to the file, making hasty notations in preparation for his closing arguments.

"I'm in a bit of a quagmire." Portia took the seat opposite his desk.

He didn't look up. "Quagmire?"

"Predicament. Quandary. Plight."

"I know the meaning of the word, Miss Tyndall."

"Hmm. Well, yes. Julia's father, Jordon Tyndall..."

For the first time since making Portia's acquaintance, Phillip noted the woman's hesitancy to speak her mind. Not good. He pushed the case file back and looked Portia in the eye. "What about him?"

Phillip knew more about the illustrious United States Senator than either of the Miss Tyndalls thought he did. He prided himself on thorough research.

"While I was in the telegraph office—visiting with the operator about who I am and who Jordon is and all about Julia, he told me every grand detail about the quake of April 19—"

"*Portia.*"

"He *felt* the tremor."

Phillip glanced at the clock. He was due in court in eleven minutes. He waved his hand impatiently, trying to hurry her along.

"I'd planned, of course, to wait to send a wire to my brother, until I had specifics about Holmes and Julia—the progress of their courtship, the wedding date, all that."

Portia whipped the strings of her handbag back

and forth in a dizzying pendulum swing. "But with Holmes out of town, I didn't think it all that necessary."

"Portia," Phillip said, trying his best to quell his frustration, "I've got ten minutes to *be* in court. Can you explain to me what the problem is, in less time than that?"

Without saying a word, she pulled from her handbag two sheets of paper, each folded twice. Phillip knew that yellow paper; only George at the telegraph office used it, to transcribe messages.

"What's this?"

"Read it," Portia urged.

"Discovered your location. Very disappointed in deception."

What? Phillip stopped reading midway through, to wave the telegram at Portia. "Deception?"

Impossible. No one but The Three knew the whole truth, and Phillip trusted his friends, completely. Who had let the secret out?

"It's from my brother, Jordon."

Phillip decided to play innocent. "What's this about a deception?"

"You see, Julia left Baltimore without her father's permission."

"That's not possible. I have Julia's—" Phillip caught himself "—I have *seen* the letters she sent. She wrote to Holmes, on four occasions. They planned this for months."

"Jordon refused to allow Julia to accept Holmes's offer. But Julia hadn't told her father *exactly* where she intended to go, only that it was to California."

So *that* was the deception. Relief lasted only a second or two.

"I can't believe I'm hearing this." Phillip pushed to his feet and paced from the desk to the window to the doorway. It was one thing for The Three to keep a few secrets, and another for Julia to do so.

He wanted to demand to know why Julia would lie. This wasn't a mere misrepresentation of facts.

Proper, respectful, level-headed Miss Julia, *lie?*

He flanked back, finding Portia's posture had wilted. Her gaze crept back to his face. She offered a weak smile that lasted only a second or two before it faded.

"*Why* would Miss Julia mislead my son?"

Portia shrugged. "Oh, I wouldn't put it in such harsh terms. It's obvious she wanted to marry him, more than she wanted to pacify her parents. By the time I found out about it, she'd packed her trunks and was prepared to leave."

Stunned, Phillip realized just how much Julia had given up, in hopes of marrying Holmes—so very much more than she'd admitted to that first night when they'd talked in the library. That more than balanced out the distress he felt at learning she'd told partial truths.

And gave him ample reason to make sure Julia and Holmes were safely married. Anxiety twisted in Phillip's gut. *Where* was Holmes? If only the kid had a stronger spawning instinct, he might manage to find his way home.

"I'm compelled to confess I may have unwittingly caused further damage." Portia's voice quavered. "You see, I wrote my brother a letter the day we arrived. Just to let him know Julia and I were together. Happily touring the west. Visiting all the grand sights."

"Did you tell him where you were?" Phillip would have seen right through the ploy, had he been in Jordon's shoes.

"Not in so many words."

It didn't matter any more. From Jordon's telegram, it was evident he'd figured out precisely where Portia and Julia had gone. When Phillip read the last two lines, his stomach bottomed out.

"I don't like his threats, Portia."

"I don't think he meant it as a threat. He's coming west. There's no doubt."

"When?"

"I haven't any idea."

Phillip's last vestiges of patience dissolved, right along with his determination to keep Portia and Julia from finding out he knew all about their family situation. "Guess, then. You're his sister. When does the Senate adjourn?"

"Senate?" Portia's eyes sparked with surprise. "Julia told me you didn't know."

"That hardly matters, given this new development." Phillip growled with frustration. "*When?*"

"We'd best prepare for his eminent arrival."

Phillip crumpled the telegram and pitched it toward the wastepaper basket. If Holmes were here, if he and Julia were already well on their way to matrimony, Phillip would have a case. As it stood, he feared Julia might pack up and return home with her father—either by her own will, or at her father's insistence.

This wasn't good. It wasn't good, at all.

He had no intention of allowing something small, such as lack of parental permission, to ruin his plans.

He collapsed into his chair and scrubbed a palm over his whiskers. *Think,* he ordered himself. There had to be a solution.

"Once Jordon steps foot in Liberty, he'll ruin everything." Portia leaned forward, her expression intense. "What I must know now, Mr. Macquarie, is how you plan to ensure Julia has a wedding ring on her finger before Jordon arrives."

"Hell if I know, Miss Tyndall. Why don't you tell me?" She seemed to be full of surprises today. Perhaps she had an ace up her peacock-colored sleeve.

"I say we meet Holmes at the depot with the whole wedding party. We'll go right to the church. Or perform the ceremony right there on the platform."

"I'd love nothing more than an immediate marriage, Miss Tyndall." Unfortunately, there was the pesky detail of Holmes not knowing he was engaged to be married.

The minute Holmes showed himself, Phillip intended to turn the kid over his knee and blister his behind. How dare he cause so much trouble?

"He should be here," Portia ranted, "not off in some stuffy courtroom in San Francisco. Tell me, what could be more important than being here, with his bride?"

Excellent argument. He couldn't agree more. Perpetuating the necessary fib, he infused his words with vehemence. "This case is critical. My son takes his responsibilities very seriously."

Portia's eyes narrowed with a hefty amount of disbelief.

"My son's a fine man." Usually, at least. "Dedicated. Honorable. And he loves your niece." He *would,* given two minutes in her presence. But that was only a matter of time. "Need I say more?"

"You're biased, Mr. Macquarie. I've half a mind to withhold this from you—" she passed over the second of her two yellow telegrams "—but I, too, want nothing more than to see my niece safely married. So we're in this together."

He snatched the slip of paper.

"Glad to hear that." As Phillip scanned the two brief lines, relief nearly brought tears to his eyes. Holmes was alive! And on his way home! The news couldn't have come at a better time. Unable to contain his relief, Phillip laughed aloud.

He scanned the brief telegram once more, frustrated as hell and utterly relieved, all at the same time. His eyes stung. Heaved a sigh of relief.

"Everything's going to be fine," he told her, wiping sweat from his brow. He stuffed his hankie back into his pocket. "I feel our luck turning for the better."

"We'll need all the luck we can get." She shook her head, setting the gaudy decor of her huge hat to bobbing. "By my calculations, we may have no time at all between Holmes's and Jordon's arrivals."

Exasperated, Phillip leaned back in his chair. "We

have no proof Jordon's left Maryland."

But he intended to get proof, immediately. He called to his clerk, seated in the lobby of the law office. "Send a message to the courthouse. Tell them I'm incapacitated."

"What are you going to do?" Portia demanded.

Phillip cranked the telephone and spoke to the operator. He paused, waiting for the connection to go through. He covered the mouthpiece with his hand. "I make a fine living, persuading people to see things my way. A five minute discussion with your brother, and he'll have no doubt Holmes is the best possible match for Julia."

"Don't be so certain. Jordon's quite opinionated about the matter."

The operator came back on the line, claiming the call couldn't go through. Something about a tornado and hundreds of telephone wires down. That was to be expected during spring and summer months.

Damn, unreliable telephone companies. Never functioning when a man needed them most. He hated it when newfangled technology proved incompetent.

Phillip ignored Portia's skeptical attitude, and pulled a fresh sheet of paper from his desk drawer. "I haven't any doubt, if I spoke to Jordon in person, I could persuade him to approve of Julia's union with Holmes. But we haven't that luxury, now, have we?"

"The telegraph is operational," Portia pointed out.

"You hurry on back there and send a wire. Find out if Jordon has left home."

"So you'll know when to expect him?"

"No, so he's aware a very important letter is on its way. He should wait in Baltimore for the missive to arrive."

"Just so *you're* aware, Jordon's at least as contrary as you are."

"I've taken on worse opponents than him and won. *Every time.*" Mentally, he mapped out his strategy, then put pen to paper. "He doesn't worry me."

Portia sighed and headed for the door. "All right, I'll track down my brother's whereabouts."

"Don't give up so easily, Miss Portia. By the time Jordon Tyndall reads this persuasive argument, he'll be *glad* Julia chose my son."

Chapter Fifteen

THE MOMENT Phillip's letter to Jordon Tyndall was posted, Phillip drove Aunt Portia back to the ranch. He used the time to assess Julia's attitude and frame of mind, given all the trouble the welcome-home celebration and Holmes's failure to show had caused.

"Tell me truthfully. Do you think Julia's becoming impatient with Holmes?"

Portia, who'd chattered like a caged monkey, until this question, suddenly clammed up.

"Say it," he urged her. "Whatever it is. I need to know."

"Julia's usually a very calm, independent person. But in the past few days, she's been sullen and agitated."

Nothing Phillip hadn't noted for himself. "You think she might give up on Holmes?"

"I haven't the vaguest, because she won't talk to me. I've tried. But she's withdrawn and irritable. I'd say it's a very good thing Holmes will be home shortly."

Phillip clung to that thought, all the way back to the house.

Once there, Phillip hurried straight to Violet. He found her in her favored spot on the west porch, reclined on a chaise lounge. Sunlight warmed her beneath a green and yellow patchwork quilt.

Although the two-story veranda shaded her face from direct sunlight, Phillip had no difficulty seeing the gray caste of her skin. Her eyelids fluttered in light sleep. A thready pulse beat in her throat.

Worry for Violet's health wrenched his heart.

At least he had good news. That couldn't help but raise her spirits and make her feel better.

Phillip pulled the folded telegram from his pocket and knelt beside her lounge. He brushed a few wisps of strawberry blond hair back from her forehead. Her brilliant locks were still as handsome as the day they'd met. Few streaks of gray marked the passage of years.

Love for his wife welled within him, making his eyes mist. He didn't want to lose her. The thought of living the remainder of his years without her filled him with despair.

She wakened, met his eye and smiled. "You're home early."

The lump in his throat made it hard to speak. "I brought good news."

"Holmes?" Her eyes brightened and she moved to sit up.

"Here." He pressed the message into her hand.

She read it, her relieved smile a balm to his aching soul.

"I have such grand hopes," Violet said, letting her eyes drift shut, "for Holmes. Julia is a wonderful girl, isn't she?"

"Yes."

"I adore her. More than anything, I want to see Holmes and Julia happy together."

Phillip kissed Violet's forehead, allowing her to

drift off again. "So do I," he whispered.

How could Phillip allow another disappointment to affect her health? She'd grown markedly more frail in the past six months. She needed her children around her.

She needed Holmes nearby. With a wife—specifically, Julia.

Violet's peace of mind was reason enough for Phillip to ensure the marriage happened. In so doing, he'd ensure Holmes's long-term happiness. Julia's brave determination to marry Holmes, despite her father's objections, would be grandly rewarded.

With renewed determination, Phillip headed back to the buggy. It was past time he made sure Julia heard from her husband-to-be. A few tender words would go a long way to making sure she was in a welcoming frame of mind, when she finally did meet Holmes, face to face.

This particular letter would take a bit of doing to get just right. The combined efforts of The Three could get the job done right, in time for supper.

"OUR CENTRAL PURPOSE is to help Julia see Holmes hasn't forgotten her." Phillip walked around the pastor's kitchen table. The square room smelled of cinnamon and sugar from Mrs. Proctor's baking. A comfortable, soothing scent that bolstered his flagging energy.

"In my experience," John interjected, "in the ministry and as a husband, women crave reassurance."

"The Three are kings among men, when it comes to reassurance, are we not?" Phillip asked.

"Kings," Luke agreed.

"So, how does this sound?" Phillip read his prized, poetic efforts. "My lonely heart pines for you. How I'll ever bear one more week of separation, I cannot say."

Luke laughed. "It's a good thing you asked us for

help. Your silly letter doesn't sound like the Holmes she knows."

"Thanks, friend."

Unperturbed, Luke went on, "You wrote the other letters. You can say those things and still sound like the same man who sent for her."

"It's a work in progress. And I'm trying to sound romantic." Phillip grabbed another of Mrs. Proctor's applesauce cookies from the plate on the table. "What do you remember about romance, anyway? You're an old fart who doesn't ever go courting."

Luke raised his white brows at John, with an expression that asked *do you believe this?* "Did you forget *my* success? Because of my wisdom, as a direct result of my guidance, Garth is a happily married man." His wide grin was full of glee. "Did I tell you Mitzi's with child?"

"Only a dozen times," John said evenly. "Oh, here's a good one. Ready?"

Phillip put the pen to paper, expectantly.

"I apologize, my dear, for keeping you waiting." John sat back, a huge grin on his too-handsome face. "That'll work wonders. Women love apologies."

Phillip nodded, scribbling the sentiment. "Then what?"

"My delay couldn't be helped," Luke suggested. "Of course, I won't give any reasons, and I haven't the courage to return home. So you'll never lay eyes on my handsome visage."

Phillip cast Luke a warning glance.

"Don't look at me like that." Luke brightened. "Hey, try this. I've waited so long to finally meet you, that one more week feels like a century."

"No," John said, "Let's get away from emphasizing how long it will be until they meet. We need to concentrate on the positives."

"Give me some positives," Phillip complained, "in specific terms I can put right on the paper."

"Compliments," John supplied. "Can't get more

positive than that. And women adore compliments."

"Such as?" Phillip freshened his pen.

"Such as," John gestured vaguely with one hand. "I admire your photograph daily. Your beauty sustains me through...my trying days?"

Luke chuckled. "That'll bring her to her knees."

"Hey, now. No need for sarcasm." John tried again. "Pop told me you're as beautiful as your portrait."

"Hey, that's good—no, it won't work. She'll think I've been in touch with Holmes, without telling her. No sense undermining the good work we're doing here." Phillip scratched through the phrase. "What else?"

Luke pressed a palm to his chest, as if pining for a long-lost love. "I eagerly await the day when we meet, face to face. I've thought of little else than the questions I want to ask. My heart desires to know everything about you."

"Nice," John said with his mouth full of cookie. "Women like to talk about themselves."

"That is nice." Phillip raised a brow, speaking to Luke. "Maybe you do know what's romantic."

"Indeed, I do. I'm an expert."

"More compliments," John suggested.

"Compliments, compliments," Phillip muttered. "That's going to be tricky. If we list specifics about her stay, like her graciousness or the party she planned, that *will* implicate me."

"That is a problem," John said. "So compliment her patience. Not just any woman would've stayed, waiting for him. Word it so he hopes the letter finds her still at the ranch, and he prays she'll be waiting for him when he returns from this harrowing business trip."

"That'll work." Phillip took down the idea, phrasing it in words Holmes would've used. "What else?"

"Mention their happy life together." John took another cookie and broke it in half. "Women love to plan for the future."

"I know we'll be happy together," Phillip said

aloud as he wrote the words, "we have many good years ahead of us."

Luke shook his head. "Word it like this. I can't wait to get home, to begin our lives together. I know you and I will find much happiness."

"That works for me." Phillip scribbled it down, lined through the extra stuff, and drew arrows to rearrange the sentence order.

He read the completed project aloud—pathetically short, considering it had taken them close to an hour to craft—and watched Luke and John's faces expectantly. "Well? Will this convince Julia to patiently wait for Holmes?"

Luke pulled a face. "It wouldn't convince melted chocolate to stick to a toddler's face."

"Thanks for the vote of confidence." Phillip dropped into his seat at the table. Doubt settled over him. An unfamiliar, most unpleasant sensation. He was accustomed to his wagers paying off, and paying off big.

Life held no reward for losers. Winning was the only option.

"It's all in the presentation." John took three glasses from the cabinet and brought out a quart of milk. "Pretty paper. The delivery matters, too. Roses. Chocolates. Women adore chocolates."

"Chocolates are good," Luke agreed. He fished a licorice whip out of his flannel shirt pocket.

"Write it down, very carefully," John suggested. "Then leave it on her bed with the flowers and candy. When she asks how the letter got there, tell her a romantic story about how Holmes sent it on the train with someone from town, and they were delivered while she was out."

"Oh, good idea." Phillip snapped his fingers. "Someone who was in San Francisco with him was coming home. A research assistant."

"Yep, that'll do." Luke leaned forward, his eyes shining with merriment. "And said research assistant stopped by Cadence Chocolatier for the finest box, and flowers too, at Holmes's express instructions."

"Absolutely." Phillip grinned, pleased with the plan. He'd shop for flowers, chocolates, and pretty paper on his way home. "This will work, my friends."

John clapped Phillip on the shoulder. "I certainly hope it does, because as of this morning, my Andrew is *miles* ahead in this race."

"Nice try, Preacher." Phillip gathered his papers and put his pen away. "You don't frighten me."

"I'm not trying to frighten anybody. I'm just reminding you of our wager. You'll be interested to know Andrew went on a shopping excursion this morning."

"What's he buying?" Luke asked, a huge grin on his face. "A gift for Lillian? Women like gifts. You said so yourself."

"Indeed they do, and Lillian's going to adore this one," John said, a smug expression on his face. "He went shopping for an engagement ring."

"An engagement ring!" Luke whispered.

"Like I said, I'm about to win this wager."

"Oh, no you won't," Phillip insisted.

"Your love letter may be flowery and full of romance," John argued, "but it won't get an engagement ring on Julia's finger."

"Buy her one." Luke smirked. "I bought my daughter-in-law's ring. It worked wonders."

"Ah, ah. No cheating." John said, most insistent. "Holmes has got to buy his own ring."

"I'm not even a tad nervous." Phillip gathered up his coat and papers. "Later on I'll give you two a full report of Julia's reaction. No doubt, she'll be planning the wedding by this evening."

John nibbled another cookie. "You keep telling yourself that. But I'm the one who'll be hearing wedding bells real soon. You don't know how much time you've got, now, do you?"

Luke chuckled.

"As a matter of fact, I do. The boy sent a telegram,

just today."

"I heard about that," muttered Luke. "And about Julia's father, too. Word is he may arrive any time now."

"And when he shows," Phillip told them both, "I'm determined he'll see a happy couple, so enamored with each other, even *he* won't consider separating them. So if this party's over, I've got flowers and chocolates to buy."

John and Luke wished him luck, but Phillip felt far from lucky. A sinking feeling tugged on his stomach, all the way to the shops. A sense of helplessness made him suspect Jordon would do something rash.

Portia was exactly right. Phillip had to get a ring on Julia's finger—and the sooner, the better.

KATHERINE DROVE the buggy up the lane toward home. "It's too late to change my mind, isn't it?"

"Pardon me?" Until that very moment, Julia had been listening to Katherine's happy chatter. Wedding dress styles. Fabrics. Lace and cording and beads.

"I know I said I was certain. Told everyone to go ahead with it"—Katherine blanched—"but now I'm thinking I've made a mistake. A very serious mistake."

Mercy, me. Julia touched Katherine's arm. If she'd changed her mind about marrying David, then she'd best make her wishes known. "This is a critical decision. One only you can make." One that would impact the entire balance of her life.

"I know," Katherine wailed.

Julia's heart twisted. She couldn't bear hearing Katherine in such misery. But what could she do?

Seconds passed. Katherine eased the team to a stop near the barn. She dropped her chin to her chest and squeezed her eyes shut. "One minute, I *was* sure. Now, the more I picture myself in that dress, I just can't do it."

Julia offered Katherine her fresh handkerchief. She imagined Katherine's first fitting for her wedding gown had sparked many emotions; anticipation, happiness, love for her intended. She simply hadn't expected a change of heart to be among them.

Katherine took the neatly folded hankie and dried her cheeks. "You think I'm horrible, don't you?"

"No, no. Not at all." She placed a comforting hand on Katherine's arm. "I'm glad you speak up for yourself."

"I know it's too late to change my mind. The plans are made. Pop's already *paid,* and this is going to upset—" Katherine gasped, wailed, "Oh, no. Here he comes."

Julia glanced toward the house. Phillip Macquarie approached, a welcoming grin on his bearded face.

"Oh, no," Julia repeated. Now?

Katherine was tangled in a painful, emotional decision. This wasn't the time for an interruption by her father. He wouldn't hear her out. Based on the argument Julia had overheard between Conrad and their father, related to the ranch, she knew Phillip Macquarie would inform Katherine of her feelings, and what she would do about them.

"There you are!" Macquarie called. "You've missed quite a bit of excitement this afternoon."

"I can't talk to him," Katherine whispered, blotting her eyes. She pressed back into the seat, to better hide behind Julia. "He'll take one look at me, and he'll *know*. He already detests David, and—"

What had David done to Katherine? She'd been happy at the dress shop, less than an hour ago. Had he said something that belatedly caused her to rethink her commitment to him? Was it bad enough to provoke her to cancel the wedding?

Phillip placed both hands on the buggy's armrest. His eyes twinkled. Julia hadn't ever seen him this happy.

She glanced toward the house. Her stomach did

an odd little flip. Was Holmes home? *Now?*

She felt shaky. Caught off guard. Unprepared.

Julia felt herself torn in at least two directions. Katherine needed her. She quickly scanned the windows, the porch, the doorway. No sign of Holmes.

"Excitement?" she asked Katherine's father.

"Yes, yes! Come right on inside, ladies."

Katherine sniffed.

"Might you give us a moment, please?" Julia offered an apologetic smile. "Katherine and I were—"

Phillip took Julia's hand, to help her down. "You'll be so surprised! Katherine, too."

If he noticed his daughter's distress, he gave no indication.

But Julia noticed. Katherine seemed to wilt on the buggy seat, and a soft, pained sigh escaped her lips.

Julia couldn't be two places at once. Katherine had chosen to confide in Julia, rather than her mother, or Alberta, or one of her girlfriends. Julia recognized and accepted what she must do.

If Holmes were waiting inside, he could wait a few more minutes.

"Mr. Macquarie."

"Hmm?" He met her gaze, confusion registering in his eyes.

"Would you be so kind as to wait in the house for us, for a few minutes? We'll be right along."

He blinked. Drew his brows together. Leaned to the right, in order to better see his daughter's face.

In her peripheral vision, Julia saw Katherine turn away.

Phillip Macquarie shoved out a sigh. "I suppose it can wait a few more minutes." Disappointment colored his tone. "You two will hurry right inside?"

Julia nodded.

As soon as her father had reached the porch steps, Katherine whispered, "We may as well go on in. He'll only hover and watch us through the windows until we do."

Evidently, Katherine had changed her mind. The conversation was over.

"Katherine. Listen." Julia waited a moment, gathering her thoughts. This young woman had become more than a sister; Julia felt strong ties of friendship, too. "Your family loves you. They'll understand."

"Not Pop. You know how he is."

"I do. And I know he wants you to be happy." If thoughts of marriage to David Orme made her that miserable—

She laughed harshly. "Happy. Right."

Julia didn't want to contradict Katherine's feelings, so she remained quiet.

Katherine set the brake and climbed down. "Let's go see what this surprise is all about." She sounded forlorn. Disappointed.

But as they walked toward the house, Katherine linked her arm through Julia's. The familiar gesture, so prevalent within Julia's own predominately female household, brought reassurance.

They climbed the stairs. Katherine paused, lowered her voice. "When we're through here, will you go back into town with me?"

Julia nodded, concerned with Katherine's hesitancy. Did she want to confront David? Did she simply need to get away from home for awhile?

Inside, Phillip met them in the hallway. The house smelled wonderful; freshly baked bread, roasting meat, potatoes, sweet fruit pie. Julia's stomach rumbled.

Phillip's whole face lit up with excitement. "Guess what was delivered while you were out?"

Julia blinked. Glanced at Katherine. Back to Macquarie. He awaited her response. She hadn't any idea. "Word from Holmes?"

"Yes!" He ushered both women to the staircase. "A most welcome telegram, telling us he'll be home on the afternoon train, day after tomorrow."

Relief washed through Julia. Finally! "That's wonderful news."

"*And,*" Macquarie emphasized, clearly ecstatic about more to come, "he sent you something special."

On the second floor, they paused outside the guest room door. It was open a few inches. Julia caught the delicate fragrance of flowers.

Macquarie pushed the door open. A *lot* of flowers. A huge bouquet, beautifully arranged in a large vase, stood on a circular table beside the bedstead. In the center of the mattress, a pale green candy box—so big, it must weigh ten pounds—propped up a pastel blue stationery envelope.

Familiar handwriting scrawled Julia's name across the front.

Holmes.

Her heart skipped a beat.

"Go on," Macquarie urged. "Read it. He sent it by private messenger, not an hour ago. I'd ask you to read me every word—" he cleared his throat "—but that's not any of my business, now is it?"

His business or not, he didn't budge. He stood with his hands behind his back, a huge grin on his face, watching everything.

Julia didn't know what to do first. Holmes's letter could wait. It'd still be there later on. But poor Katherine needed support now. And companionship back into town. Julia feared if she let the opportunity pass, it may not come again.

Phillip blinked. "Oh, pardon me." He headed for the door. "I should leave you to your privacy."

He cast Katherine a meaningful glance, *let's go,* but Katherine pretended not to notice.

"Have a seat," Julia suggested to Katherine, as her father shut the door behind himself.

Katherine took the chair near the dressing screen. Julia waited for Katherine to pick up the threads of conversation, if she so chose.

Julia smelled the blossoms, admired their beauty, and smiled to herself. Holmes would be home in two days! The certainty of it warmed her clear through. She set his letter aside—she'd read it when she had a moment to herself—and lifted the candy box lid.

Julia's hunger flared. Her tummy grumbled. Her mouth watered.

And oddly, an image of Conrad, sipping sarsaparilla, and wolfing down perfect squares of nutty fudge leapt to Julia's mind. And right along with it, came the remembrance of her suspicions that Conrad had felt something for her.

In wake of that thought, her insides tingled.

Shame on her, thinking about Conrad, when Holmes had just sent her this very thoughtful gift of candies and flowers and probably a love note. Proper courting gifts. From the man who would be her husband.

Pushing thoughts of Conrad aside, she selected a nougat-filled milk chocolate and offered the box to Katherine.

Abandoning her chair, Katherine chose a piece, then sat on the edge of the bed. She ate in silence. "That's delicious." She peered at the pale pink nougat inside. "This must be a new kind."

Julia finished her coconut crème. "Hmm."

"I know you want to read your letter," Katherine mentioned, a plaintive note in her small voice, "but I just keep seeing Miss Worth and her seamstresses sewing madly on a dress I'm never going to wear."

"My letter can wait." Julia tucked the precious, unopened envelope from Holmes, into the top drawer in her dresser. "I'm happy to go with you."

"I really should let her know. Immediately."

"I understand." It seemed odd Katherine would show concern for the seamstress's work, given her whole future was shifting, changing forever. "And I certainly don't mind."

"Thank you." Katherine's step seemed a little to quick, a little too bright, as they headed back out to the rig.

"Where are you going?" Phillip appeared in the

kitchen doorway, a brandy sniffer in his hand. "Is there a problem?"

"Ah," Katherine began, then cleared her throat. "I've forgotten something quite important at the dressmaker."

Phillip turned to Julia, his expression reflecting impatience that she'd leave, so soon after receiving Holmes's gifts. Apparently, he wanted her to fawn over his offerings. Squeal and fan her face and spend all afternoon rereading his love letter and getting fat on chocolates.

Macquarie took a step closer. "You enjoyed what Holmes had to say? You anticipate his arrival with fondness?"

"Oh, yes. Everything is just as it should be," Julia assured him, even as Conrad's face popped into her mind. Again.

Conrad, in the soda fountain, unsure and tormented.

Conrad's unease, as she'd offered a truce that afternoon beside the geyser.

"Anything you can share with his old man?" Macquarie wanted details. And reassurance. Julia could see that much.

She thought of the letter, tucked safely in the bureau drawer. Perhaps it was best to let him believe it was too private, rather than admit she hadn't put Holmes first. "A very sweet love note. Very dear to my heart. And quite private."

His grin broadened. He sipped brandy. Saluted Julia with his crystal snifter. "Glad to hear it."

"Well said. Now, come on," Katherine urged, tugging Julia behind, and out to the buggy.

"What will the dressmaker do with my wedding gown?" Katherine asked a few minutes later. She flicked the reins and urged the matched pair of Saddlebreds into a smooth canter. "It's not even finished."

"You've already paid for it. I imagine that's up to you."

"Well, I don't care what becomes of it. I think I'll ask her to try to sell it to someone else." No trace of bitterness in Katherine's tone, contrary to Julia's expectations.

"That's a fine idea." Julia hoped Katherine wouldn't attend one of her friend's weddings, only to find the bride in the gown Katherine had planned to wear for David Orme.

"I'm going to order the silk. Oh, yes," Katherine emphasized, her spirits rising almost instantly. "The silk. That choice feels ever so much better."

Julia didn't understand. Had she missed something? "Silk?"

Katherine turned to Julia, meeting her eye. "The ivory silk Miss Worth showed us. That's the one I want."

Comprehension swept through Julia, bringing welcome relief. All along, she'd been sure Katherine's heart was breaking over a ruined romance with David. Julia tried to hide her surprise, but soft laughter escaped her lips.

"What?" Katherine asked.

"Nothing." Julia bit her lip. But kept smiling. David and Katherine would be just fine. And Holmes would be home, in less than two days' time. Everything would be absolutely right with the world again.

"*What?*"

"You want a different wedding dress."

Katherine nodded, turned. "What did you think I meant?"

Chapter Sixteen

THE MOMENT Phillip caught sight of Holmes stepping off the train, he forgave everything. He no longer minded that Holmes had caused a tremendous amount of grief.

He was home.

Warm, welcome relief flooded Phillip, washing away years of anxiety. Holmes, back in Liberty. To stay.

He'd see to that.

His firstborn looked happy and healthy. Violet would be thrilled to see him, as would the rest of the family. Especially Miss Julia.

After careful deliberation, he'd decided the direct, full-disclosure route to be the safest. It was a delicate situation, one that required diplomacy. Knowing Holmes as he did, he expected a protest.

From day one, Holmes had made it a habit to refuse anything Phillip suggested. The kid had fought him tooth and nail about everything from serious matters such as his education to piddly nonsense like whether or not brown cows gave chocolate milk. Holmes, a Macquarie through and through, argued simply for argument's sake.

Holmes had never shied away from confrontation—a hallmark of an excellent attorney. He admired that characteristic in his son.

Hence the plan to broach the subject in a public setting. Holmes wouldn't argue, much, if they had an audience.

Again, he checked Julia's letters, safely tucked into his coat pocket. First, he'd introduce Holmes to Julia on paper, then in person.

Phillip shook Holmes's hand, then caught him in a back-pounding hug. Emotion clogged his throat. "Welcome home, son."

"Thanks, Pop. Glad to be home."

Exactly what he needed to hear. "Good to have you back." He walked with Holmes across the platform and toward the street. Holmes's trunks could wait. "Hungry?"

"Starved."

"The Goldmine?"

"Sounds good."

A thick, juicy steak would satisfy the appetite. A bottle of wine would soothe them both. They'd have some pleasant conversation and talk about the news in town. By the time they had dessert, Phillip would have Holmes prepared to hear about Julia.

Phillip drove the buggy the six blocks to the restaurant. Once they were seated in a quiet corner, Holmes relaxed visibly. He seemed tired, but genuinely pleased to be back in Liberty. He'd already mentioned the law office, twice. A very good sign.

This late in the afternoon, only three other tables were occupied. The dining room smelled heavenly of quality beef, baking potatoes, and fresh bread.

The red gingham tablecloths and padded seat

covers were a new touch, but the delightfully rich Monterey Jack cheese biscuits were the same. The hot, buttery bread fairly melted in Phillip's mouth.

While they waited for their meals, Phillip filled their wine glasses. "You heard about Doc Tibbs's heart attack?"

"How's he getting along?"

"He'll live. I heard the new doc's on his way up from San Francisco." Phillip sipped the velvety smooth red wine. "Delicious."

"Firm tannis," Holmes added.

"You won't find this excellence anywhere else on earth." Ah, there was no place like home.

He made a mental note to order several cases from the local winery for Holmes's wedding reception.

Holmes set down his goblet. "Gabriel will switch over to the new doc?"

"We're hoping so." No guarantees, yet. But Phillip wasn't above paying the new doctor handsomely to continue Gabriel's training right here in Liberty. But that was a worry he'd have to dwell on later, once he got Holmes safely settled.

When their food arrived, Holmes dug into his thick steak—The Goldmine specialty—and ate with single-minded attention. Phillip admired that trait in his son. They said little until the waiter took away their dishes.

The boy's exhaustion showed in his lack of conversation. By the slump of his shoulders and dark smudges beneath his eyes, it was evident the kid was worn out. Final exams at the conclusion of his last, demanding year at school. A cross-country journey. Far too many miles stretched between here and Boston.

Over coffee and generous slices of carrot cake, Phillip decided the time was right to introduce Holmes to his bride. He withdrew Julia's four letters and passed them to his son. His pulse kicked up a notch.

"What's this?" Holmes leafed through the envelopes, noting the broken seals. "These are addressed to me. At Harvard."

"Indeed, they are." Phillip couldn't resist smiling. Holmes would be pleased with Julia. The darling girl had presented herself very well in the letters.

Full of anticipation, he palmed his beard and leaned back in his chair. "Read them."

Holmes read the first, but only a few paragraphs. He paused to examine the photograph of Miss Julia Tyndall. After several seconds passed, he looked up from the likeness. "What have you done?"

The boy didn't sound testy. Just baffled. "Read the rest," Phillip urged. "She has quite a lot to recommend her. Daughter of a United States Senator."

"I know that." Holmes scanned the rest of the letter, then the newspaper column Julia had sent, detailing a reception she'd hosted, in honor of her parents' wedding anniversary. "But the question is, why do you?"

Sharp kid. Nowhere in Julia's letters, or in this one newspaper clipping, was her father's profession ever mentioned. Phillip had found that quite odd. "You know who Senator Jordon Tyndall is?"

"Why wouldn't I? He's one of Harvard's most distinguished graduates."

This was fantastic news! Phillip could hardly contain himself, but he forced himself to give Holmes time to peruse Julia's photograph. After a moment, Holmes refolded the papers and tucked them back into the envelope.

Phillip watched his son's expression closely, with much anticipation, and an equal dose of trepidation. He didn't seem duly impressed with the ideal Miss Julia, or her father.

Any moment, he expected Holmes, being Holmes, would have plenty to say on the matter.

Holmes wasn't the kind to simply accept an opportunity, especially one like this, without rebuttal. Phillip's other sons might believe great and wonderful things just happened, like manna from heaven, but not

Holmes.

He waited for Holmes to rebel.

And waited.

Holmes seemed to consider the situation, likely preparing a defense. A little slow on the draw, but he'd learn, given time and experience.

Phillip turned the wine goblet stem between his fingers.

No resistance, whatsoever?

This seemed a very good omen, indeed.

It was all he could do to allow Holmes time to properly read the second letter. Patience, he urged himself.

Holmes set aside the second letter, met Phillip's gaze and held it, revealing very little.

Made a father proud, to notice his son had confidence. That particular ability would serve him well in the courtroom. And when meeting with new clients. As well as established clients who expected the mature counsel Phillip had always provided.

Seconds passed. Across the restaurant dining room, the door opened and a couple left. A warm breeze wafted across the floor. A quick glance assured Phillip there were still plenty of people in the restaurant—at least four—to encourage Holmes to limit the volume of the impending argument.

If there would be an argument.

A somewhat sad smile—due completely to his exhaustion, no doubt—crept up Holmes's handsome face.

Ah ha! Recognized the magnitude of his good fortune, did he? That was more like it!

Come on, son. Thank me, and let's go home and meet your bride. Phillip leaned back, grinning like the happy Pop he was.

Holmes chuckled. It seemed the good food had worked some magic, breathing life back into Holmes's travel-weary bones.

"I've met Senator Tyndall," Holmes said.

Surely he'd misunderstood. "You've *met* him?"

"He gave a series at lectures at Harvard. His alma mater."

Why hadn't Kinsley told him this? His old classmate, now teaching at Harvard, had been Phillip's eyes and ears while Holmes was there. Nabbed Julia's letters, sent them on to Phillip. Posted letters Phillip wrote from Boston, to Baltimore. Had Kinsley not known Miss Julia was the senator's daughter?

"Did you speak to the senator?" Phillip demanded. Was this why Jordon Tyndall had been so against Julia's journey west and her impending marriage to Holmes? "What did you say to him?"

A dozen unseemly possibilities raced through Phillip's mind.

"I met him at a reception. I doubt he'd remember me."

Phillip eased back against his chair, pressed a hand over his heart, and willed it to slow. He held Holmes's gaze for a long moment. "Did he mention his daughter to you?"

"No."

"Are you certain?"

Irritation marred Holmes's features. "Don't know, Pop. Relatively certain."

"When, exactly was this?" Before or after Julia asked her father's permission to travel to California?

Holmes cast his gaze upward, apparently considering the question. He huffed out a breath. "Early in the year. February, I believe. Perhaps the first week or two of March."

Perspiration dampened Phillip's brow. He blotted his forehead, then stuffed his handkerchief back into his pocket. Chances were Tyndall hadn't even known he'd met Julia's intended husband. Besides, it didn't matter. All that mattered now was moving forward with the plan.

"Why does this matter?" Holmes asked, showing mild concern.

Oh, it mattered, all right. Tyndall was on his way. Holmes would have to meet his father-in-law-to-be once more. And he simply must make a favorable impression.

But first things first. "I'm glad to hear you've met Miss Tyndall's father. Good for you. Now how about you read the other letters? She's a charming lady."

With an expression of mild amusement, Holmes forked up another bite of cake. He chewed, swallowed, and licked the rich cream cheese frosting off the tines. "I know what you did to Garth Wakefield. Everything from the plot to the paper marriage. Is that what you did?" He indicated Julia's letters.

"Paper marriage?" Phillip brushed the suggestion away. "Of course not. I wouldn't presume to make that final determination on your behalf."

"Not with Judge Morley watching your every move." Holmes was sharp; a chip off the old block.

"Yes, he is." Although disgruntled, Phillip saw no sense denying it. He had no secrets from his son.

"I thought so. Just to clarify, there is no paper marriage, no proxy marriage, nor marriage of any kind."

"Not yet."

"I see your confidence hasn't waned in my absence."

"Of course not. I merely sorted through the applicants—"

"Applicants?" Holmes asked.

"I sent out newspaper advertisements."

"Miss Tyndall did mention it, I recall," tapping the first letter. "Go on." A hint of a smile played over Holmes's mouth. It seemed he knew a lucky strike when he saw one.

"I know the demands of Harvard Law. You hardly had time to sleep, much less pursue a social life."

Holmes nodded as he swallowed a bite of carrot cake. "You've given this a great deal of thought."

"I have. Out of concern for your happiness." He'd had months to think things through, to prepare this most important opening argument. "I couldn't expect you to make time for young ladies, given the rigors of your education. You've the time, now, for pursuing other interests."

"Such as a wife."

"Exactly." Father and son thought alike. Could almost read each others' minds. They'd make a fine team, defending the law, side by side.

"And family," Holmes added.

"Absolutely. You're ready for that stage of life." And ready to settle down. In Liberty. But Phillip saw little sense in pushing the issue, just yet. He'd hand-picked Julia to do that for him.

"Yes, I thought I was."

"Was?" Oh, no. That didn't sound so good. Doubt edged in, pushing aside Phillip's sense of well-being. "What does that mean? Julia's precisely the type of young woman you would've chosen for yourself, if you'd had the time."

Holmes drained his coffee and accepted a refill from the waiter. He stirred sugar and cream into the dark brew as if his thoughts were centered squarely on unfaithful Miss Daphne Browning, that ill-mannered, low-bred, conniving tart.

That would *never* do. Miss Browning was absolutely not the right kind of woman for Holmes. He deserved honesty. Integrity. Virtue.

This issue, if swept under the rug, could spell disaster for Holmes's future with Miss Julia. No matter how distasteful, it had to be dealt with.

"I assume you had the misfortune," Phillip said, choosing his words with care, "to hear of Miss Browning's unfavorable choice."

At this, Holmes looked up. "Unfavorable? Why?"

"Because she'd given you her word—"

Holmes waved that away, "Is her husband mistreating her?"

That drew Phillip up short. He didn't know if Daphne was happy, and he didn't care. He also had no intention of giving Holmes the idea Daphne wanted to be freed from her hapless union. "All I care about, son, is *your* well-being."

Holmes considered this for a moment. He nodded, smiling sadly. "This is why you did it."

"Sent for Miss Julia? Yes. Absolutely. You deserve better than that Miss Browning."

"Mrs. Clark," Holmes corrected.

"I don't care what name she goes by, she would have made you unhappy. You know that don't you?"

"I do."

He must keep Holmes focused on the here and now. "But on the other hand, Miss Julia is an amazing woman. True. Honest. Endowed with integrity and virtue. With her, marriage is guaranteed a happily-ever-after."

"Hmm?" Holmes's attention drifted back to Phillip and the topic at hand.

It must be somewhat of a shock for Holmes to return from his ordeal in the east, obviously still reeling from Miss Browning's unfaithfulness, to find a bride waiting for him. And not just any bride. An ideal, well-suited, intelligent and educated, society-bred beauty.

Holmes's attention seemed dangerously far away. "No one in Boston makes carrot cake to rival The Goldmine's. You know that?"

"Yeah, I do. Everything tastes better here. I bet you haven't had a decent meal since you were last home."

Holmes shrugged, listlessly looking through Julia's letters, lying on the tabletop beside his empty dessert plate.

A bell tinkled as another group of patrons entered the restaurant. On the opposite side of the room, a lady laughed at something her companion had said.

But Holmes ignored all that and picked up the last two letters.

Phillip was pleased Holmes seemed to read them with attention to detail.

The wait gave Phillip plenty of time to collect his thoughts and prepare for Holmes's counter attack. It would come, eventually. He found the challenge invigorating.

Still, Holmes kept reading. By the time he'd finished the fourth letter, he seemed resigned.

Resigned wasn't exactly what Phillip had been going for. Where was the anticipation? The excitement? The gratitude?

"From this last letter," Holmes said, "I gather two interesting bits of information."

Phillip waited.

"One, she sent letters to me, in Boston, that you have in your possession. Interesting, given they're addressed to me, and I never saw them."

"I have friends."

Holmes raised a brow.

There was no sense withholding information at this point. "Kinsley's an old school chum."

"Ah." Holmes nodded. "Never once let it slip."

"I knew I could count on him."

"And he posted your letters to Miss Tyndall."

"Right."

"Which brings us to my second point." Holmes indicated Julia's last letter. "From this, I suspect she's already arrived."

"She has." Too full to eat another bite, Phillip pushed his dessert plate away and took one last sip of coffee. "She's been anxiously awaiting your arrival for more than two weeks."

"Most unfortunate."

"Oh, she doesn't mind. Not at all. She's anxious to meet you," he grinned, remembering all the reassuring conversations he'd had with Miss Julia, "especially after the candy, flowers, and nice letter you sent her from San Francisco a couple days ago."

"I did?"

"Yes, sir. And you should've seen—"

"I was in San Francisco?"

Phillip nodded, and finished his train of thought. "—the excitement. The ladies have a grand welcome home party all planned for you."

"No, Pop, I—"

Phillip leaned forward, anxious to impart all the good news. "Guests. A big supper. I've ordered wines and—"

"You didn't."

"Of course I did. This is a happy occasion! I see no reason to spare any expense, any effort. We couldn't be happier you're finally back with us."

Holmes drew in a deep breath, let it go slowly, and shrugged.

That was it? A shrug?

Phillip searched Holmes's face, but got nothing more. He may not be snatching up his coat and running for the buggy, but he hadn't flat-out refused to meet Julia, either. This, at least, was something Phillip could work with.

Perhaps he ought to be glad Holmes was too worn out to argue. He couldn't delay much longer. The women were waiting at home, expecting them. "Are you ready to meet Miss Julia?"

Holmes seemed to mull that over, for the space of a few seconds. "We must get our stories straight first. It's clear you wrote to her. I'd best know what *I* said. I'd hate to come across as forgetful."

"Indeed." Yes! Holmes, cooperating. Holmes, eager to meet Julia. "Oh, I knew you'd be thrilled with her, son. This is all going to work out so well. You'll see."

"Pop, listen. She seems like a nice girl, but I—"

"She is!"

Holmes remained quiet for the space of several seconds.

Phillip bit his tongue, rather than interrupt. He wanted to sing Julia's praises. He wanted to regale her accomplishments and assure Holmes of her sweet temperament. But he made himself wait for Holmes to continue.

After another long moment, Holmes finally said, "I don't see any reason for her to get hurt."

"No, of course I—"

Holmes gestured for Phillip to wait. "Like you said, she seems to be a good match, the kind I *might* have chosen for myself."

Smart boy. It seemed Harvard had given Holmes perspective. "Indeed, she is. I knew that all along. That's why I chose her."

"She has no idea, does she?"

A twinge of conscience poked at Phillip, but he shoved it aside. "None. But I had the best of intentions. I only signed your name to those letters to speed along the process. Now, I know you may not like that I signed your name—"

"I think it best we don't tell her all that, up front."

"My thoughts, *exactly*." They did think alike, didn't they?

"So what did you tell her?"

Leaning a bit closer, Phillip confided all the details he'd sent to Julia.

Holmes listened carefully, nodding at intervals. No big smiles, no shouts of joy, but all that would come soon enough.

"I gather you didn't officially offer marriage."

"Son, I assure you, no. But you know how women are." Stark recollection of how much Miss Julia had forfeited in order to come west, in order to marry Holmes, rushed to the forefront. It was only right he let Holmes in on that detail. Particularly so, given the immanent arrival of her father. So in painstaking detail, Phillip recounted all he'd learned from Julia that first night, peppering it with Portia's disclosure of Jordon Tyndall's displeasure with Julia's trek west.

Holmes took the news with aplomb. Maturity. Decorum. With Miss Julia's acceptance of a forthcoming proposal a sure thing, Phillip would've expected a bit more enthusiasm.

But he wasn't worried.

Once Holmes met Miss Julia in person, nature would take its course. These two young people were a match made in heaven.

"Are you ready to meet her?" Phillip tossed money onto the table.

"No time like the present."

Chapter Seventeen

"READY TO MEET your groom?" Aunt Portia fairly bubbled over with enthusiasm. She hadn't been able to sit still, or stop talking, for the past thirty minutes. She'd fussed over Julia's hair, and dusky purple suit, forcing her to make Holmes wait a customary half hour.

Portia shook out a wrinkle in Julia's skirt and gave the rest of the matching ensemble a quick check. She pushed up on her toes to rearrange the angle of a curl by Julia's ear.

Julia had indulged her aunt in this ritual. But she couldn't help smiling at Portia's complete lack of concern with her own appearance. Her charcoal-colored wool dress needed a hot iron. Portia, in all her attention on Julia's clothing, hadn't noticed.

"I'm ready." Julia came up with a smile, and prayed it looked sincere.

"Now, remember," Portia counseled, "you were half in love with Holmes, merely from reading his letters. For *him,* you were ready to give up everything—" she ticked the items off on her fingers "—your parents and their esteem, the familiarity and comfort of your childhood home, your inheritance, a comfortable future as a governor's wife. For what? All for a chance to find marital happiness with a man of your own choosing."

"None of those desires have faded." If anything, they'd doubled in intensity.

Why did Portia doubt that?

"I'm glad to hear it."

"Well, it's true." She felt as though Portia needed convincing. Had something happened, to make Portia fear things wouldn't work out?

"Starch and steel, Dolly." Portia's voice rose with fervor. "This is the time to remember those tender affections, the very emotions that convinced you to emancipate yourself from your father's delusions of matrimony to that rising politician. The adoration that caused you to accept Holmes's proposal."

What had gotten into Portia? "I remember. Clearly."

Portia grinned. "The time has come to give every ounce of effort to secure the future *you* chose."

"Yes, of course. Portia, why the pep talk? You act as though you expect—"

"One never knows when things will run amok. When unexpected, uh, things, people, what have you, will present themselves and muddy the waters."

"What are you worried about? What has happened?"

Portia averted her gaze. "Nothing. Nothing at all."

"Yes, it has. Tell me."

Portia signaled the end of the conversation by marching to the door. "We've kept Holmes waiting long enough. Shall we?"

Julia kissed her aunt's powdered cheek and hugged her quickly. "Holmes and I are going to be fine.

His last letter satisfied me. Would reading it make you feel better?"

"Now?"

"I don't see what another two minutes will hurt."

Portia opened her mouth. Closed it. "Holmes is *waiting* for you." She led the way into the hall.

Grinning, Julia followed.

In the parlor below, male voices blended in laughter as they exchanged news. Phillip. Gabriel. And another rumbling baritone that must be Holmes.

"I've got to get back," Gabriel said to the others. Julia caught a glimpse of him as he passed through the foyer below. His boots thudded on the highly polished floors. Denim and faded chambray, so much like Conrad that her heart hiccupped. His footsteps receded into the back of the house. A door opened and closed.

Phillip continued his conversation with Holmes, evident by the topic of Harvard Law. The two bantered back and forth in good-natured camaraderie. Someone laughed.

This was it. The time had finally come.

Julia's nervous stomach shivered.

Portia escorted Julia down the staircase and to the parlor doorway. She gave a little squeeze on the elbow for luck and whisked her inside.

Late evening rays slanted through the west-facing windows, casting the formal room in golden light. Sheers danced at the open windows. Phillip and the man she supposed to be Holmes were alone, seated in matching chairs before the cold fireplace.

The conversation between father and son halted in mid-sentence. Two pair of male eyes turned her way. Phillip's jovial face lit up. Appreciation flickered through Holmes's expression. They rose to their feet in unison.

"Miss Tyndall." Phillip hurried to welcome her. He took her hand in a show of formality, bringing her into the center of the room. "It is my greatest pleasure to introduce you to my son. Holmes, Miss Julia

Tyndall." Julia hadn't ever heard Phillip sound so happy about anything. "And her aunt, Doctor Portia Tyndall."

"Ladies," Holmes said. His rich baritone sounded remarkably similar to his brothers. Very much like Conrad's. "I'm pleased to make your acquaintances."

"As are we," Julia answered. She'd greeted thousands of her father's political associates. Meeting Holmes felt no different than any one of them.

No flicker of interest, no tingling of nerves, nothing.

Surprised, she paid him full attention. She was supposed to *feel*. Just as she had on the train platform, the day of her arrival.

Holmes's hair, parted neatly down the center, was a few shades lighter than Conrad's rich russet. Thinner, too. Trimmed much shorter. His fair skin hadn't seen as much sunlight as of late, nor was he as broad beneath his well-tailored black wool suit. But the familial resemblance was undeniable. Same square jaw. Similar hue of green in his kind eyes.

Of course she'd call Holmes handsome. He looked far too much like Conrad. Without the distinction. Slimmer. Paler. A watered-down, less-appealing version of his brother.

Mercy, me.

This was all wrong.

Even if it was, clearly, Holmes's profile she'd memorized in the sepia-toned portrait.

Yes, she'd hoped he would be like Conrad, that he would appeal to her in every fundamental way. She'd taken it as a good sign that Conrad interested her. Holmes was supposed to evoke all the same emotions, only much better.

Instead, she simply saw the unfavorable comparisons.

She didn't want to see Conrad in every angle and plane of Holmes's face. This was Holmes, whom she'd chosen.

That was all that mattered.

Wasn't it?

Portia's encouraging words fled right along with Julia's confidence.

Somewhere in the turmoil, she noticed Holmes seemed pleased by her appearance. Welcoming, even. But full of earnest affection? That was a stretch.

Given his warm letters, the eager-to-make-your-acquaintance note he'd sent from San Francisco, accompanied by chocolates and flowers, she'd half-expected a kiss on the cheek. Something more than an appreciative once-over that she'd received from every male visitor she'd greeted as her father's hostess.

Phillip must've picked up on the tension. "Portia, let's you and me skedaddle. We'll leave these two to get acquainted."

"You run along." Portia parked herself in an upholstered chair. "I'll stay right here."

"We can trust them." Phillip offered Portia a hand up, which she pointedly refused. "We'll be in the kitchen, to prepare a repast. You can almost hear everything from back there."

Julia sensed Holmes's gaze on her profile. He seemed to soak in every detail. Not an unfamiliar sensation. Not a welcome one, either.

"And leave these two without a proper chaperon?" Portia sounded delighted at the prospect, but didn't stand up.

"I'm not talking about plucking and roasting a chicken, Portia." No one provoked Phillip the way Portia seemed able to do. "Alberta's got the cheesecake all done, set out all pretty on little china plates. All we've got to do is bring it out here."

Phillip's obvious attempts to leave Julia alone with Holmes embarrassed her. Utterly focused on helping them along, he tried *too* hard.

Portia, ever indifferent to manners, propped her tiny shoes on a needlepoint footstool. "The kids might need a bit of help to keep the conversation afloat."

Holmes chuckled softly, escorted Julia to the

settee, and took a seat beside her. “We won’t have a bit of trouble finding a topic of conversation, will we, Miss Tyndall? We’ve already been introduced through letters.”

“Indeed.” She offered a polite smile. “It seems we know each other already.”

“Then I’ll just listen.” Portia grinned, eagerness shining in her eyes. She brushed Phillip’s arguments away. “I won’t interrupt the happy couple. I promise.”

“Fine. I’ll go get the cheesecake, myself.” Phillip stalked out of the room.

Portia giggled, rubbed her hands together, and leaned forward in her chair. “Do begin, Mr. Macquarie, with how you came to choose my niece as your bride. This is a story I must absolutely hear.”

“Yes, certainly.” Holmes leaned back, settling in comfortably. He seemed to gather his thoughts for a moment. “After reading through all the respondents, I knew Miss Julia was the best choice for me.”

He turned to Julia then, and met her gaze.

Julia stared into green eyes, so much like Conrad’s, and tried to feel something, *anything,* for him. She offered a warm, encouraging smile.

He smiled back. Appealing. Engaging. Inviting.

A hint of attraction flickered through her mid-section.

This, she could work with.

All they needed was time to really get to know one another. And remember their growing affection nurtured through correspondence.

This was the man she’d given up everything for, determined to be blessedly happy. She’d known she could love him, and that he would come to love her, too. He was the man she wanted for her husband.

With renewed confidence, she promised herself that in less than twenty-four hours, she’d be well on her way to falling in love with her husband-to-be.

IN MOST CIRCUMSTANCES, Conrad would agree a healthy conscience was a man's greatest asset. A sense of right and wrong kept a body on the straight and narrow, and out of trouble. The problem was, he'd gotten off that path. He'd flirted with danger and gotten trampled in the process.

As Conrad went about his morning's work, he decided he deserved it.

All around him, the crew efficiently ran the morning's milking through each of three De Laval cream separators. Some operated the hand-powered motors, others fed milk into the rapidly spinning bowl. They joked as they worked. Laughter echoed against the high ceiling and rattled in Conrad's aching heart.

He checked the tubing that drained butterfat away from the main body of the first machine. Skimmed milk flowed through the lower tube, opaque and fluid. He moved on, to the second and third machines, trying his best to concentrate on his work.

He wanted nothing more than to forget. *Ha!* Like *that* would ever happen. Jealousy had a way of clinging like flies.

Ever since Holmes's arrival the previous evening, and all the hoopla that followed, Conrad had been in a sour mood. Irritated because Julia was so all-consumed with Holmes, she'd completely ignored everyone else.

After supper, Holmes and Julia had gone for a walk, arm in arm. And hadn't come back for almost two hours.

Then they'd sat up, talking out on the porch. Conrad had heard their mingled voices, peppered with laughter, long after dark.

Did any of that stop him from thinking about Julia? Missing her? Reliving the fun they'd had together?

She'd wanted to be friends.

Maybe that asinine plan had worked for her, but

the consequences for him were too great.

He went through all the motions; checking the filling holding tanks, evaluating the quality of the butterfat, pausing to dislodge a stuck valve, cleaning the centrifuge bowls between batches.

But nothing distracted him from the thoughts swirling in his head. Holmes and Julia. Together. Courting. Falling in love.

If that was the way it was meant to be, why did Conrad care? All during Silas's courtship and marriage to Nadine, Conrad hadn't been bothered. At all.

So why the obsession? This was exactly what he'd wanted. For Holmes to get himself home, and tend to his own bride.

Too late, he realized Gabriel had spoken to him. The familiar hum of machinery, the rumble of male voices, and the slosh of milk and cream had all faded to silence until that moment.

"Sorry, what did you say?"

"You don't look well."

"I'm OK."

Gabriel searched his face for a few seconds, his attention turning quickly from a casual observer to doctor-in-training. "You coming down with something?"

"No, I'm all right."

"Maybe you should go back to the house."

Nope. Holmes and Julia were there. Together.

Despite knowing that, his heart turned over at the mere thought of seeing her again.

He was stupid, if he thought showing up and trying to be friendly with them would do any good. Every time he saw them together, his agitation grew worse.

All he needed was to stay away. And immerse himself in work until his inappropriate urges subsided. And then stay away some more.

Gabriel tested Conrad's brow for fever, pulled back Conrad's left eyelid for a better look at the eyeball, and grunted. "You sick to your stomach?"

Conrad swatted Gabriel's hand away, shook his head.

"Got the hurries?"

He knew what was wrong with him. And it wasn't anything Gabriel could fix. "What is this, Doctor? An interrogation? I told you I'm fine."

He expected Gabriel to walk off, in a fit of temper. He wouldn't have been surprised if Gabriel said something smart. But contrary to Gabriel's usual manner, he merely stood there, as if looking for the source of the problem.

"Let's get finished here. We don't have time to stand around, talking about nothing." Conrad slammed the lid on the holding tank.

A few of the other men looked up, noted the interchange between brothers, and pointedly ignored it. Just as they always did.

Gabriel headed for a quiet corner, gesturing for Conrad to follow. Why he trailed after his nosy brother, he couldn't say.

Gabriel kept his back to the crew. "Want my advice? No, I didn't think so, but I'm going to say it anyway. Go talk to her. I'll cover for you here."

Was his problem that evident? Great. Just great. He pretended he didn't know exactly what Gabriel meant. "Ma? Why would I want to tell her I'm sick?"

"Miss Julia, you wuss. March right up to the house and talk to her."

Immediately defensive, Conrad demanded, "Why would I want to do that?" No way would he speak to Julia, especially with Holmes within earshot. There was nothing to say. Nowhere for a conversation to go.

"Just act like you're there for a bite to eat. Talk to both of them. Maybe Holmes will have gone into Liberty."

Conrad glared at Gabriel. Was this how it had been with Gabriel and Sally?

"He does have work to do at the office," Gabriel

suggested.

Conrad had already made up his mind. A long time ago. Julia belonged with Holmes, and nothing Conrad said or did would ever change that. Nor did he want to. There was no honor, no decency in coming between them.

Conrad called himself every kind of fool for falling in love with the wrong woman.

He knew where to draw the line. He would not make excuses, he would not rationalize, would not justify his behavior. He'd learned that lesson good and well from Gabriel and Sally.

"You're wrong, Gabriel. I've just got a lot on my mind. Finances. Schedules. It has nothing to do with Miss Julia."

"Uh huh. You keep telling yourself that."

"I know what's what. And I suggest you leave me alone." With that, he headed into his private office and slammed the door. He flung the window open and gulped outside air.

Gabriel, who never was too bright, waited all of thirty seconds before he knocked on the door. Conrad ignored him. He didn't like anybody taking one look at him and making that accurate of a diagnosis. Conrad's troubles were none of Gabriel's business.

Seconds passed. Gabriel yelled through the door, "If you change your mind, I'll—"

"Go away."

For a moment, Conrad figured Gabriel would stay glued to that spot until Conrad cried uncle. A few seconds passed. Gabriel's footsteps retreated.

Conrad ground his molars in frustration. Gabriel couldn't possibly understand. How could he? During their last fight, Gabriel had made it evident he'd never suffered a pang of remorse, just welcomed Sally's affections, and to hell with Conrad and his broken heart.

Conrad was a better man than that. He knew right from wrong. He'd made the only honorable decision.

The only thing left to do was follow through.

Chapter Eighteen

TWO DAYS AFTER Holmes's return, Julia strolled arm in arm with him through the orchard. The air was fragrant, the breeze gentle. Early summer leaves fluttered.

After a few minutes of lapsed conversation, Holmes spoke. "Any last minute party details I might help you with?"

"I have your brothers and some of the dairy hands moving furniture on Friday morning."

"I can help with that."

"And a few more invitations to deliver in town. It seems your parents have decided this party should be larger than their first attempt."

"I'd be delighted to deliver them for you," he said. "I'll take care of it this afternoon, when I go to the office."

Phillip had mentioned an important appointment,

that morning over breakfast. Holmes had promised to meet his father in town.

"Thank you. You're very kind."

With the welcome-home celebration coming up, it was kind of him to ask what she needed. The genuine show of support meant a great deal to her. He seemed to be just as responsible and loyal, as thoughtful and steady as his family had boasted.

So why wasn't she more endeared to him? He'd shown courtesy. Volunteered help. Interested in all the details. Was eager to be of support in every way.

He may not be as warm and gregarious as he'd presented himself in letters, but his solemnity wasn't the greatest concern.

Something weighed upon his mind. It wasn't the party or the preparations. No, it was something else, altogether. And she had no idea what it might be.

She wondered if she knew him, at all.

Falling in love with him, Julia realized, proved more difficult than she'd anticipated.

Holmes led the way down the gently sloping path between fruit trees and headed back toward the house. It wouldn't be long until he'd need to leave.

Holmes's gaze rested on hers, for the briefest of moments. Was that a flicker of pain in his eyes? "You're a lovely woman, Miss Tyndall."

The compliment seemed genuine. He'd phrased it properly, with no suggestion of anything untoward. But her heart hadn't forgotten the way Conrad's attention had made her feel. Beautiful, for who she was in whole. Independent of the face or figure, family name or fortune. No, not just independent of those curses...*in spite* of them.

Holmes's attention lingered on her face. He seemed to be drinking in every feature. The moment stretched uncomfortably.

"Thank you," she murmured, averting her gaze.

"I see the resemblance."

Her footsteps faltered. She'd heard it before, far

too often. But from Holmes? She'd thought he hadn't known. She'd been very careful not to mention any connection. Tyndall was a common enough name.

"Your father," he prompted. "You take after him. I mean that in the most complimentary of ways."

Julia's stomach clenched. No, no. This couldn't be happening. "You never mentioned an acquaintance with my father."

"Acquainted is a strong word. I heard him speak at Harvard. Quite an inspiring lecturer."

Why hadn't he mentioned this in his letters? In her gut, she feared he'd chosen her, amongst all his candidates, on the sole qualification of her parentage.

Precisely what she'd tried desperately to avoid.

In that moment, her estimation of Holmes Macquarie plummeted.

Why? Frustration hummed in her veins. Vibrated with every step she took.

"We were lucky," Holmes rambled on, "to have the senator give a series of thought-provoking lectures."

"When was this?" She had to know. If her father had only spoken there recently, then Holmes couldn't have based his decision upon that ill twist of fate.

"A few months ago? February, perhaps March. It's all running together."

Julia's heart skipped a beat, then two. They'd begun corresponding by then. But Holmes's offer of marriage hadn't come until early April. The timing cast a very poor light on Holmes's motives.

And made Julia out for a fool.

Disappointment washed over her in heavy waves.

The pathway brought them to the edge of the orchard. Holmes opened the fence and ushered her through ahead of himself.

She watched his profile for several long seconds, wondering if at the moment he'd made the familial connection between her father and herself, if he'd whooped with joy. He'd netted a senator's daughter!

In her experience, most aspiring politicians were

lawyers first. And most aspiring politicians were looking for a step up—which often involved finding a well-connected wife.

All her efforts to conceal the trappings other men couldn't see past, in the desperate hope she might find a husband who would love her for herself, an unmitigated waste.

Despair overwhelmed her. Blindly, she turned toward the house. A hundred thoughts collided in her head. Questions she should ask; words she doubted she could force beyond the lump in her throat.

"Miss Julia, wait a minute." Holmes caught her by the arm, arresting her progress with his gentle hold. "What is the problem?"

The man hadn't a clue! Bewilderment slackened his features.

She couldn't hold back, couldn't soften the frustration. "You sent for me, *because* I'm a Tyndall."

Holmes had the nerve to chuckle.

Oh! of all the patronizing responses! She wrenched free and marched toward the house.

He fell into step beside her. "That's not what happened at all."

"No? I am aware you received more than one response to your newspaper advertisement. I'm certain I was your most appealing candidate, on the sole merit of my father's connections."

"Stop right there." Holmes's tone was gentle. But he sounded frustrated, just the same. "That's not true."

She met his gaze, narrowed her eyes in disbelief, and was startled by the obvious pain etched there. Ah, there it was. Indecision. He was trying to decide if he should admit his folly.

"I knew it!"

"No, Miss Julia, you don't know anything." He drew a deep breath. Considered, apparently, how to approach his stupidity with diplomacy. "I know it looks that way, but I assure you the choice was based on anything but that."

"Oh?" She folded her arms. Tapped her foot. Wondered why she'd been foolish enough to trust him with her true name. She should've made up an alias, to conceal her identity.

"You're precisely the kind of woman for me. College educated. I do enjoy a spirited discussion about all topics."

"And?" Why would she make this easy for him? He'd better have more reasons than that.

"You've lived in Massachusetts. So have I."

This mattered to him? "Thousands of women have lived in Massachusetts."

"You've got enough spunk and fire to survive as a Macquarie. Here. On this isolated ranch. With my odd family, who—" He tossed up a hand, gesturing behind Julia's back. "Great. This proves my point."

She turned to find Conrad headed straight for them. Tall. Determined. Focused all that intensity squarely on her.

But Holmes wasn't finished—oh, and neither was she. "Here he comes, even though we're obviously in the middle of a private discussion."

Julia grappled with her self-control, aimed all of her attention squarely on Holmes. "Why, then, did you send for *me?* If not for my father's notoriety?"

Holmes took both of her hands in his, brought them together. His gaze locked with hers. "Your sweet temperament," he said, quirking a half-grin. "I'm serious, Miss Julia. Your letters were captivating. Interesting. Special in a way I find it hard to explain."

"Those are pallid reasons, one and all."

At that moment, Conrad joined them. His wind-tossed hair shone in the sunlight. He seemed broader, more solid than she'd remembered. More alive. He braced those long, strong fingered hands on his hips.

He looked completely wonderful.

He split a glance between his brother and Julia; he knew he interrupted an important discussion.

Holmes wouldn't be deterred. "You stuck with it,

for weeks," Holmes emphasized, drawing her attention back to him, "before I made it home. You're patient. But I already knew that, from your letters. Those same letters convinced me you're the kind of woman who will make this place her home."

Julia watched Holmes's features, really looked at him. He wasn't bluffing, wasn't telling stories. He *meant* what he said.

"I *need* someone who *wants* to be in California. Someone who will support my decision to work in this little town and build a life here."

Julia's temper ebbed. Fast. How could she argue with any of this? His declarations were honest. Heartfelt. Just as they'd been in his letters to her. She had no doubt he told the truth.

"Do you believe me?" Holmes's tone had turned pleading. He obviously needed her to understand.

Conrad shifted his weight from one foot to the other. Crossed his thickly muscled arms. Did he think ill of her for making Holmes appeal for understanding?

She squeezed Holmes's hands, pulled free, slipped her hand into the crook of his elbow. She may have sounded like a traitor, but she hadn't intended to. "Yes."

From the corner of her eye, she noted Conrad's watchful gaze, taking in the conversation, watching them both too closely.

Several seconds passed. At last, Holmes nodded, dismissing the conversation. Turned to his brother.

"You're headed to town," Conrad said to Holmes. "Can you drop some equipment at the blacksmith's before your appointment? I've got it loaded in the wagon."

"No problem." Holmes seemed relieved at the change in subject. Calmer. More like himself.

Fragments of his letters rushed through her mind. Everything he'd said just now, all the reasons why he'd sent for her, matched perfectly with things he'd written. So he admired her father; that wasn't all that mattered.

He wanted to remain in California. Here. Where

they would build a life together. Where most people had never heard of Jordon Tyndall.

He wanted the same things she did.

He'd convinced her of all that, in his letters.

His assurances ought to soothe her irritation, shouldn't they?

There wasn't anything amiss with Holmes. She'd chosen him for good, solid reasons. They had a beautiful future ahead of them, even if he had too much easterner mixed in with too little California dairyman.

While the brothers talked over details of the errand, she couldn't help but note the similarities in height, their characteristic Macquarie features.

Conrad's blue cotton shirt, soft from many washings, molded to his broader frame. Holmes's woolen suit, necktie, fashionable white shirt. Such stark contrasts.

But the subtle differences were more telling. Conrad's voice was deeper, rougher. Holmes's features more refined, his shoulders narrower, his manner more staid.

Julia found her attention riveted on Conrad, soaking up the less-noticeable details. About him.

He smelled of sunshine and wind and horses. He'd rolled up his shirt sleeves, baring strong forearms. Her gaze slid upward, to his familiar, dear face.

She found herself loving the copper hues in his hair and golden bronze of his skin, the meandering ruddy scar winding through the stubble of his red beard, and the sheer size of him. His presence enlarged him somehow.

She noted the light sprinkling of freckles across his straight nose and high cheekbones. The breadth of his jaw. His even, white teeth. Full, masculine lips.

She didn't need to glance at Holmes to know his bottom teeth were overcrowded. Conrad's mouth held her attention fast.

He offered his brother a smile.

Predictably, Julia's insides tingled with warmth.

Conrad's handsome smile consistently elicited such a response.

"Good." Conrad clapped Holmes on the shoulder. "See you tonight." He met Julia's gaze for the briefest of seconds. "Ma'am." He strode toward the creamery.

Ma'am... as if they were no more than strangers.

Disappointed, Julia forced her attention away from Conrad's retreating back. She felt Holmes's gaze on her profile, knew a much stronger pull toward Conrad.

Her heart squeezed. She felt queasy, lightheaded, so mushy in the middle, she wondered if she'd be able to remain standing.

What was wrong with her that she felt the *right* emotion for the *wrong* brother?

Did she want to fight it?

She swallowed. Met Holmes's gaze. Whatever she'd wanted to find there—hope? affection? attraction?—all she glimpsed was kindness.

Plain, ordinary kindness. Compared to the vibrant connection she'd known with his brother, Holmes's lack of something more left her feeling bereft.

Would affection grow between them? In time?

Did she dare risk it?

"Where are the invitations you want me to deliver?" Holmes led her toward the house.

"On the kitchen table."

"I'll get them," he offered, smiling. "Consider the task completed."

The moment she took his arm, she knew the startling truth.

This kind, considerate, reliable man may not be such a great fit after all.

No matter how much she'd wanted him to be, he wasn't the cowboy of her dreams.

He wasn't the man whose life, whose soul was the perfect complement to her own.

He wasn't Conrad.

How could she possibly consider a future with

Holmes, when her heart had chosen his brother?

SHE WANTED CONRAD, instead.

The stark realization had hummed through her from the moment of recognition. On the garden pathway. Seeing the two men, side by side, had caused something to shift within her. Something immense.

The moment Holmes had driven the wagon down the lane, she'd wanted, *needed* nothing more than to find Conrad. It took thirty minutes of searching, but she finally found him half an hour later.

There was no denying it; she wanted *him*.

He stood tall, boots spread, hands splayed on hips, talking with a ranch hand beside the pasture fence. His brimmed hat shaded his face. He stood nearly in profile. Something about his agitated stance and occasional movement reminded her of the day her train arrived and she'd observed him through grimy windows.

Yes, she'd been undeniably attracted to him, from the beginning.

But her feelings had blossomed into so much more than appreciation for his muscled form and rugged appearance. It was the man beneath that exterior that had captured her heart.

He'd made her laugh, he'd begun riding lessons, captivated her attention, understood her. He'd wanted to know her, inside, for the woman so very few knew.

In contrast, Holmes paled. Significantly.

Holmes may have captured her interest in letters, but Conrad had earned her affections in the minutes and hours and days spent together in Holmes's absence. Conrad commanded her affections. There would be no changing that now.

What would Holmes think? She'd have to tell him.

She weighed everything she knew of Holmes from

his letters, the many hours they'd walked arm in arm, sat in the parlor coming to know one another. Frankly, she couldn't foresee Holmes having anything stronger than a moment's disappointment over losing her.

Hardly enough emotion to build a loving marriage on.

That truth resonated through her, confirming her decision. What choice did she have but to act in the best interest of Holmes, herself, and Conrad? Holmes wouldn't be any happier with her than she would be with him. But declaring herself would allow for Holmes to find far greater happiness with someone else, and allowing her beautiful beginning with Conrad to blossom.

She focused on only him, still many yards away. Joy unfurled. Like wings of a butterfly, a soft, calm confirmation settled upon her. Yes, *he* was the right one for her. She could see that now.

She'd given up everything—home, family, esteem of her parents, inheritance, her place in Baltimore society—all so she might exert her right to choose her own husband. Gregory hadn't been right for her, and regrettably, neither was Holmes.

It might be uncomfortable and somewhat inconvenient to inform the Macquarie family, but not insurmountable.

It would all work out.

As long as Conrad wanted her in return.

Her stomach fluttered in anticipation.

From this distance, she could hear little bits of Conrad's conversation with the ranch hand. It seemed their discussion was wrapping up. A handshake. The worker headed toward the barn.

No time like the present. *This man,* her cowboy, so much more than she'd ever banked on finding. Affection swelled, overflowed. Her smile came so easily.

He noticed her, turned in her direction. Smiled. But the happy response faded much too quickly. "Miss J," he murmured by way of greeting when she'd come within a few feet of him.

He broke eye contact, kicked the toe of his boot into a clump of grass beneath his feet. Unsure? He hadn't been uncertain of himself, at least not around her… until Holmes's return.

Surely that was a good sign?

Her grin widened. She couldn't help it, not with Conrad so close, not now that she knew her own mind.

"I need to talk to you." That wasn't quite right. "*We* need to talk." Nervousness vibrated through her. Her plan to confide her change of heart hadn't seemed so forward until this moment.

"All right."

Heat arched between them, sizzling through her like an electric shock. Every nerve was tingling, every fine hair standing on end.

He gazed at her profile. Remained silent, waiting for her to speak.

Julia glanced at him, briefly met his gaze. Something lurked there. He guarded his emotions closely. But for a moment she glimpsed a wistfulness.

A wave of dizziness rolled through her. The gentle lull of breeze through the nearby stand of trees echoed loudly in her ears.

This wouldn't get any easier. She simply had to broach the subject. "I must ask you...ah, a quest—, an *important* question. A personal one."

Conrad was quiet for the space of a few heartbeats. "All right. Ask."

Her heart pounded. Never in her life had she been so forward with a man. Doing so felt oddly liberating. And frightening. Both empowering as she grabbed hold of the destiny she chose with both hands...and yet so full of risk.

What if he didn't want her?

There was no denying the connection between them. Yet he might do just that—deny it. He'd been pushing her away hard and fast for days. She had to believe he'd only done so because of Holmes.

He *would* understand she'd chosen, wouldn't he?

With her heart pounding against her too-tight corset, she felt winded. Ridiculous, given the leisurely walk. And the shade. Simply had to be Conrad's nearness. And the intense emerald green of his eyes boring into hers.

Conrad cast her a sideways glance. Removed his hat, raked his fingers through his hair, spun the brim around his hand.

"I've had..." she cleared her throat, "the most amazing discovery."

He leaned back against the fence, propping one boot heel over the lower rung. He tapped his hat against the raised thigh. "You have a question. For me. And a discovery."

She nodded. Why wouldn't the words come? Aware of his intent gaze on her face, she couldn't bear to let him see the desperation, the need that overwhelmed her.

Compelled to look away, she turned her attention to his free hand, hanging loosely at his side. Masculine. Broad. Veins marbled the sun-kissed, callused skin.

He shifted his weight against the wooden rail, brushing his arm past hers, evoking a sudden urge to slip her hand into his.

Her heart pumped vigorously. Did she dare?

The act would communicate what she could not articulate.

The grove of trees rustled with the movement of small animals, the dance of the breeze through vegetation. Not another living soul in sight. In this isolation, she felt more bravery than good sense.

It was easy to forget Holmes, altogether.

She swallowed hard and closed her hand around his.

Conrad couldn't have been more stunned, had Julia announced she loved him.

But try telling his stampeding heart this affectionate touch and *Julia's* affection itself were not the same thing.

Reflexively, his grip tightened about her slender fingers. What did this mean?

"Julia?" The plea came out hoarse and strained.

Her hand. In *his.*

Such a small, simple touch shouldn't feel so incredibly good. Shouldn't make the breath catch in his chest as if he'd been thrown from the saddle and landed hard.

Despite the kick in the chest, happiness erupted within him. The emotion had come on suddenly, with remarkable force. He'd never experienced anything like it before.

The wind tossed a loose curl into her face. She tucked the lock behind her ear and offered a shaky smile. Sunlight filtered through the trees, illuminating the pale flawlessness of her skin.

The world faded away, leaving nothing but the two of them. With it disappeared the faint rush of wind, the dance of leaves and undergrowth. Her body's heat, so near, warmed him through.

"Would it be all right?" she whispered.

He bent his head closer, to better hear her.

"If I..." her voice faint and uncertain to his ear, "change my mind?"

"Right." He'd known they shouldn't hold hands. It wasn't a good idea. They weren't little kids and this sure as sunrise wasn't about friendship. He moved to release her, but her grip tightened.

"What I mean is, is it all right with you?" Determination glinted in her eyes. Her voice got a lot more backbone behind it. "May I...choose you?"

"*Me?*"

Never, in all his life, had he been so stunned.

Or so overcome with joy.

He wanted to shout, but he couldn't draw a breath. His heart seemed to give out, beating ineffectually against his ribs.

He glimpsed interest in Julia's eyes—no, *more*

than that—something akin to need.

Cupping her face between his hands, he tunneled his fingers into her hair. *She wants me.*

Me.

A bark of laughter erupted, his emotion as sharp as could be.

Impossible.

She stepped closer, pushed up on her toes, and brought her mouth a mere inch from his own. Her small hands gripped the shirt at his sides.

The sapphire of her eyes sunk deeper as her pupils expanded. Up close like this, he could see a navy blue ring around her irises, more purple at the moment. In those beautiful eyes something else shone there. An emotion he never thought he'd see turned on himself.

Is this what love looks like?

Anticipation hummed in his veins. What would her lips feel like, against his own?

She pushed up on her toes, her gaze dropping to his mouth.

Anticipation zinged straight from his hands entwined in her silken hair to the toes of his boots. The promise of a kiss had never been this magical with Sally.

As quickly as the memory, the old emotions entangled with Sally barely tolerating him, treating his kisses like something to put up with, it all washed away.

The promise of Miss J's kiss...he could taste how good it would be. Oh, yeah, *he wanted.*

He wanted Julia. His answer was yes. Yes!

No! With the suddenness of a lightning strike immediately overhead, the fog cleared.

Gabriel and Sally.

Holmes.

She belonged to Holmes.

Craving slammed into him, hot and sharp.

Her lips, a mere inch from his own. Her beautiful eyes had closed. Surrendered. She wanted him, wanted his kiss. *One* kiss—surely that wouldn't...

Whoa, Nellie.

He wasn't *that* weak. But hell, he felt it.

At the last possible second, he averted his course. His lips grazed her cheek. He felt her draw breath, her face turn toward his.

She wanted his kiss, sought it still. Amazing. *Unbelievable.*

He groaned aloud, the yearning chased hard and fast by guilt.

Guilt. A hundred times worse than the remorse he'd felt a few days ago or the week before that. How could he have allowed this to happen?

His fingers tightened in her silky, fragrant hair. Hunger melded with desperation in his gut. In that moment, he realized one taste would never be enough.

Self-loathing churned within him. How pathetic, that Julia's timid show of affection immediately stole his good sense, his ability to reason, and his conscience.

What made him suppose he could steal a kiss, and his relationship with Julia might remain unchanged?

After this, how could he possibly look at her like a sister?

With alarm, he realized he still held her. He started to free his hands from her hair, but she stilled him, gently bracketing his face.

She stepped so close, her bosom pressed against his chest. "It's all right."

She intended to kiss him!

"No. I can't." If he let this happen, how would he ever look Holmes in the eye again?

One kiss could permanently damage Holmes's marriage.

That was a serious consequence.

"I want a kiss, Conrad." His name, warmed by her ardor just about made him cave. She pressed warm lips against his jaw. "I want *you.*"

"*Julia—*"

Her kiss nearly wiped out his ability to think like a rational man. He wanted to give in, to take and to give.

Oh, how he wanted her. He craved her kiss, the

touch of her skin, the promise of forever. Dammit, he wanted it all. Her body, her heart, every ounce of her affection.

He wanted to keep her for his very own.

Why must she belong to his brother?

Temptation sunk claws deep into his soul.

But the ramifications reached far beyond Holmes, Julia, and himself. The spoiled marriage would affect the whole family. He didn't want to consider what the fallout would do to his mother.

Although it ripped his heart out, he set Julia away.

"Conrad?" Concern roughened her voice.

His heart twisted. He couldn't risk looking her in the eye. His tenuous control would snap, given the tiniest leeway.

He knew what he had to do. What choice did he have? He headed back toward the dairy. "I can't."

Her breath caught on a strangled cry. "I don't see why not."

Slowly, he turned to face her. Anguish marred her beautiful face. Her eyes filled with frustration, disillusion, pain.

How could he make her understand?

His heart jumped into his throat and lodged there. "The one thing I cannot, *will not* do is steal you from my brother."

She took two strides closer, pushed her little palm against his chest, impatience coloring her words. "I am *not* his. It's impossible to steal me from someone that doesn't have me."

Pain ripped through him as he stalked back up the road, putting as much distance between them as possible. He refused to look back.

He halted. As much as he wanted to, he couldn't leave her. Not like this. He had to explain, to make her understand. This whole mess affected the family, would affect the family forever. He must make himself perfectly clear.

Breath rasped deeply in and out of his chest. How

had they come to this? Though sunlight bore down on his bare head, and the early summer day warm, it seemed an icy wind cut through him. He shivered.

Her hand settled on his back. That simple touch nearly broke his resolve.

He'd made a serious mistake in talking alone with Julia. Especially after that argument she'd had with Holmes before he'd gone to town.

Conrad berated himself for thinking he could spare her a minute, answer a question. It hadn't been anything more than his desperate desire to spend a stolen moment with her.

Had his conscience been asleep?

Not anymore. It was wide awake and berating his stupid, stupid mistakes.

"Look at me," she said, so softly he almost hadn't heard.

He closed his eyes. If he looked at her, he feared he'd crumble. He wanted her affection, her attention so desperately, he doubted he could do the right thing.

When he did not obey, she marched around in front of him, gripping both of his forearms with surprising force. She turned her face up to his, locking their gazes.

A long moment passed. Her dark blue eyes sparked with frustration. "I asked," she paused, for emphasis, "if I could *choose you.*"

He shook his head, but couldn't make himself pull away from her touch, from her gaze. Didn't want to.

"I've spent hour upon hour in Holmes's company since he returned," she said.

Even as she gave words to what he'd known to be true, jealousy flared in his gut. Hated it. Hated himself.

Her tone gave no room for argument. "He's nice. A gentleman. But *I feel nothing* for him."

Unwanted pleasure fought back the rising jealousy.

Still, her gaze tangled with his. "It's my choice whom I marry, Conrad. *My...choice.*"

"I know," he forced through his tight throat.

"I've changed my mind." Her grip on his arms tightened.

He couldn't restrain himself. He had to touch her. Cupped her elbows, locking them together in an almost-embrace.

"You can't abandon him." All the aggravation and rejection he'd suffered with Sally's desertion swamped him, clawing at his throat, making breathing difficult.

She didn't seem to register what he'd said. "I choose *you,* Conrad."

Wonder, wretched and horrible, burned through him with the destructive force of an earthquake. Caught in its force, he didn't respond in time.

"The question," she stated with emphasis, "is do *you* want me, too?"

Hell, yes.

Handsome Holmes, with his unblemished face, could have any woman he wanted. He had a fancy education. An attractive law degree. His opportunities for happiness were limitless. Undoubtedly, he'd have hundreds of women to choose from.

Conrad, in stark comparison, couldn't imagine marrying anyone but Julia. She was the only woman to see *him,* not his scar. She should be *his* wife, the mother of *his* children.

After Sally, he'd refused to think about marriage. Would never marry. Had no desire to even try.

Until Julia, he doubted he'd ever feel this way about anyone; he'd *known* no decent woman would ever want him. Ever.

She, his brother's bride, was his once-in-a-lifetime.

No amount of rationalizing would make it any different.

Thou shalt not covet thy neighbor's wife. He could quote the whole biblical passage word for word. Unfortunately, to Conrad's way of seeing things, that command covered his brother's not-yet-wed bride.

May God forgive him.

He could make excuses; weakness of the flesh, the circumstances that brought them together, his own lack of foresight. But no excuse could justify kissing her. The line between right and wrong was definite, razor-sharp, and immovable.

He'd crossed the line. Unwittingly, foolishly—but none of that mattered.

Guilt made bile rise in his throat.

It wasn't fair.

Life *wasn't* fair. He'd barely lived through that god-awful lesson the first time.

"Miss J," he rasped, "listen to me." Somehow, his hands were no longer on her elbows, cradling her arms. To his dismay, he found his big, clumsy hands cradling her face. Her skin felt like satin. Smooth and warm and perfect.

Longing redoubled. He swallowed. Tried to release her, couldn't.

She nodded, eyes shining with hope. Happiness.

He hated himself for hurting her.

"Not two months ago," he began, trying to find the right words, "Gabriel decided it was his right to steal Sally's affections from me."

"I know. Your sister told me."

He shook his head. She didn't know; she couldn't. No one knew. "Sally was *mine.* Nothing official. Not yet. But that didn't change the way I felt about her."

Compassion softened the sapphire blue of Julia's eyes. Sadness for his loss. *Damn it!* Why did *her* comprehension have to feel so good?

"Gabriel *didn't care* that Sally was mine, don't you see?" Old fury welled within him, making it too hard to look Julia in the eye. It was all too intimate.

He eased her against his shoulder, circling his arms about her back. It was better that he didn't have to see pity on her expressive features.

"I loved her." But what he'd felt for Sally was so watered down compared to his unwanted, unbearable awareness and reactions for Julia that he could see now, in stark black and white that it hadn't been love. "At least I *thought* I loved her."

"Oh, Conrad."

"I didn't lose only Sally that day. I lost my brother, too." And that was the heart of the matter. What he needed her to understand. "Gabriel stole Sally's affections, and in coming between Sally and me, he ruined our relationship as brothers."

Grief over the whole mess turned as sour as week-old milk in his mouth. He couldn't think about his relationship with Gabriel right now—what mattered was Holmes. And Julia.

Julia's slender arms moved around his waist. Held him close. Her feminine fragrance enveloped him as her hands splayed against his back. She fit against him so precisely, so perfectly. Slowly, as if fearful he'd bolt, she rested her cheek against his collarbone, snuggled her forehead against his throat. This unequaled, amazing woman, in *his* arms.

Right where he wanted her.

Right where she did *not* belong.

"My relationship with Gabriel is ruined. I can't, I won't, do the same thing to Holmes." He'd heard Holmes vow to Julia, in the garden just an hour ago, that he needed *her*. Just as she was, to fill all the empty corners in his life and heart.

Against his chest, she sighed. Her soft curves seemed to settle in closer. She was listening, but did she *hear* him?

He shouldn't hold her like this. It was torture, knowing she *thought* she wanted to be there. But she wasn't his. Nothing had changed.

Clasping her narrow shoulders, he eased her away from him. A crack opened up in his heart. The rending hurt like hell. Stung far worse than the pain he'd felt after Sally.

"I'll simply tell Holmes the truth, that I want you, instead." Her shy smile twisted in his gut.

She couldn't possibly know how deep her words cut. *I want you.* He heard the conviction in her words, the truth behind the sentiment.

Wanting him and loving him were two very different things, but his foolish heart didn't seem to understand.

He clenched his jaw, wishing he'd never started on this path to destruction. Weeks ago, if he'd kept to his work and left Julia to her own devices, he never would've come to care about the woman behind the pretty face. He might have never found himself so in love, his good sense lost.

Love.

In love with his brother's bride.

Oh, God. It was *true.*

He wanted to scream at the injustices that had driven him to this point, but knew it was a hell of his own making.

He groaned. "*No.*"

Her beautiful smile faltered. "I don't see why not. I doubt he feels anything for me beyond kindness, perhaps a bit of responsibility."

He had to explain himself better. If she could understand, she'd see there was no other way. He took a big step back, breaking all contact between them. He pinned Julia with his gaze. "It's not right. Holmes doesn't deserve betrayal."

She wasn't listening. Shaking her head, taking a step closer to him. Hands up, in a pleading gesture that broke his heart.

"*He* wants you. *He* found you, first. *My brother* is a good, honorable man, and I will not disgrace him"—or myself, *God!*—"by taking you from him. I'm trying to do the right thing here."

His chest burned with angst that flashed into a white-hot fire with the first tear that spilled down her cheek. *He* had made her cry; a first tear. Never had he seen her weep.

She straightened her already perfect posture.

Drew a breath. Shaking, she whispered, "You want me, don't you?"

To tell her the truth would damn them both, undeniably hurt Holmes. Make him, Conrad, every bit as callous and heartless as Gabriel.

No matter how desperately he wanted to grab every ounce of happiness he could, with Julia, he simply would not.

He looked her in the eye, shored up his resolve, and lied. "Might fancy a kiss, Miss J." Emotion would give him away. He forced a smirk.

The pressure had built in his chest until it was excruciating. "Want to keep you?" *Yes!* He'd never wanted anything more. "*No, thanks.*"

Chapter Nineteen

AN ACHING CONSCIENCE, Conrad decided two nights later, caused more sleeplessness than a broken bone.

He ought to know. A nip of brandy had almost knocked Conrad unconscious just before Doc Tibbs had set his busted leg. Conrad had been ten years old, and it had hurt like the dickens.

Unfortunately, this was different. Several glasses of the stuff downed in an attempt to forget hadn't dulled the constant ache in his chest.

There was no point in lying abed, waiting for sleep to ease his heartache. That wasn't going to happen. He doubted he could get drunk enough to blot out the memories.

His bare feet whispered along the floorboards as he circled lap after lap on the upstairs wrap-around veranda.

Stars glittered in the black heavens. Silvery moonlight cast shadows in the yard. Despite the cold, nighttime wind and familiar scents of freshly turned soil, harvested alfalfa, and Ma's lilacs in full bloom he could still smell Julia's perfume.

The fragrance lingered. Teased. Mingled with the fine hum of good brandy in his veins.

Despite every effort, he recalled the satin of her cheek beneath his lips, the rush of anticipation as she threaded her fingers between his.

So he walked. Like he always did, whenever responsibilities and problems weighed heavily on his mind.

He passed Julia's bedroom window for what seemed like the hundredth time. He pointedly refused to peer inside. Instead, he kept his attention on the wind-tossed oak and barn beyond.

He wouldn't look. He didn't want to catch so much as a glimpse of her form under bed quilts.

He turned the corner and strode around Ma's chaise lounge and past his parents' darkened bedroom windows. Precisely twenty five paces took him beyond Silas's vacant room, to flank left once more. He strode beside Katherine's room, then Gabriel's, and Holmes's at the corner.

The house remained dark and silent. The whole family slept peacefully.

He rounded the corner and drew up short, instantly sober.

Julia.

Standing on the veranda. A mere five feet away. Blocking his path.

Her long, wavy hair caught in the breeze, lifting and flirting about her face.

Her face, cast half in shadow, half in pale moonlight, made his gut tighten with longing. It seemed an indulgence, decadent beyond any measure of decency, to stare at her beautiful face.

He'd missed her. Desperately. In every last

intervening hour since he'd almost kissed her beside the pasture fence.

He hadn't known how badly he missed her, until that very moment.

How had he ever supposed he could kill his feelings for her? They'd taken root so deep in his soul, it frightened him. How would he ever survive living in this house, alongside Holmes and Julia as husband and wife?

She took a hesitant step toward him. Her pale, summer-weight robe covered her from neck to wrist to ankle, but left her feet bare.

Images of her naked lower leg, creamy white in the shade beneath the trees, burned through his memory. His heart lurched and knocked frantically against his breastbone. Emotions he'd barely tamped down surged to the surface. Every last trace of liquor burned out of his blood.

She held his gaze, completely unsurprised, as if she'd expected him. Had she been lying in bed awake, watching him pass at regular intervals?

Suddenly aware of his nakedness, he wished he'd pulled on more than a pair of Levi's. Better yet, he wished he'd left the house to walk the fields.

If he'd exercised half the brains God gave him, he never would've tried to sleep in this house, anywhere near her.

He considered making a run for it. He could vault over the railing and scurry down the ivy-covered lattice to the ground below.

What a stupid idea.

So he'd bumped into her. No harm done. He intended to make sure it stayed that way.

"Nice night." His voice sounded gruff, deeper than normal. Giving her a wide berth, he headed past her to the safety of his own bedroom, planning to lock the French door between them.

"Yes, it's beautiful out." She hugged herself against the cool wind. "Conrad," she added hastily, "I have one question."

Last time she'd asked a question, he'd gotten himself into a heap of trouble.

"Not a good idea." He moved to pass her. Three steps, and he'd be safely inside his bedroom.

She detained him by planting a palm in the middle of his bare chest. "Wait. Please."

The warmth of her touch, shockingly intimate, lanced through him. Gooseflesh prickled all over his wind-chilled body. Reflexively, he grabbed her hand.

The wind caught her wrapper and brushed the hem against his bare feet. Her sleeve skimmed his arm.

Her delicate scent provoked memories he didn't want. His hands in her hair. The almost-kiss that nearly destroyed him. The overwhelming need to taste her lips, to accept and to give. His pulse rushed through his veins.

She took a half step closer, slipped an arm about his waist, and brushed her bosom against his chest. The unnerving contact sent heat coursing through him. She felt so warm, alive, intoxicating. He moaned as her sweet-smelling hair caressed his cheek.

"I've missed you," she whispered, a split second before she reached up and pressed her lips to his.

Her confession ruined his tenuous hold on decency. His determination turned to rubble at the shock of her kiss.

It began sweetly, leisurely. The wondrous texture of her mouth made him moan. His lungs demanded air, but he couldn't breathe.

Kissing her connected them in a way he could scarcely define. It evoked an urgency within him he'd never felt before. It felt wicked and forbidden, yet miraculously, perfectly right.

Love for Julia rushed through him. He ached, needing her nearer. With his hand gentle upon the nape of her neck, he bid her closer.

She responded with eagerness, tightening her embrace, parting her lips. In that moment, he realized she wanted this as much as he did. The knowledge compounded his pleasure.

Mine.

Their kiss erupted from chaste to reckless in that instant. His tongue slipped inside her mouth. He backed her against the pillar, his hands in her long silken hair.

Consumed with hunger, he trailed kisses along her jaw, her neck, her ear, barely registering the textures and tastes before he took her mouth once more.

He hugged her tightly. Her softer body yielded to his. Several wonderful, earth-stopping seconds passed.

The momentum seemed to slow, the miracle of their kiss stretching as if time had stopped completely. She nibbled at his lower lip, pressing a series of soft, tantalizing kisses along his jaw. Her every touch brimmed with affection for him, and acceptance for the man he was.

And that stunned him. Completely uprooted everything he'd always believed about himself, about his worth.

Never once, in his meager experience, had he encountered anything like it. Lifelong insecurities quieted at her touch. It empowered him, moved him, uncovered another layer of loneliness and need.

Desire robbed him of sanity. He kissed her with brazen possessiveness. The privacy and darkness fed his complete disregard for propriety. He wanted everything she offered, and more.

They could run away together. Leave family behind. Then nothing else would matter.

Some part of his brain still functioned, screaming at him to see reason.

This was madness.

He could never steal her from Holmes.

The weight of what he'd allowed to happen—what he was still doing—crashed upon him. Horrified by his lack of inhibitions, by the enormity of his transgression, he ripped himself away from her. He nearly stumbled in his haste to put distance between them.

She followed, taking his face in her hands. A soft whimper. Another kiss. She wrapped her arms about his neck and drew herself flush against his chest.

He groaned, grappling for strength to obey his conscience. Heaven and everything he ever wanted on one side, and all respect and decency on the other.

"Julia," he moaned.

She responded with a deep, throaty sound that shot fire through his veins.

Desire flared.

Lamplight flooded through sheer curtains of Holmes's bedroom window.

PANIC SURGED through Conrad, slamming his heart into a gallop. He grabbed Julia by the wrist, and pulled her into the shadows.

Had Holmes seen them together? Had he overheard their brief words? Guilt burned through Conrad's gut. Had he heard Julia's throaty moans?

Conrad clenched his jaw and swallowed a curse. His conscience shouted condemnations.

There was no way to take any of this back, no way to erase what had just happened with Julia. Sick to his stomach, Conrad realized he'd made *the worst* mistake of his life.

Julia didn't seem to see it the same way. She snuggled close, wrapping warm, soft hands around his arm.

Any second, Holmes would barrel from that door and throw a punch Conrad would fully deserve.

He freed himself from her embrace, pulled her further from Holmes's window. When they were at a safer distance, he glanced back at the glowing rectangle of light and saw Holmes's shadow pace between lamp and windowpanes.

Second after second dragged past, and after some time, Conrad determined his brother must be oblivious because he stayed inside.

"This is wrong," Conrad whispered to Julia and meant it. He knew he'd put himself in this mess, and blamed no one else. "I never should've touched you, never should've—"

"Yes, you should have," she whispered, slipping easily into his arms. Feminine, soft curves pressed close. "Things are finally right."

The battle still raged within him. He'd been through all this before. Too many times. The answer remained the same.

She and Holmes had written to each other for more than six months. They'd chosen each other, based on fundamentals of a solid relationship. Holmes had proposed marriage, and Julia had accepted.

Holmes had his entire future planned. The law partnership. A proper, lovely wife. For him, it was time to settle down and raise a family.

No way in hell would Conrad yank that out from under his brother.

Even though it meant he'd never have those gifts for himself.

Julia rested a soft cheek against Conrad's chest.

Gently, his heart rending, he set her away from him. "I will not do this. It's wrong."

"Improper, maybe." In the moonlight, he glimpsed her smile. She brushed a palm over his bare chest. "But daylight will come, and we can—"

"No." This reeked of danger. Compelling beyond anything he could bear.

He wanted a future with her so badly, he couldn't recall all the reasons why he must refuse. That scared him worse than anything had in a long while.

"—spend time together," she whispered, "when we're modestly dressed."

"No," he repeated, panic showing in his voice.

"Absolutely not."

"Holmes won't mind. He doesn't feel passion for me, I assure you. We'll find a way to tell him."

Her hapless comment evoked painful memories of Sally and Gabriel. He knew now that he hadn't loved Sally, but the betrayal still chafed. A fresh wave of panic lurched through Conrad. "Don't tell him, Julia. *Don't.*"

"Why not?"

Confessing would be a terrible mistake. It might make them feel better, but it would destroy Holmes. Conrad would have no part of that. "We have no choice. We must pretend it never happened."

"You just kissed me." She sounded hurt. "I know the difference between brotherly and—"

"It cannot happen again." He held her gaze for a second or two. "Do you understand me? It's wrong. You belong with Holmes."

She stilled. "His kisses don't move me. Yours make me feel—"

Conrad motioned for silence. He didn't want to hear it. The weight crushing his conscience was already too great.

He doubted he'd ever forget her kisses and the way they made him feel. A hundred years from now, it would still haunt him. Of that, he was absolutely certain, because love like this didn't dry up and blow away. The emotion had taken root in his soul, entrenched so deeply, he had no hope of ever cutting it free.

Given a lifetime, he'd never find another woman he loved the way he loved Julia, nor did he want to try. He couldn't admit any of that to her.

He'd gotten sucked in, again, to this destructive trap. He knew he could never be alone with her again, never have a personal conversation, and most important—never touch her again.

Never.

He'd said it before, made vow upon vow. But this time, he meant it. No more polite conversations. No more tempting fate. He'd proved himself too weak.

There was no other way.

"It's over between us, Miss Tyndall. Nothing like this will ever happen again."

Chapter Twenty

MORNING'S FIRST RAYS of light glowed upon the horizon. Julia leaned her cheek against the cool windowpane and watched Conrad's confident stride as he left the house.

He didn't glance back.

She knew he never would.

He'd made himself quite clear. The rejection, severe though it was, pained her far worse, knowing their kisses had been filled with genuine emotion.

She'd meant every bit of it.

More importantly, so had he.

But there was no room for misunderstanding, no room for hope, no room for her in his life.

He strode out of her line of vision, and she closed her eyes.

And wished she could stop loving him.

JULIA CHOKED on her wine. Coughing, she clutched her goblet. "A double wedding?"

Katherine had to be *kidding*. A joke, made in too much wine.

"Why, yes!" Katherine rushed on, talking louder and faster than the other thirteen friends and family members gathered around the dining room table. This simple family supper conversation had gone terribly wrong.

David's panicked, "Sweet Kathykins?" barely got Katherine's attention.

Katherine clutched both of Julia's hands in her own. "You don't mind sharing, do you, Julia? It'll be a wonderful day. It's already yours, too, what with all your planning and work and we're going to be sisters anyway."

Violet Macquarie obviously liked the idea. She leapt from her chair and threw her arms around Holmes.

The thought of the wedding happening so soon slammed against Julia's ribs. She wasn't ready. Didn't want to wed Holmes.

Mercy, me. "Katherine, I—"

Phillip Macquarie cut in. "Another toast, everyone! To our Miss Julia, whose affection for our Holmes brought her all the way from the Atlantic seaboard."

Silas applauded and whistled. His wife, Nadine, called out, "Hear, hear!"

The family raised their wine goblets and drank to that. The noise level doubled.

"Oh, Holmes," Katherine gushed, "you'll just love the beautiful bridal satin Julia had made in Baltimore. It's absolutely stunning."

Holmes didn't have a chance to respond before interrupted by Olaf, who rose halfway out of his chair to offer a handshake. "Congratulations, son."

His pale face registered shock. “Thanks.”

Olaf dropped back into his seat at Portia’s side. “These Tyndalls are fine people. *Fine* people. You’ll be a happy man with Julia at your side.”

Katherine squealed with excitement. “And Holmes, you’re going to *love* the wedding we’ve planned. And the cake—oh, my!—you won’t believe this big cake we ordered. We can get another groom’s cake. Chocolate and raspberry? Just for you?”

This couldn’t be happening. One minute, the family was enjoying a sumptuous supper and spirited conversation. The next, they were planning *her* wedding.

Without her consent.

In shock, Julia turned to Portia for help, finding the batty woman guzzling wine and ignoring Olaf’s kiss upon her cheek.

Holmes’s parents were too busy congratulating each other to notice anything else.

Gabriel, seated between Conrad and the notorious Sally Tibbs, spoke to Conrad. In less time than it took to say hello, the two brothers were in a heated argument.

Julia couldn’t worry about that at the moment; she was caught in an undertow. If she didn’t do something—fast—to make everyone see reason, these crazy plans would sweep her out to sea.

Before Julia could open her mouth to protest, Phillip bellowed loud enough to be heard by all. “This is the best idea I’ve heard in a month of Sundays. Holmes, what have you got to say to your lovely lady?”

Holmes blinked. Glanced at Julia, but didn’t seem sold on the idea, at all. “OK,” he managed. “Why not?”

He called *this* a proposal? Where was the sincerity? This got worse by the moment. He didn’t want to marry her, any more than she wanted to marry him!

She watched, open-mouthed and stunned, as Holmes didn’t so much as wait for her answer.

The cacophony exploded in a storm of well-wishing and congratulations.

Although still stinging from Conrad's rejection, she thought he'd say something in her defense. He knew her loyalties were divided. He *knew* she didn't want to marry Holmes.

But he didn't so much as glance in her direction. He continued his heated argument with Gabriel.

Julia scanned the rest of the faces surrounding the dining room table. Everyone was too delighted to notice her desperation.

The entire family assumed she'd marry Holmes, without further ado. Why wouldn't she? She'd come to California to marry him, and that's precisely what was about to happen.

They might not object, but she did. "Wait, everyone, please."

If anyone heard, they gave no indication. What was she supposed to do? Whistle? Scream? Throw her china dish to the floor in a show of tantrum?

Across the table, Conrad threw his napkin onto his unfinished supper plate. He shook his head with obvious disgust. Without so much as glancing at her, he shoved back from the table and headed for the door.

His fury made her chest ache. She wanted him to stay. She wanted to go after him. What could she say, if she did?

Absolutely nothing.

How many times could she swallow her pride and beg him to love her?

There wasn't a thing left to say.

"Conrad?" his mother called after him, but he didn't pause.

Portia raised her wineglass, the deep red contents listing nearly to the rim. "To our happy bride and groom!" She sounded a little tipsy. "Our *second* pair, that is."

"To our happy bride and groom!" the family echoed.

As Conrad escaped the house, the back door

banged against the siding. It rebounded, whipping shut with a clatter.

Gabriel, Sally, and Olaf turned toward the sound of the slamming door, but everyone else seemed captivated by the sight of David kissing Katherine. Deeply.

The way a man in love kissed the only woman he'd ever want.

Much the way Conrad had kissed her... right before he broke her heart.

Phillip gestured for Holmes to get on with it, too.

Laughter rippled through the family. Portia clattered her knife against her crystal water goblet.

Everyone knew what that tinkling signal meant. Before Julia could protest, the others had joined in. A crystal cacophony. A dozen pairs of expectant eyes. Waiting for a very public kiss.

Holmes leaned close. He hesitated for the briefest moment, a question in his eyes.

What choice did she have?

Conrad didn't want her. Pain sliced through her resolve to get through this family dinner. *He didn't want her.*

Apparently Holmes did.

In his own way.

She'd come to California to marry him. This was what she wanted, wasn't it? Her romance with Conrad had been brief and wonderful—so incredibly wonderful—but it was over.

Holmes had been her first choice, she reminded herself. An intentional, carefully thought-out decision, based on solid information in his detailed letters.

Now, he was her best chance—truthfully, her only chance—to keep the life she'd chosen. Besides, it was the right thing to do.

She met him halfway, let her eyes drift shut, and pressed her lips to his in a shallow mockery of a kiss.

As with the other two times he'd kissed her, she felt absolutely nothing.

"I'VE NEVER SEEN a young couple more in love than Holmes and Julia are," Phillip told John and Luke during their traditional weekly poker night.

The Three sequestered themselves in John's kitchen, surrounded by all the necessities: good food, excellent brandy, cards and chips, peace and quiet.

OK, "in love" was a bit of a stretch.

But the two of them were almost smitten with each other. Everything was progressing nicely; the kids had a wedding date set, Violet hadn't ever been happier, and Holmes's future as content husband and father was just about guaranteed.

And said wedding date was closer than any nuptials Andrew could pull off. So the forty dollars was guaran-*damn*-teed.

Success hummed in his veins, along with the smooth brandy, and he couldn't resist gloating. "Julia's parents—the illustrious Senator Jordon Tyndall and his lovely wife—are on their way, even as we speak, from Baltimore."

John plunked down his brandy sniffer. "They're coming?"

"I told you I had good news." Phillip puffed once more, enjoying the flavorful cigar, basking in the glow of success, and thriving on his friends' reactions. "They've decided to attend the ceremony. Gave Holmes their blessing! Violet and I couldn't be more pleased."

Luke raised his brows in silent amusement.

John sipped brandy.

The others may not want to talk about the lovebirds anymore, but Phillip wasn't done touting his own success. "You should've seen the pair of them together this morning. All sweet conversation and smiles."

John shuffled the cards, then offered the deck to

Luke to cut. "I did see them together. They didn't look all that enamored."

Luke took a bite of flaky almond cookie. "These are even better than usual." He popped the rest into his mouth.

"Don't be such a doomsayer." Phillip anted a white chip into the center of John's kitchen table. The others tossed in their own. "They've publicly announced their engagement. That has a way of changing things."

Julia was a Baltimore society lady; couldn't expect her to make a big romantic show of affection for his son in front of everyone, now could they?

All in all, a free ticket to bask in his personal triumph. "You should've seen them tonight at supper. Talking about a wedding trip to San Francisco."

John dealt each of them five cards with an easy flick of the wrist. "San Francisco? *Julia?*"

"Yes, Julia. My daughter-in-law is excited to tour all the famous spots."

"I'm just surprised she wants to spend her honeymoon in a city, that's all." John set down the deck. "I thought you said she liked the open spaces and countryside."

"It's not carved in stone." Phillip sorted his cards, not about to admit he'd embellished their talk more than a little. Did it really matter where they went on their wedding trip? No. How 'bout that! A big dog, straight off the deal.

"Pass." Luke tapped his cards into a neat stack and reached for another cookie.

Feeling lucky, Phillip tossed two chips into the pot.

"Open, already?" John considered his cards a minute. "Sure of yourself tonight, aren't you?"

"Oh, yes. My son's about to marry the prettiest girl on the planet. They're blissfully happy. Spend every waking hour in each other's company. I've practically got more grandchildren on the way." It was only a slight exaggeration. "I'd say that's about as good as it gets."

John kept his gaze on his cards. He moved one from the edge of his hand into the center. "I'm not convinced Holmes is all that happy."

"You're not his father," Phillip insisted, "so you can't be expected to know everything. I, on the other hand, am certain I'm right."

Phillip saw no reason to mention Violet had brought up concerns about Holmes's moods, too. So they had a difference of opinion on the matter.

He refused to believe anything was amiss. There were legitimate, solid reasons why Holmes wasn't the young man they'd sent off to school. Couldn't the others see the boy was still tired from his trip, and a little overexcited with the whirlwind courtship?

That did *not* indicate something was wrong.

On the contrary, it merely suggested Harvard had taught Holmes the maturity to take life seriously, and the wisdom to follow his heart.

John shrugged, and tossed in his bet. "Have you two talked about the whole arrangement? Does he want to marry Julia?"

"Of course he does! Like I said, he's blissfully happy. He's done with the rigors of school. I handed him an excellent partnership. He's falling in love with a beautiful woman, whom is the best match he could possibly ask for. And he's getting married in eight days."

Luke discarded four cards and drew replacements.

Phillip usually tried to read Luke's lousy poker face, but tonight, he had more important things on his mind. He pinned John with a glare. "Stop looking at me like that. I'm not going to talk to him about problems that don't exist."

"All I'm saying is Holmes deserves a chance to say no to this marriage." John glanced up. "You want to draw?"

Phillip hated John's way of provoking guilt, all the while trying to sound like a peacemaker. So he refused the bait. He considered his cards once more. "Stand pat."

"Suit yourself." John discarded two cards, drew more, and fit them into his hand.

"The happy couple is finalizing wedding plans," Phillip argued, "holding hands, whispering sweet nothings in each other's ear. It's the sweetest, most romantic courtship I've ever witnessed."

"If you say so." John did have a gift for evoking guilt, without being obvious about it. He would've made a damn fine attorney.

"I say so. Eight days, John," Phillip needled, "and you better cough up that full forty dollars."

"Looks to me," Luke muttered under his breath as he cast Phillip a pitying look, "like you're going to be the rotten egg."

"There you go again," John accused, "banking on a jury's verdict before it's out."

"This is infinitely more certain than banking on a jury." Phillip grinned, leaned back in his chair, and placed his bet. "I'm positive about my son's future with my soon-to-be daughter-in-law. And my forty dollars to finance Holmes's wedding trip to San Francisco."

John's expression dampened. "If this is all about the money—"

"It's a matter of principle," Phillip countered. "It's not the forty dollars, but *winning* that matters. Because winning equates with successfully securing Holmes's future happiness."

The others didn't seem convinced.

"And I am winning. Just ask Andrew. He'll tell you there's no way he's getting married in the next week, but Holmes is. That's exactly what we wanted, from the beginning."

Luke peered over his spectacles. "I had a talk with Andrew this afternoon."

"A talk." Phillip puffed his cigar. Excellent flavor. He savored it for a moment, watching the others for a response. "And did he tell you he's getting married in the next week?"

John and Luke exchanged one of those looks that

meant they were in on something together. Something devious.

"What did you two talk about?" Phillip demanded.

"Just gauging the race, that's all." Luke pulled a licorice whip from his shirt pocket, pulled off a fleck of flannel lint, and took a bite. He chewed, grinning like a little kid.

Fine. Phillip had no intention of allowing them to bully him. "Go ahead and gage this race, if you want. It should be obvious who's in the lead. The double ceremony's all scheduled, isn't it, Pastor?"

John nodded, solemnly. "It's on my calendar. I'll raise." John tossed his chips into the center of the highly polished table. A generous, confident bet.

Phillip took a second to consider his own hand, and the odds that John had anything better than a big dog. Not likely. "What, so now you're keeping secrets? Or a sore loser?"

"Me?" John's dimples deepened as he laughed. "Oh, all right. Andrew and Lillian had supper with the missus and me last night."

"So?" Phillip felt no threat, whatsoever. But he wanted to know what he was up against, just the same. "I thought you were going to announce he'd actually *bought* an engagement ring, not just shopped for one."

John's expression showed no hint of amusement. "They want us to counsel with them, weekly. Provide insights and instruction before their wedding."

Phillip couldn't help it—he laughed out loud. "What's this all about? No, I'll tell you what's behind this. Your son's scared to death of commitment. Holmes and Julia will have a dozen children before Andrew even makes it to the altar."

He chuckled...until he witnessed the look that passed between Luke and John. One of those brief exchanges that revealed a mother lode, without uttering a single word.

Luke tapped his cards into a neat stack and tossed them, face down, onto the table. "I'll drop."

Phillip stared at both of them. "What aren't you telling me?"

John left his cards on the table and went to the kitchen counter to refill his snack plate. He returned a moment later with a stack of almond cookies, two little ham sandwiches, and a buttermilk doughnut.

Only once John had taken a bite of doughnut did he answer the question. "Luke and I have discussed the matter, and we believe Julia deserves to know The Three sent for her, not Holmes."

Phillip couldn't believe his ears. "Why would we do something stupid like that?"

John didn't even hesitate. "Because I'm a man of conscience."

"So *now* you develop a conscience, eight days before the wedding."

John chewed, swallowed. "I'm going to pretend you didn't say that."

"Then I'm going to pretend," Phillip informed him, "that you're not suffering a fit of conscience over a pesky detail."

"It's not a pesky detail," John said with confidence. "Last night, I'm sitting at this very table, counseling my son and his wife-to-be about honesty within their relationship. About how important it is to communicate, to trust one another, to always tell the truth. And I'm thinking, good grief, I've condoned the worst kind of secrecy in a marriage I'm about to bless in one week's time."

"The two situations are completely different," Phillip argued. He didn't want to hear any of this. But John's sermon sunk in, quick and deep, like water into parched soil. It dashed his euphoria, undercut his confidence, and completely ruined his sense of well-being.

Phillip figured Luke, basking in his own son's wedded bliss, would surely come to his defense.

Luke chewed his licorice and shrugged. He offered no help, whatsoever.

"Julia is perfectly happy." Phillip reminded the others. "Delighted to have Holmes in her life. The pair of them are anticipating their rapidly-approaching wedding."

Holmes would be happy with Julia. He *would.* The two of them were meant for each other.

Phillip shoved aside the nagging doubts. He'd know, if his son were unhappy. Holmes had spine. He had character. He knew how to stand up for himself, always had. He wouldn't be bullied into a marriage he didn't want.

John refused to answer. He held Phillip's gaze, waiting for Phillip to suffer the same pangs of conscience. He'd have to wait a very long time.

"I'm don't have a problem with any of this," Phillip informed them both. "I know exactly what I'm doing, and I'm proud of it, because it's the right thing."

Still, no response. Phillip's conscience prickled with apprehension. But he'd be damned if he'd admit it.

"There's no point, whatsoever, in spoiling Julia's happiness. Or Holmes's."

Luke shrugged. He finished off his licorice whip. "So, where were we with this deal?"

Phillip raised the bet, throwing in three more chips. The drive of competition aggravated his dark mood. "I'll tell you where we are. No one's going to fold. Understand me? We're *one week* away from the I-do's. I see no reason to spoil everything now."

John picked up a few chips from his own stack. "I'll see yours, and raise." He held Phillip's gaze, in silent challenge.

So he thought his moral high ground was the winning way to go, did he? If any circumstances justified the suppression of evidence, this situation with Holmes and Julia was it. Nothing could make Phillip change his mind.

"Show me what you've got," Phillip said.

John shrugged and flipped over his hand. A royal flush. The grand mother of all poker hands. Phillip remembered, very well, the last time John had held this winning hand. He'd damn near crowed long before the showdown.

John raked in the pot, a cocky grin on his too-handsome face. So *now* he showed all the tell-tale signs.

Phillip struggled to maintain his composure. He swallowed a curse. He *detested* losing. Especially to his friends.

Luke reached for Phillip's cards. "What you got? Big dog? Not bad—" he chuckled, throwing salt in Phillip's wound "—for a losing hand."

Chapter Twenty-One

ABRAHAM LINCOLN, Conrad had read, was quoted as saying, "A man is only as happy as he makes up his mind to be."

The philosophy made good sense.

As Conrad worked with Holmes to carry borrowed dining room tables into the house, he talked himself into his new positive frame of mind. No more dwelling on the negative. He was through calling Holmes a lunkhead. From here on out, there would be no more pangs of jealousy.

He offered Holmes a big, amiable smile. "How's your day going? This is going to be some party!"

There was no point being a grump about things he couldn't change—including Holmes's marriage to Julia. In keeping with Lincoln's philosophy, Conrad could decide to live alongside his brothers and their wives in harmony.

Pop had always planned for every last one of his kids to stay in this house after their marriages. He liked the old-fashioned idea of two and three generations under the same roof. It was Pop's dream. He'd built this spacious house in order to make it possible.

Silas may have escaped Pop's plan, by moving next door to his wife's parents. But Holmes, the ever-obedient son, would do as Pop wished.

In Conrad's new optimism, he saw his diligent efforts could make it work.

This was what his parents desired. Moreover, it was what Julia wanted.

The sooner everything got back to normal, the better.

With his newfound positive attitude firmly nailed in place, Conrad felt much better. Optimistic. In control.

Almost as if the storm had finally passed him by.

Sunshine and blue skies abounded. He felt like whistling a bright melody. There were countless things to be thankful for, things he might not have noticed, if he'd allowed his misery to consume him.

Take the heavenly aromas drifting out of the summer kitchen, for one. The barbecued Cattleman's Shredded Beef was something to look forward to. He loved the rich, tangy, garlicky sauce. He could almost taste it.

He'd heard talk of Cadence chocolate-topped cheesecake with fresh berries and whipped sweet cream. If that wasn't something to anticipate with much relish, he didn't know what was.

Tonight, the house would be filled with friends and family, excellent food, and superb wine. By itself, any one of those things would've been something to smile about.

"Beautiful day, isn't it?" Conrad asked Holmes. "Warm. Plentiful sunshine. Nary a cloud in the sky."

Holmes grunted.

Perhaps it was Conrad's determination to find happiness in the moment, but Holmes's silence seemed markedly pronounced. Usually talkative, vibrant, and friendly, Holmes didn't seem like himself.

Conrad's good mood slipped. "You OK?"

Holmes walked backward as they carried the table through the yard. In the direct sunlight, his coloring looked pasty. As if he'd been locked in a classroom far too long. "Sure."

"You don't look too good. Still tired?"

"What?" He blinked, clearly caught unaware by the question. "Oh, yeah. Just tired."

Conrad didn't believe it. Not for a minute.

Little things gave Holmes away: the slump of his shoulders, the vague lack of attention he gave to conversation, a waning appetite. He'd eaten part of a sandwich at noon, but he hadn't enjoyed the meal. Could be he was nervous about his upcoming marriage, but Conrad figured there was more to it than that. He hoped it didn't have anything to do with what had happened between Conrad and Julia.

Guilt flooded in, sharp and immediate.

And Conrad shoved it back under the rug.

If anyone had a long list of things to be happy about, Holmes did. Today, the world revolved around him. He was about to greet a hundred guests, all anxious to welcome him home. He'd finished school with honors, had a full partnership handed to him on a silver platter, and his future was secure in every way. To top it off, within the week, he'd take Julia to wife.

All in all, a charmed life.

What did Holmes have to be down about? Conrad wasn't about to ask. No, sir. He clung to his determination to make this whole living side-by-side thing work out. The only way to do that was to mind his own business, especially when it came to anything remotely personal.

Particularly if it had anything to do with Julia.

Some odd sense made him suspicion that it did.

Together, he and Holmes situated the first table in the front parlor. The whole household hummed with activity. Hired women carried in armfuls of ironed tablecloths and napkins. The windows stood open to allow drafts of fresh, sun-warmed air inside. Cut lilacs stood in several vases, lined up on the sideboard for use as centerpieces later on. The blossoms filled the sunlit rooms with delicate fragrance.

Despite the commotion, Conrad noticed Julia the moment she entered the parlor. A smudged white apron covered her navy blue work dress. Tiredness dampened the usual light in her eyes. With a soft smile, she tucked a loose lock of hair behind her ear.

She looked wonderful.

Conrad's heart forgot he wasn't supposed to be happy to see her. He had the sudden urge to go to her. To do what, he didn't know. But he felt a distinct, urgent tug in her direction.

Her gaze settled on his for a fleeting moment.

Her smile seemed to fade in that brief second before she turned to Holmes.

Chastising himself, Conrad glanced away. He accepted an armload of linens one of the ladies handed to him to place on the settee behind himself. He didn't want to notice the interaction between Holmes and Julia, but it was impossible to ignore.

Answering Julia's summons, Holmes crossed the room to her side. She looked up into Holmes's face, bestowing the smile Conrad remembered too well, then spoke to him in lowered tones. Conrad couldn't help but note the confidence between them. The familiarity. And closeness.

Holmes leaned down, to better hear something Julia said.

That fast, Conrad's good mood evaporated in the wake of jealousy searing through his veins. All Holmes had done was walk up to Julia and talk to her. He hadn't touched her, hadn't kissed her, hadn't embraced her.

Yet.

But this was only the beginning.

He may have thought he could paste on a happy

face and pretend he didn't love Julia. How could he survive watching the two of them together, day after day, loving each other, growing closer together, sharing all the things he wanted but could not have?

Making up his mind to be happy would *never* make everything OK.

Life in this house would be unbearable. Torture, day in and day out. An absolute hell.

In that moment, Conrad knew he could never survive watching Holmes be a husband to Julia. No amount of positive thinking, no choice to be happy, would ever change that.

Blindly, he headed away from them and through the open front door.

He had to get out of there. Go far, far away.

He bumped into Gabriel on the threshold. Two straight-back chairs in Gabriel's arms blocked his path, but Conrad pushed past.

The chairs thudded to the floor. Gabriel called, "Conrad?"

Ignoring everyone else, Conrad entered the house through the side door into the library. He thundered up the stairs, taking them two at a time.

Below, Julia's laughter mingled with Holmes's. Conrad's gut clenched at the sound.

In light of everything that had transpired, it was almost a relief Pop had refused to sell the dairy and surrounding property. At least Conrad still had his money in the bank.

That spread over in Lake County was looking better all the time. Far enough away from Julia that he wouldn't have to see her living with Holmes. Wouldn't have to hear her laughter. Wouldn't live every day of his life in utter torture.

Gabriel, being Gabriel, didn't bother to knock before he walked into Conrad's room. He watched as Conrad shoved the bare necessities into a satchel.

Conrad expected a lecture. Undoubtedly, Gabriel wouldn't take kindly to Conrad skipping out of the welcome-home, nor all the work before and after the shindig.

To his surprise, Gabriel said nothing. He simply watched.

Conrad glanced at his brother as he headed for the door. "Tell Ma and Katherine I'm sorry."

"Tell them yourself."

He should. But he couldn't. His windpipe twisted closed. How could he explain his reasons for leaving?

Gabriel indicated the hastily packed bag. "You planning on spending more than a couple days away?"

It wasn't fair to Ma or Katherine. His conscience wrenched. Someday—he couldn't promise how soon—he'd beg their forgiveness for running out before the party. And before the weddings.

He couldn't trust himself to speak. He nodded.

"You planning to miss the weddings?" Gabriel's voice echoed with disappointment. "You'll break Ma's heart. And Katherine's. You ought to tell them you have feelings for Julia."

"No." He turned a lethal gaze on his brother. "And neither will you."

Julia's laughter echoed up the stairs, aggravating Conrad's agony. He could easily imagine the light in her eyes, the expression on her lovely face.

God, he *loved* her.

Nothing could make him watch her pledge her life, and her heart, to Holmes.

With something that looked far too much like empathy, Gabriel squeezed Conrad's shoulder. "You sure you're doing the right thing?"

With a dark glare, Conrad pushed past his brother. He couldn't talk about this. He had to get away from this house and its madness before it consumed him.

Gabriel held his ground. "Think about it, Conrad. Are you sure?"

Conrad stared his brother down. Every ounce of pain he'd suffered over the past weeks had been about doing the right thing. "Absolutely certain."

AFTER MANY of the guests had said their goodbyes, Julia went in search of Holmes. Throughout the evening's festivities, it became evident she must ask him one specific question, and accept the consequences.

Perhaps half an hour earlier, she'd seen him visiting with an older gentleman on the porch outside the dining room. Cooler night wind raised gooseflesh on her arms as she stepped through the door. Two ladies visited beside the porch railing. She exchanged pleasantries with them, then noticed Holmes, about twenty feet down the side of the house.

He sat alone in a wicker chair and stared into the darkness. Light spilled through windowpanes, emphasizing his complete stillness. Romantic strains of Schubert's *Unfinished Symphony*, played by the string quartet, mingled with conversation inside the house.

"There you are." She offered a warm smile as he glanced up.

His blank expression persisted for the space of a second, then cleared. He'd loosened his necktie and unbuttoned his collar, handsome in his well-cut suit. Always well mannered, he stood. "Am I needed inside?"

"No. Everyone's content."

The guests were enjoying themselves, but it was evident Holmes wasn't. If her suspicions were correct, he wasn't any happier about the cascade of wedding plans that swept them toward the inevitable ceremony than she was.

"May I join you?" she asked.

"Yes, of course."

Chair legs scraped over painted floorboards as he pulled a second chair closer to his own and offered it to her.

She sat and cradled her wineglass between her

hands.

He took his seat and stared out over the yard for several moments. A chill breeze tousled tree limbs and carried the soothing smells of the clean out-of-doors. Everything smelled so fresh, so good here.

Inside, laughter erupted. Phillip carried on a boisterous conversation with one of his contemporaries. He accepted hearty congratulations for Holmes's return and the upcoming weddings. The men must've wandered deeper into the house, for their voices faded, leaving the dull murmur of mingled conversations and the continued, familiar strains of music in the background.

"Your parents seem pleased with the evening," she said. How she hoped it was so. A few long looks from Holmes's parents had her worrying. She supposed the pain from her father's criticism of galas she'd hosted for him colored her assumptions.

Distracted, he took a few seconds to answer. "The party's been a tremendous success. Thanks," he murmured, sincerity evident. "You did a great job."

Sweet, kind Holmes. His lower expectations might be his greatest quality.

Julia hadn't any difficulty noting the sadness in his tone. He tried to mask his discontent, but he wasn't the same man who'd written those letters, bright with hope for their future together.

"What's wrong, Holmes?" She watched for his response.

"Nothing," he said after a moment. "Nothing at all."

She gathered her thoughts, and tried again. "We've been swept away by Katherine's excitement, pulled into her grand plans for a combined ceremony. We've not had the chance to talk about it."

A few seconds passed. Then he asked, "What would you like to discuss?"

"Marriage is a serious commitment," she said softly.

"Yes, it is."

"Too important to rush into. Wouldn't you agree?"

He seemed to think that over. "I know ours wasn't a conventional courtship."

"No, it wasn't. But I came to know you well enough, through our letters, to see you're merely pretending to be happy now."

"I'm happy," he insisted, too quickly.

"You've made gallant efforts, all day, to convince everyone of that. The family. Your numerous guests. I believe you might have succeeded."

"You doubt me?"

She doubted him, yes. And herself. What was she doing, going along with this farce of an engagement? Pretending—just like Holmes was—that they had any prospect of a life together?

"I care about you," she told him, potently aware caring wasn't enough. It never would be. "But I want to be happy. Don't you?"

He didn't answer.

Obviously, he was just as leery of a union as she was. She'd hoped they could arrive at a mutual decision. Much better that way. But if they both continued with this charade, they could well end up wedded. "Holmes?"

Distracted, he pulled his blank stare from the darkened yard and finally focused on her face. "Hmm?"

He merely needed to see she had doubts. That's all it would take. He'd be sure to agree, once he could see she wasn't keen on the idea any longer. "Let's put it off for a while, shall we? I'm not ready for this commitment, any more than you are."

"Not ready? Nonsense." His chuckle sounded forced as he took her hand. His touch, warm and firm, didn't excite her. She may as well be holding her young nephew's hand—not an encouraging thought.

She looked away from his smooth, soft hand, painfully similar in shape and size to Conrad's.

"I never meant to worry you," he went on, "especially with your parents on their way here, the invitations out, and announcements already in the newspapers. It was unkind of me to cause you a moment's concern. For that, I apologize."

She noted these weren't declarations of love. Or even hope for a contented, companionable union. He'd mentioned only duty and responsibility.

She held Holmes's gaze, remembering that his letters had persuaded her to run away from home, defy her father, and bank everything on her future with him. There had been a time, not so distant, when she would've done anything to become his wife. My, how her perspective had changed.

The time had come to ask the question that had nagged at her, all evening. She ought to feel trepidation, but surprisingly, didn't. Perhaps the calm came because she already knew the answer, and it didn't frighten her. She yearned to hear it, because it would free them both.

"I need the truth, Holmes Macquarie. Do you honestly *want* to marry me?"

A man and his wife strolled through the yard, arm in arm, toward the line of waiting buggies and wagons. Julia watched them talking and laughing together, to give Holmes time to respond.

When Holmes remained silent, she studied his profile. Lamplight warmed the coppery hues of his hair, cast golden shadows along his jaw and cheekbone. Her heart tumbled at the familial likeness he bore to Conrad.

He closed his eyes for a second or two. To hide his reaction? To collect his thoughts? For courage?

The moment stretched, and it became evident he wasn't going to answer. He couldn't, because her hunch had been correct. Since the time he'd invited her west, and that very moment, his affections had changed.

What a relief!

She set her wineglass on the windowsill in order to place her other hand atop their joined ones. She squeezed in silent support.

"It's all right," she told him. "I know you don't

want to marry me, and that's OK, because I don't—"

"No, no, Julia. You misunderstand." He sounded strained and worried.

"But you—"

"I *want* to marry you," he vowed, giving a valiant effort to sound convincing. "You're precisely the kind of woman I *need* for my wife. I couldn't have chosen better, had we known each other before."

How was she supposed to respond to that? "But you don't love me. And I don't—"

"Julia," he said, leaning closer. His grip tightened on her fingers. "Frankly, I'm glad that's the way it is. And I'm glad we can be open with each other, and approach our union without emotions to entangle everything."

She shook her head, not wanting to talk about any approaching union. She was still caught back on the absence of love issue.

"You're right," he went on. "I'm not myself. And you deserve to know it's over. She doesn't need to come between us."

Surprised, Julia completely forgot the thought she'd been holding onto.

She? She, who?

In that instant, something subtle shifted within her, making sense of all the confusion. The puzzle pieces slid into place—Holmes's delayed return from San Francisco or wherever he'd been, his somber dispositions, the elusive differences between the man she'd come to adore through his letters and the man she'd finally met in person.

She'd never guessed he'd fallen in love with someone else.

Had she known him, at all?

She found it didn't matter. Relief, welcome and sweet, flowed through her. She wanted to laugh. Unlike hearing Conrad's confession about Sally Tibbs, Julia didn't feel one iota of jealousy knowing Holmes had loved another woman.

"Forgive me, Holmes, but if you love someone else, how can you profess a desire to marry me?"

He couldn't hold her gaze. Despair dampened his features. "She didn't want me."

Empathy flooded through Julia. The details of his loss were irrelevant. Her aching heart bonded to him with an immediate affinity.

Two of a kind.

How ironic, that the very circumstances that kept Holmes and herself from fully committing were what made her feel closest to him.

"How long has she been gone from your life?" Probably a year, because that coincided with his newspaper advertisement. Perhaps even longer. Regardless of the length of time, there may be a chance this woman would reconsider.

He shrugged.

In that moment, she understood what she had to do. She and Conrad had no chance of a future together—he'd made that perfectly clear—but she saw no reason at all why Holmes shouldn't be happy.

Weeks of unsettled anxiety swept aside, making room for a welcome sense of peace. Finally, she had a very good reason to call off their farce of a wedding. "We can't possibly consider going through with the marriage. It's not right."

"Now, hold on," he insisted. "There's no reason to cancel our plans."

"No reason? You love her. You should be with her, not me."

He met her gaze fully. "No, Julia. *This* is where I should be."

"I find that quite hard to believe—"

"She's no threat to you." He sounded certain. "She made it very clear she wants nothing more to do with me. Whatever was between us is over."

She hesitated. Considered everything he'd said. "I'm sorry." She meant it. How well she understood the pain of rejection.

His face, cast half in lamplight and half in shadows, turned away. "Don't be. It wasn't your doing."

He drew a deep breath. "I opened a correspondence between us, suggested marriage, and invited you here. You're a lovely, kind woman—exactly what I hoped you'd be, and what I need. I'm a man of my word. My offer stands."

This marriage proposal wasn't phrased as a question, any more than his first had been. Why *would* he ask? He believed they'd reached an agreement, months ago. She knew her letters had strongly implied her intention to become his wife. A unwritten promise. But a promise, just the same.

And he fully expected her to keep it.

"You forfeited a great deal," he reminded her. "For me. I won't see you disappointed. I see no reason why we shouldn't be married on Saturday. I promise you, Miss Tyndall, my full devotion and unerring fidelity."

What, precisely, was she supposed to say to that? Her only argument—*I love Conrad, not you*—would prove useless. Given Holmes's confession, he clearly believed love for someone else was an inadequate reason to call off a wedding.

Before she had time to come to any conclusion, whatsoever, Holmes stood and gently tugged her to her feet. "It's time to go inside and say goodnight to our guests."

Like every lawyer and politician of her acquaintance, he'd made his closing arguments. His whole demeanor announced the conversation was over. Settled. Put to bed. He'd never broach the subject again.

Unfortunately, she was unprepared to give a rebuttal.

Oh, but she would. Before her father showed up and wrested the chance away from her.

Holmes could count on it.

Chapter Twenty-Two

ON THE DAY Julia had run away from home, she had never anticipated such happiness when she saw her father again. Especially not before she wore Holmes's wedding ring.

Relief and joy flooded through Julia as she hugged her mother, then her father on the front steps of the Macquarie front porch. Tears filled her eyes at the sweet reunion.

Almost a day preparing her rebuttal and she was no closer to finding the right words to convince Holmes she truly didn't want to wed him. After all, she couldn't very well divulge Conrad's role in the demise of their budding romance. She would not come between the brothers that way.

Now that her parents were here, everything would be all right.

"I'm glad you're here, Daddy."

He would intercede. Undoubtedly, he would insist she return home with him. And make it quite clear he wouldn't allow her to marry the likes of Holmes. He would save her—and Holmes alike—from Holmes's misguided honor.

She could count on it.

Her father held her gaze for a moment, his handsome smile so dear and familiar. "I'm glad to be here, Dolly."

Yes, everything would be all right again.

Bolstered, at peace, Julia made proper introductions. "Father, Mother, this is Holmes Macquarie. Holmes, my parents, Senator and Mrs. Jordon Tyndall."

If Holmes were intimidated, it didn't show. He offered a handshake. "It's a pleasure to meet you again, sir."

"The pleasure is mine." Her father returned the handshake with vigor. His smile, sincere and warm, made Julia's stomach tumble. "I'm delighted to finally make acquaintance with the man my daughter has chosen."

THREE DAYS after her parents' arrival at the ranch, Julia lay in bed beside Portia and watched the faint play of moonlight over the plastered ceiling and walls. Silver beams made Holmes's most recent bouquet appear blue and gray in the surreal light coming through the window. The floral fragrance lingered, a haunting yet pleasing scent.

It reminded her she was supposed to have affectionate feelings for her groom.

Portia's soft, rhythmic breathing gave way to a moderate snore. The older woman could sleep through anything. An earthquake could rattle the house's foundation, and Portia wouldn't feel a thing.

Julia turned over, putting her back to her aunt, and vigorously fluffed her pillow. She snuggled in beneath the covers, trying to get comfortable.

It was hopeless.

Everything was supposed to be OK by now. But it wasn't.

Two days before the wedding she didn't want, her parents and her groom were the best of friends. Jordon Tyndall, who didn't care for most of the people he met, had taken an instant liking to Holmes.

Her parents were sound asleep in Holmes's vacated bed, probably dreaming of Julia's future as Mrs. Holmes Macquarie. Holmes had graciously given up his comfortable bed to Julia's parents. He'd taken the narrow bed in his brother Silas's unused room.

This close to her nuptials, Julia's thoughts ought to be centered around her groom, but she found herself tortured, almost constantly, by thoughts of Conrad.

A half-dozen times in the past few days, she'd thought she'd heard his voice, only to discover it was one of his brothers speaking. She was tired of seeing him everywhere she turned. Because it was never really him.

He was gone.

Had been gone since before the welcome-home party. One minute, he'd been setting up tables, the next, he'd vanished.

No one knew where. Nor when he'd return.

Memories of the time they'd spent together, the ease with which they'd talked about all sorts of things, the riding lessons he'd given, and his kisses haunted dreams and waking hours alike.

Mostly, she remembered his kisses.

How, exactly, was she supposed to justify *that?* She couldn't make excuses. She couldn't even confront Conrad, just to make sure her feelings for him weren't serious, because he'd disappeared sometime the afternoon of Holmes's welcome-home party—six days earlier. Gabriel had passed a vague message to the family, something about dairy business that had taken Conrad away.

She didn't want to care. It shouldn't matter. But she did care and it did matter.

Her emotions still warred between humiliation at his rejection and loving him more than she ever had.

How could she possibly live on this ranch, in this house, with Conrad as a brother-in-law?

The very thought was insane. Unthinkable. Ludicrous.

Loneliness engulfed her. The future stretched forward in an endless stretch of disappointment. The magic of the great American west, the joy of embracing her new adventurous life with her very own cowboy had lost its glamour.

She tipped onto her back and kicked to loosen the constrictive covers around her feet.

She wasn't about to marry Conrad, so she should stop missing him so badly. His absence should've given her peace to approach the wedding with proper anticipation. Instead, her sanity was nearly shot.

Portia's breathing caught on a sudden cough. As her aunt came awake, Julia lay perfectly still. She wasn't in any mood to explain her sleeplessness.

"Julia?" Portia whispered.

A second or two passed. Julia didn't want to answer.

"Dolly, what is it?"

Julia sighed. "Can't sleep."

"Getting cold feet?"

"No."

Apparently Portia saw right through that lie. She shifted a little. "What's there to fret about?" She yawned, clearing the sleepiness from her voice. "I never would've thought I'd see the day my brother changed his mind, but change it he did. Phillip Macquarie has a gift for persuasive arguments, hasn't he?"

Julia had heard all about Phillip's letter to her father. This may have been the only documented case of

Jordon Tyndall allowing someone else's platform to sway his convictions. His party, should they ever find out about it, would be appalled.

"Hmmm." Julia turned over to face her aunt. "Apparently, he's more gifted than I'd thought."

Portia giggled with delight. "I think it's fabulous Jordon's eyes are opened. I'd say Phillip's letter arrived just in time."

A most unfortunate turn of events.

"I think it carried a great deal of weight," Portia surmised, "to hear a fine attorney's argument for Holmes. Of course, you already knew all those wonderful things about him, long before your father decided to open his eyes to possibilities outside the realm of the promising Gregory Gerritsen."

"Gregory will be troubled to learn he's lost Father's esteem." Her dad had groomed Greg for years, expecting more than an ally; he'd chosen him for a son-in-law.

"He'll be sorry he's lost you."

"Only because I'm a Tyndall. And he lost me months ago."

Portia rose and propped her head upon a cupped palm. "I believe he cared for you, in his own way, but that's neither here nor there, because you chose Holmes."

"Hmm." Holmes was all of those wonderful things Portia had mentioned. And more. He was kind. And considerate. And the thought of sharing a marriage bed with him brought on waves of unsettling distress.

"Dolly, what's the matter?"

How could she explain the anxiety that tied her in knots? Plain and simple, the man she'd chosen, wagered everything in order to have, wasn't right for her.

He may be, superficially, the things she thought she wanted in a husband. But she didn't love him. And he didn't love her.

Why couldn't anyone *else* see that?

The whole household scurried around, completely

oblivious to her anxiety. Katherine, wrapped up in her own joy, noticed little else. Phillip was delirious with anticipation. Julia didn't know why this should surprise her—her *own parents* were so absorbed with getting settled and helping with final preparations, they hadn't any inkling of her distress.

It had taken a sleepless night of tossing and turning to alert Portia to the idea there might be a problem.

"It's just cold feet," Portia determined. "Holmes is a wonderful man. Intelligent. Gracious. Handsome."

That made Julia feel worse. She'd wanted to love Holmes. Planned on it. Wagered everything on her future happiness, here, as Holmes's wife. But everything had gone wrong.

Simply put, Holmes wasn't Conrad.

"I don't love him," Julia confided.

"Hmm. Complicates things, then, doesn't it?"

Julia groaned. "Why didn't I say something, the moment Katherine brought up the idea of a combined ceremony? I should've told her I wasn't ready. I should've interrupted the conversation, made a scene, and put an end to it. But I got sucked in by the undertow, and next thing I knew, I was adrift, out to sea."

"Hmm."

"Drowning."

"Ah."

"I need a life raft."

"Yes."

"You're no help, Portia." Julia let out her breath in a huff, and dropped onto her back. "What am I going to do?"

"You're looking for sage advice?"

"If you've got some, I want to hear it."

Portia hesitated. "Do you, indeed?"

Uneasiness swept through Julia, again. No, she wasn't entirely sure she wanted to know what Portia thought. If there were an easy way out of this fix, Julia would've discovered it by herself.

"All I know is I'm glad I've lived my life alone, rather than wed merely for the sake of marriage." Portia settled back in, tucked the covers beneath her chin, and sighed with contentment.

Julia agreed with her aunt's viewpoint. She felt the same way. If she'd merely wanted security and support and children, she could've been married years earlier.

"Twice, I received marriage proposals," Portia continued. "And twice, I made the same decision."

"Twice?" Julia hadn't heard a thing about Portia having had a romance, much less proposals of marriage.

"You think I'm making up bedtime stories, just to amuse you? Yes, two proposals. From very decent, eligible bachelors. But I wasn't about to marry just because somebody asked me and just because my parents expected me to accept."

That sounded like Portia. Thumb her nose at tradition. Do her own thing, rather than settle for less than she deserved.

"You did the very same thing," Portia said after a moment. "You ran away from home, risking alienating your father in the process, so you wouldn't have to marry a man you didn't love."

Ooh. It was a reminder she needed desperately, even if she wasn't prepared to hear it.

That was precisely why she'd left home. She'd refused her father's choice of husbands, because she'd been determined to marry for love. Because she didn't want to live in a loveless marriage. Because she'd known what she wanted, and Greg hadn't been it.

How could she have forgotten?

What had changed, that she'd so much as *consider* marrying Holmes, whom she didn't love, and who didn't love her in return?

If she dared, she'd walk away, right now. "I'm supposed to get married in two days. It feels like a death sentence."

"Technically, a day and a half."

"Changing my mind this soon before the ceremony is a far sight better than a day or two after."

"Yes, that's certainly preferable," Portia muttered.

"This isn't just about Holmes and myself. Holmes's good parents have their hearts set on it." She loved them, even if she didn't quite love Holmes anymore. Without him, she'd lose the chance to marry into this family.

"You're not marrying Holmes's parents," Portia insisted.

Violet anticipated, with much joy and rejoicing, the marriages of two of her children in the white church in the center of Liberty. Phillip had warmed to the idea of Katherine's union with David, and seemed quite happy about all the wedding plans.

The day would be special for the whole Macquarie family, but especially for Katherine. "I don't want to spoil Katherine's special day."

"Katherine, like all brides, won't notice or care what anybody else is doing."

That made Julia chuckle, despite her anxiety. Portia was right. She couldn't marry Holmes, merely because she'd given tacit approval, nor because she adored his family and wanted to remain here.

Marriage was forever.

She could not, in good conscience, trap herself or Holmes in a union based upon so little. It wouldn't be fair to either of them.

She might have always fancied herself in love with Holmes, never known better, if it hadn't been for Conrad.

He'd changed everything.

He'd changed her.

Unfortunately, Conrad was the only man she could see herself with, and he'd rejected her. Even if he were at home, nothing would change. He'd made his position very clear.

"Oh, Portia." Julia's eyes stung with the threat of

tears. A lump the size of her fist closed off her air. Still, she knew she'd made the right choice. "I can't go through with it. I can't marry Holmes."

Portia patted Julia's hand in a show of comfort.

A minute or so crept past. The sturdy house settled. Wind brushed branches of the great oak against the roof.

Finally, Portia spoke. "Is it possible you'll come to love him, given time?"

Interesting question. If she and Holmes were to live elsewhere, away from Conrad, could she grow to love Holmes?

She lay still, considering the possibility. A moment passed, and she had her answer. A soft, simple impression that her capacity to love may be limitless, but it had one finite focus. Whether tomorrow or a lifetime from now, she knew that would never change.

Her heart belonged to Conrad, although he didn't want it. He didn't want her. He never would.

Tears, held back by sheer willpower over the past week, spilled. "No."

She knew what she had to do; she'd return to Maryland. What she didn't know was how she'd manage to break the news to everyone else.

"I should tell Holmes." Julia tried to swallow the tightness in her throat.

The wedding rehearsal wasn't for another eight hours or so. She'd have ample time to find Holmes alone, before then. Despite the pain it would cause everyone involved, she'd find a gentle way to confess she couldn't marry him.

"He should hear it from me first."

Portia sighed, snuggled deeper into the covers. "I would hope so."

POT-BELLIED CLOUDS stole the last vestiges of

midday sunlight. The incessant drizzle had lasted all morning, and showed no signs of letting up.

Conrad sat at a dining table near the window, his cold meal forgotten. No one's roast chicken was as good as Ma's, not even Katherine's. Certainly not this fare he'd paid too much for. Seemed he'd lost his appetite somewhere between home and here.

Could be the gloomy weather, or the unrelenting homesickness, but Lake County didn't appeal. The spread he'd seriously considered buying wasn't worth the asking price. At least not to Conrad, who knew what home looked like, and that place wasn't it.

He'd thought looking over that tract of farmland and moving forward with his life would be a comfort, but it'd only aggravated his loneliness.

Lit lamps on each table reflected back dully from the window panes.

So little light in his darkening world.

A wagon lumbered past, the team slogging along the muddy street. The driver had his coat collar turned up around his ears to ward off the wet.

He accepted a refill on his coffee, determined to sit a spell and hope the worst of the rain passed. Jupiter was dry and warm at the livery. No need to rush anywhere.

No one waited on him.

His room at the boarding house was small, sparse, and lonesome. The only view, a neighboring brick building.

The door opened, bringing a rush of cool, humid air. Conrad didn't turn to see who came in. He didn't know more than a handful of souls nearby; no sense turning to say hello.

Rain pocked the standing puddles.

Damn, but this town was ugly.

The hardware store across the way needed a fresh coat of paint. Beside it, awnings adorning the apothecary had faded to a nondescript shade that might have once been blue.

Nothing like the well-tended shops in Liberty.

Yeah, well, no place on earth was as wonderful as home.

Somebody hung his pommel slicker a coat peg, plopped his sodden hat on a spare chair.

Then pulled back the empty chair at Conrad's table.

Pulling his musings from the puddles, he found Gabriel, dripping water and frowning

The kid collapsed into the seat. His chin hadn't been shaved. Looked half-drowned, like he'd swum across the county line, rather than ridden.

"You look like hell," Gabriel muttered.

"Could say the same about you."

He didn't want to be glad to see his brother. Didn't want to acknowledge his arrival eased the homesickness.

So he scowled. "What are you doing here?"

"Came to fetch you home."

Conrad shot his kid brother a darker glower. "Why?"

"You going to eat this?" Without waiting for a response, Gabriel pulled meat off a leg bone and stuffed it in his mouth. Chewed vigorously.

Must've left about dark last night and ridden straight through. Despite the foul weather. Had to have had a mighty compelling reason to do something like that.

Panic flared. "Ma? She OK?" Her heart had been giving her grief, her coloring scary as hell.

Gabriel gestured with a chicken wing he'd all but stripped clean. "Worried about you. But fine." Another glance communicated *the wedding, fretting about that.*

He didn't want to think of the wedding. Couldn't.

So he signaled the waitress over. Ordered another hot meal and coffee for his brother. The kid was hungry enough to need it, too.

It didn't sit right with him to see the kid cold, wet, and hungry. Certainly not on his account.

"No need to worry," Conrad assured. "I'm here 'cause I want to be."

"Nope. You're *here* because Julia's *there*. And she's with Holmes."

Too much truth. If Gabriel could see it, it's possible the rest of the family could, too. Not something he wanted to contemplate.

He pulled a coin from his pocket, dropped it on the table. Pushed back his chair. Time to go.

"Sit down." Gabriel didn't even look up from the cold spuds he shoveled into his mouth.

"I've heard enough."

"I didn't ride a long, hard night to say howdy-do and eat your cold leavings." Anger lurked in Gabriel's tone. Anger and something far more uncomfortable. Something akin to concern. Or caring.

As the server set a hot, fragrant plate of roast chicken in front of Gabriel, Conrad sank into his chair. He didn't want to fight with his brother anymore.

The woman filled both coffee cups. Took Gabriel's order for two slabs of cherry pie.

Once she'd left them in peace, Gabriel picked right back up where he'd left off. "You've had nearly a week to sulk. It's time to come home."

It might *never* be time to go home.

He doubted he'd have the stamina to live in the same house, not even the same town as Julia, with her forever lost to him.

"It's not up to you." He had no intention of explaining himself. Not to Gabriel.

Gabriel stilled, his fork halfway to his mouth. Gravy dripped back onto his plate. His gaze snared Conrad's.

"No, it's not," Gabriel finally admitted. "But I won't sit by and watch you ruin your life."

Conrad snorted, anger rising faster than he thought possible. "I'm *not* ruining—"

"There's *nothing*—" Gabriel interrupted.

"—*my* life."

"—for you here." He plunking his laden fork into his meal.

Sad. Yet undeniably true. "I'm doing what I have to."

"You've had time to buy that ranch you came here for. Haven't yet. Know why?"

Damn, pushy kid. Thought he knew everything. Followed him here, checked up on him. Who'd he been talking to, anyway? "I'm sure you're fixing to tell."

"You don't want that ranch. You don't want to live here." Gabriel gestured at the bleak scene through the window.

No sense arguing.

"This isn't the life you want."

Might as well, given what he wanted most could never be his.

God, would the sharp pain brought on by every thought of Julia, *ever* fade?

Gabriel must have seen some of that, clear as day on Conrad's face, because he reached across the table toward him.

Conrad expected a brotherly chuck to the shoulder. Or a strong grip that communicated support. What he got was an open-handed smack on the cheek.

"Ow! What was that for?"

"You just gonna lie down and accept the way things are?" Gabriel demanded. "You just gonna let Julia marry Holmes?"

When he put it like that, he sounded downright cowardly. Not one bit honorable. "Yeah."

"You're an idiot."

He swallowed, hard. Wanted to hurt Gabriel back. "I'm not the hard-hearted, bride-thieving kid brother you are."

The insults tasted sour as week-old milk in his mouth. Brothers didn't give up on each other, didn't go their separate ways like a man could when things didn't work out with his girl.

If he were honest with himself, he wouldn't blame

Gabriel for the trouble between them. Truth was, Conrad had made a mountain out of the Sally debacle. A mountain that stood solidly between himself and his brother. Shameful, that.

Gabriel was still the same kid brother, whom he had loved... *still* loved—no matter what. Nothing could change that. Not even a woman. Certainly not Sally.

The very moment the hateful accusations were out of Conrad's mouth, Gabriel stilled.

Conrad's shot had hit the mark, and he instantly regretted it. "I didn't mean that."

He was ready for a counter-strike. For a fist. Hurled accusations. To hear the door slam behind Gabriel as he left.

The last thing he anticipated was Gabriel's sudden laughter. Hearty, full-bodied, roiling laughter that drew the attention of every person sitting in the gloomy restaurant. To punctuate his amusement, he slapped a palm against the table.

"Get over it," Gabriel ordered, still grinning widely. "You don't even *like* Sally. Julia's the one you're all tied in knots over."

True. All true. Conrad scrubbed a palm down his face. "Precisely why I'm here, as you so aptly put it."

"The reason *I'm* here," Gabriel sobered a little, "is you're my brother. Don't know why, given that mean mouth of yours, but I love you."

"Yeah." His throat closed, tight. That bond was in their blood. For keeps. He loved Gabriel; he'd missed his companionship, his friendship.

Gabriel's attention had wandered to the storm outside. Taking in the contentment on his brother's face, Conrad had a most unpleasant realization.

He hadn't cut himself off from only Gabriel, but from the whole family. He had no one to blame for his current miserable state but himself.

One thing he'd seen too clearly during this lonesome week; family was *all* that mattered. Sad that it had taken leaving them to see that.

He *did* love his brothers, all of them. Loved his parents. His baby sister, whose wedding was tomorrow. He'd shoved all of these precious emotions under the rug, right along with the unwanted love he couldn't control; love for the one woman who'd hold his heart forever.

Lightning blazed overhead, brightening the gloomy building and street beyond with an eerie light. Thunder followed with hardly a second to spare. That strike had been close.

Too close.

The din of conversation around them spiked. Exclamations of worry, delight, hysteria from a pair of young girls. Even a whoop of elation.

Another brilliant flash of lightning, booming thunder almost simultaneous. Rain sluiced from the sky as if someone had opened an irrigation gate. Water poured off the roof, flooded the sidewalk and washed into the muddy street.

The waitress set two warm wedges of dried cherry pie before them. It smelled heavenly, but the crust wasn't as golden as Katherine's. Not as thin or flaky.

Gabriel was right; Conrad wanted to go home.

Needed to go home to his family.

Love was too precious, too important to treat like rubbish.

So where did that leave him?

Either completely alone, where he could bury the emotions that eviscerated him...or he could return home. Where he had the joy and angst and companionship of brothers and sister, parents, neighbors.

And Julia.

If the only way she could be part of his life was as a sister-in-law, wasn't that better than nothing at all?

He might not survive it.

Gabriel tucked into his pie. "This is good."

Conrad pricked the crust with the tines of his fork. His appetite good and gone.

"Eat up. We've got a long, treacherous ride ahead of us."

Conrad gave a listless shrug. "Think you've convinced me, eh?"

Ignoring the question, Gabriel put another huge bite of pie in his mouth. Chewed. "I'm thinking we ought to hunker down here tonight. You got a room somewhere?"

"Yeah."

"Don't want to risk the horses until the storm lets up."

He didn't want an answer, and Conrad didn't give him one.

Rain pounded on the roof, the sound rising to a roar. Came down with such a vengeance, he couldn't hardly see the storefronts on other side of the street.

"You going to eat that?" Gabriel gestured with his fork at Conrad's pie.

In answer, Conrad pushed it across the table.

Dread chilled him from the inside out.

Sitting through the wedding ceremony would be utter torture. After that, there was no telling how long he could tolerate living at home.

He made no promises, made no plans past the celebrations.

All that would have to wait.

BY THE TIME Julia finally caught a glimpse of Holmes, the wedding rehearsal was set to begin.

The notion had occurred to her, numerous times during his conspicuous absence that morning, that he'd taken off.

Holmes stood in the doorway, taking in the commotion of the whole wedding party—Macquaries, Tyndalls, Ormes, plus many close friends—and grinned. The big, happy, delighted grin of a man who was about to get everything he wanted.

Oh, if he only knew.

In keeping with Holmes's buoyant mood, the sun's rays brightened, streaming through the stained-glass windows. Jewel-toned light puddled on the shiny floor and plastered walls.

If Julia believed in signs, she might have mistaken this as an indication Heaven smiled on her ill-fated union. The brilliance lasted the space of several seconds before it faded, leaving the church interior almost gloomy.

Julia hesitated to approach Holmes. Her conscience pained her. The last thing she wanted to do was hurt him, or any of his family. But her determination hadn't wavered. She must call off their wedding, and she intended to do it with as much kindness and sincerity as she could manage.

Strains from the pump organ piddled out in the middle of a bar. The organist adjusted a knob or two. The pipes wheezed back to life.

Portia, with the patience of a toddler, gave Julia a shove toward Holmes. "There he is. You march right on over there and talk to him."

"Wish me luck." Julia made her way down the congested aisle and past the knot formed by Mrs. Orme and her daughters.

The hum of conversation grew louder as Phillip and several others took note of Holmes's arrival. Julia would've sworn she heard Violet, visiting with the pastor's wife a good thirty feet away, sigh with relief.

"Holmes!" Phillip handed his grandson back to Silas, and headed for Holmes.

All conversation petered out. Every eye swiveled toward the door. Spontaneous applause echoed in the church.

Holmes's grin widened. "Good afternoon, everyone."

More cheers. Many responded with delighted greetings.

Phillip shook Holmes's hand with vigor. "There's our happy groom. Eager as they come, aren't you, son?"

Holmes responded, but in the commotion and buzz of conversation around her, Julia missed his precise words. But she had no difficulty discerning Holmes's hearty laughter as he accepted a bear hug from Silas. The brothers pounded backs.

Mercy me, Holmes seemed the quintessence of a happy bridegroom.

"Where you been?" Silas demanded, loud enough for all to hear. "Ma thought you'd left your bride at the altar."

Laughter sparkled through the gathering.

Violet gasped. "I thought no such thing."

Julia excused herself past a few more guests. Two elderly women—David Orme's aunts?—took notice of her and eagerly stepped aside.

"I never doubted him," Phillip announced. "My son's a man who keeps his word. Wouldn't get here on time? It never occurred to me."

"Did you doubt me?" Holmes asked as Julia reached his side. His voice was laced with teasing warmth, reminding her of Conrad.

Selfishly, she was relieved Conrad hadn't come today, so she wouldn't have to witness his disappointment. It would be hard enough to break the news to everyone else here that only half of the wedding would go forward.

Rather than answering a question that didn't need a response, Julia quietly told Holmes, "We need to talk."

Holmes's giddy smile faded, revealing concern. "Yes, yes of course."

Phillip, oblivious to Julia's intentions, announced, "Let's get started. Everyone, in your seats. Holmes, get yourself up to the front. Senator? You've got a daughter to walk down the aisle." He motioned for Julia's father to hurry on back. "Music!"

The organist nodded, then pumped out jubilant strains.

"Yes, now." Julia took Holmes's arm and tugged him through the doorway, into the vestibule beyond. "This is important."

"All right." Holmes headed for the far side of the sunlit room.

Phillip, prepared to practice walking Katherine down the aisle, appeared in the doorway, a pleased grin on his whiskered face. "I know you haven't seen each other all day, but the guests are waiting, you two."

Phillip patted Katherine's hand, tucked into the crook of his arm. "Ah, here's your father, Julia. You two line up right behind us."

Julia held up a finger, indicating she needed a minute. She whispered to Holmes, "In the cloak room?"

"OK. Sure."

Julia caught a glimpse of her father's concerned expression, just as Holmes closed the cloak room door securely behind them. Inside, dust motes danced in the watered-down shaft of daylight filtering through a single, high window. Muted strains from the organ reverberated in the still air.

Holmes's contented grin lingered. With one fingertip, he brushed a curl back from Julia's cheek. "I know what this is about, and I want to assure you I'm very sorry."

Relief flooded through her, as welcome as a warm breeze in June. She'd been so agitated over the Macquarie family at large—none of whom seemed remotely aware that she and Holmes were woefully mismatched—that she'd doubted Holmes would be any different. That had made her mistake his joy, his contentment, for that of an expectant, happy groom. Instead, he'd been happy, because he'd arrived at the same decision as she! The thought brought an instant, genuine smile.

"Forgive me?" Holmes asked.

"Yes, I—"

A brisk knock sounded on the door. "Julia?"

Her father opened the door and peered inside,

getting a good look at the two of them, standing in the little room, lined on all sides with coat pegs, quite unsupervised. Julia hadn't any trouble reading her father's mind, and knowing exactly what caused his furrowed brow.

"Holmes and I needed a moment alone," she explained.

"There'll be plenty of time for that, after the ceremony."

Julia split a glance between her father and Holmes, who seemed inclined to let her do the explaining. An awkward moment passed. "There won't be a ceremony—at least, not for us."

"I don't understand," her father said. So calm, so rational, just as she'd expected. It was good she could break the news to him, before the others.

"I thought you forgave me," Holmes said, touching her arm. "I didn't intend to make you worry this morning, I assure you, I simply needed a few hours to get my head on straight. And I did. I'm ready."

Oh, no. She'd mistaken his words, so certain he'd come to the same decision as she. She swallowed the sudden dryness in her throat, unable to meet his gaze.

"Julia?" Holmes's warm hand settled on her forearm.

So like Conrad's touch.

And so terribly wrong.

Her heart hammered rapidly against her breastbone. "I'm sorry," she managed. "I can't go through with this, and I thought that's what you were telling me, also."

"Can't go through with this?" her father repeated.

"Can't go through with *what?*" Phillip bellowed. He elbowed Julia's father aside, his broad frame nearly filling the doorway. He made a menacing figure, when he wanted to. "Holmes, what did you say to your bride to make her say something so preposterous?"

"I apologized," Holmes assured, quickly.

"Smart man." Phillip palmed his beard and

seemed to regroup. "Happily married men know how to apologize, and do so at every opportunity."

"I apologized," Holmes clarified, "for being late. But it seems Julia has changed her mind."

Julia cringed, waiting for Phillip's reaction. Behind the anxiety, she hadn't any trouble hearing the utter lack of concern in Holmes's tone. He didn't seem to mind, at all, that she didn't want to marry him.

"Of course she hasn't," Phillip said, completely dismissing the issue. "Smart brides know how to forgive and forget. Holmes's apology is most sincere, I guarantee you that."

"Mr. Macquarie." Julia made sure she had Phillip's attention. "Please understand. I've changed my mind, and it has nothing to do with—"

"*Changed your mind?*" Phillip parroted, his voice unnecessarily loud. "Impossible. What kind of a bride changes her mind, at a time like this?"

"Julia." Her father nudged Phillip to the side, dropping his voice to a harsh whisper. "Have you any idea how many people are out here? Are you trying to embarrass yourself?"

Chapter Twenty-Three

TWO FATHERS blocked the only exit from the tiny, airless room.

Embarrass herself? The only embarrassing thing about this was two fathers' reactions to a very reasonable decision. It was *her* decision to make.

Julia found it hard to breathe. Heat flushed up her throat. "This isn't about the guests, Father. It's about what's right and what's wrong."

"You made your choice," her father continued. "A very fine one, indeed. I couldn't have chosen better for you, if I'd tried. Now I suggest you live with it."

Stunned, Julia couldn't come up with a retort before the chance slipped away altogether. The organ's jubilant tune sputtered to an abrupt halt. Footsteps pounded closer on the wood floor. Questions mingled. Everybody wanted to know what the hold up was.

"Speak up, Dolly!" Portia's voice, full of

confidence and cheer, cut through the din. "Those of us in the back can't hear."

Heat flushed through Julia. She hadn't expected, or wanted, an audience.

"What is this about?" her father asked, his voice lowered. "Why change your mind at this late date? You got *precisely* what you wanted."

"Of course she did!" Phillip bellowed. "These two are blissfully happy with each other! She chose my son, almost a year ago."

It wasn't a year, it was six months. And neither she nor Holmes were blissfully happy.

Julia's father frowned. "I'm well aware of that."

"What's the problem?" Katherine, somewhere in the crowd now packed into the vestibule, asked aloud. The poor girl sounded distraught. David attempted to soothe her with gentle tones.

"The problem—" Julia identified the voice of Phillip's friend, Luke Wakefield, "—is John's about to be forty dollars richer."

"Absolutely not!" Phillip cast a heated glance over his shoulder.

"Looks like a done deal from where I'm standing," Luke added.

"Not on your life! There will be a wedding—a *double* wedding." Phillip turned expectant eyes on Julia. "Miss Julia just needed a minute alone with Holmes. All brides and grooms want a stolen moment alone, don't they?" He gestured for support.

Lukewarm applause trickled through the mob. It died within seconds.

Julia squared her shoulders and faced her would-be father-in-law. Her conscience ached, just as she'd known it would. "I'm sorry, sir, but I—"

"You're *happy,*" Phillip insisted. "Aren't you, Holmes? Of course you are. Now come on out here." He cleared the doorway, fully expecting Julia and Holmes to vacate the cloak room forthwith. "We've got a wedding rehearsal to get underway, then a very nice luncheon to attend at the hotel, then a—"

Holmes stepped past Julia and clamped a hand on his father's shoulder. "Pop. Practice walking Katherine down the aisle, hmm?"

"But *you,* Holmes." Phillip's distress seemed to worsen. "You and Miss Julia..."

His expression—crestfallen and grief-stricken—wrenched Julia's conscience. Never, in all her life, had she caused this kind of pain. She didn't care at all for the way it made her feel.

Calm, sure, Holmes responded. "Katherine's wedding's still on. Let's not spoil her special day."

Good, kind-hearted, gracious Holmes.

Phillip shifted his weight, offering a glimpse of the crowd at his back—specifically Gabriel. In that briefest of moments, Julia glimpsed his disappointment, plain as day. He shook his head and turned away.

In the silence of the crowd pressing close behind the two fathers, Julia was certain she heard Violet Macquarie weeping. *Oh, mercy.* It wasn't supposed to be like this. Not any of it. Just as she'd feared, her decision was hurting the family she'd come to love as much as her own.

"I'm *sorry,*" Julia whispered, and she'd never meant anything more.

"The wedding's tomorrow," Phillip soothed. "You two have come so far, made so many plans, have such a glorious future ahead of you. I hate to see you throw it all away."

The pastor pushed his way between the fathers' shoulders. "Shall we discuss this matter in private?" Honest concern warmed his words.

"Oh, no you don't." Phillip pushed his friend back into the masses. "I'm not about to let you talk them out of getting married."

"Hey, now," the pastor said, his tone filled with worry. "I'm trying to help."

Julia glanced at Holmes, trying to convey her honest apologies. In his eyes, she witnessed acceptance.

And relief. He winked—a quick gesture that spoke volumes and assured her he truly was OK with her choice. What an amazing, wonderful man. In that moment, she felt a fast friendship with him.

He would make someone a wonderful husband.

No matter how badly she'd disturbed and hurt the rest of the family, she had the small comfort of knowing Holmes wasn't saddened by her decision.

Relief washed through her, vibrant and sweet. Breaking the news had been the hardest thing she'd ever done, but without doubt, she knew she'd done the right thing.

"No need to talk it over," Holmes told the pastor. "Miss Tyndall's made up her mind. I, for one, accept her decision."

"I second the motion," Luke Wakefield crowed, clapping a hand on Phillip's shoulder.

"Good," Pastor John said. "It's decided."

PHILLIP TOOK A tremulous breath, in an attempt to control his temper. How could his glorious plan, within hours of fruition, collapse before his very eyes?

He held Holmes's gaze, then glanced at Julia. How dare they look at him with pity? Worse, how *dare* they look so damned relieved?

This was a travesty!

What more could he possibly say? He'd belabored his point. He'd rephrased and counter-argued until he had no choice but to concede defeat.

Bitter ashes, indeed.

"Give us some room," he announced to the crowd pressing too close. How was he supposed to think, with John and Luke breathing down his neck? "Everybody, take your seats."

The horde began to trickle back into the chapel.

But most everybody kept their beady little eyes pinned on Phillip. As if they expected the show to continue.

The front door opened, letting in a slice of sunshine and a gust of cooler air. Phillip wished someone would prop it open wide. Fresh air would do them all a world of good.

"What do we do now?" John asked of Phillip, voicing the question evident on nearly everybody's faces.

"We practice," Phillip said, too riled to think straight. "The wedding's still on."

"But he said—" Luke started to argue.

"I know what he said," Phillip interrupted. "And I know what she said. No need to rehash the argument. Katherine and David deserve a rehearsal, don't they?"

"Holmes!" An unfamiliar woman's voice, coming from the direction of the front door, was nearly got lost in the hubbub. "Holmes, I know you're in here. Show yourself."

What now? Whoever she was, her tone of voice made it obvious she hadn't come to offer congratulations.

Phillip glanced at Holmes, the question poised on the tip of his tongue. Holmes's expression was an odd, disturbing mixture of joy and dread. Two emotions that had no business camping together on the same face.

The crowd of friends and family parted, apparently loathe to get between this woman and Holmes.

A strawberry blond, nearly as short as Portia, pushed her way through. Her expensively tailored, rust-colored traveling ensemble hugged her trim figure. Instantly, Phillip surmised that getup, and the furious woman wearing it, had come from the east coast.

Holmes may have said something to Miss Julia—Phillip couldn't be sure, but it sounded like another "I'm sorry"—then pushed through the doorway and out into full view.

He was sorry? Oh, this did not bode well, not at

all. Dread settled in Phillip's gut, dragging down whatever fragments of hope he still harbored.

"Susannah." Holmes took a halting step forward. "You're here. I can't believe—"

Phillip groaned and scrubbed a palm down his face. He couldn't bear to look. He didn't want to know who this woman was to Holmes, nor did he want to witness the censure on the faces of the impromptu jury—especially the senator's.

A loud crack sounded. Stunned, Phillip peeked between his fingers in time to see the little lady shudder.

She'd slapped Holmes across the face. Hard.

Someone gasped. The audience fell utterly silent.

Holmes, despite everything, tried to take Susannah in his arms.

Phillip winced. A groan slipped between his clenched teeth. No matter how sorry Holmes thought he was, Phillip was infinitely more remorseful. He didn't dare meet Julia's gaze, couldn't bear to see the pain on her face. She must have realized there was another woman, and that was why she'd called off the wedding.

The woman in question evaded Holmes's embrace. To Phillip's eye, she seemed quite unconcerned with the fact nearly fifty people watched with morbid curiosity.

Somewhere in the crowd, Portia chuckled. Someone else cleared their throat, while one of the other women tried to hush Portia.

"Might you explain," this Susannah woman demanded, "why I followed you all the way to California, to accept your *proposal* of *marriage*—"

Marriage proposal! Phillip clenched his eyes, heard the collective intake of breath all around him, and braced himself for much, much worse to come.

The senator made a sound of derision. "What *the hell* is this, Holmes?"

What the hell, indeed! Why hadn't Holmes breathed a word about this woman?

"—and I find you on the brink of marriage?"

Susannah's voice shimmered with outrage.

Holmes lifted both hands in supplication. "You refused—"

"No, don't answer. I don't want to know. If you'd marry someone else this quick, then you're not the man I thought you were."

"Well said," the senator added. He cast Phillip a sharp look that left no room for doubt. It seemed Tyndall's esteem of Holmes and the whole Macquarie family had plummeted. To an all-time low, no doubt.

"I'm not marrying her," Holmes said to this Susannah person, his tone soothing.

"Don't look at me like that, Macquarie." Susannah was softening, Phillip could see that. "I wouldn't have you, either."

Sounds of sympathy came from the onlookers. Others bellowed a hodgepodge of humiliating comments; they weren't pleased by Holmes's abandonment of Julia, virtually at the altar.

John and Luke, flanking Phillip on either side like sentinels, cast him a look that clearly proclaimed him an idiot. He didn't need their censure; they were in on it, too!

Despite the fact the others owned at least half the blame, Phillip's conscience was consumed by fire.

What had he done?

He couldn't understand why his good son, in the wake of Susannah's rejection, had gone along with the plan to marry Miss Julia? *Why* would he do such a thing? It was as plain as day the boy was in love with this little spitfire named Susannah.

Sick to his stomach, Phillip watched as tears welled in Susannah's eyes. "Did you love me, at all?" she asked of Holmes.

Holmes nodded, reaching for Susannah again. This time, she went willingly into his arms. Her fists clung to the back of Holmes's suit coat.

Compassion tugged at Phillip's heartstrings. He couldn't help but care about this girl he'd never met, simply because his son loved her. And because she obviously loved him.

"The question," came Holmes's muffled voice, "is do you love me?"

Phillip didn't hear the girl's answer, but the resounding chorus of "Ahhs" from their audience made it clear she'd responded in the affirmative.

"You knew," the senator said to Julia, clearly meaning Holmes's relationship with Susannah.

"I did." She sounded sad. Wistful. Quite forlorn.

Phillip cringed. No wonder she'd called off the wedding. What woman would want to marry a man who loved somebody else? He wanted to scream at the injustice.

Phillip nudged John. "Why am I always the last one to learn something so damned important?"

No one answered his plea.

No wonder the boy had been so docile. So disheartened. All along, he'd been nursing a broken heart. Grieving over this woman who'd rejected him.

How *dare* she reject his son? Didn't she recognize outstanding husband-material when she saw it?

Finally, when it was too late, Phillip understood everything.

In that instant, he recognized that Holmes hadn't merely noted Julia's appeal as a wife; he'd given up hope of reconciliation with a woman he'd chosen for himself. He'd decided to do the right thing by Miss Julia and honor the pledge given her. Knowing Holmes and his misguided sense of honor, the boy likely would've taken the secret of Phillip's involvement to the grave.

Bile rose in Phillip's throat. May heaven forgive him. He'd come within a hair of destroying his son's happiness.

Holmes kissed Susannah then, in full view of the entire wedding party. Sounds of appreciation flitted through the family. But not everyone was happy for Holmes; a few raised their brows, some muttered exclamations or shook their heads.

He caught Violet's eye across the crowded vestibule. His dear wife was conflicted, he could see that. *Dear, sweet Holmes,* she communicated clearly, silently. Followed immediately with *Oh, poor Julia!*

Phillip felt a tug on his sleeve, turned to see Julia taking his arm in a show of comfort. He grasped her hand and shook his head. Dismay overcame him.

Miss Julia straightened her posture, although clearly troubled. Her brow furrowed. Regret brimmed in her beautiful eyes. She looked beaten. Exhausted. Heartsick.

Guilt overwhelmed Phillip, consumed him. He wanted to make restitution, wanted to patch things back together, but knew there was absolutely no way to manage that. This would never be all right for the dear girl.

She'd sacrificed *everything*, because of his meddling. Dammit, but he should've listened to John the other night.

She'd given up home, parental trust, her future. Banking on her chances with Holmes, she'd parted ways with a man her father had chosen for her. Probably good, a decent husband candidate. And for what? Only to be forced to set Holmes free, because he was in love with someone else.

Phillip stared the truth in the face and knew he'd caused Miss Julia, whom he'd come to love like his own daughter, irreparable harm.

She may have been the first to apologize, but he was the one who was sorrier than he could possibly say.

JUST AS NIGHT claimed the last traces of dusk, Conrad and Gabriel handed off their mounts to ranch workers. They trudged up the stairs onto the back porch.

Weariness throbbed in every muscle and ached in

every joint. Had he ever been so damned tattered, in all his life?

Mud clung to his boots, his denims. The rain had finally let up, but the mess remained. He couldn't wait to peel off the damp, filthy clothes and take a hot bath.

The house was awash with lights burning in most of the rooms. Windows stood open, all along the back of the house to let in early summer's fresh air. Homey aromas of Ma's cinnamon buns greeted him, increasing his hunger pangs tenfold. His mouth watered, remembering the way those buttery rolls, drizzled with icing, melted on his tongue.

It beat tinned beans and meals purchased along the roadside. Good food was a small consolation, considering everything else he'd suffer over the next twenty-four hours.

Conversation, punctuated with female laughter, carried through open windows. Katherine, David, Silas, then Holmes. Conrad caught himself straining to hear Julia's voice mingling with the others.

Who was he trying to fool? Returning home—aside from being the right thing to do—had been moronic.

Why had he thought coming back here would ease his conscience? Seemed he was doomed to suffer for the rest of his life.

On the porch, both he and Gabriel pulled off muddy boots and wet socks.

Gabriel opened the door for them both. Conrad drew a breath for strength and entered the washroom. He tried to avert his gaze from the kitchen, where most of his siblings sat around the table, nibbling cinnamon buns and sipping fragrant coffee.

Too tired to talk, he and Gabriel washed up, side by side. Like old times.

Conrad toed off his boots and decided he wasn't hungry enough to go in there. He wasn't ready to see Julia. Not yet. Instead, he'd head upstairs and drop into bed.

"Oh, no you don't," Katherine argued, her voice carrying from the kitchen. "Don't you pin that one on me. I wasn't anywhere around."

Holmes's rich timbre filled the kitchen as he laughed. "Your memory's fading, Pipsqueak. I recall the precise details. I saw you steal that hen from the coop and hide her, cage and all, under your bed."

Katherine squealed the way she did when somebody tickled her, Silas most likely. Still treated her like she was in braids.

"Couldn't bear to see her in a stew pot, eh?" Silas's deep baritone. Katherine's girlish laughter was full of delight.

Conrad remembered the circumstances, too well. He'd been the one to talk Katherine into hiding the chicken she'd called Squawkers from Ma's ax. It'd been a six-year-old's desperate attempt to save a treasured pet.

"That wasn't the only time you got caught with chickens in the house," Holmes said. "Easter morning, you got the harebrained idea—"

"Conrad!" Katherine's chair scraped back.

Everybody turned in his direction.

He offered a half-hearted wave, leaned his weary bones against the door jamb.

"Hey, you're home." Holmes's smile brightened. "Get in here and tell these oafs I had nothing to do with the Squawkers incident."

Conrad wasn't about to admit his part in the fiasco. "You're guilty, as charged."

Gabriel pushed past, helped himself to a pair of cinnamon buns and a glass of milk.

Katherine giggled and tore a strip of cinnamon-laced bread from her bun. "Ha! Told you so."

"You were what, two, when this happened?" Holmes retorted. "I doubt you remember anything. And I'm glad you're getting married tomorrow, moving out, and leaving me in peace."

Katherine squealed and slapped at Holmes's

shoulder. Beside Katherine, her husband-to-be, David, chuckled.

Try as he might, Conrad couldn't keep from heading for the doorway, where he'd have an unobstructed view of the table. And Julia.

To his surprise, he noted Julia's absence, and immediately relaxed a little. He guessed she'd already retired for the night, and that suited him fine.

But seated beside Holmes was a young woman who resembled Katherine and Ma enough to be a distant cousin. Little, fair-skinned, with glossy red-gold waves pinned up in a fashionable do. Her coffee-brown eyes twinkled with happiness.

She gave him a quick smile. "Good evening, Conrad. Gabriel." The same east coast accent as Julia. Similar cut of clothing.

The reminders were almost as bad as glimpsing Julia, herself. He nodded, surprised she'd call him by his given name. "Ma'am."

"Introduce me." She jabbed Holmes in the ribs with an elbow.

"Conrad, Gabriel," Holmes said with evident pleasure, "allow me to introduce Miss Susannah Byron."

"She's from Boston," Katherine added.

Miss Byron smiled. "Pleased to meet you both."

Uncomfortable with five pairs of eyes trained on him, he headed for the stove to get himself an iced bun. They smelled heavenly. He piled two onto a plate and licked a bit of sugar off his thumb. Mmmm. Better than he'd remembered.

Belatedly, he noticed his siblings had fallen quite silent.

Gabriel paused after wolfing down one bun. "Care to tell us whatever it is that needs explaining?"

Conrad turned to find Katherine's attention on her coffee cup. David twirled a fork on the wooden tabletop. Silas and Holmes shared one of those looks that spelled trouble.

Mad, were they? He'd been gone all of six days,

not even a week. If they'd heard he'd looked at that parcel of farmland...

Conrad sighed. "All right, I'm sorry." He found he meant it. "Yes, I looked over that piece of farmland, intending to buy it, but I'm back in time—"

Silas cut him off with a wave of his hand. "You missed the excitement today. Miss Byron made a grand appearance at the wedding rehearsal." Silas always was the most outspoken of the bunch.

Conrad didn't know what to say, so he took a big bite of cinnamon bun and scanned the five faces that watched him expectantly. He didn't enjoy being out in the cold. "Am I supposed to remember you, Miss Byron? Because I don't believe we've met."

"Miss Byron and Holmes," David Orme said evenly, "will be married tomorrow in our joint ceremony."

Chapter Twenty-Four

CONRAD BLINKED. He was saddle-weary, exhausted, and starving. But he knew he'd heard right. He held Holmes's gaze and swallowed without bothering to chew. "*What?*"

Holmes smiled like he'd just been crowned king, and looped an arm around the little strawberry blond's shoulders. As if he didn't care one way or the other about Julia—his *bride,* for hell's sake!

Julia. His heart seemed to seize in mid-rhythm.

She didn't belong to Holmes, not anymore. She was free to move on, released from her commitment and engagement. Elation surged through Conrad's very being.

That was a good thing, wasn't it?

Couldn't be, 'cause fury rode hot and hard on its heels, all directed squarely at Holmes.

How could Holmes sit there, with a smug grin on

his face, and completely disregard Julia's feelings? He'd exchanged letters and invited her to come west.

Only to abandon her because perky Miss Byron showed up *today?*

The urge to protect and defend Julia brought on a blast of indignation that obliterated every other emotion.

Conrad's chest heaved as he fought to control his temper and failed. As he plunked the dessert plate onto the counter top, it snapped into two. "And what of Julia? Where is *she?*"

He heard the razor-sharp edge to his words, and so did everyone else.

"Conrad," Katherine soothed, "it's not like—"

"It's not like what?" he demanded of Holmes. "It's not like she wasn't already your wife?" He shook his head, refusing to hear any answer Holmes might give. "You make me sick."

Holmes stood, patting Susannah's shoulder. Conrad leveled a venomous gaze at the woman who'd singlehandedly destroyed Julia's happiness.

She had the good sense to hold her tongue.

"Outside," Holmes ordered. He didn't wait to see if Conrad followed.

Hell yes, he followed.

In the few seconds it took to head down the back stairs, Conrad's temper flashed white-hot. For the first time in more than ten years, he threw the first punch.

His fist hooked Holmes's jaw, snapping his head back. Holmes stumbled, scrabbled for footing in the muddy yard, and lunged.

Conrad caught a jab squarely in the gut. He grunted and snared Holmes in a headlock. "*What* are you thinking? You invite Julia here, get to the altar, then toss her aside like rubbish?"

"You don't know what you're talking about." Holmes lunged, throwing all his weight into an effort to wrest free.

Conrad tightened his hold, dropped his brother to

his knees. "Fight like a man, you weakling. You've spent too many hours in a classroom."

Holmes bucked, tossing Conrad off. With a feral growl, he drove a shoulder into Conrad's kidney.

Pain erupted behind Conrad's ribs. Air whooshed out of his lungs, but he managed to remain upright. Bare toes slid through wet grass and cold mud.

Grabbing Conrad's shirt, Holmes flipped him onto his back. "Shut up and listen. You're wrong."

Conrad landed hard. Furious, Conrad yanked his brother off his feet and pinned him. "No. *You* listen," he shouted into Holmes's face. "How *dare* you?"

Conrad was dimly aware the others had come out to the veranda. Gabriel hollered for them to break it up, but seemed inclined to let them finish.

Holmes locked both hands around Conrad's neck and squeezed. "I swear, Conrad, I thought I was doing what was best."

He broke Holmes's grip with some effort. "Best for who? You don't care about Julia."

"For the record, I proposed marriage," a grunt as he caught an elbow to the ribs, "to *Susannah* before,"—*whoof*—"left Boston," blocked another punch, "before I'd even *heard* Julia's name."

"Rotten excuse." Conrad plowed a fist into Holmes's face. "You're lower than a dung beetle. Worse than a—"

With renewed strength, Holmes wrested free. "What are you, Julia's champion? Her guard dog?" His breaths came in ragged gasps. "You act like you're...in love with her." Accusation gave way to awe, to understanding.

No, no, no. This was *not* his fault. He had no intention of admitting anything. He swiped his sleeve across his bloody lip. His fresh bruises and battered ribs ached like hell, but far less than his broken heart.

Time to turn the blame back around, where it belonged. "You deserve whatever you get, because you sure as sunrise don't deserve Julia."

But then, neither did Conrad. A few stolen kisses couldn't span the chasm between them. He'd been gone a week. Refused her. No telling what she thought of him now.

"Well, would you look at that," Holmes murmured, his voice vibrating with awe. "That's the best news I've heard in a month of Sundays." He shoved Conrad off him, stood, brushing off his trousers.

Conrad wanted to knock the idiotic grin off his brother's face.

"You're *in love* with her."

This time, he didn't hesitate, not even for a second. "Yes, I am."

Holmes grinned, wincing as his abused lip split further. "*Why* didn't you say something?"

"What? Hand over the bride, and nobody gets hurt? Shoot, Holmes, I was trying to do the honorable thing and stay out of it. Besides, she doesn't want the likes of me."

Holmes, still chuckling, he offered Conrad a hand up. "Does Pop know you stole my bride?"

"Did *not*."

Holmes laughed again, a happy, joyful sound that doubled Conrad's fury. No, quadrupled. The chump didn't deserve a sliver of happiness, not after what he did. "How dare you laugh—"

"Hold on," Holmes urged. "I never heard Miss Tyndall's name, not until Pop mentioned her the day I got home. I didn't send for her. *He* did."

What?

Dumbfounded, Conrad's ears rang as if Holmes had clubbed him in the head with a length of fencepost. He clung to his balance by force of will.

"*Pop* sent for Julia?" Didn't make a lick of sense. "You wrote to her, for months."

Holmes nodded. "Pop did it all. Signed my name."

Pop.

That conniving, idiotic fool.

"You know what he and the others did to Garth

Wakefield, don't you?" Holmes asked.

"I know enough." He'd heard The Three—Pop and his cohorts—had decided Garth Wakefield needed a wife and had taken matters into their own hands. An illegal paper marriage and much to-do later, Garth Wakefield was a happily wedded man.

"The Three targeted me next," said Holmes. "I figure they decided I was a hopeless cause and in desperate need of their assistance. Little did they know I'd found the perfect woman, but she turned me down—"

Conrad paced two steps toward the house, then flanked back, his thoughts in a jumble. He held up a hand, interrupting Holmes's babbling. "Pop sent for Julia."

"Oh, yes. He's guilty."

Conrad had spent so long believing Holmes wanted Julia, that he knew he ought to be furious at Pop. But the urge to shout a grand *alleluia!* was too powerful. All that suffering, pointless. He'd stayed away from Julia, denied himself, denied *her*—all for nothing.

Was it even possible she'd be interested in more than a few forbidden kisses? In more than friendship? "Does Julia know?"

"Not from me, she doesn't." Holmes gingerly touched his jaw. "Did you have to hit me?"

"Had no choice, you blockhead."

"Suppose not." Holmes offered a handshake as a peace treaty.

Conrad hesitated, but only for a second. Over their clasped hands, Conrad stared Holmes full in the face. "I don't understand. What possessed you to go along with their con?"

"What was I to do?" Pain tinged Holmes's words. "Pop persuaded a decent, innocent lady to believe I'd written those letters. Was I supposed to disillusion her? Who am I to dash her dreams? Besides, the woman I love refused me. At least *someone* was interested. So I figured, why not?"

"It would've saved us all a great deal of trouble." Maybe not Julia, who'd wanted to marry Holmes, at least in the beginning. Conrad's heart wrenched.

Holmes shook his head. His shoulders drooped. "Probably."

Conrad kicked at a tuft of grass beneath his bare feet. He wanted to curse and bellow. Weeks and weeks of torture, all because Holmes's sense of honor was as overblown as his own. "You're a wuss."

Holmes chuckled. "Her attention felt good, given the rock-bottom state of my affairs. Miss Tyndall's a prime catch. Excellent wife material."

Conrad swore. "You would've married her, only for that?"

"I believed I had little choice but to go through with it. But in the end, she didn't want me."

This was welcome, startling news. "What?"

"She called it off. Told me she couldn't marry me."

"What did you think she'd do? Fight Susannah off?" Conrad shook his head with disgust. Holmes didn't know Julia, not at all. "She's a *lady.* Unlike you, she's not the kind to settle fights with her fists."

"Before all that," Holmes argued. "She cried off before Susannah made her appearance."

"Before," Conrad repeated, glancing toward the porch where Susannah and the others watched in silence, listening to every word.

"Yes."

"Did she know Susannah was on her way?"

"I don't see how she could have. Susannah claims she came to the church, directly from the depot. Susannah sent no wires ahead, no letters, no communication of any kind."

Conrad wanted to believe Julia had turned Holmes away for self-serving reasons. Was there any possibility, any at all, that Julia might honestly be interested in *him,* instead?

Holmes's story gave Conrad hope, but something within him still screamed *impossible.*

After all, he was no great catch.

Scarred.

Landless.

Insignificant.

Rough around the edges.

Despite all that, she'd kissed him. *Him.* As if she might actually love him.

The very thought yanked the rug out from under him. His stomach tumbled end over end, finally coming to rest in the vicinity of his toes.

It all seemed too good to be true. There could be any number of explanations why she'd cancel the wedding, but he gave voice to only one. "She must've found out Pop sent for her."

"Not a chance. You should've seen the way she looked at me this afternoon. She didn't know."

Conrad narrowed his eyes. "Looked at you like...how?"

Holmes brushed that off. "You know Pop would never admit to any wrongdoing."

"Hmmm." Conrad nodded, rubbing the back of his neck.

"I figure she had her reasons for calling it off. From where I stand, makes perfect sense."

Impatient, Conrad grunted. He didn't much like thinking Holmes understood Julia better than himself. "What?"

"*You,* blockhead."

"Me? I didn't get in her way. I did everything possible to stay out of it."

"Unlike some people, who shall remain nameless, she's not the kind to marry when she loves someone else."

Conrad's stomach tingled, fell. "Like who?" His voice sounded gruff. Urgent. Pathetic, but a bit of reassurance sounded mighty fine.

"It's obvious she loves *you*, Conrad, although why, I can't imagine."

Conrad grabbed hold of that possibility, suddenly

desperate to find her. He couldn't keep a fool's grin from spreading across his face. "Where is she?"

"Upstairs, I think. Packing her trunks. She's leaving in the morning."

Without hesitation, Conrad bounded up the porch steps, two at a time. Everybody parted letting him through easily.

Didn't care one whit if he tracked mud into the house. He had to see Julia, now.

He hadn't a clue what he'd say, or how he'd ask the questions burning in his soul, but knew he had to do whatever it took to make things right between them.

TRYING HER HARDEST to focus on everything she'd gained rather than what she'd lost, Julia took her riding habit from the wardrobe and laid it carefully in the half-packed Saratoga.

For a few weeks, she'd lived her dreams.

She had memories to treasure. Most of them revolved around Conrad, and that was something she'd have to live with. She folded her exquisite white satin wedding gown with care, wondering why she bothered to take it home.

On the other side of the bed, Portia tucked her own belongings into her mismatched trunks.

"Portia, once again, you don't have to return home with me." Julia's stomach ached at the thought of separating her aunt from Olaf, who so obviously loved her.

"Who said I was going back to Baltimore?"

"You're *not* going to Olaf's place?" Her unconventional aunt just might move in with her beau. She'd never cared what people thought. Why would she start now?

"Heavens, no. Central America awaits."

Julia paused, a suit folded over her arm. "I see."

"Olaf's put his land up for sale." Portia grinned. "He threatened to follow me to the ends of the earth. You should've seen your father's face when he heard that."

Portia perked up, suddenly still. "Did you feel that?"

Julia may have sensed a subtle shifting. A groaning of the earth. Perhaps she had. "Maybe."

"Oooh. There it is again!" Portia's eyes rolled heavenward, in utter bliss. "I tremor. Seismic activity!"

Julia tucked the skirt and jacket into her trunk and returned to the wardrobe for another. She didn't want to let the thread of their conversation go. This was important. "Mr. DeLaigle loves you."

Portia blinked, seemed to come back to the conversation. "Jordon told me I should stick with Olaf."

"I agree."

"I'm not giving up my independence, love or not," Portia argued. "I have research to do. A teaching position at the college to maintain. I don't have time for marriage, and I told Olaf so."

Julia wondered how long Olaf DeLaigle would follow Portia around before she gave in and married him. Knowing Portia, it might take her ardent suitor quite some time.

Downstairs, a door banged open. Katherine's excited voice melded with David's. Masculine footfalls pounded up the staircase.

Seconds later, a fist pummeled the guest room door. "Julia?"

Her heart tumbled. Conrad?

Portia beat Julia to the door, and opened it a crack. "Ah, look who's here."

With her heart in her throat, Julia peered over Portia's head. *Conrad.*

He was home!

She rushed toward him, hauling herself up short after two strides. Fresh blood smeared from the corner of his mouth. Mud smeared one cheek, dirtied the front of his shirt, both hands, his denims. His bare feet were filthy.

His breaths came in rapid, deep pulls. Fire blazed in bloodshot eyes. A deep bruise was forming on his jaw.

He'd never looked more wonderful.

She'd thought she'd never see him again.

A moment passed. He didn't speak. He simply stared at her, his expression slowly softening.

She wanted to ask if he was all right, but the question was unnecessary. Obviously, he was hurt.

"Looks to me like you'd best come in." Portia opened the guest room door wide, leaving Conrad and Julia to stare at one another.

Portia carried another armload of clothing from the wardrobe to her trunk.

"Unpack your trunks." Conrad's tone, rough and strained, left no room for argument. "You're staying."

What was this about? First, he informed her they weren't friends, now, that she must stay? She supposed his displeasure was based on more than her decision to leave; he didn't want her to leave Holmes.

Apparently, he hadn't heard of the significant change in wedding plans.

Portia said, "Julia's parents have purchased four tickets on the morning train. We see no sense attending the ceremony."

"Where are they?"

"The tickets?" Portia slammed a trunk lid. "Jordon has them—"

"Julia's parents," Conrad said, impatient. "Where are they?"

"In town," Julia answered. "At the hotel." They'd made quite a bit of noise about their refusal to stay under Phillip Macquarie's roof one more night. But Portia had insisted—just as loudly—that it was absurd to leave comfortable lodgings before morning.

Conrad held Julia's gaze for the space of several seconds.

Why did he want her parents?

She felt compelled to explain, even though the rest of the family would share the details, soon enough. "Holmes wants to marry Susannah—"

"I know." For a moment, it seemed as though he might pull her close. "Where are Holmes's letters?"

"His letters?" she asked. "Why—"

"Where are they?"

She took the stack, tied with a yellow ribbon, from the desk.

Conrad wiped his dirty hands off on his shirttails, pulled one letter from its envelope. He let the rest fall onto the bed. "Do you know whose handwriting this is?" He scanned through the pages.

An odd question. "Holmes's."

He shook his head.

"Not Holmes's?" She didn't understand.

He removed another letter. "Pop wrote these."

Julia held Conrad's gaze for a moment, and knew he was serious. If anyone ought to recognize Phillip's—and Holmes's—penmanship, Conrad certainly would.

Why would Phillip write Holmes's letters? It didn't make sense. She had no doubt Holmes—a graduate of Harvard Law—could read and write exceptionally well.

Portia examined the letters. "I don't understand."

"Give me half a second." Conrad's long strides carried him to his bedroom next door and back before she could figure out what he'd gone after. He opened a small, leather-bound book. "Pop wrote this."

Julia took the book from his hands, scanned the familiar script inside the front cover. She knew every curl, every twist, every cross on every *t,* every dot on every *i.* She shook her head and lowered herself into a chair.

The truth stared at her, evidenced by birthday wishes penned by a father to his son in the front cover of this book.

Chapter Twenty-Five

NUMB, SHE OPENED her mouth, then closed it again. She couldn't find any words.

She didn't want to believe Phillip had written the letters, signed Holmes's name, lured her into this whole arrangement, and persuaded her to remain loyal with another love note accompanied by chocolates and flowers.

Apparently, that was precisely what Phillip had done.

It might be unbelievable, unconscionable, but knowing Phillip Macquarie, she shouldn't be surprised.

One look at Conrad's expressive face, and she knew this was what he'd come to tell her.

She supposed she ought to feel humiliated, incensed, to learn the entire affair had been Phillip's illusion. If Holmes and their future as husband and wife mattered to her, at all, she supposed she would have felt all that, and worse.

Why on earth had Holmes gone along with Phillip's scheme? He could've told her the truth, on a dozen different occasions. He very well could've mentioned it in the cloakroom at the church. But he hadn't.

And neither had Conrad.

Had they both been in on it?

Humiliation crept in, making it impossible to look at either Conrad or Portia. If only she'd known this, she might have been playing with a full hand. But no, they'd kept it from her, until it was almost too late.

Oh, if she'd only known!

"It seems logical," said Portia, "that Holmes had ample opportunity to confess the truth."

Conrad made a rough sound of agreement.

Anger rode hard on the heels of Julia's humiliation. This was the last thing she wanted to discuss, especially with Conrad in the room. "It doesn't matter anymore, Aunt Portia."

"It most certainly does! Why didn't Holmes tell the truth?" Portia's voice rang with irritation. "He had occasion. Repeatedly."

"He should have." Conrad's gruff voice filled with affection. Concern. For her.

She didn't want it. Neither could she resist. Her frustration crumbled as quickly as it had appeared.

"Did *you* know?" Portia demanded.

"No." Conrad's attention was fully on Julia. "Only learned about it moments ago."

"I expected better of Holmes," Portia announced, a tad on the loud side. "I believed him a man of integrity, now it's evident he's a liar, through and through."

"He perpetuated the lie our father told, in order to do what was best by everyone." Conrad shook his head, clearly disgusted.

Julia closed her eyes, reclined against the headrest. Holmes had been too honorable to renege on promises he hadn't made. Conrad, too loyal to his brother, hadn't allowed himself to pursue her.

What a sad, miserable ending to her glorious adventure.

"I'm not amused," Portia announced. "Are you telling me Holmes *actually believed* he was doing the right thing? I know precisely where he got his warped sense of right and wrong, and it was *not* from your mother's side," she told Conrad. "You boys learned it from your father's tarnished example."

"Pop's not all bad," Conrad said.

"Oh, he most certainly is." Portia headed for the door, clearly on the warpath. "He deserves every ounce of comeuppance, I tell you."

"Aunt Portia." Julia didn't want a bigger spectacle than they'd already caused. Poor Phillip had seemed ready to collapse after the scene in the church vestibule. "It's all right. It's over."

"Oh, no, it's not. Where is he? I've got a thing or two to say to him."

Conrad tossed the counterfeit letters onto the bed. "I don't know. Just got home."

"He can't hide from me." Portia stormed into the hallway with a rustle of taffeta. "Phillip Macquarie! Show yourself!"

"You're going to stand by," Julia asked Conrad, "and let my aunt assault your father?"

"I agree with her. He deserves whatever he gets."

Julia was a believer in consequences, and found she didn't mind that Portia fought this particular battle in her stead.

She'd rather stay here with Conrad.

For just a few more minutes.

She held his gaze, wishing things had turned out differently between them. For a moment, she could almost forget their estrangement, set aside the tumultuous weeks since Holmes's return. For the space of a heartbeat, they were still friends.

Mercy, she'd *missed* him. Yearned for his

companionship, the sound of his voice. She closed her eyes, not sure whether she should be grateful for this last chance to see him, or to weep.

"Phillip!" Portia's voice echoed through the upstairs hallway. An answering commotion came from the first floor.

Conrad closed the bedroom door and strode toward Julia in that loose-hipped stroll that branded him a cowboy. His tired, bloodshot eyes watched her with an intensity that sent chills up her spine. He offered his hand.

She ran her gaze over his callused palm and the familiar curve of blunt fingers. She glanced at his face, questioning. He'd made his feelings for her quite clear before his abrupt departure.

No matter how desperately her heart wanted to justify all that as his overactive sense of honor, she held herself back from believing he wanted more than a handshake.

But she wasn't ready to say goodbye.

"Take my hand, Miss J."

Oh, no. This wasn't a good idea. Her heart still ached with his rejection. Why give him the chance to destroy her, again?

He waited.

She wasn't sure she wanted to accept comfort from him. Even as a friend. It would be too painful. Better to keep her distance.

Hesitantly, she met his gaze.

How was she supposed to find the strength to resist an expression so filled with hope and kindness? And...love?

With uncertainty, she slipped her hand into his.

Warm, rough fingers closed over hers and urged her to him. He brought her knuckles to his lips for a lingering kiss.

Her heart skittered. Words of love hovered on the tip of her tongue. She wanted little more than to fling herself into his arms and pick up where they'd left off before Holmes interrupted their romance.

"Thought you could hide?" Portia bellowed from the top of the stairs.

"Why would I hide from you?" Phillip's voice echoed through the stairwell. Heavy footsteps resounded as he climbed to the second floor.

Portia lit into Phillip, starting at the top of her list of reasons why he should hide, had he the sense of a gnat.

Ignoring the tirade, Conrad brought Julia's other hand to his lips and pressed a kiss there, too.

Her breath caught. "Conrad, I—"

She completely forgot whatever it was she'd intended to say. How could she think, when he looked at her that way? He released her hands and took her face between his palms. Slowly, he closed the distance, his bare toes against the point of her shoes.

What did all of this mean? Her pulse accelerated. Until moments ago, she'd believed they had no possibility of a future, but now she wanted desperately to believe in miracles.

"I'm sorry." He spoke softly, with fervor she couldn't mistake. "I'm sorry. About everything. Pop's idiocy, Holmes. *Me.* I swear I had no idea what they'd done. I only wanted to do the right thing."

Warm acceptance rushed through Julia. Forgiveness came easily; he'd done nothing wrong. She nodded, awash with emotion.

In the distance, Portia's embattled conversation continued, but Julia couldn't think straight, much less care. Phillip could fend for himself.

"Kiss me," Conrad whispered.

Tears gathered in her eyes, but her smile widened. "You told me you'd never kiss me again."

"I was wrong. More sorry about that, than anything else."

"Good. It's forgotten."

"So kiss me."

"I'm savoring this perfect moment."

"Savor faster." He brushed his lips against hers.

Tingles erupted, sizzling along her nerves. The delicious tastes of cinnamon and sugar lingered on his mouth. She brought her hands to his strong forearms to steady herself.

Slipping his arms around her, he deepened their kiss, immediately awakening all the longing she'd forced aside and tried to forget.

"You're mine," he told her, against the tender spot beneath her ear.

"Mmmm."

"You!" Portia accused shrilly from the hallway. Such a cacophony erupted among the Macquarie clan, their voices were indecipherable.

Far too soon, Conrad pulled away. Concern dampened his eyes. "I know I don't have much to offer. No land or house of my own. But I have money in the bank and the dairy turns a good profit."

Was he headed toward a proposal? She didn't dare hope.

"I know."

"I'll buy land of my own," he rushed on, "a place we can call home."

We. Quite possibly the most beautiful word Julia had ever heard. It didn't matter where they lived, where they called home, if they had the hope of a future together.

"We," she whispered.

"What?"

"You said *we*." She touched his dear face. Bruised, bloodied, dirty. More appealing than ever.

He covered her hand with his. Over rough beard stubble and endearing, perfect scar.

His vibrant emerald eyes clouded. He swallowed.

She held his gaze. Love for him swelled, spilled over in a single tear. As she had that day at the side of the lane, she told him what was in her heart. "All I see is you."

He drew a tremulous breath. Smiled. "You really

don't mind, do you?" By the look in his eye, she knew his feelings for her ran deep.

"Why would I mind? Thought all I was getting was a cowboy, but now you say you have money in the bank, a plan for our future."

He kissed her wrist, then held both her hands tightly as he dropped to one knee. "Miss J?" A long moment passed. He gazed at her with adoration, with awe.

In the hallway and staircase outside the bedroom door, a whole chorus of Macquaries railed at Phillip. Portia egged them on.

Conrad hadn't paid them any attention. He focused solely on her.

Happy tears stung her eyes. Weeks of loneliness and doubt seemed to lift in that moment, freeing her soul.

She waited, expectantly, hoping she knew what was coming, and wishing he'd hurry it up.

"I won't allow you to return to Maryland."

"My bags are packed. My wedding is canceled." *Please, give me a reason to stay.*

"I love you, Miss J. Marry *me.*"

Tears filled her eyes. She squeezed her eyelids closed, tried to swallow, then nodded.

A chuckle vibrated through his chest. "Is that a yes?"

Again, she nodded. "Yes! I love you, Conrad Macquarie."

Portia's voice drifted in, making it clear she refused to back down. "Need I remind you, Julia came here for a husband? Because of your egocentric, fabricated, *preposterous* scheme?"

Conrad laughed out loud. He leapt to his feet, swung Julia around and around. Nothing had ever felt as wonderful as his arms about her.

Phillip's remorse, evident in his placating tone and his string of apologies, did nothing to pacify Portia.

"I suggest," Portia announced, "you do something

about it."

Conrad seemed oblivious to the argument, seemed to see only Julia. "Don't listen to them," he whispered against her mouth. "'Cause I've got plenty to say, and I want you to hear me. I missed you. Worse than you can imagine."

"I have a fair idea."

"I've loved you," warmth shone in his eyes, "far longer than was decent, no matter how hard I fought it. When I say you're mine, Miss J, I mean it."

She wanted to hear and to treasure everything he said. Even worse, she wanted his touch, his kisses. "You're doing too much talking. Any minute, Portia's bound to remember she left us alone."

"Right."

"Portia!" Phillip bellowed, making the windowpanes rattle. "You're infuriating. What, exactly, do you want me to do?"

"You have two sons left—Conrad and Gabriel!" Portia announced with finality. Apparently her batty aunt didn't care that Conrad and Julia could overhear every word exchanged. "Do whatever you must, but Julia *deserves*—after all her planning, after all her work!—to be wed in tomorrow's ceremony."

"Tomorrow?" Phillip sounded dumbfounded. "Gabriel's sweet on Sally Tibbs. I can't very well ask him to abandon her, now can I?"

Conrad grinned and shook his head. "Pop's an idiot," he whispered against Julia's neck.

She chuckled, snuggling up close. "He's a dear."

"And," Portia went on, her voice ringing with authority, "you know Julia deserves to have her parents present. They've traveled the full breadth of the continent to see her wed."

"How is this my fault?" Phillip demanded.

"You wrote that persuasive letter to Jordon, and don't you deny it!" Portia barely paused for breath. "You impersonated Holmes, writing letter after letter to Julia."

"Hold on, now, Portia—"

"You say Gabriel's taken. Fine." Portia paused for emphasis. "I suggest you persuade Conrad to become the bridegroom."

"By tomorrow?" Phillip's voice squeaked with distress.

"What will it take to persuade you to marry me tomorrow morning?" Conrad asked. "I have no intention of allowing Pop to talk you into it, not before I do."

"A kiss is a fine way to begin a persuasion."

"Gladly. But I want the details settled."

"Later."

With a smile on his face, he gathered her close. "Tomorrow, Miss J."

She rose on tiptoe and pressed her lips to his. She couldn't resist teasing him, just a little. "That's rather sudden, isn't it?"

His kiss, tender and demanding, convinced her there wasn't anything sudden about it.

"Tomorrow," he told her between kisses, "cannot possibly come quickly enough."

PHILLIP HELD his tongue. Regrouped. Stared down Portia, who refused to budge even an inch. "I find it hard to believe Julia will *want* to marry Conrad. He isn't her type."

Portia turned to the rest of the family, clustered together on the staircase, for a view of the proceedings. Her expression clearly said, "Ha!"

"Husbands are not interchangeable!" Persuasive argument, that.

Violet, bless her soul, smiled in her special way, offering silent encouragement.

Holmes slipped his arm around Susannah's shoulders and pressed a kiss to her crown.

"I'm right," Phillip insisted. "Julia and Conrad may have been friendly at one time. Cordial. Pleasant. But they've hardly spoken to each other since Holmes returned from school."

"And *whose* fault is that?" Portia demanded.

With a bedlam of tangled responses—unanimously identifying Phillip as the culprit—the family sided with Portia.

Phillip cut off the rabble-rousing. "*I* didn't tell them to stop talking to each other. Conrad is the most hard-headed of the lot. He does whatever suits him, despite—"

"On the contrary," Portia stated, "Conrad is a man of uncommon integrity. And in this family, that's the highest of compliments."

Phillip growled with frustration. "Portia!"

"It's all clear to me, after witnessing Conrad's interaction with my niece just moments ago, that they have tender feelings for each other."

Gabriel finally stopped chattering to David and Katherine. "Yeah, Pop. Conrad's been in love with Julia from the beginning."

"Impossible." Growing ever more aggravated, Phillip tossed up his hands in exasperation. "There would've been some indication. It's evident they don't even like each other."

Gabriel snorted. "Conrad's so in love with Julia, he can't think straight."

"Love?" Violet asked, stunned. Met his gaze. *Our Conrad, in love with Miss Julia? Is it true?*

Phillip blinked. And tried to imagine Miss Julia and Conrad—in love?

With each other?

He held out two hands, gesturing for silence. "*When* did this happen?"

"Ah, ah, ah," Portia chided. "What you have been too clueless to notice, is their friendship suffered *because* of their romance."

"I'm not clueless," Phillip argued. He saw little

reason to take Portia's word as gospel. "Where is Miss Julia? I'll speak to her about this."

Portia indicated the closed guest room door behind him. He raised a brow? "In there?" he whispered.

Everyone nodded.

Apparently, Miss Julia would've heard every last word.

He cringed, but made sure the rest of the family didn't see him do it. Well, no sense knocking now, was there? He opened the bedroom door.

Given the sight that greeted him—Miss Julia completely enveloped in Conrad's embrace, sharing the kind of kiss that left no room for doubt—his old heart hopscotched over a few missed beats.

He gladly conceded to Portia. "Fine. Julia can marry Conrad. Tomorrow. I believe he won't put up much of a fight."

Conrad broke the convincing kiss, and grinned at Phillip. Julia tucked her head against Conrad's shoulder.

Phillip couldn't be sure, but he thought he heard Miss Julia whisper something quite endearing to his son.

Watching the pair of them together, so obviously in love, made a heart-warming sight. More than enough to make an old man sigh with contentment.

Content or not, he was still aggravated. "*Why,*" he demanded of no one in particular, "am I always the last one to hear my children are in love?"

Chapter Twenty-Six

ON THE GLORIOUS day the Macquarie family celebrated the marriages of three children, Phillip sat with Violet on the front pew of the white church in Liberty.

At his other elbow, the illustrious Senator and Mrs. Tyndall. The pair held hands. The sweetest expressions softened their faces.

One minute together with Julia and Conrad, and they'd given their blessing.

No persuasive argument needed.

Phillip could see why. Just looking at those two, anybody could see the two had found the kind of love most folks just dreamed of.

Violet snuggled close to his side and dabbed her eyes with a lace-trimmed hankie.

While the combined ceremony unfolded before their view, Phillip handed his wife three envelopes. One addressed to each of their newlywed kids.

Violet took a peek inside the first card. *You're retiring?*

Thank God for this woman, his cherished wife. Her color looked much better. Beautiful, in the glow of the setting sun streaming through stained glass windows.

He swallowed to ease the tightness in his throat. Whispered, "Eventually."

It made perfect sense to give Holmes the law practice as a wedding gift. Just as buying Silas a house next door to his wife's parents had been the right congratulatory present.

Violet read the other two gift cards, then gave Phillip's arm a warm hug. Nestled close to her, he couldn't help but grin. Her squeeze told him she approved.

Making his wife happy was one of the simple pleasure of his long life.

Katherine didn't need or want the practice or the dairy. But she and David would enjoy a wedding trip to Europe, as much as anybody. He'd called David a lot of names, outside Katherine's hearing, of course. In this letter he'd referred to him as Son. His only baby girl deserved at least that much.

Phillip watched the proceedings, his gaze landing on Conrad. Pride welled within him. A man couldn't ask for a finer son.

He must have told Conrad a hundred times he wouldn't sell the dairy. That didn't mean he couldn't make a wedding present of it.

Excellent way of keeping his son and daughter-in-law close to home.

It would be sweet to see Conrad's face when he and Julia opened his gift.

PHILLIP RAISED his wine goblet and announced to his friends, "I win. Time to settle your debts, preacher. I believe you bet me forty dollars I couldn't bring this marriage to fruition."

"I don't owe you a nickel." John brandished a steak knife. "Not one penny."

Any other day, Phillip would've responded with outrage. But today was thrice blessed. "We had a gentleman's wager."

"With very specific rules. That bet was based on bringing about Holmes's marriage."

"Holmes *is* married, Andrew is not," Phillip agreed, enjoying the tidy, circular logic. "Therefore, I win."

He reclined in the plush upholstered chair, basking in the glow of hundreds of candles reflecting off china and crystal. Jubilant strains of Mozart in the background added to his pleasant mood.

"Happenchance." John shook his head, denying Phillip's hand in the matter. "You hadn't a thing to do with that marriage, thank the good Lord."

"I sent the boy to Harvard, didn't I? I paid for his education. Without my assistance, he never would've met his lovely bride."

Across the crowded Orme Hotel Ballroom, Holmes and Susannah stood beside a linen-covered table of other young couples, visiting. Had quite the bruise on his jaw, but from the smile on his face, the kid felt no pain.

The two of them looked so happy, so fulfilled, it made Phillip glad Holmes had found her. Not exactly the lady he'd chosen for Holmes, but perfect for him, just the same.

"I still win," he informed Luke and John. "Hands down. There's the bride I chose, in bridal satin, sitting at the bride's table, married to my son."

"Ha!" John exclaimed. "Wrong son. Therefore, *I* win."

Phillip ignored the outburst. He was too busy

admiring Julia, radiant in bridal white, her supper forgotten. With her head bent close to Conrad's, she listened intently to him. Wrapped up in their own world. Anyone could see these two were an ideal match.

How had he missed the love blossoming between them?

Until he'd seen Conrad's busted lip, the eye swelling shut, he'd had no clue the boys had anything to fight about. He would never understand why they had to resolve their arguments with fists. Could've talked it out, fought like gentlemen. With words.

Ah, well. Boys will be boys.

He couldn't help but grin. Mixed it up, they did, but neither one of them could have looked happier today, standing up in church with their brides.

Seated beside them at the rectangular banquet table, David and Katherine laughed together. His lovely daughter, in ivory silk and a crown of blossoms and ribbons in her hair, scooted closer to her groom.

Phillip grudgingly admitted—but only to himself—that Katherine seemed quite grown up. A woman. Emotion tightened his throat. What had become of the little girl in braids?

Phillip couldn't say which pair of newlyweds looked happier. It did his old heart good to see his children settled. Last year, Silas had married Nadine. Then Holmes, Conrad, and Katherine, all married, in less time than it took to issue a bench warrant.

Relaxing in his chair, Phillip basked in the joy only a parent could know on this splendid occasion. Taking another sip of wine specially ordered for the occasion, he raised his glass, offering a third toast.

Maybe it was his fourth.

"A toast," he said happily, noticing a hint of slur in his words. This excellent vintage made him as happy as the blessed occasion did. Good stuff. He'd have to order more from the local winery at the first opportunity.

Luke and John raised their glasses.

"To two beautiful daughters-in-law and the only

son-in-law I'll ever need."

Luke's laughter rang a bit too loudly. He downed the rest of his wine. Refilled his glass. Topped off John's, too. Liked it, did they, when someone else paid the tab?

Luke absently rubbed his belly, as if his indigestion had flared up from the rich food and abundant drink. "You won, did you? As I see it, you didn't get your way at all. Your kids have minds of their own. Mixing up who married who and all that."

Phillip waved that away, in too pleasant a mood to nitpick details. "All that matters is I got *three* kids married off, in one shot. *Try* to top that, boys."

"One hundred percent of mine are wed," Luke argued. "You can't say the same. You're only four out of five, whatever percentage that is."

Phillip took another sip, shaking his head at Luke's attitude. "You've only got one son, period."

"Gabriel may have every intention of marrying Miss Sally Tibbs," John advised between bites of fried chicken, "but until they've said their I-do's, there's no telling what might happen."

"You're speaking from experience, I see," Phillip retorted. "I would've thought, with all this wedding fervor, your Andrew would've at least set a date with Lillian."

"He has. Didn't I tell you?"

"Ha!" Phillip laughed aloud. "I don't believe you. You're the worst liar in California. Worst, west of the Mississippi."

"I am not!" The wine had put a bit of color in John's cheeks. And fervor in defense of his rotten lying.

Luke chuckled. "Don't be a chicken liver. Admit it. You lost, fair and square. Andrew's still a bachelor. Without help, Andrew will *die* a bachelor."

"We ought to do something about that." Phillip set down his fork and knife, too full to eat another bite.

John spread butter over his roll. "Oh, no you don't. Andrew and Lillian will be just fine. Sooner or later."

"You tell me he's shopping for an engagement ring. You say they're seeking premarital counseling." Phillip chuckled, wondering what his own boys did, premaritally, that lead to marriage a hell of a lot quicker. "Talk. Talk. Talk. Ten long, arduous years of talk, and it's leading nowhere. Nothing ever comes of it."

"I'm a patient man. They're making strides in the right direction." John leaned back in his chair, nibbling the roll. "There's no reason to intervene."

"No reason?" Phillip couldn't understand John's lack of concern. "Time's a wasting. With neither Andrew nor Thomas showing any hint of giving up bachelorhood in favor of marriage, you may not live to see grandchildren."

"Have I told you Mitzi's expecting?" Luke asked.

"Yes," John said tartly. "Several times."

Luke clasped John's shoulder in one hand and Phillip's in the other. "*I'm* going to be a grandfather."

"I was a grandfather, first," Phillip reminded them. "I won that race, too. Do you want to be last in *everything?*" he asked John.

"Don't mind if I am." But his expression soured, and it was clear he did mind, terribly.

Luke pushed his plate away. "Look at our grand successes. Two attempts at matchmaking, and two sons well-married. We've honed our skills. The next romance will be particularly simple. Easy."

"Hey, now," John said, "there's no reason to meddle with Andrew and Lillian."

"How can it be called meddling?" Luke asked, his features full of innocence.

Phillip chuckled. Luke, guileless? Not when he had his sights set on abruptly ending a man's bachelorhood.

"We might have introduced complete strangers last couple times around," Luke continued, "but there's no need here. Andrew and Lillian have already chosen each other."

John shrugged. "That much is true."

"What's the harm in shoving Andrew off his patootie?" Luke asked. "Then everything will follow a natural course."

"Absolutely not." John signaled the end of the conversation by filling his mouth with juicy fried chicken. He chewed with obvious displeasure.

"He needs a little shove," Luke argued. "There he is, helping his mother serve wedding cake, like he does at every wedding. Always the cake-server, never the groom. I don't know how many more receptions Lillian will sit through, watching her intended slice wedding cake."

John kept his gaze on his plate. He pierced fried chicken, scooped mashed potatoes, and dredged the combination through gravy. "Mark my words, he'll be married before we know it."

Luke chuckled, his eyes sparkling with the promise of a new adventure. "Of course, this wedding will *probably* happen with or without our help. I merely suggest we expedite the process."

Taking note of Lillian seated at a table with her mother, a few other young ladies, and an old widow or two, Phillip noticed something quite interesting.

"Would you look at that." Phillip gestured with a dip of his head. "Notice who snagged Lillian's attention?"

Lillian's gaze was pinned on the new doctor, standing beside one of the old widows at that very same table. Probably discussing her gout.

From here, it sure looked like Lillian's gaze wasn't simply attentive... but downright admiring.

"I have a most entertaining idea," Phillip commented in an off-handed sort of way as he turned back to his cohorts.

John's silverware clattered onto his Orme Hotel signature china plate. His jaw dropped. It would've been comical if he hadn't chosen that precise moment to inhale a chunk of chicken.

Choking, coughing, both hands at his throat, John heaved to his feet in panic. His chair toppled over backwards.

With so much revelry, grand music, and laughter, most of the wedding party was clueless to John's plight. Phillip pounded John between the shoulder blades.

On the fourth whack, the offending fried chicken came up. John coughed hard. Gasped. Plunked back down in his seat. Wiped his eyes with his purple napkin. Blotted his lips.

Through it all, Luke leaned back in his chair, hands laced over his belly. As if John hadn't just about died, Luke commented, "You thinking what I'm thinking?"

John tossed his napkin onto the table, covering the hunk of chicken that had cut off his wind. "This is not," John emphasized, wiping his lips with the back of a shaking hand, "another Daphne Browning incident."

"No, indeed," Phillip agreed, reasonably. "Yet it's an ideal...method, shall we say, of nudging Andrew—"

"No," John argued, most unreasonably.

"The new doc's just our man." Luke chuckled. "Look at him, would you? Handsome devil. So personable. And unattached."

"My thoughts, precisely." Oh, this was fun. Matchmaking with someone else's son was a delight.

"No." John said more loudly. "No."

"You hear something, Phillip?" Luke pointedly ignored John. "I think I hear a dog barking. Sounds like 'no, no, no.'"

Phillip chuckled. "You know, friend, we don't actually *need* permission from the father of the would-be-groom to give his boy a much-needed, much-deserved shove."

"What do you need?" John demanded. "A wager? I'll bet the forty dollars you owe me," he said pointedly to Phillip, "that Andrew and Lillian are married by Christmas. All on their own."

"What forty dollars? I don't *owe* you."

"You lost the bet. Pay up."

"I'll hold the forty for now," Phillip said. "And collect yours when Andrew still hasn't married Lillian, come New Year's Day."

"You, my friend," John said with the first genuine smile since the conversation began, "had better save your pennies. Once you see Gabriel and Sally married, you might not have two coins left to rub together."

"Bah," Phillip mumbled, shaking to seal the bargain. "I got this reception two-thirds the price. The Ormes covered their own ballroom."

This gathering had to be the largest party ever held in Liberty. The ballroom was more crowded than he'd ever seen it.

He laughed, feeling the momentary pinch in his billfold, but able to ignore it. If he'd learned anything in his sixty-plus years, he knew one important truth.

Wealth wasn't measured in dollars and cents, but in the number of cherished faces around his dining room table. If a man didn't have a posterity, what did he have?

That was a simple, priceless blessing John hadn't fully experienced.

Not yet.

But he would. Phillip caught Luke's eye, a grin spreading over his face. It gave an old man something to look forward to.

~ THE END ~

Please *share* this book with a friend.
Lending is easy with a paperack book.

Please *recommend* this book.

Please share your thoughts on this book with friends.

Please post a *review.*
Reviews from readers make all the difference to those browsing and buying, as well as to writers. Please take a moment and leave an honest review—as few as 20 words will do.

Easy links to post reviews

on Amazon
http://amzn.to/1j4yXNY
(case sensitive)

AND
on Goodreads
http://bit.ly/1tozNQG
(case sensitive)

or other eRetailer where you purchased this book, such as *Barnes & Noble*
http://bit.ly/1wmkDqf
(case sensitive)
(Scroll down to "Customer Reviews")

Books By

KRISTIN HOLT

please see

www.KristinHolt.com

And while you're there, please sign up for a newsletter,
to *be the first to hear about new releases.*

The Menace Takes a Bride

A Sweet Historical Mail Order Bride Romance
(Rated PG)
The Husband-Maker Trilogy, Book 1

Garth is willing to wait for the right woman to come along. *His father isn't.*

Garth Wakefield may be pushing thirty, but he's not about to settle for just any wife, in spite his father's claim that unmarried men over the age of twenty-five are a menace to society. Garth knows he's anything but a menace; he owns a lucrative business, is an honest and upstanding citizen, and would never dream of misleading any of his female friends.

When it comes to matters of the heart, he wants it all. Passion, enduring love, and happily-ever-after. When Garth's impatient father forges a paper marriage, Garth suddenly finds himself saddled with a bride. Worse, Mitzi has full control of his fortune and business.

While Garth works desperately to free himself, his delightful bride entwines their lives and hearts until he can't bear to see her go. He's found everything he's ever wanted in the most unlikely of people, his own not-completely-legally-wed wife. But can he convince Mitzi to marry him all over again, for love this time, before she learns the marriage is a hoax?

The Menace Takes a Bride

is available
for your Kindle
http://amzn.to/1oySj27
(case sensitive)

also in paperback
Amazon.com
http://amzn.to/1pvCgRX
(case sensitive)

for your Nook
AND
Paperback
BN.com
http://bit.ly/1sZLA1L
(case sensitive)

The Doctor Claims a Bride

A Sweet Historical Mail Order Bride Romance
(Rated PG)
The Husband-Maker Trilogy, Book 3

She's promised to the other guy...

~ ***Coming Soon*** ~

for your Kindle
and
in paperback

Check the author's book list for availability:
http://amzn.com/e/B00FPXLSLW
(case sensitive)

About the Author

Kristin's love of books and reading began as a preschooler. She arrived home after her first day of Kindergarten frustrated to tears that they hadn't taught her to read (though her parents already had). Today, she devours several books a week, always searching for more authors to add to her keeper shelf. The advent of eBooks made that keeper shelf take up significantly less room, thus ensuring her husband is less aware of the book addiction.

Kristin has worked as a Registered Nurse (Labor and Delivery, Maternal-Child), Childbirth Educator, magazine article writer, Weight Watchers Territory Manager and Leader. Through it all, writing remained her first love. She lives north of Salt Lake City with her husband of twenty-five years, three college-age kids who haven't completely moved out, a daughter dancing her way through high school, and a Vizsla named Snickerdoodle.

Find her at www.KristinHolt.com.

And while you're there, please sign up for a newsletter, to *be the first to hear about new releases.*

A Sweet Historical Romance Novella
(Rated G)

Miranda sneaks home after a long absence, determined to avoid her former fiancé. But Hunter wants far more than his old role as brother-in-law-to-be. Abundant Christmas spirit, matchmaking mothers, and hometown holiday celebrations conspire against Miranda's plans for a quiet, at-home Christmas.

Her heart doesn't stand a chance.

is available for your Kindle—
http://amzn.to/1fcxAOj
(case sensitive)

also in paperback
at Amazon.com
http://amzn.to/1iitikl
(case sensitive)

for your Nook
AND
Paperback
BN.com
http://bit.ly/1jfsLDP
(case sensitive)

A Sweet Historical Mail Order Bride Romance (Rated PG)

Forty Bachelors.
Fifteen Brides.
What could go wrong?

Evelyn is in a pickle.

In less than five months, Evelyn Brandt will be an unwed mother. Her parents discover her secret and send her away on the next west-bound train. They insist she deliver the child on the other side of the continent where the disgrace won't harm her father's business empire and the family's social standing. She'll be allowed to return home after the child is adopted by decent people *and* her corset fits properly once more.

Sam's in charge of the Bride Lottery, and the competition's fierce.

It's too bad the mail order bride agency failed to round up even half their order, 'cause every man on the mountain wants a bride—except Sam Kochler—so he's saddled with enforcing the rules. He received bios of each lady the agency sent, so when Evelyn steps off the train, he's a tad curious and a mite too interested.

The tougher the competition becomes, the worse some fellas behave, and it's not long before Sam finds himself courting Evelyn—only to protect her while she makes up her mind. He won't allow himself to fall in love and still doesn't want a wife...or so he keeps telling himself.

Is available as an eBook at Amazon.com

http://amzn.com/B00MACH28Y
(case sensitive)

Paperback edition coming soon!

GIDEON'S *Secondhand* BRIDE

A Sweet Historical Mail Order Bride Romance Novella
(Rated PG)

The last thing John Gideon wants is another wife.

Mere weeks have passed since John buried his wife, but he must trudge forward. For the sake of his three little ones, he has no choice but to remarry. His mail order bride must agree—this marriage will be strictly business.

Permilia is desperate to flee the bonds of marriage...

The War Between The States cost Millie her kind, gentle husband. He came back in body, but his soul was ravaged by war. To save herself and the life of their toddler son, she leaves her abusive husband though she has nowhere to go, no money, no family. A single option surfaces—a farmer has sent for a mail order mother, housekeeper, and helpmeet. It's a marriage in name only, so she justifies disappearing into the west and keeping her secrets.

...a marriage her husband vowed she'll never escape.

Oliver Owens warned Permilia the only way she'd leave him would be through the undertaker. It's only a matter of time before he catches his runaway wife.

He doesn't want a wife.
She doesn't want a husband.
Marriage of convenience?
Perfect.

is available ***for your Kindle***

http://amzn.to/1vn2ryK

(case sensitive)

also in ***paperback***—

Amazon.com

http://amzn.to/1krJpm0

(case sensitive)

for your Nook

AND

Paperback

BN.com

http://bit.ly/1oxvC8y

(case sensitive)

Made in the USA
Las Vegas, NV
08 March 2022